Discover the series you can't put down . . .

'If you like your conspiracies twisty, your action bone-jarring, and your heroes impossibly dashing, then look no farther – the Ben Hope series is exactly what you need'

Mark Dawson

'Deadly conspiracies, bone-crunching action and a tormented hero with a heart . . . Scott Mariani packs a real punch'

Andy McDermott

'James Bond meets Jason Bourne meets *The Da Vinci Code*'

J. L. Carrell

'Non-stop action – this book delivers'

Steve Berry

'Full of authentic detail and heart-stopping action – a real thrill ride'

Ed Macy

'Scott Mariani is an awesome writer'

Chris Kuzneski

THE PRETENDER'S GOLD

Scott Mariani is the author of the worldwide-acclaimed action-adventure thriller series featuring ex-SAS hero Ben Hope, which has sold millions of copies in Scott's native UK alone and is also translated into over 20 languages. His books have been described as 'James Bond meets Jason Bourne, with a historical twist'. The first Ben Hope book, *The Alchemist's Secret*, spent six straight weeks at #1 on Amazon's Kindle chart, and all the others have been *Sunday Times* bestsellers.

Scott was born in Scotland, studied in Oxford and now lives and writes in a remote setting in rural west Wales. When not writing, he can be found bouncing about the country lanes in an ancient Land Rover, wild camping in the Brecon Beacons or engrossed in his hobbies of astronomy, photography and target shooting (no dead animals involved!).

You can find out more about Scott and his work, and sign up to his exclusive newsletter, on his official website:

www.scottmariani.com

By the same author:

Ben Hope series
The Alchemist's Secret
The Mozart Conspiracy
The Doomsday Prophecy
The Heretic's Treasure
The Shadow Project
The Lost Relic
The Sacred Sword
The Armada Legacy
The Nemesis Program
The Forgotten Holocaust
The Martyr's Curse
The Cassandra Sanction
Star of Africa
The Devil's Kingdom
The Babylon Idol
The Bach Manuscript
The Moscow Cipher
The Rebel's Revenge
Valley of Death
House of War

To find out more visit **www.scottmariani.com**

SCOTT MARIANI

THE PRETENDER'S GOLD

avon.

Published by AVON
A division of HarperCollins*Publishers* Ltd
1 London Bridge Street
London SE1 9GF

www.harpercollins.co.uk

A Paperback Original 2020

First published in Great Britain by HarperCollins*Publishers* 2020

A catalogue copy of this book is available from the British Library.

ISBN: 978-0-00-823601-4

Typeset in Minion 11/14 pt by Palimpsest Book Production Limited, Falkirk, Stirlingshire

Printed and bound in UK by CPI Group (UK) Ltd, Croydon CR0 4YY

MIX
Paper from
responsible sources
FSC
www.fsc.org
FSC® C007454

THE PRETENDER'S GOLD

PROLOGUE

'Can you believe this crap?' Ross Campbell muttered to himself as he stared through his rainy van windscreen at the narrow rural road ahead, winding onward for endless miles into the murk. The December cold and rain were showing absolutely no sign of letting up, and he had the prospect of a good soaking to look forward to when he reached his remote destination.

What a bummer. What a drag. Of course, this job would have to land on him on the dreichest, dreariest and most depressing day imaginable. Today of all days, marking exactly twelve months since Katrina had left him to run off with that rich bastard cosmetic dentist from Inverness.

Ross strongly felt that he should instead be slouched in his armchair at home, nursing his smouldering resentment in front of the TV with a few bottles of Broughton's Old Jock at his elbow. Yes, he was still feeling sorry for himself. Yes, he was taking it badly and allowing his chronic anger to get the better of him. And anyone who had a problem with that better keep their opinion to themselves. Got that, pal?

But however Ross felt he should be spending this miserable winter's afternoon, his duties as partner in the firm of McCulloch & Campbell, Chartered Building Surveyors, obliged him to be here. His task: to scout and assess the western perimeter of the development site within the Loch Ardaich pine forest, right out in the sticks thirty miles north of Fort William. Like it hadn't already been scouted and assessed a dozen times already, but what was the point of complaining?

The closer he got to his destination, the more aggressively the rain lashed his windscreen. The road narrowed to a single-track lane in places as it followed an endless series of S-bends along the forested shores of Loch Ardaich. The heather-covered hills rose high all around, their tops shrouded in mist and cloud. Now and then he passed a lonely cottage or the deserted ruins of an old stone bothy. On a clear day you could sometimes spot an osprey circling over the waters of the loch, or even an eagle; and it wasn't uncommon for a red deer to suddenly burst from cover and leap across the road right in the path of oncoming traffic, scaring the wits out of the inattentive motorist. Ross had lived here all his life, though, and for him the scenery and fauna of the remote western Highlands that drew thousands of visitors each year from all around the world held little wonder or fascination.

At last, the wire-mesh fence and main gates of the development site appeared ahead. The adverse weather conditions had kept most of the protesters away, but the diehards were still grimly hanging on. Ross gave a groan as he saw the small crowd huddled in their rain gear by the gates, ready to wave their sodden banners and scream abuse at any vehicles entering or leaving the fenced-off construction zone. Ross would have bet money that Geoffrey Watkins was among them. Come up all the way from England to stir up as much trouble as he could, Watkins was the most militant of the lot.

Ross personally didn't have a lot of time for the environmental nutters in general, though he had to admit they might have a point on this occasion. It had certainly been one of the more contentious projects his firm had been involved in, and he'd often wished that his senior partner, Ewan, hadn't agreed to take it on. The plans for Highland Manor, an eighteen-hole championship golf course and gated community estate with million-pound homes for wealthy retirees, had attracted no small amount of anger from locals. Two hundred acres of ancient pine forest had been earmarked for destruction under the scheme, sparking furious resistance and attempted legal action by one of the larger and more organised ecowarrior groups. The environmentalists had lost their legal case in court months ago, but in spite of the ruling against them were still gamely doing all they could to disrupt the development. Their methods had been creative enough to cause protracted and extremely expensive delays. The company who'd initially landed the contract had been brought to a virtual standstill by the legion of protesters who had invaded the site, chained themselves to trees, lain in the path of bulldozers, harangued the foresters and generally made it impossible to get the excavations underway. When the company had built a scale-proof fence worthy of a prison compound and brought in security personnel to eject the protesters, the ecowarriors had simply sharpened up their game by sabotaging construction vehicles, slashing tyres and setting an awful lot of valuable machinery ablaze, until in the end the company execs had been forced to cut their losses and give up.

Three more construction firms were now in competition

to decide which lucky crew would take their place. All the while, persistent rumours abounded of a lot of dirty money changing hands and palms being greased for the project to be greenlit. If you believed the gossip, certain local officials were going to do well out of the deal – if and when it actually got completed. The situation was a mess.

Ross was driving his company van, a little white Peugeot Bipper with the chartered surveyor firm's logo proudly emblazoned on its side, a magnet for trouble. Not much wanting his vehicle to be attacked and pelted with missiles, he slipped away from the main gates and detoured around the site's western perimeter to a small side entrance the protesters had, mercifully, chosen to leave unguarded today. He parked the van and listened to the rain pounding the roof. The ground was turning to slush out there, appalling even by the normal standards of a Scottish winter. Beyond the fence stood the thick, dark forest, ancient and forbidding. Local folklore held spooky old tales of bogles and sluaghs and other evil spirits and hobgoblins that lurked in the woods, preying on the hapless. What a load of shite, Ross thought, but he still didn't much fancy having to venture inside.

He changed into his wellies and tugged on his raincoat before getting out of the van, then took the plunge. Moments later, he'd undone the padlock holding the side gate and let himself through the fence, closing it behind him before setting off at a trudge towards the trees.

The forest was very dense and hard to walk through, and Ross was certainly no hardened outdoorsman. He tripped and stumbled his way for nearly quarter of a mile using a GPS navigation device to orient him towards the western boundary. Without the GPS he'd soon have been hopelessly lost, probably doomed to wander for ever. Overhead the tall trees swayed in the wind and their branches clacked and clashed like the antlers of fighting stags in the rutting season. Deep, deep in the forest he swore out loud – who the hell could hear him, anyway – as he had to clamber over a slippery, moss-covered fallen trunk that blocked his path with no other way around except through a mass of brambles that would have stopped a tank. He cursed even more vehemently a few metres further on, when he was forced to negotiate a steep downward slope where part of the ground had been washed away by floods of rain, exposing tree roots and a great deal of rotted and richly odorous vegetable matter.

Damn and blast. Why'd this have to happen to me? At least, if it was any consolation, the rain had stopped.

He was halfway down the slippery incline when he lost his footing. He windmilled his arms to try to regain his balance, to no avail. Next thing he was tumbling and slithering through the gloopy mud, desperately grasping at roots in an attempt to halt his descent but unable to stop himself until he'd rolled and somersaulted all the way to the claggy, squelchy bottom.

'Oh, for God's sake!' he yelled as he managed to sit upright, caked from head to toe in wet, cloying, dripping, freezing cold filth that dripped from his fingers and matted his hair. 'I don't bloody believe it!' Followed by a stream of much more profane invective.

But then his words abruptly died in his mouth as a very strange and unexpected sight caught his eye.

He reached out and raked in the dirt to uncover the rest of the shiny, glinting object whose corner was peeking up at him from the ground next to him. Something hard and small and thin and round, which he picked up and held up to look at more closely. As he wiped dirt off it, a stray beam of sunlight penetrated through the pine canopy above. It reflected off the object in his fingers, and it was as though someone had shone a golden light in his face. He gasped in astonishment.

Then, moments later, he was finding more gold coins in the mud. Dirty, but perfect and beautiful. Six, seven, eight, nine, ten of them. The torrential rain flood that had washed away part of the bank must have disturbed them from their hiding place. How long had they lain undiscovered in this remote and little-travelled neck of the woods?

Suddenly, Ross Campbell's unlucky tumble and getting clarted up to his oxters in muck had become the best thing that had ever happened to him. As fast as he could stuff the coins into his coat and trouser pockets, more kept appearing all around. Within minutes he'd collected dozens of them. It was so incredible he was laughing and hooting to himself like a kid. When he'd loaded all he could carry into his pockets he struggled back up the slippery bank with his booty, vowing he'd return to dig up the hundreds more he was certain lay buried there.

The journey back to the van seemed to take him about half the time. He was so dazed and ecstatic that he barely noticed the brambles and treacherous terrain, and didn't think for a single moment about his filthy, wet clothes or the fact that under them he was soaked to the bone. Reaching the van, he piled into the driver's seat and dug some of the coins from his pocket to re-examine more closely. They were old, really old. He was no expert, but he was certain they must be worth a ton of money. A bloody fortune, lying there in the mud for hundreds of years, just waiting for him to come and find it.

Ross could hardly contain himself. The day's task was almost completely forgotten. He'd just tell his business partner Ewan that the weather was too awful to get the job done, and promise to return as soon as possible. He had the exact location marked on his GPS device.

In the meantime, he needed to get home as fast as he could. A hot shower and a cup of tea, before he caught his death. Then he'd spend the rest of the afternoon, and probably the evening, cleaning up, counting and re-counting his glorious loot. What might the coins be worth? Hundreds of pounds each? Thousands? The numbers escalated in his head until it made him dizzy. Fantasies were already forming. He could picture himself quitting his job, for a start, then getting out of this godforsaken shithole and making a bee-line for somewhere with warm sandy beaches, palm trees and beautiful bikini-clad girls, maybe never to return. Fuck Katrina and her dentist! He'd show them.

He'd need to get the coins independently valued, of course. The internet would only tell him so much. But it would have to be discreet. And preferably done by an expert in another part of the UK, maybe in Edinburgh or London. Someone who'd never be told the precise location of the discovery. Nor would anyone else, certainly nobody local. As it seemed that he alone knew about this, he meant to keep it that way. The last thing Ross wanted was for others to come searching. And with the Loch Ardaich development project so conveniently put on hold, he'd have plenty of opportunity to come back here as often as he liked to hunt for more treasure.

With a trembling hand Ross started up the van engine, then took off in a rush. He couldn't wait to get home. This was, beyond a shadow of a doubt, the most wonderful and exciting day of his entire life.

It would also prove to be one of the last. He didn't know it yet, but he would never live to see his fantasies come true. Nor did he have any idea of the chain of events his strange discovery was about to set in motion.

If Ross Campbell had not found the gold coins that had lain hidden all this time in the forest, people would not have been hurt or killed. None of the things that were about to happen would have taken place. And the men who were soon to be drawn into the web of danger would not have become involved.

One man in particular. A man Ross Campbell would never meet.

A man called Ben Hope.

But Ross Campbell had found them, and now the storm was coming.

Chapter 1

Eleven days later, the clouds were gone and the sky was bright and blue. But none of the assembly who had gathered at the cemetery in the village of Kinlochardaich to watch the interment of the coffin was smiling.

What an unspeakable tragedy. Ross Campbell had been a much-loved member of the community, even if he had been going through some personal ups and downs in the last year and not always the cheerful and carefree soul he'd once been. It was hard to keep secrets in this close-knit community, and everyone knew that his former long-term girlfriend, Katrina Wilson, was now living with someone else in Inverness. Then again, those who had spoken to Ross in the few days leading up to his untimely death reported that his mood had radically improved all of a sudden. For reasons that remained unclear he'd seemed strangely happy, even jubilant, as though he'd finally broken free of the emotional troubles that had plagued him since his relationship breakup. It seemed so ironic that, just as his life appeared to have turned a corner, he should fall victim to such an awful accident.

It was 'Patch' Keddie, the one-eyed birdwatcher who was one of the community's more colourful fixtures, who'd discovered the body floating face-down among the rushes at the edge of Loch Ardaich while on his solitary wanderings in the countryside with backpack and spotting scope, four days earlier. Shocked and upset by the grisly discovery, Patch had hurried to a spot where he could get phone reception and called for an ambulance, but it was already far too late.

It appeared as if Ross must have been exploring the loch-side when he'd slipped and fallen into the water. His surveyor's van was later found quite a distance away, parked by the fence of the Highland Manor development site. This had sparked much puzzled debate about what Ross was doing down at the water's edge, a good quarter of a mile or more from the location he'd been surveying. Perhaps he'd wandered over there just to enjoy the magnificent views. In any case, having never learned to swim he had little chance of escaping the freezing cold water. He wasn't the first victim to have been claimed by the depths of the loch.

Among the mourners at the graveside was Ross's partner in the firm, thirty-four-year-old Ewan McCulloch. Head bowed and grim-faced, Ewan was visibly shaken to the core by the loss of his business associate and friend. Though they'd only worked together for five years, like most folks in this close-knit community with relatively few incomers they'd known each other for nearly all of their lives.

Other attendees at the funeral included Ross's stricken parents, who now lived near Inverness. Mrs Campbell had wept bitterly throughout the gruelling church service and was so crippled with grief that she could barely remain upright to watch her only child's coffin go into the ground. Her husband bore his agony in stoical silence, but the expression in his eyes was ghastly to see.

Katrina Wilson, the ex-girlfriend, was conspicuous by her absence. Nobody was terribly surprised that the untrustworthy little cow had not bothered to show up. Also present were Mairi Anderson, the surveyor's office administrator; William and Maureen Reid, who ran the Kinlochardaich Arms, the village's one and only pub; Rab Hunter, the local mechanic who'd known both Ross and Ewan since primary-school days; Patch Keddie, tears streaming from his one eye; and Grace Kirk.

Grace was a couple of years younger than Ewan, had attended the same primary and secondary schools and then left for a time to pursue a police career in the big city. She'd returned to her birthplace a few months ago and was the only female officer in the area. Today she was off duty and out of uniform, hiding her reddened eyes behind dark glasses as she stood in the back of the crowd with her hands clasped and shoulders drooping.

When at last the gut-wrenching ceremony was over, there were solemn handshakes and hugs and commiserations and more tears before the assembly began to disperse. Poor Mrs Campbell had to be virtually carried away to the waiting car. Ewan had been hoping to say a few words of thanks to Grace Kirk, but when he turned away from the grave he saw she'd already gone. He shared a quiet moment with Rab Hunter, who clapped him on the arm and said, 'Rough times, man. You okay?' Once you got past the intimidating muscles and the piratical beard and earring, Rab was a big softy at heart. His eyes were full of tears and he kept blinking.

'Yeah, I'm okay,' Ewan lied.

Rab shook his head and blinked once more. 'I still cannae get my head aroond it, you know? He was here with us, and now he's gone.'

'I can barely believe it either,' Ewan replied, truthfully this time. He, too, was having a hard time adjusting to the reality of Ross's death. They parted, and he walked slowly back across the cemetery grounds and past the old grey stone church to where he'd parked his van. It was a little white Peugeot with the company name on the door, identical to the one Ross had been driving. Ewan didn't have a car of his own. His only personal vehicle was a rundown old camper, currently off the road and somewhat neglected. Maybe one day he'd get around to it.

As Ewan headed homewards he was asking himself the same question he'd been asking for days: What on earth was Ross doing down there at the lochside? He couldn't have been lost; he knew the area as well as anyone. Ewan didn't believe he was admiring the scenery, either. Ross couldn't have given a damn about such things. Had he been drinking? A couple of times in the months since Katrina had left, Ewan had thought he could smell alcohol on Ross's breath during work hours. Maybe he should have reached out to his friend, offered support, but he'd said nothing at the time. Now he feared that Ross's emotional state might have been more serious than anyone had supposed.

At the back of Ewan's mind was the unmentionable thought that wouldn't go away.

Suicide. Was it possible?

Surely not. Ross wasn't the type to top himself. But then, every man has his breaking point. What if Ross had simply reached his? What if the apparent uplift in his spirits during his last few days – and yes, Ewan had noticed it too – was really just a desperate man's last-ditch attempt to disguise the bleak despair that was consuming his heart and soul?

If that was true, then Ewan had truly failed his friend.

'Oh God, Ross. I'm so sorry.'

When Ewan got home to the small house in which he lived alone, he went straight to the kitchen and poured himself a stiff whisky from a bottle a client had given him the Christmas before last. He wasn't much of a boozer, but

12

this could be a good time to take up the habit. He sat down heavily in a wooden chair at the table, gulped his drink and then poured himself another. Mixed up with his grief was the bewildering issue of how the business was going to continue with just him as a solo operator. There was already too much work for two partners, especially if the massive undertaking that was the golf course project went ahead. Ross's sudden absence left a gaping hole that threatened to swallow Ewan up, too.

He had been unable to do any work since receiving the news of the death four days ago. He had no plans to go into the office tomorrow either. Nor the next day, most likely. Let's just sit here and drink, he thought. By the time he'd finished the second whisky the edge was coming off his pain and he decided that a third would help even more. He knew he'd probably regret it, but what the hell.

Ewan woke up in the darkness. The phone was ringing. What time was it? He must have been asleep for hours, and had no recollection of having moved from the kitchen table to the living room couch. His head was aching and his mouth tasted like the contents of a wrestler's laundry basket. He should never have drunk so much. Bleary-eyed and disorientated, he managed to get up, turn on a light and stumble across the room to answer the phone. Who could be calling?

He picked up. 'Hello?' he croaked.

There was silence on the line. Ewan repeated, 'Hello?'

Chapter 2

'Is that Ewan McCulloch?'

The caller spoke in a local accent. His voice was throaty and deep, marked by a pronounced lisp that somehow sounded familiar to Ewan, though very distantly so. He tried to think where he might have heard the voice before, but couldn't place it. His head was spinning from the whisky. Glancing at his watch he saw it was nearly midnight. He managed to get it together enough to reply, 'This is he. Might I ask who's calling?'

'Never mind who I am,' said the lisping voice. 'It's what I know that should concern you. It's what I saw. I cannae keep it tae myself any longer. It's not right.'

Ewan blinked, paused a beat in confusion. 'I'm sorry? I don't understand. What are you talking about? Do I know you? Look, it's very late and I'm kind of tired.'

'Shut up and listen tae me. I'm talkin' aboot yer man Ross Campbell. That was nae accident, get it?'

'No, I don't get it,' Ewan replied, thoroughly bewildered. 'What are you trying to say?'

'And in case you thought he did it tae himself, think again.'

'Who is this?' Ewan demanded. 'Are you sure I don't know you? Have we met?' The more the caller talked, the more Ewan was certain he'd heard the voice before, as if in some other life he could barely remember.

14

'They killed him.'

'They *what*? Say that again.'

'You heard me,' the caller went on tersely. 'The basturts caught him in the woods, dragged him doon tae the loch and tossed him in the water tae make it look like he drowned hisself.' He let out a sigh. 'There. Now you know the truth.'

Stunned, Ewan carried the phone back to the sofa and slumped into it. Was he dreaming? No, the caller sounded perfectly real. And very sober, serious and sure of what he was saying. 'But . . . you're talking about . . .'

'Aye, I am. That's what this was. No other word for it. Cold-blooded murder.'

'I . . . what . . . how . . .?'

'How do I know?' the caller finished for him with a sour chuckle. 'Because I was there, that's how. Fishin' for salmon that it's not my right tae fish, if you get my meaning. I was checkin' my nets when I saw these five men appear from the woods. Thought they were a bailiff patrol at first, so I hid deep in the bushes, wonderin' how the hell I was gonnae get away. They've caught me before. But they didnae see me. They had other business on their minds.'

Ewan pinched the bridge of his nose and squeezed his eyes shut, desperately trying to think straight. 'I . . . this is just insane.'

'It was near dark,' the caller went on. 'But I saw the whole thing clear. As they came closer it wiz obvious that the fifth man, he wasnae one o' them. They were holdin' him by the arms like he was a prisoner. He was fightin' and strugglin'. Yellin' at them tae let him go. But the poor guy couldnae get away from them and he never had a chance. They hauled him tae the edge o' the bank. I couldnae believe my eyes. Didnae want tae watch. Next thing there was a big splash as

15

he hit the water. Two o' them were carryin' boat hooks with long metal poles, them telescopic ones. He tried tae drag himself up the bank but the fuckers kept pokin' him and shovin' him under. Again and again. Took five, six minutes. Maybe longer. I wanted tae do somethin' tae help. But I was scared what they'd do tae me. Then when he stopped fightin' and I could see him floatin' in the water, they prodded him a few more times tae be sure. I heard one o' the basturts laugh. Then they turned an' walked back tae the woods. And that was the last I saw o' them.'

Ewan couldn't speak, could barely even breathe. His mind was swirling from much more than a bellyful of booze. Ross, murdered? Was this some kind of crazy dream? Ewan dug his fingernails into his flesh and nipped himself until it hurt, but the caller went on talking.

This was no dream.

'I could've gone tae try an' pull him from the water,' the caller said. 'But I knew he was dead already. I was shocked. Ma heart was thumpin' so bad, I thought I was gonnae faint. So I just waited until they were gone, and then I legged it. Ran like hell, an' kept runnin'. I wish I hadnae, but that's what I did. I just wanted no part o' it. It wisnae until the next day, when they found the body, that I even knew who they'd murdered. Been frettin' over it ever since. Cannae shut it oot o' ma head.'

At last, Ewan was able to marshal his wits together enough to ask the obvious question. 'These four men. Who were they?'

There was a pause on the line as the caller mulled over his reply. When he spoke again, he sounded scared. 'I'm sorry, Mr McCulloch. It would be mair than my life's worth tae tell you another word.'

'You recognised them, didn't you?'

16

Another heavy pause. Then, 'Two o' them. That's all I'll say.'

'Please,' Ewan said. 'I need to know.'

'Forget it. I've already told you too much. Goodbye.'

'Hold on. Don't hang up. Please! If you don't want to tell me, then at least report what you saw to the police. Better still, we could go there together. Tell me who you are. I could meet you somewhere, right now. We could drive up to the police station in Fort William first thing in the morning.'

'Mr McCulloch—'

'We don't have to tell them about the salmon poaching, if that's what you're worried about. Under the circumstances I don't think they'd even be bothered about—'

'Look, I just wanted you tae know the truth o' what happened,' the caller said. 'Or as much o' it as I dare tae tell. Dinnae make me regret that I called you. Nobody except you has any clue what I witnessed. I intend tae keep it that way. And if you have any sense, you'll keep this tae yourself too. That's all I have tae say. Good night, God bless and good luck.'

And Ewan was left holding a dead phone. He tried dialling 1-4-7-1-3 to find out the caller's number and call them back, but the information had been withheld.

It was only just gone midnight, but Ewan was certain he'd get no more sleep. He couldn't even close his eyes. He frantically paced the floor, his mind awhirl. Was this some kind of sick joke? The enormity of the mystery caller's claim was staggering. Ludicrous. Impossible.

And yet . . . what if it were true?

As he went on pacing for the next hour, Ewan reflected on the trouble and anger that the golf course development scheme had stirred up. A lot of folks in these parts were furious about it, not least the self-proclaimed ecowarriors who, vowing never to give up the fight, had plagued the construction company until they downed tools and walked away. A few months back, someone had made a threatening anonymous call to the McCulloch & Campbell office, saying their firm would regret it if they remained connected with the project. Of course, Ewan had reported the call to the police in Fort William, who'd appeared to do nothing about it. For the next several weeks he had kept expecting to find his car tyres slashed or an office window broken, but nothing more had come of it and he'd quickly forgotten the episode.

However, a lot of other people, including Mairi the firm administrator, had been convinced that it was only a matter of time before someone got seriously hurt. Some of the protesters were a militant bunch. Who knew what they might be capable of?

Breaking windows and vandalising construction machinery were one thing. Murder was something else entirely. But given that both Ewan and Ross were widely known to be associated with the project, albeit only indirectly, what if . . .

Jesus. Maybe it was true!

The more Ewan thought about it, the deeper his panic grew. He wanted to call Mairi to tell her. But he didn't want to alarm her until he could be more certain of his facts. Who to talk to, then? The police again? Perhaps Grace Kirk? Even if he'd had her number, she'd only think he was crazy. He had no real evidence. What if it was all a lie?

It took a long time for Ewan to think of who to call for help and advice. His uncle was retired and had been enjoying a quiet life in the Italian countryside for the last few years, with his Neapolitan wife Mirella. He'd always been there for his nephew, since Ewan's parents had passed away. He'd spent his career in the army, though he'd seldom ever spoken about the things he'd done and his crazy adventures back in those days.

Though you weren't supposed to talk about it, everyone in the family had known Ewan's uncle was no ordinary soldier, but was involved for a long time in the secretive and hidden world of Special Forces. He was older now, but still strong and wise, a rock you could cling to. Someone you could truly confide in.

Yes, that's what Ewan needed to do.

He soon found the number in his address book. Feeling a little more settled, he managed to doze off for a few hours on the sofa. At six in the morning, seven a.m. in Italy, he brewed a strong coffee, then picked up the phone.

Chapter 3

Ewan's uncle was called Archibald, but nobody called him that. For some reason that had never been too clear to Ewan, the name his uncle had always gone by was Boonzie. Boonzie McCulloch. Ewan thought it might have been an old army nickname that stuck.

It was a great relief to hear his voice on the phone. Despite having lived for years in Italy, Boonzie's accent was still as strong as the day he'd left Scotland. He was delighted to hear from his only nephew. But Ewan thought his uncle sounded tired, his voice a little weaker than the last time they'd spoken.

After spending a couple of minutes on the usual pleasantries, Ewan bit the bullet. 'This isn't just a social call, Uncle. I wish it was. Fact is, I've got a problem.'

'What kind o' problem, laddie?'

'The kind I need someone like you to advise me what to do about.'

Boonzie listened calmly and quietly as his nephew related the whole story: Ross's death, Ewan's initial speculations about possible suicide, and the anonymous phone call from the man he could only refer to as 'the poacher', which had blown away all the previous theories about the drowning and left him, Ewan, in such a quandary. He told it exactly as it had happened, leaving nothing out. When he finished,

Boonzie methodically broke down the facts and went through all the questions that had been flying around Ewan's mind. Was this real? Could it be some kind of prank? How plausible was the witness's claim? Could it be verified? Was there any way to identify this mystery caller and get him to come forward, or at least reveal more about what he'd allegedly seen?

Nobody with a background as tough and dangerous as Boonzie McCulloch's could have survived as long as he had without being extremely cautious. He was nobody's fool and his mind was as sharp as the wicked double-edged blade on a Fairbairn-Sykes commando dagger. But after a long discussion, Ewan's uncle could come to only one conclusion. 'I trust ye, laddie. If it sounds real to you, then it sounds real to me.'

'Part of me wishes you'd dismissed the whole thing as total bollocks,' Ewan said. 'I'd have been happy to believe you, and try to forget this nightmare ever happened.'

'Ye say this person sounded familiar,' Boonzie said thoughtfully.

Ewan replied, 'I thought so at the time, yes. I was sure I'd heard his voice before somewhere. But the more I try to remember where, the less sure I am about it. I might have imagined it. I'm going out of my head with confusion. What the hell am I going to do?'

Boonzie's reply was unhesitant. 'Do nothing. Sit tight and wait for me tae get there.'

Ewan realised how foolish he'd been not to anticipate that this would be his uncle's instant reaction. 'No. I can't accept that. I'm not asking you to drop everything and come here. I just thought . . . to be perfectly honest I don't know what I thought.'

'Aye, well, two heads're better than one. Give me a day to

sort things oot here and make the travel arrangements. I'll be with you as quick as I can.'

'I hate to drag you away from your home.'

'The middle of winter's no exactly the busy season for us,' Boonzie said with a chuckle. He and Mirella had a seasonal business growing tomatoes and basil, which they canned into purée and pesto for the restaurant trade in their region of Campobasso. They'd never be millionaires, but it was a blissfully peaceful life and exactly what the couple wanted to be doing.

'All the same. I feel like shit about it.'

'Wheesht. It's the least I can do. We'll have this thing worked oot before ye know it.'

Despite his sense of guilt Ewan was already feeling much better. 'And then? Take it to the police?'

'Maybe. First let's make sure we know what's going on here. One step at a time, Ewan. One step at a time.'

'Thanks, Uncle. You've no idea how much this means to me.'

'I promised yer father on his death bed that I'd look after ye, Ewan. That's what I mean tae do. You're like the son I never had.' The fearless Boonzie McCulloch wasn't afraid of sounding corny, either.

'Och, stop it. You're embarrassing me.'

'I mean it. So you stay put, keep yer head doon and dinnae move a muscle until I get there. Okay?'

'I will.'

'Swear?'

'Absolutely.'

But despite his promise, as the hours passed following their conversation Ewan found it progressively harder and harder to sit twiddling his thumbs waiting. The morning seemed to drag on for ever and he didn't know what to do with himself. Impatience was building like steam pressure inside him. Shortly after eleven a.m. his rising tension was suddenly interrupted when his landline phone rang again, louder than a train whistle, making him jump.

As he hurried over to pick up, the thought hit him that this could be the poacher calling back to say he'd had second thoughts and would agree to meet and tell him the rest of what he knew. Or else maybe it was Boonzie, telling him he was already at the airport and would soon be winging his way to Scotland. Boonzie to the rescue!

It was neither.

'Oh, hello, Mr Campbell.' Ewan felt awkward talking to Ross's father and didn't know what to say. The agony of the man's grief was palpable over the phone line. He sounded like death.

'It's about Ross's van,' Mr Campbell explained. 'It's still here and I suppose you'll be needing it back.'

Ewan had forgotten all about the van. For some bizarre reason the police had had the recovery service tow it to Ross's place. Now that he was effectively running the business alone for the foreseeable future, Ewan had little use for two company vehicles, but he replied, 'Oh, aye. Yes, I suppose I will.' Then he gritted his teeth and asked how he and Mrs Campbell were doing.

Not well, came the predictable answer. They were both sleep-walking through a nightmare. Eileen was on heavy medication and pretty much comatose. Their doctor was waiting for them back in Inverness, where they would be returning that afternoon to pick up the pieces of their life. Ewan offered some more lame condolences and said he'd come right over and collect the van. Not a task he particularly relished, but at least it'd get him out of the house for a while and give him something to do.

23

Ross had held a mortgage on a small ground-floor flat in a handsome double-fronted stone house a couple of doors down from the Kinlochardaich Arms, on the other side of the village. It was within easy walking distance of Ewan's place, and he set off on foot. The wind was cold; he wondered if snow might be on the way.

Seeing the white Peugeot Bipper van parked outside Ross's flat brought a lump to Ewan's throat. Mr Campbell appeared at the window, and came outside a moment later to greet him with the same grim-faced demeanour as before. They shook hands and spoke only briefly. Ross's father handed over the set of vehicle keys that had been among his son's possessions recovered by the police. Then Ewan got into the van and drove off, feeling miserable.

With nothing better to do when he got home, he set about cleaning out the inside of the van. Ross had not been the tidiest of people. His flat had always been a tip and he kept the company vehicle like a pigsty: crumpled fish and chips packaging tossed negligently into the back, crushed empty Coke cans rolling about the floor, crisp packets stuffed into the glove compartment, dirt everywhere. Tons of dirt. It looked as though his friend had been wallowing about in a bloody farmyard. Tutting and shaking his head, Ewan chucked the rubbish into a bin bag, then went and fetched the vacuum cleaner and started dejectedly hoovering out all the bits of dried mud. *Honestly, Ross. Sorry to say it, but what a slob you were.*

Ewan was cleaning beneath the driver's seat when he came across the strange object that had somehow made its way under there. He picked it up and stared at it.

'Holy shit.'

Chapter 4

The gold coin seemed to glitter between his fingers with a life of its own. Ewan had never seen anything like it before. He turned off the hoover and sat at the wheel of the van to examine the coin more closely. Its markings were ingrained with dirt, as though it had not long ago been dug up out of the ground. But they were still clear enough for Ewan to make out. One face bore the head of a regal-looking individual with long, flowing locks of hair and a noble, patrician profile. Inscribed around the circumference were the letters LVD.XV.D.G.FR. ET NAV. REX. The reverse of the coin was inscribed with a crown and more writing: CHRS.REGN. VINC.IMPER.1746.

None of which meant anything to Ewan except the obvious 1746 date mark. And the fact that it was most definitely not a piece of brass. But now the question was burning inside him: what on earth had Ross been doing with it?

On an impulse, he got out of the van, knelt down by the open driver's door and reached an arm under the seat to see what else might be under there. To his even greater amazement his fingers closed on a second coin. As with the first, he stared at it for a long moment. It was virtually identical except for the date mark, which was a year older.

Where could Ross have possibly found these? Surely, not

even an inveterate slob would leave valuable gold coins lying around for any length of time in their car. They couldn't have been here long. Perhaps this explained where all the mud had come from. Was this what Ross had been doing on his trips into the countryside, rooting up old coins?

Scotland as a whole was incredibly rich with history, but nowhere more so than this region. Myths and legends of buried treasure had for years drawn legions of dreamers and speculators to the Loch Ardaich pine forest and surrounding glens looking to get rich in other ways, armed with metal detectors and shovels and divining rods and God knew what else. Nobody had ever found anything of significant historic interest, barring a few rusty old arrowheads and, on one exciting occasion, a medieval Scottish claymore sword so decomposed that it looked like a rotted stick. Gradually, the treasure hunters had dwindled to a bare few – while the sceptics and naysayers became both more numerous and vociferous. 'There's nothing there' had become the received wisdom.

But it looked as though Ross might well have proved the naysayers wrong. Why hadn't he shared the news of his discovery?

Reflecting, Ewan felt a pang of betrayal. He'd always considered Ross his friend. Friends didn't hide things from one another. Ross's deliberate act of secrecy smacked of mistrust and deviousness. What did he think, that Ewan would try to steal his precious coins? Claim his share, because they'd been discovered on company time?

But hold on a minute, Ewan thought. This wasn't making any sense. What were the coins doing lying about in the van in the first place? Who wouldn't have brought them inside and made sure they were safely hidden away? Which meant, or implied, that the reason Ross had left these two particular coins in the van was that he didn't know they were there.

Which in turn also meant, or implied, that the reason he didn't know they were there was that he'd accidentally dropped them, in his typically clumsy and negligent style, while his attention was taken up with something else. And what else could possibly have distracted him in such a way?

One logical answer sprang to mind.

More coins.

Ewan could picture it perfectly. Ross, delirious with greedy joy at his find, scrambling home in such a rush that the gold was literally slipping through his fingers. How many more coins could he have found? Enough, obviously, that he hadn't bothered even counting them until he got back to his flat, or else he'd surely have missed these two. Dozens of them? Scores? Who could say?

But then Ewan had another thought that made his blood turn cold.

If these two coins represented only a minor fraction of Ross's haul, as logic suggested, then where were the rest? What if Ross had had them on his person, keeping them close, when the alleged killers struck? What if the killers had taken them?

And worst of all, what if the gold was the reason they'd killed him?

Suddenly this whole dreadful thing made some kind of sense.

Ewan pocketed the pair of coins and pulled out his phone to call his uncle. No reply, and no messaging service on which to leave a voicemail. Ewan only had the Italian land-line number to reach him on. He wasn't even sure if Boonzie possessed a mobile. Knowing him, perhaps not. There was an email address for him and Mirella, but Ewan had given up sending messages to it long ago.

Ewan couldn't stand passively waiting any longer. He had

to *do* something. People must be told about this. Now there was not only a potential witness to the crime, but a likely and compelling motive to boot.

Kinlochardaich had a church, a pub, a garage, a small convenience store and its own tiny primary school with about twenty-five pupils, but it had no police station – something many residents regarded as a blessing. The only cop hereabouts was Grace Kirk, and so Ewan clambered into his van and drove hurriedly over to the rented cottage in which she lived alone, just beyond the outskirts of the village. He was a little nervous about going to see her. They hadn't been alone together since they were both sixteen years old and sort of, kind of, on-and-off going out. Not that it had been much of a relationship. A bit of hand-holding, a few awkward kisses and some sweet talk, nothing more serious. But Ewan had secretly worshipped and pined for Grace for years afterwards, and in fact was willing to admit to himself that he'd never quite got over her. The news of her return to Kinlochardaich a few months back had got him rather worked up, though he'd never had the courage to speak to her, let alone ask her out again. The local gossip mill had it that she and Lewis Gourlay, a regular of the drinking fraternity at the Arms, were an item. Ewan stubbornly refused to believe the rumour.

In the event, he needn't have felt nervous because Grace wasn't at home. Ewan's remaining option was now to drive the thirty miles south-east to Fort William, the nearest town of any real size, and talk to the police there. The journey took an hour, thanks to the narrow and winding roads.

The police station was a generic slab-sided office building located out of town near Loch Eil, with misty hills looming in the background. On arrival Ewan blurted out his story as best he could to a duty officer, who became thoroughly confused, asked him to calm down and showed him into an airless, windowless interview room with a plain table and four plastic chairs. Locked in the room and made to wait, Ewan felt strangely like he was under arrest. The beady eye of a video camera watched from one corner.

Half an hour later, the door opened and in walked two middle-aged plainclothes men who introduced themselves as Detective Inspector Fergus Macleod and Detective Sergeant Jim Coull. Macleod was a large burly man with a neck like an Aberdeen Angus bull and a florid complexion, and Coull was a smaller sandy-haired guy with a brush moustache, lean and whippy in build, whose hands never stopped moving. They sat at the table and asked him to run through the account he'd told the duty officer.

Ewan patiently laid the whole thing out to them in detail. They listened gravely and Coull scratched occasional notes on a pad he kept close to his chest. When Ewan reached the part about the coins, the detectives asked if they could see them.

'I only brought the one with me,' he said, showing them the slightly newer one from 1746. It was a lie; the other was still in his pocket, but some mistrustful instinct made him keep it hidden. The detectives examined it with impassive faces, then Macleod asked if they could hang onto it as evidence. Ewan, who had seen this coming, reluctantly agreed. Coull put the coin in a little plastic bag and assured him it would be well looked after.

'Don't forget to drop the other one into the station when you get a chance,' said Coull.

'Of course,' replied Ewan, thinking he'd do no such thing.

'Now tell us again about this poacher who claims to have witnessed the alleged incident,' Macleod said, leaning across the table with his chunky square hands laced in front of him. The term 'alleged incident' grated on Ewan somewhat, but he patiently and politely repeated what he'd already told them.

'Like I said, that's all I know about the man. I don't know his name, or exactly who or what he saw, other than he witnessed four men pushing Ross into the loch and deliberately drowning him. He couldn't swim, anyway.'

'Couldnae swim, eh?' Coull asked, glancing sideways at his colleague as though this were some suspicious detail critical to cracking the case. By now Ewan was starting to get peeved by their lacklustre response. He asked them what they intended to do about this, now they had the facts of the matter before them.

Macleod heaved his thick shoulders in a shrug. 'To be honest, Mr McCulloch, I would hardly say we had the facts. What you're reporting is essentially no more than hearsay. These are very serious allegations and require more than this kind of flimsy anecdotal evidence to support them.'

'Well, if you wanted something more substantial to go on, you could try to identify the witness, for a start,' Ewan said.

'Alleged witness,' Coull corrected him.

'Okay, *alleged* witness,' Ewan said with a flush of impatience.

'And how do you propose we do that, Mr McCulloch?'

'Given that he seems to be in the habit of poaching salmon on the loch, he might not be that hard to find. He told me he'd been caught before. So maybe he's already on file somewhere. I mean, you must have a database of all the people who've been prosecuted for that sort of thing.'

'You'd have to narrow it down to something a wee bit more specific,' Coull said. 'We don't know when he was caught, or doing what exactly, or where. That's an awfy lot of potential names to trawl through, each one of which would have to be processed individually. You're talking an enormous expenditure of manpower.'

Ewan stared at him, thinking, *Isn't expending manpower what the police are meant to do when somebody gets murdered?* 'Okay, but it must be possible to identify him one way or another. Then maybe you could find out what he knows. Maybe in exchange for turning a blind eye to what he gets up to. Like a plea deal.'

'That's not what a plea deal is,' Coull said, like a real smart-arse.

'Whatever you call it, then.'

Macleod pursed his lips and breathed heavily. 'I see. You've got this all worked out, haven't you, Mr McCulloch? Maybe you should be doing our jobs for us.'

'There's a thought,' Ewan snapped back and instantly regretted it.

The interview didn't get any more productive from that point. Twenty minutes later, Ewan left the police station wishing he'd never gone there. On the long drive homewards he was wondering angrily why the hell he'd agreed to let them hold onto one of the gold coins as 'evidence', if they had little to no intention of taking the murder claim seriously.

Oh, what the hell. Boonzie would soon be here to help set things straight.

But there was no phone message waiting for him when he got home. Ewan's heart sank in dismay.

He spent the rest of the day trying to alleviate his frustration with mundane tasks like fixing the broken wall tile in the bathroom. That evening he immersed himself in the internet, typing in search keywords like GOLD COINS LOCH ARDAICH PINE FOREST and noting down whatever he could find on a pad. There wasn't much. Then he began checking out numismatical websites, a strange and obscure corner of the web devoted to the study of old currency.

Researching the coin's inscriptions and 1745 date mark online he was able to determine that what he had in front of him was what was known as a *Louis d'or*, a gold Louis, the eighteenth-century precursor to the later French Franc. Its value, from what he could glean, was something in the region of five thousand pounds. Holy crap.

French coins buried in Scotland? Ewan investigated the history behind that, too, and made more notes. Lastly he spent a while hunting for information about illegal salmon fishing in the vicinity. Again, he discovered a few details, though nothing specifically useful to him, and scribbled them down on his pad.

He looked at his watch. Getting late, and still no word from Boonzie. Ewan didn't want to pester his uncle by trying to call again, but maybe he could send an email. Thinking Boonzie ought to know about the coins, he used his phone to take a photo of it, then attached the image to a brief message that just said, 'Ross found this. It gets weirder. Hope you get here soon.'

He watched the message go, and felt suddenly very alone and empty. In a sudden fit of hopeless rage he ripped the page out of the notepad, screwed it into a ball and flung it at the wastepaper basket. It missed, and rolled into the corner. He was too despondent to care.

He was beginning to worry that maybe his uncle wasn't coming at all.

Chapter 5

Early next morning, with the surveyors' office still closed and having heard nothing from his uncle, Ewan decided to drive over to the golf course development site and take a look around. He avoided the ubiquitous crowd of demonstrators who never seemed to tire of camping by the main entrance, and sneaked around to the same discreet spot on the perimeter fence where Ross's van had been found. He quietly let himself in through the locked side gate and spent a while wandering among the woods. The chances of finding where Ross had made his fateful discovery were pretty slim, and he knew it; he didn't really know why he'd come here except for something to occupy his mind.

From the southern edge of the forest's tree line he made his zigzagging way down the steep, heathery slopes to the lochside. The sky was pale and the air was chilly, making his breath billow in clouds. The craggy hilltops that surrounded the loch like the defences of prehistoric fortresses were wreathed in mist, now and then a shard of sunlight breaking through the cloud and casting a golden streak across the rugged landscape. All his life Ewan had marvelled at the magnificent scenery, but it was now forever tainted by the tragic event that had taken place here.

He hung around for a while, ambling up and down the

bank in the vague hope of spotting the mysterious poacher. Which was a silly bit of wishful thinking, at best. The loch was twelve miles from end to end and it occurred to him that, of course, the spot where Ross was found wasn't necessarily the same place where the witness claimed to have seen him being killed. The body could easily have floated some distance. To make matters worse, it was unlikely that the poacher would visit the same location twice in such a short time, even under normal circumstances. The fishing rights on the loch were tightly controlled by the Fisheries Board, whose tough bailiffs were known to patrol the shores regularly.

In short, Ewan knew all too well that he was wasting his time here. Utterly demoralised, he trudged back through the woods and reached the van just as it started to rain again. He slumped in behind the wheel and drove off.

He hadn't gone far when he noticed a car in his mirror, following him along the twisty, otherwise empty road. The chunky Audi four-wheel-drive seemed to have appeared out of nowhere – but then Ewan hadn't been paying a lot of attention. Now that it had caught his eye, he watched it in the mirror and thought it was following him much too closely, like fifty miles an hour on these tricky little roads wasn't fast enough for this guy, and he was aggressively trying to get past. *Okay, okay, you pushy bastard*, Ewan thought, slowing to forty and edging a little to the side to let the guy overtake.

But instead of passing him, the big Audi slowed down too, matching his speed and remaining right on his tail, almost bumper to bumper. What was this clown playing at? Not liking this one bit, Ewan sped up again to widen the gap between them. Like before, the Audi stayed right with him, accelerating at the same rate he did. Ewan didn't want to take his eyes off the twisty road for too long, but kept glancing in the mirror. All he could see were two vague shapes behind the Audi's rainy windscreen. 'Come on, then, do you want to overtake me or not?' he yelled.

Then, suddenly, the Audi swerved out to one side and came surging by him with a roar. Just as he was feeling glad to be shot of this tailgating hooligan, the Audi abruptly sliced across his path and its brake lights flared crimson through the rain.

With his heart in his mouth Ewan stamped on his own brakes and twisted the steering wheel to avoid a rear-end collision. But the road was slippery, he was travelling too fast and he felt his wheels lose traction. He cried out in panic as the van went into a skid. The verge flashed towards him. His front wheels hit the grass with a thud and the nose of the van ploughed through several feet of dirt before smashing hard into the drystone wall that divided the verge from the neighbouring field.

The force of the impact threw Ewan violently forwards in his seat and the exploding airbag punched him in the face. Dazed, he saw stars. He was only dimly aware that his engine had stalled and the front end of the van was a buckled mess embedded in the remains of the drystone wall. Through a mist of confusion, he sensed someone approaching; then his driver's door being wrenched open and the cold air flooding into the cab. The shape of a large man leaned down towards him and reached inside the car. Ewan heard the clunking sound of his seatbelt clasp being released. Next thing he knew, two strong hands grabbed him by the collar and he felt himself being hauled roughly out of his seat.

Ewan did what he could to resist but he was disorientated and still in shock from the accident, and the man was much bigger and stronger than he was. Ewan felt himself being bodily dragged along the wet grass, then dumped hard on the ground at the roadside. He heard car doors opening and shutting, and became aware of more men gathering around where he lay gasping and blinking.

All he could do was gape helplessly up at them. Four unsmiling faces stared back. The men were each wearing bulky quilted jackets, black woollen beanie hats and black gloves. Two of them, including the man who had dragged him from the car, were total strangers.

The other two, he realised with a jolt of paralysing terror, were not.

One of the men he recognised grinned down at him and said, 'Hello, Ewan.'

Chapter 6

It was later that morning that a taxicab driven by a local man called Duncan Laurie picked up a traveller at the tiny Spean Bridge railway station on the West Highland Line. The passenger was an older man, lean and grizzled with a salt-and-pepper beard and white hair buzzed so short it looked like a military crew cut. He gave Duncan an address in the village of Kinlochardaich, a few miles away, loaded his own single travel bag in the boot of the car and sat in the back.

Duncan had been driving cabs for a long time and he was pretty good at sizing people up. His passenger had the look of a tough customer. Not a particularly tall or large man, but he was one of those work-hardened gruff little guys who seemed to be made out of wood and leather. Not someone to be messed with, Duncan thought. But there was nothing menacing or threatening about him. He had an air of stillness and calm. A man who meant business. Though he was obviously a Scotsman – from Glasgow or thereabouts, judging by his accent – he looked more as though he'd spent the last several years in a warmer climate, like Greece or Spain. At first glance he could even have passed for a native of the Mediterranean region, except for those flinty, hooded grey eyes, the colour of a battleship. Eyes that seemed to watch everything, drinking in his surroundings and missing no detail as they set off north-westwards along the scenic glen road towards Kinlochardaich.

'You're no from around here, I'm guessing,' Duncan said by way of initiating conversation.

The flinty eyes connected with his in the rear-view mirror and the passenger replied with a monosyllabic 'Nope.'

'Here to visit, then, aye? Got friends and family in Kinlochardaich?'

The passenger gave only a slight nod in response. Not much given to small talk, seemingly. Maybe he was tired after his long journey from wherever. Or maybe he just wasn't keen on questions. But it would take more than a bit of dourness to quell Duncan's sociable nature.

'Name's Duncan. Duncan Laurie. I live over in Gairlochy.'

'McCulloch,' the passenger said quietly. 'Boonzie McCulloch.'

'Good to meet ye, Boonzie. If you need a taxi ride during your stay, give me a call, okay?' Duncan plucked out a business card and handed it back over his shoulder.

'I'll do that,' Boonzie replied, taking the card. Then he said no more until they reached the quiet streets of tiny Kinlochardaich.

The taxi pulled up at the address. Boonzie retrieved his bag from the boot, paid his fare and thanked Duncan for the ride. The taxi sped off. Boonzie glanced around at the empty village street, which looked as if it hadn't changed much in the last century or so, and reminded him of the Scotland of his youth. Misty mountains were visible in the background and the air was tinged with the scent of woodsmoke from chimneys.

He checked the address his nephew had given him over the phone. This was it: 8 Wallace Street. A modest grey stone terraced house, a far cry from the rambling old farmstead Boonzie and his wife Mirella called home, but not a bad wee place. He was happy that his nephew had made something of himself. The boy had been dealt a rough hand, what with losing his mother at such a young age and the death of his father not many years afterwards. There wasn't a day that Boonzie didn't think about his late brother Gordon. Though he'd never spoken a word of it to a living soul. Boonzie was like that.

He rang the front doorbell and waited, smiling to himself in anticipation of meeting Ewan again. It had been a while.

No reply. Boonzie tried again a couple of times, then noticed that the parking space in front of the house was vacant and wondered if Ewan had gone off somewhere. Which was a little vexing. Boonzie had called from a payphone at Inverness airport earlier, and left a message to tell Ewan when he'd be arriving. If Boonzie had been carrying a mobile he'd have tried calling him on it again now, but he detested the damn things and prided himself on being the last man on the planet who didn't own one.

His thoughts were interrupted by the sound of a sash window squeaking open overhead. He stepped back from the door and looked up to see a thickset woman with curlers in her hair, leaning out from the neighbouring house's upstairs.

'Excuse me, but are you lookin' for Ewan McCulloch?' she called down to him, and Boonzie nodded and said he was. 'I'm Ewan's uncle,' he explained.

She said, 'The police were here before.' She pronounced it the Scottish way, 'polis'.

Boonzie frowned. 'The police?' What was this about? Hadn't he said to Ewan not to call them until he got here?

What the woman said next shocked him. 'Aye. Ewan's been hurt. He's been taken to the hospital in Fort William.'

'Hurt? What happened?'

The neighbour shook her head. 'Dunno, but it sounds bad. Happened this mornin'. You should get over there quick.'

Boonzie was reeling, but outwardly showed no flicker. He retrieved the business card from his pocket and asked, 'Mind if I use your phone?'

An hour later, Boonzie jumped out of Duncan Laurie's taxicab for the second time that day, ran up the steps of Fort William's Belford Hospital, slammed through the entrance into the reception area and hurried to the front desk. 'Ewan McCulloch was brought in here today. Where is he?'

'Are you a relative?'

'I'm his uncle, Archibald McCulloch.' Boonzie normally disliked giving his real name, but at this moment Ewan's wellbeing was all that mattered to him. 'Was he in an accident? Is he badly hurt?'

'Take a seat over there please, Mr McCulloch. Someone will come and speak to you in a minute.'

Wild horses couldn't have made Boonzie sit down for an instant. He paced furiously for seven and a half minutes before a weary and overworked-looking doctor wearing blue surgeon's scrubs finally appeared from a doorway down the corridor. The medical receptionist hurried over from the desk, conferred quietly for a moment with her and pointed in Boonzie's direction.

Boonzie saw the doctor's eyes snap onto him. He clocked the expression on her face. He knew instantly that what she had to tell him wasn't good news.

The doctor came over. She had fair hair tied in a tight bun, and a staff name badge that identified her as Dr Fraser, head surgeon. Before she could speak, Boonzie collared her with 'So, tell me. Is my nephew dead?'

'He's alive.' But the way she said it was full of concern. Boonzie stood and listened with gritted teeth and balled fists as Dr Fraser told him what had happened to Ewan.

'He's suffered an epidural haematoma, fractured cheekbones, a broken jaw, broken collarbones, a compound fracture to the right arm and another to the left leg, plus a severely dislocated shoulder and massive bruising. But he's lucky to be in as good shape as he is. I thought we were going to lose him.'

In some ways the story sounded like a terrible echo of what Boonzie already knew about the fate of Ross Campbell. The doctor related how a local resident, who happened to be driving along the lochside road that morning to visit a friend, had stumbled upon the car wreck and the inert body lying by the roadside in the pouring rain and called 999. A former nurse, she'd checked the victim's pulse, recognised the seriousness of his injuries and known to do all the right things. If not for her intervention and the good fortune of finding him in time, Ewan might well not have survived.

Just as with Ross, everybody's first assumption had been that the victim had suffered an accident. The doctor explained: 'That was how it initially seemed when he was brought in. It wasn't until I examined his injuries more closely that I realised . . . of course I notified the police right away. They're looking into the matter even as we speak.'

'Realised what?' Boonzie asked. The muscles in his throat were clamped so tight that he could barely speak.

'I'm sorry to say there's more to this,' Dr Fraser replied. 'Your nephew appears to have been the victim of a deliberate, possibly premeditated and very violent assault. Judging by the extent and pattern of his injuries, I'd say there were at least two attackers. Maybe more, I don't know. What I do know is that the injuries look as though they were inflicted with one or more solid impact weapons. Something with a round profile, like a baseball bat.' She shook her head. 'Frankly, I've never seen anything quite so vicious before. Things like this just don't happen in this region. Basically they beat the poor man to a pulp and left him for dead.'

Boonzie digested that information with the fear and rage inside him starting to turn to ice-cold water in his veins. He was silent for a few seconds. Then asked tersely, 'Will he survive?'

'I don't have the facilities for complex neurosurgery, so I had to trepan the skull. That's when—'

'I ken what trepanation is,' Boonzie said. Many years earlier, in a bloody little jungle war that officially never happened and was now largely forgotten by all but the men who'd fought and watched their comrades die in it, he'd seen an SAS medic desperately trying to save the life of a badly concussed soldier in the field by drilling a hole in his head to relieve pressure on the brain. The soldier had lived, but he'd never been the same again.

Dr Fraser glanced at her watch. 'He came out of surgery just over an hour ago and is in intensive care right now. So far he seems to be doing fine, under the circumstances, but we'll have a better idea of his prognosis once he regains consciousness. Obviously it's the brain injury I'm most concerned about. The coma might last hours, or it might last days, weeks, or longer.'

'Or for ever.'

'There is that possibility, which we need to be prepared for.'

'What are his chances, fifty-fifty?'

'I wouldn't like to speculate, Mr McCulloch. Things could go in any number of ways and it's far too soon to tell.'

'I appreciate your honesty, Doctor,' Boonzie growled.

'In such cases the relatives are always notified. But it seems it's not been possible to locate a next of kin.'

'I'm his only family. Can I see him? Even for a moment?'

She hesitated. 'You might find it upsetting to see him in his condition.'

If the good doctor only knew the slaughterhouse horrors that Boonzie had witnessed in his lifetime. 'I can handle it,' he replied.

'Just for a moment, then. Come this way.'

Chapter 7

A couple of hours earlier, while Ewan McCulloch was still on the operating table, a phone conversation had taken place. It was a very private and secret call, but if anyone on the outside had been listening they'd quickly have worked out which of the callers was the subordinate, and which of them was clearly in charge.

'What part of this do you not understand? Your instructions were to beat the truth out of him and then kill him. It's not rocket science.'

'We tried to get it out of him. He didn't seem to know anything.'

'So not only did you come back empty-handed, you also left him alive. Are you stupid?'

'It wasn't our fault. I told you, a car turned up before we could finish him off. We had to leg it before we were spotted.'

'Yes, yes. I get the picture. Four tough guys, scared of some bloody old biddy on her own. What a bunch of pathetic cowards.'

'What were we supposed to do, beat the shit out of her as well, in broad daylight? And what if someone else had turned up too?'

'The road past Loch Ardaich isn't exactly the M25. You could easily have handled it.'

'Well, we were unlucky, that's all. Credit where credit's due, chief. We took care of the other moron for you, didn't we? No problems there.'

'Yes, you did. But now I'm wondering if you didn't just get lucky with Campbell. Maybe I should have called Hacker back home from Korea to take care of the job. He doesn't depend on luck.'

'You had your reasons. Hacker works for you personally. You didn't want to be too closely connected with it.'

'Evidently, that was my mistake, trusting a bunch of useless fools on the outside with the simplest of tasks. Did I not pay you enough, perhaps?'

'Give us a break, will you? We didn't do a bad job of searching McCulloch's house. In and out, twenty minutes, nobody any the wiser. If he'd had any more coins stashed away, we'd have found them. And as for him, you don't have anything to worry about. He's in a coma. People in comas don't say much.'

'They're also known to come out of them.'

'I don't think that's likely. We hit him pretty hard. He's got something called an epidural haematoma. Bleeding on the brain. They're operating on him even as we speak. Chances are, if he ever does wake up he'll be a drooling vegetable, sucking on a tube for the rest of his life.'

'You'd better hope you're right about that. Because you've got just as much to lose as I have if he suddenly remembers who worked him over and starts blabbing. Next thing the trail leads back to me.'

'That would never happen.'

'Damn right it won't. I want you to keep a close watch

on things there at the hospital. If Ewan McCulloch so much as bats an eyelid or twitches a finger, I want to know about it. And then I'll expect you to finish what you started. We're not taking any chances here.'

'Killing a man inside a hospital, that won't be easy. Not with doctors and nurses coming and going twenty-four-seven.'

'Don't you watch the news? Medical staff kill patients all the time. If the National Health Service's finest can do it, you can do it. I don't care how it's done. I just want him permanently out of the picture. Whatever it takes. Understand?'

'I understand.'

'That's wonderful to hear. Now stop wasting my time, and don't ever screw things up again. Not while you're working for me. Or you'll end up in a lot worse state than Ewan bloody McCulloch.'

Chapter 8

Boonzie left Belford Hospital with the dreadful image of Ewan, lying crumpled and shrivelled in bed covered with tubes and hooked up to machines, deeply imprinted on his mind. Dr Fraser hadn't permitted him into the intensive care isolation unit and strictly allowed him only a few moments to peer through the thick glass window at his nephew inside.

A few moments were enough. He contained his rage as he walked outside into the windy, rain-slicked car park. Looking around for Duncan Laurie's taxicab, he saw it was gone. The guy had obviously got tired of waiting.

The time was approaching midday. Boonzie's body told him he was hungry but he wasn't interested. He was thinking about his next move, and that he'd need to rustle up some form of transport of his own, when someone called his name from behind. 'Mr McCulloch? Hold on a minute. Can I talk to you?'

He turned to see a woman emerge from the hospital entrance and hurry over to him. He guessed she was in her early or mid-thirties. She was wearing jeans and a rain jacket, and the cold wind blew her long dark hair in streams across her face as she approached. She brushed it away. Boonzie could see she was upset. He had no idea who she was, or how she knew his name.

'I'm Boonzie McCulloch,' he said. 'How can I help ye,

lassie?' When you got to Boonzie's age, everyone younger than forty-five was a lassie or a laddie.

She introduced herself as Grace Kirk and said she was a friend of Ewan's. 'I came to see him, but they wouldn't let me. They told me his uncle was here visiting. Family members only.'

'There's nae much tae see, lassie,' Boonzie said gravely. 'He's in a bad way.'

'Is he . . . will he . . . ?'

'He's alive. Whether he stays that way, or whether he'll have any kind of a life after this, is anybody's guess. Dr Fraser seems tae know what she's doing. I trust her.' That was a big thing to say, coming from Boonzie McCulloch.

Grace buried her face in her hands. 'Oh, God.' She fought with her emotions for a moment or two. When she looked up, her eyes were moist and pink. 'I can't believe something like this could happen to him.'

'I need tae go and talk tae the police,' Boonzie said. 'Do ye know where the station is?'

'I do. I work there.'

'Ye're a policewoman?' Boonzie thought she didn't look the type, but then again, what did he know?

She nodded. 'I'm off duty at the moment, but my shift starts in an hour. Now they won't let me see Ewan, I was about to head back there. You could follow me in your car.'

'If I had one, I would.'

'Then why don't I give you a lift?'

Grace drove an ancient green Land Rover that was speckled with mud on the outside and as crudely minimalistic as a motor vehicle could be on the inside. 'I'm afraid it's not exactly luxury,' she said as they climbed aboard.

Boonzie liked it. 'The hours I've spent in these things. Takes me back, I can tell ye.'

She understood. 'Military?'

'Aye, long time ago. I live in Italy noo.'

'Nice place to retire to.'

'Retire? Me? Not on yer life.'

'I'm sorry, I thought—'

'Ye thought I was old.' *Maybe I am*, he reflected.

'I apologise. What do you do?'

'Grow tomatoes,' he replied, then changed the subject. 'So I take it ye're no one of the officers looking intae what happened to Ewan?'

'I'm too close to it,' she replied wistfully. 'They wouldn't have me on the case, knowing we were friends. Plus, I'm only a constable. DI Macleod and DS Coull are leading the investigation.'

'That'd be who I need tae talk tae, then.' He looked at her. 'So you and Ewan must know each other pretty well?'

'Once upon a time,' she replied, a little evasively. 'I've only just come back to this area after working away down in Glasgow for a few years.'

'That's where I'm from. Born and bred.'

She flashed a sad smile. 'No kidding? I never would've guessed.' Then the smile was gone again, like a ray of sunshine swallowed up behind fast-moving clouds. 'This place is heaven to me. I can't believe something like this could happen here. Especially not to someone like Ewan.'

'Aye, well, it did.'

When they got to the police station, Grace led Boonzie inside and before long he was being shown into an interview room with the two officers in charge of the investigation, who introduced themselves as DI Fergus Macleod and DS Jim Coull. Boonzie thought that a Detective Inspector and a Detective Sergeant were a lot of horsepower to allocate to a simple assault and battery case, albeit a serious one. They invited him to sit, but Boonzie had done enough sitting on his journey to Scotland to last him a while, and remained standing. Grace hovered in the background, still out of uniform, while the detectives ran through their standard patter with Boonzie, designed to placate and reassure and instil trust, using phrases like 'bring to justice' and 'leave no stone unturned'.

Boonzie cut to the chase with, 'So do ye have any suspects yet?'

'Not at this time, Mr McCulloch. It's still very early days.'

'Seems tae me ye're looking at two related crimes,' Boonzie said. 'Ewan had reason tae believe that what happened tae his business partner Ross Campbell was nae accident. Now someone's oot tae get him, too.'

'We know about your nephew's suspicions regarding Mr Campbell's death,' Coull said. 'He was here two days ago, telling us the whole story. I should say it was quite a tale. Something about a salmon poacher working the loch at the time of the alleged incident. Also about some gold coins that were in Mr Campbell's possession.' Coull added the last part with a raised eyebrow and an expectant tone.

Ewan's visit to Fort William police station was news to Boonzie. The gold coins were even more so. He said nothing for a moment as he wondered why Ewan hadn't mentioned them. It could all have happened since they'd last spoken, while Boonzie was attending to certain matters before setting off.

'I gather you and he have been in contact,' Macleod said. 'Just out of interest, he didn't happen to mention anything about the coins to you, did he? Such as, where exactly Mr Campbell might have found them?'

It sounded to Boonzie as though the cops were fishing for particular information here, though he had no idea what or why. 'No, it's the first I've heard o' it. What've gold coins got to do with this?'

'I'm afraid that's a police matter,' Macleod said, clamping on the lid with something that looked a little too much like a satisfied smile. 'Concerning a separate investigation.'

Thirty-three years in the military, twenty-six of them as an NCO climbing up the ranks of the British Army's most elite regiment, had honed Boonzie's skill at reading people. Neither Macleod nor Coull was making a good impression on him. He sensed they were holding back. He didn't like being kept in the dark.

'A separate investigation? So ye're saying ye dinnae see these two cases as connected?'

'Again, it's too early to say, Mr McCulloch,' Coull replied in a smarmy, condescending tone that made the bristles on the back of Boonzie's neck prickle even more. Coull added, 'And as we're not generally in the habit of divulging the details of our ongoing police investigations to the public, might I suggest that you go home and let us take care of it? Rest assured, we'll find the men who did this.'

Boonzie grunted. 'Aye, we've heard that shite before.'

Macleod said sharply, 'Meaning what?'

'Meaning that I havnae come all the way here from Italy tae be given the brush-off, while my nephew's lyin' in a hospital bed wi' a face like raw minced steak an' a stoved-in heid he might never recover from. Ye've had two long days tae investigate what Ewan told ye aboot the poacher, and it seems tae me as though ye've done bugger all but sit on yer big fat arse' – pointing first at Macleod, then swivelling his accusatory finger like a turret-mounted fifty-cal Browning to aim at Coull – 'and yer wee scrawny arse.'

With the cops momentarily too stunned and outraged to utter a reply, Boonzie glowered at them both with steely

51

disapproval and added, 'There's more tae this than meets the eye, and if the police cannae be bothered tae find out what, then I damn well will.'

Standing in the background, Grace Kirk hadn't spoken a word. Boonzie thought he saw a flicker of amusement curl her lip, but then she quickly suppressed it.

There were no such smiles from the two detectives. Macleod was the first to bounce back. 'You're not showing a lot of respect for officers of the law, Mr McCulloch.'

'Ye get what ye're due, son. Nae mair, nae less.'

'I hope you're not getting ideas about pursuing any sort of private citizen's inquiry,' Coull said, with cheeks flushed the colour of cheap wine. 'The police take a very dim view of that kind of thing.'

'Then ye'd best stay oot ma road,' Boonzie grated. 'There's nae room for amateurs in this kind of business.'

'You're warned, McCulloch!' Macleod stood up aggressively from his chair. He was four inches taller and considerably wider than Boonzie, and was all hard-eyed and tensed up like a silverback gorilla ready to attack. It was a display of intimidation most men would have shrunk away from, but Boonzie did not shrink away. He stared at Macleod, calm and cold, and kept staring until the cop seemed to deflate and sat down again without another word.

At which point, the discussion was over. 'I'm sorry, lassie,' Boonzie said to Grace, and walked out of the room.

Chapter 9

Grace caught up with him again in a quiet corridor as he made his way back towards the station reception. Boonzie said, 'I suppose ye're gonnae give me a hard time for what happened in there.'

She shook her head, more in disbelief than in disagreement, and despite all the sadness of the moment he saw the same twinkle of mirth on her face as she'd tried to mask in the interview room. 'Honestly, Mr McCulloch. What a way to speak to my superiors. Big fat arse and wee scrawny arse?'

'Didnae take it too well, did they?'

'You tell it like you see it, that's for sure.'

'Is there any other way?'

'What was all that stuff about a salmon poacher? I didn't understand.'

Boonzie was often slow to trust people, but he got a good feeling about Grace Kirk. He briefly ran through what Ewan had told him about the strange phone call he'd received the evening of Ross's funeral.

'Do you think it's true?' she asked, deeply perplexed.

'Ewan's nae liar.'

'But was the poacher telling the truth? What if it was just a stupid hoax? Some idiot calling to stir things up?'

'I dinnae think so. Ewan thought he knew him.'

Grace stared at Boonzie. 'Knew him? From where? Who is this person?'

'Ewan couldnae place the name,' Boonzie said. 'All we know is, the poacher is someone with a secret. Who needed tae get it off his chest and warn Ewan tae watch his back.'

She shook her head in disbelief. 'The whole thing is insane. This is Kinlochardaich. Murders don't happen here.'

'Until the day they do,' Boonzie replied.

'And what's with the gold coins? I didn't understand that part either.'

'Nor me, hen. Ewan never mentioned anything.'

'I don't like this one bit. Please. I'm asking you. Won't you just go home and let the police handle this situation?'

Boonzie's face hardened like granite. He replied, 'I came here tae help Ewan. It's too late for that. But I'm no leavin' until I find the people who did this.'

Grace could see that no force on earth could change his mind. She paused, glanced over her shoulder as though to check nobody was watching, then quickly took a slip of paper from her pocket and pressed it into his hand. It was a grocery receipt, on the back of which she'd scribbled a phone number.

'That's my personal mobile. Will you call me if you need anything?'

Boonzie said, 'Like what?'

She flushed slightly, shrugged. 'Ewan and I . . . we were close once, a long time ago. We weren't much more than kids back then. Anyway, he often used to talk about you. Said you were like a father to him. After what's happened I just thought – just between you and me, you know? – that if there's anything I can do to help . . .'

Boonzie was touched by her words. It didn't surprise him to hear that she and his nephew had known each other better than she'd let on at first. He didn't miss a lot, and had noticed the way she talked about Ewan. He also got the impression that she wasn't overly impressed at the way her provincial cop colleagues were handling the case. But he kept all that to himself and replied simply, 'That's very kind of you, lassie. I appreciate it.'

'Just please, don't go poking around too much.'

'Because of what those clowns Macleod and Coull might think?'

'No, because you seem like a nice man, and there are obviously some nasty characters about, and I wouldn't like to think of you getting hurt. There's been far too much of that already.'

He smiled. 'I've come across a few nasty characters in my time, and I'm still here. Dinnae you worry aboot me, lassie.'

A door swung open and a pair of uniformed officers stepped through it, talking. One of them smiled at Grace. The other just looked, then glanced at Boonzie. Grace said, 'I'd best get ready for my shift. Where are you headed now?'

'Back tae Kinlochardaich.'

'Will you be okay? Not many buses go out that way.'

'I'll be fine.'

'You take care, all right?'

Boonzie thanked her again, and watched her hurry off. He was a straight-ahead kind of man who either liked people or he didn't, and he'd decided that Grace Kirk was one of the good ones.

She'd been right about the buses, too. It was nearly two hours before Boonzie finally got back to the village. On his way out of the police station he'd stopped at the reception desk and, as next of kin, been given an envelope containing some personal effects Ewan had had on him when they'd brought him in. There wasn't much: wallet, loose change, keys. No phone. Boonzie guessed that the detectives were hanging onto that, for what it was worth.

As he unlocked Ewan's front door to let himself inside, it felt wrong to be here alone. Boonzie wanted his presence to make as little impact as possible on his nephew's home. If he had to stay here a few days, he'd kip on the sofa rather than use a bedroom, and wouldn't use the kitchen. Boonzie had been trained to sleep rough, live off the land and leave no trace of his passing, and spent many years instilling those same skills into others. Old habits died hard.

But the moment he stepped inside the house, such thoughts were forgotten as he saw the obvious signs that someone else had been here. Someone not as worried about disrupting the place.

Ewan's house had been completely turned over.

Chapter 10

Boonzie had seen burglaries before and knew immediately this was something different. Whoever had broken in had been searching for something. Drawers had been rifled, sofa cushions slashed and the stuffing pulled out. Even the carpets had been pulled up as though someone wanted to check the floorboards. It was a mess. This had been the work of more than a single intruder. More likely two or three, working in tandem to ransack the place and get out fast.

Boonzie soon found the intruders' entry point, a broken utility room window in the rear, overlooking a weedy yard filled with bins, junk and a parked camper van. Access was through a lane that cut between the backs of the houses. The intruders had reached through the smashed glass to open the window and climb in. He secured the window shut and then returned to the main rooms, where most of the damage was, to look for any clues.

Ewan had used the small dining area off the living room as a basic home office, with a little workstation desk against one wall. Boonzie noticed the empty space on the desk, a rectangle of dust where something had been removed. There was a printer and scanner, a nest of tangled wires, a pair of disconnected computer speakers and a monitor screen, but the computer itself was missing. The intruders had taken it.

But who were they, and what had they been looking for?

Boonzie considered reporting this new development to the police, then changed his mind. Why complicate matters, especially with those two useless idiots in charge of the case? He already knew what he had to do, and they'd only get in his way.

Saddened by the state of the place, he set about tidying up as best he could. As he worked he found a balled-up piece of notepaper lying in the corner behind a wastepaper basket. Uncrumpling it to see what it was, he found that it was covered in handwriting he recognised as Ewan's.

Boonzie had left his reading glasses at home in Italy, and had to peer closely at the paper to read what Ewan had written on it. The upper third of the page was a scrawl of notes Boonzie didn't really understand. Something about 'Louis d'or', and some dates and other names that meant little to him. Below that were some jottings about local history, dating back to the eighteenth century, featuring a few famous names that Boonzie did recognise, though it was unclear why Ewan had been taking such an interest in the subject. The notes at the bottom of the page switched away from history and were about illegal salmon fishing in the area. Underneath Ewan had scribbled in capitals the words 'WHO IS THE POACHER??' and underlined them so hard he'd scratched right through the paper.

Boonzie smoothed the page flat, folded it neatly and put it in his pocket. Then turned to look around him at the wrecked room. Until now he'd managed to keep a handle on his emotions. The image of Ewan in the intensive care unit flashed into his mind, and he thought how his nephew might never awaken from the coma these people had put him into. Rage boiled up inside him.

'Bastards,' he muttered.

Boonzie put his hand on his chest as he suddenly felt an

odd sensation behind his ribs, followed by a jolt of pain that made him let out a low groan. He swayed slightly on his feet and reached out to support himself on the back of a chair. He waited a few seconds for the pain to subside, then walked slowly into the kitchen to find a glass and fill it with tapwater. He used it to gulp down the last couple of pills from one of the little bottles he now carried everywhere with him. He hated taking them. There was a fresh bottle in his pocket. He tossed away the empty.

When he felt better, he went to pick up Ewan's landline phone and called Mirella. 'It's me. Just checking in. You okay?'

She was happy and relieved to hear from him. They spent very little time apart, as a rule, and she told him how much she was missing him.

'Listen, hen, there's bad news. It's aboot Ewan.' Boonzie quickly filled her in on all that had happened, and shared his belief that the same people who killed Ross Campbell had tried to kill him, too. He told her about his meeting with the cops, and how he'd decided to pursue this himself.

Mirella was shocked and worried, but her greatest anxiety was for her husband caught up in the middle of this situation. 'Promise me you'll take care.'

'You know I will. Always.'

'How do you feel? Are you taking your medicine?'

'Och, I'm fine,' he said, brushing off her concerns. 'Strong as an ox.'

Mirella knew how stubborn he was, and that he didn't like being fussed over. More matter-of-factly she said, 'Something came for you. An email, from your nephew. He sent it last night. I only saw it today.'

'From Ewan? What aboot?'

'Hold on, I'll read it to you.' A pause, while Mirella carried the phone over to the computer and pulled up the email.

'Okay, here it is. It just says, "Ross found this. It gets weirder. Hope you get here soon."'

'Ross found what?'

'There was an attachment with the email. I opened it. It's a photo of an old coin. It looks like gold. Why would he send you that? Has this got something to do with what's happened to him and his friend?'

Boonzie didn't want to burden Mirella with more concerns, so he reassured her that it would all be sorted out soon.

'I hate you not being here,' she said with a sniff.

'I'll be back home before ye know it, pet.'

'Call me every day. Don't let me sit here worrying.'

'Twice a day,' he promised. Then he repeated once more how much he loved her. Which he truly did, no less than the day he'd first laid eyes on her and fallen hard. He reassured her that things would be fine and not to fret. It was hard to say goodbye.

When the call was over, Boonzie sat thinking for a long time. These damned gold coins just wouldn't go away. They were clearly vital to understand what was going on here, but he wouldn't know where to start with something like that. By contrast, Ewan's notes about salmon poaching had given him an idea. If he could find the poacher, he could begin to unravel this whole thing. And there was no better time to start than right away.

The first thing Boonzie needed to do was sort himself out some wheels. He went back to the utility room with the broken window and looked again at the camper van parked in Ewan's back yard. It was old and dirty and neglected-looking, but ideal for his purposes. He didn't want to stay in the house. If he'd thought the men who had ransacked it might return, he'd have felt differently and wanted to lie in wait for them, but he knew they wouldn't be coming back here. The camper van would give him a mobile base from which to pursue his objective, wherever it led him.

Boonzie was a man of many talents, even if a lot of them were underused these days. Among the skills he'd learned in the regiment was fixing old vehicles, the kind that soldiers making their way deep behind enemy lines might have to commandeer. He found the camper keys on a hook in the hallway and went out to inspect it.

A quick look around the vehicle confirmed his first impressions. The camper was equipped with two berths, sleeping bag and blankets, a stove, heater, and even a tiny washroom with a chemical cassette toilet. A little travel-stained and threadbare, but not too grotty and sheer bloody luxury compared to some of the places he'd been forced to make camp in his life. The engine wouldn't start at first, but an hour later he had the corroded battery connections fixed up as good as new and the diesel glow plugs switched for a new set he found in the house, and the old girl coughed into life at the first twist of the key. He left the engine running to put charge into the battery, and returned to the house.

It was mid-afternoon and the light was already beginning to fade. After living in Italy so long he'd almost forgotten how early the winter evenings fell, this far north. Back in the house he worked through the plan that was coming together in his mind. Certain additional items were required in order to put it into action. He dug a copy of the Yellow Pages out of the wreckage of Ewan's living room and soon found what he was looking for. The place he had to go next was more than an hour's drive away, but he would make it.

Boonzie locked up the house, climbed aboard the camper and drove out of the yard and into the street. By nightfall, he'd have the things he needed.

Then he'd be ready to go hunting.

Chapter 11

While Boonzie was making his preparations, another phone conversation was going on between the same two individuals as before.

The underling reported, 'There's been another development, chief.'

His superior replied, quite irritably, 'What kind of development?'

'Someone else is on the scene. An old guy. A relative of McCulloch's.'

'I thought McCulloch didn't have any family.'

'Turns out he does. An uncle. His name's McCulloch, too. Lives in Italy. Arrived here this morning.'

The superior heaved an impatient sigh. 'Okay. Now tell me why I need to be concerned about some old guy who lives in Italy.'

'Because he's isn't just any old old guy. He's probably twice as fit as most men half his age. A right hard case.'

'And why is this a problem?'

The underling said, 'Firstly, he isn't buying the accidental drowning theory about Campbell. He seems to think the cases are connected.'

'I wonder where he got that idea. The poacher?'

'His nephew told him the whole story.'

'To be expected, I suppose. Go on.'

'Uncle McCulloch's got a bit of an attitude problem. Not a happy chappie. And he's intent on pursuing his own investigation.'

'I see. One of those.'

'But here's the worrying part, chief. The guy is ex-military. Retired British Army non-com. We tried to get into his MoD file and hit a brick wall. Classified shit. You know what that means.'

'Why the hell should I know what that means?'

'It means trouble,' the underling replied. 'Now, it so happens that I've got a brother-in-law who works for the Ministry. I was able to call in a favour and—'

'I'm a busy man. Why don't you just cut to the chase and tell me what you found out?'

'Well, I've got McCulloch's whole bio here in front of me. And like I thought, it turns out this bastard was no ordinary soldier. I really think you should listen to this.'

'Let's hear it, then.'

'Born in Glasgow in 1953. Joined up at seventeen and was accepted into the Parachute Regiment two years later, in 1972. Did five years with them before he passed selection for 22 Special Air Service in February, 1977.'

'You're telling me that this moron Ewan McCulloch had an uncle in the SAS. Great. Just great.'

'He served with them for twenty-six years. Counter-hijack and counter-terrorism specialist. A hell of a record, chief. I mean, you name it, he's been there and done it. Operation Nimrod, 1980. The Iranian Embassy siege. Then the following year in Gambia, he was one of the special ops team who went in and rescued the President's wife and kids from leftist rebels. Falklands War, 1982, he was with D Squadron for the famous assault on Pebble Island, when they destroyed half the Argentine air force in just thirty minutes.'

'Oh, wonderful.'

'In '87 he was taking out IRA insurgents in Northern Ireland. Same year, his SAS unit got deployed to end the Peterhead Prison riot, here in Scotland. Blew their way in and stopped it before the rioters even knew what was happening. Four years after that, it was Operation Desert Storm, search-and-destroying SCUD missiles the Iraqis were trying to lob into Israel. Then in Bosnia in 1997 he was with the unit that shot dead a Serb war criminal called Simo Drljaca.'

'This just keeps getting better.'

'The following year they did a snatch mission in Serbia against another war criminal, Stevan Todorovic. Tracked the guy to a remote hideout in the mountains, kidnapped him in the dead of night and whisked him back into Bosnia to be arrested. After that, in 2001, yer man was sent to Afghanistan for Operation Trent, fighting against the Taliban—'

'All right, all right, I get the picture.'

'There's probably more, all kinds of black-ops crap that nobody without a top-grade security clearance even knows about. He finally retired in 2003, rank of Colour Sergeant. Moved to Italy with his wife, been living there ever since.'

'And now he's honouring us with his company here in Scotland. Lucky us.'

'It's a worry. Someone with this bastard's skills could be dangerous, if he starts sniffing around.'

'I'd call that an understatement. All thanks to you, I might add.'

'Chief, this guy would've turned up even if we'd killed McCulloch. In fact that would've probably made things worse.'

'I'd say it's bad enough as it is, don't you? Where is he now?'

'At his nephew's house. Baird followed him there earlier and he's watching the place. I spoke to him just before I called you. The old guy is still there. What should we do? You want him taken care of?'

'If I said yes, what makes you think you're up to the job, after last time?'

'This will be different. No more screwups.'

'He needs to disappear. Gone. Vanished. Not a trace. The sooner the better, before he starts talking to too many people and drawing attention.'

'Baird can handle it. Knife job, quick and dirty, no witnesses, while the old guy's still at the house. He won't even see him coming.'

'No. Baird's just a violent retard. From what you say, the old guy will chew him up and spit out the bones. I think you'd better pull Baird off McCulloch's tail before he gets spotted or somehow manages to mess things up for us. I have other plans.'

'Like what?'

'It takes a pro to deal with a pro. I'm sending in Hacker.'

Chapter 12

The Normandy coast
Two days later

Ben Hope had always been a runner. In his mindset, if you weren't constantly moving forwards, you were going backwards. That had never been an option for a person of his restless disposition, who needed to keep pushing hard from one challenging goal to the next. Somewhere deep in his mind he believed that, like a Great White shark, if he stopped moving, he'd sink to the bottom and die. He'd made himself physically fit from his mid-teens onwards, running and cycling and rock-climbing as though he was being chased by demons. That was before he'd joined the British Army and stern, shouty men in PT Instructor insignia took him to the next level and beyond. During his career he'd been able to achieve a degree of fitness, motivation and commitment that was off the charts. Now, all these years later, he still ran every day.

He liked to vary his routine. Sometimes he could be found pounding the woodland tracks and undulating wildflower meadows around the rural thirty-acre compound he co-owned here in France, a place called Le Val. Other times, he would drive out to this long, lonely stretch of beach just a few miles away on the coast. The beach was where he'd come today, to stretch his legs and put himself to the test during some downtime.

Winter was the season in which Ben liked running the most. A cold wind was blowing in off the sea, carrying pockets of squally rain that soaked him to the bone. This was his element, and the physical discomfort just made him push harder. The adverse weather on this chilly December day meant that the beach was totally deserted except for him and his German Shepherd, Storm, who loved nothing more than to tag along after his master on these punishing work-outs with his tail wagging and his long pink tongue lolling out. Ben loved the emptiness. It allowed him to run at his peak and be alone with his thoughts.

A couple of times a week, as he was doing today, he liked to raise the endurance bar an extra notch by carrying a bergen weighed down with forty pounds of sand. Back in the day, he and his Special Forces comrades used to hump much greater loads than that for endless miles both in training and in combat. This was taking it easy by compar-ison. But it was enough to keep him in better shape than most of the much younger guys who came to be put through their paces at Le Val.

Ben co-ran the tactical training facility with his business partner and close friend Jeff Dekker. Jeff's career had followed a parallel course to Ben's, serving for years in the Navy's Special Boat Service. Along with ex-soldier Tuesday Fletcher and the rest of their team they were kept busy by all the military, police and private close protection personnel who travelled to their quiet corner of rural Normandy from all over the world to hone their skills and learn from the best.

Ben finished his run and returned to where he'd parked his new car among the dunes on the approach to the beach.

It was the latest in a line of BMW Alpina high-performance sedans, dark metallic blue. As much as he favoured the marque, he seemed to keep trashing them. The last one had been shot to pieces in a gun battle outside Alençon, a few months earlier. He blipped the locks open as he trudged up the loose sand. His body felt loose and pumped. Ten hard miles, and he was barely out of breath. Not too shabby. The dog was more tired than he was.

Ben dumped his bergen in the back of the Alpina, drank half a litre of bottled spring water, then changed out of his sandy running shoes. As he was getting ready to head back to Le Val he saw that he had a new voicemail message waiting for him on his phone.

It was from Jeff. He didn't sound very happy, but that was no surprise since he'd fractured a bone in his wrist during a training exercise two weeks earlier, and was currently confined to desk duties with a cast and sling. Yet Ben could tell instantly from his tone that something else was wrong. Jeff sounded uncharacteristically worried. All he said was, 'Call me back soon as.'

Ben did, right away. 'Got your message. What's up?'

'Boonzie's wife called the office number just now.'

'Mirella?'

'Yeah. Tuesday got the call and passed it on to me. There's some kind of problem. She seemed pretty upset.'

'Did she say what kind of problem?'

'No, she wanted to speak to you about it. I think you'd better talk to her, mate. It sounds serious.'

It made sense to Ben that Mirella would rather talk to him, since Jeff didn't know Ben's old comrade Boonzie and his Italian wife as well as Ben did. But it didn't make sense to Ben that it was Mirella, rather than Boonzie himself, who'd called. Something was obviously wrong.

Rather than let it wait until he got home, Ben punched Boonzie and Mirella's landline number into his mobile. He sat in the car, watching the waves rolling in as the call connected and he heard the Italian dial tone. Storm had jumped into the back and was panting hot breath in Ben's other ear and trying to lick his face. He gently pushed the dog away as Mirella's voice came on the line, saying, 'Pronto?'

Jeff had been right. She didn't sound good at all.

Boonzie had learned Italian shortly after moving to Campobasso, and rather stubbornly insisted on speaking it with her all the time, so Mirella had never got to perfect her English. Which was fine, since Ben spoke Italian very well. 'Mirella, it's Ben.'

She sounded even more distraught, on the point of tears, as she thanked him for calling back so soon.

He asked, 'What's wrong?'

'It's Archibald.' Mirella never called her husband by his nickname. Given that Boonzie would typically threaten dire violence against anyone else who dared to refer to him any other way, very few people did.

Ben steeled himself for the news that his dear old friend had fallen critically ill, or had received some terrible medical diagnosis, been given a week to live or was already dead. Not that Boonzie was particularly ancient. Even if he had been, the grizzled old warrior was one of those people you expect to live for ever, carved out of granite and as enduring and immutable as a mountain range.

But Mirella's reply shocked him even more. 'He's missing.'

Ben stayed grimly silent as Mirella told him the story that had played out over the last few days. She explained how Boonzie had travelled to the Highlands of Scotland to visit his nephew Ewan, who'd been having some trouble. Ben hadn't even known Boonzie had a nephew. He went on listening as she described the backstory of Ewan's partner in the surveying business, recently drowned in an apparent accident that Ewan thought he had reason to suspect to be foul play.

The more Mirella talked, the faster the words came streaming out. Ben had to close his eyes and focus hard to keep up with the stream. He interrupted her flow with, 'Hold on. Why did he think that?'

'Because he received an anonymous phone call from a person claiming to be a witness to a crime,' Mirella replied. 'They said they saw some men murdering Ewan's friend.'

As she went on explaining what she knew about the mystery witness, Ben listened hard and tried to make sense of it all. 'So Boonzie – Archibald – went there to help Ewan do what? Track down this salmon fisherman guy?'

'And find out what happened to Ross. But now Ewan is hurt, too. Archibald thought the same people who killed Ross had tried to kill him.'

'Are the local police involved in this?'

'He went to speak to them, but he wasn't impressed. He decided to go his own way. You know him, how independent-minded he can be. And he doesn't trust the police, at the best of times.'

Ben certainly did know him, and could also resonate with his reasons for going it alone. But it sounded like Boonzie had got himself into something bad, and that worried Ben. He asked, 'When did you last speak to him?'

'Two days ago. He doesn't use a mobile phone. He called me from his nephew's house. That was when he told me what happened to Ewan, how badly he was hurt, and how the police weren't going to be of any help. Then I told him about the email that had come for him.'

'What email?'

'From his nephew.' Mirella repeated to Ben what she'd already told her husband, reading out the short text of Ewan's message verbatim. She described the image file that Ewan had attached with it. 'It was a photo of a gold coin. The thing that Ross was supposed to have found. That's all I know.'

Ben frowned at the mention of the coin. In his experience, gold and murder went together like strawberries and ice cream, and this made the suspicions of foul play seem more plausible. He said, 'Can you send me the image file?', and told her the email address to send it to.

Mirella was marginally more savvy with newfangled gadgetry than her technophobe husband. 'I'm doing it now.'

Moments later, the email pinged into Ben's inbox. He put the call on speaker while he opened up the file and scrutinised the picture. It was a good photo, focused sharp and up-close. No question that it was a gold coin. An old one, showing the date 1745. Probably valuable, though at this point Ben had no clear idea.

'What the hell is this about, Mirella?'

'I don't know,' she replied helplessly. 'Archibald didn't say much when I told him about it. But he sounded as though it was no surprise. Like he already knew something.'

'Did he say what he was going to do next? Where he was heading after Ewan's house?'

'If he had a plan, he didn't tell me what it was. He just promised me he'd be home soon, and not to worry. But I am, Ben. I'm so desperately worried. He promised to keep in touch. Said he'd call twice a day to tell me where he was and what was happening. But it's been two whole days and I haven't heard anything from him at all! I keep imagining all kinds of terrible things. I'm going crazy here on my own. I had to talk to you.'

Ben said nothing for a few moments, thinking about his

friend. Boonzie McCulloch was one of the toughest old war dogs Ben had ever known, and he'd known a few. The kind of guy you'd thank God was on your side, and not the enemy's. Boonzie was also famously reticent when it came to talking about his past exploits. Ben was certain that even Mirella knew only a fraction of what her husband had been through, and survived, in his time.

'He's pretty resilient, Mirella. The fact that you haven't heard from him might not mean he's in trouble. It's possible that he's gone to ground for a while, and can't call you. Maybe he will, any time now. And then everything will be okay again.'

'There's something else,' she said, in a voice that sounded hollow, drained of energy. 'Something he'd never have wanted me to tell anyone. He made me swear to keep quiet about it. Like if it was never talked about, it wouldn't be real any more and it would just go away. But it is real. And it isn't going away so easily.'

'I don't understand. What are you talking about?'

And then she told him about Boonzie's illness.

Chapter 13

Mirella said, 'I could tell he was having a problem. He seemed tired a lot more often than usual, and sometimes he looked pale. Something was obviously bothering him, but he kept insisting that he was fine and would get irritable if I pestered him about it. Then about six months ago, he finally confessed that he'd been getting increasingly severe chest pains and was becoming worried about them.'

Ben asked, 'How serious is it?'

'I persuaded him to see a private specialist in Campobasso. The doctor ran some tests and soon diagnosed heart disease. Said there was a risk of cardiac arrest if the condition was left untreated. Archibald just brushed it off, didn't want to accept the diagnosis. When we got home, he wouldn't even talk about it. I was so angry and upset. That man is as stubborn as a mule.'

Tell me about it, Ben thought. He waited anxiously to hear more.

'Anyway, of course, the pains got worse. Eventually he agreed that something had to be done. Two months ago, he went into hospital to be fitted with a pacemaker.'

This was news, even though Ben and Boonzie kept in touch regularly. 'I spoke with him just six weeks or so ago.

I thought he sounded a little tired, but he never mentioned a single word to me about operations and pacemakers.'

'And he'd have hated anyone knowing. Even more than he hates having it. He's not as strong as he used to be, and he has to take all these pills every day. Of course, he works twice as hard to prove himself. But he's struggling, Ben, I can tell. He's been getting fainting attacks. I read that some of these defibrillation implants can malfunction sometimes, or that all kinds of complications can happen, even a year after the operation. When he told me he needed to go to Scotland I begged him to stay, but he wouldn't listen. What if something happened to him there? Why else wouldn't he have called me again in two whole days?'

'We don't know that, Mirella,' Ben said, lowering his voice to sound more reassuring.

'I already called the hospital, in case he might have been taken there. It's in a town called Fort William. The only patient there with the surname McCulloch was his nephew Ewan. But that doesn't mean nothing has happened. The town is miles from where Ewan lives. It's a remote place, deep in the hills. Archibald could be out there somewhere, with nobody to help if he got into trouble. He could have fainted again, or had a bad attack, and nobody might even know about it until—' Mirella's voice had reached a peak of anxiety and now broke apart into a sob.

Ben was quiet for a long time. Then he said, 'Tell me the name of the place.'

She read it out for him, struggling with the strange foreign spelling. Ben noted it down and was instantly putting together his plan.

'Here's what we're going to do, Mirella. I'll get there as quickly as I can. You need to stay by the phone and call me immediately if you hear from him. Okay?'

'Yes, of course.'

'I need as much information from you as possible to help me find him,' Ben said. 'For example, did he rent a car at the airport?' Knowing what kind of vehicle Boonzie was using would be a useful asset. The registration number, even better. There were ways of bluffing that kind of knowledge out of rental companies.

'He went by train.'

Ben considered the kind of remote local stations the area would have, not a car rental outlet for miles around. 'Then how's he travelling?'

'I don't know. I'm sorry.'

'Don't worry about it. What about other contacts there? Does he know anyone else in the village, did he mention any names to you? A friend of Ewan's, perhaps? Or maybe he booked a place to stay, like a hotel or guesthouse?'

'He never mentioned anything about that to me.'

Ben said nothing. He'd have little to go on when he got there. But that wasn't anything new to him.

Mirella said, 'I don't know how to thank you for this, Ben. I didn't know who else to turn to. I couldn't go to Scotland alone. I wouldn't know where to begin.'

'You don't have to,' Ben told her. 'That's what you have me for. Finding people is what I do best, and I *will* find him. That's a promise.'

And that was how, within just a few hours, Ben was getting ready to set off on another unexpected mission. They had a habit of coming his way just when he was settling back into a steady routine and life seemed comparatively normal and peaceful. He never turned down people in need of his help. And he sure as hell wasn't going to fail to be there for one of his oldest and closest friends in the world.

Back at Le Val, Ben's work schedule for the next few days

was quickly rejuggled. Classes were cancelled, while others had to be reassigned to the stalwart Tuesday Fletcher, who was already covering for the workload Jeff couldn't handle with one arm in a sling. Needless to say, both men would have happily dropped everything and closed Le Val's doors to come with him to Scotland, but Ben wouldn't have it. Even Jeff had to admit he wouldn't be of much use with a fractured wrist.

'Anyhow,' Ben said, 'it's hardly a three-man job. The old bugger is probably having the time of his life up there, and just forgot to call home.'

Privately, he wished he could be that confident. A tingling sensation was gnawing inside him. It was a sense of deep foreboding, as though some part of his mind predicted that he was walking into danger. He tried to shake off the feeling, but it hung over him like a cloud.

Cherbourg was the nearest airport to Le Val, and the first available flight to Inverness was leaving late that evening. Ben booked his ticket online, then packed a few items into his battered, much-travelled canvas army bag. It was going to get chilly up north. Thermal gear and winter socks? Check. His warmest pair of waterproof combat boots? Check. Cold weather Norgi Top? Check. Spare packs of cigarettes? Essential. After sharing a light dinner with Jeff and Tuesday in the cosy surroundings of the old farmhouse kitchen, no wine, he shrugged on his old brown leather jacket, said a warm goodbye to Storm and walked out to the Alpina with his bag.

The winter's night was crisp and frosty, and the forecast had threatened snow. As Ben drove to the airport he kept glancing at his phone in its cradle on the dash, plumbed into the car's speaker system in readiness for Mirella's call to say that she'd finally received contact from Boonzie and all was well. He would have loved nothing more than to be able to turn back towards home. But the call didn't come, and turning back was not an option. He chain-smoked Gauloises cigarettes all the way to Cherbourg to alleviate his worry. That didn't do much good, either.

Ben's plane was on time, for what it was worth. The flight was a frustrating twelve-hour marathon that took him a staggered route via Lyon and Amsterdam and soon made him wish that he'd just driven the thousand or so kilometres direct. He checked his phone at each stop-off. Nothing from Mirella. Then, after a delay to clear snow from the runway, he finally boarded the KLM jet for the third leg of his journey.

Every wasted hour only made him fret all the more. When they eventually got into the air, Ben closed his eyes and tried to sleep, but he couldn't force his mind to relax. Old memories flooded his thoughts. Some good, some less good. Some very nasty indeed.

A number of years had passed since his last journey to the Scottish Highlands. It had been back in 2004, at a time when he'd not long been out of the regiment. His objective on that occasion had been to spring an unannounced visit on a former Special Forces commanding officer, a man named Liam Falconer. That trip had not gone well, at least not for Falconer and several of his entourage. That was the price he'd paid for having involved himself in some secret operations he shouldn't have, dark and shadowy even by the standards of the black-ops world Ben had just left.

Men had died. Ben had been the one who had killed them. He did not enjoy taking lives. It was something he had been trained to do out of necessity, and he did it proficiently enough to have ensured that he'd been the only person to walk out of that situation.

He hoped nothing bad awaited him in Scotland this time around, but he sensed that he was hoping in vain. The feeling of foreboding had not left him. It was growing deeper and more threatening with every mile he came nearer to his destination. The same familiar adrenalin-tinged dread he'd experienced so many times in the past as a soldier heading into the heart of war.

Boonzie McCulloch, where the hell are you?

Chapter 14

At last, too many long and grinding hours after leaving France, Ben's plane dropped down out of a cold grey sky and he got his first glimpse of Inverness. The quiet airport lay seven miles from the city and had once been a military airfield. Now it was the Gateway to the Highlands and Islands, standing in lonely isolation against a backdrop of misty hills and the distant North Sea.

Disembarking, Ben was glad he'd brought warm clothes. The piercing wind felt as though it was roaring straight down from Iceland, and the sleet promised to turn to snow if the temperature dropped any lower.

His first action was to call Mirella and find out what he already knew, deep inside: still no contact from Boonzie. It was now the third day since she'd last heard from him. 'I'll find him,' Ben assured her.

But he had to get there first.

He hunted for a car rental place and was relieved to find a small independent firm that obviously hadn't heard about the near-blanket ban imposed on him by most of their larger competitors. For some peculiar reason the latter seemed to object to having their vehicles returned to them riddled with holes, burnt or blown up. But he resolved to take extra care this time around.

The village of Kinlochardaich, Boonzie's last known location, lay seventy miles inland to the south-west. Ben required a car that could get him to his destination as quickly as possible and was rugged enough to handle the remoter parts of the western Highlands in winter, since there was no telling what kinds of roads or conditions he might meet out there. The answer to his needs was a big, chunky Mercedes four-wheel-drive. Fast and comfortable, a tad luxurious for his needs, but sturdy as hell.

His route was the A82, one of the most famous highways in Scotland since for miles it closely hugged the shoreline of Loch Ness, home of the fabled creature. Ben was too concerned about reaching his target to take in the views across the rippling, mysterious waters of the loch. With the wipers slapping away the sleet and the Merc's heater belching full blast he ripped by the ruins of Urquhart Castle and the village of Drumnadrochit, empty of holidaymakers at this time of the year but peppered everywhere with signs for Nessieland and monster theme tours. From Fort Augustus the road followed the Caledonian Canal through Glen Mor and along Loch Lochy. More endless, beautiful scenery that Ben flatly ignored as he pressed the big Mercedes along. Road signs were bilingual, in English and Gaelic.

Rather than rely on GPS he had a map of the area imprinted on his mind. The seventy miles took him just over an hour, by which time his winding path had led him deep into ever-remoter country and his car was alone on the road for long periods. The thickening sleet slapped the windscreen and the outside temperature fell to just above zero, but inside was a bubble of warmth. His first glimpse of his destination was the eastern edge of Loch Ardaich, its restless grey waters surrounded by forest and rocky hills whose tops were shrouded in mist. He followed a lonely signpost directing him towards the village of Kinlochardaich, and not long afterwards he was making his way through the quiet, narrow streets.

The houses were mostly grey stone, settled into themselves with the passing of a century or more. He passed an old church with a graveyard, and a village filling station with a workshop and a couple of pumps, a village shop and post office; and soon after that he found the street whose name Mirella had given him.

Ewan's address would have been one of Boonzie's first ports of call when he arrived here, aside from visiting his nephew in the hospital, so it would also be Ben's. He parked in an empty space directly in front of Ewan's home, which was in a terraced row right on the street. He got out of the Mercedes, stretched his legs and back after the drive, lit up a Gauloise and then locked the car and walked up to the house. The sleet had died off, but the wind was chilly and Ben thought he could smell snow in the air.

As expected, the house was closed up. Ben peered through the front room window but couldn't see anything through the net curtains. He came away from the front door and walked a little way up the street to where a gap between the houses led, he guessed, around the back.

His guess was right. Ewan's back yard was a small area of wasteland, weedy and neglected. Ben stood for a moment, drinking in details. He noticed the patch of ground where a vehicle had stood until recently. A van-sized vehicle, judging by the spaces between the bare-earth wheel impressions in the dirt. A single dark oil stain had bled into the ground, the lack of individual splotches telling him that the vehicle had not been moved for a long time prior to being driven away.

He also noticed the discarded set of diesel glow plugs that

81

someone had pulled out of its engine and tossed into the weeds. They weren't rusty enough to have been there longer than a couple of days. Nearby lay a crumpled strip of emery cloth, reddened from where someone had been polishing up corroded metal.

Ben wondered whether it might have been Boonzie who took the van. He was good at fixing old vehicles, and having travelled up by train he'd have needed some form of transport to get around in. It made sense.

As he pondered Boonzie's movements, he spied the broken window at the back of Ewan's house, and walked over to examine it. Someone had obviously let themselves in through the window. Ben reached his arm carefully through the jagged teeth of glass and tried the window catch from inside, but it had since been locked. He wondered about that, too.

The back door was securely bolted from the inside, which might explain why whoever had broken in opted for the window. Three minutes later, Ben had followed their example, but without breaking anything or leaving any trace. What the SAS had taught him about covert entry had been only the beginning of his education. If life had gone differently, he could have been a pretty successful cat burglar.

Inside, Ben found what he'd been afraid he might find. Every room of the house had been thoroughly trashed by a person, or persons, who had evidently been searching for something. Ben noticed that somebody else had since briefly attempted to clear up the living room. His curiosity about who that someone might have been was answered when he found an empty pill bottle lying on the floor. It hadn't been left here by the intruders, that was for sure. The label was printed in Italian, and showed that the pills had been prescribed to SIG. A. McCULLOCH. The 'SIG.' short for 'Signore' and the 'A.' for Archibald.

Boonzie had been here, all right.

Ben guessed that he might have been given the house key by the police, being next of kin to Ewan. Then since he hadn't booked anywhere else to stay, Boonzie might have come here intending to use his nephew's home as a base. Ben wondered if the shock of finding the place in such a mess had caused Boonzie to need to pop the last pills in the medicine bottle. That was a potentially worrying detail. But whatever the case, Boonzie had evidently changed his mind about staying here, and wasted no time in moving on. To where, was another question.

Ben searched the wreckage of the living room until he found what he was now looking for. Ewan McCulloch's household documents, including house insurance, bills, receipts and credit card statements, had already been given the once-over by the intruders and were scattered about under the upturned drawers of his desk. Ben was more interested in vehicle papers. He supposed that anything like company car or van paperwork would be kept at Ewan's business premises, but that anything related to a personal vehicle would have been sent to his home address. Again, his guess was right. Among the scattered documents was a registration document, expired insurance renewal letter, road tax reminders and old MOT certificate for a Ford camper van. The log book identified it as being fifteen years old, which probably explained why it had been sitting off the road for a while and had needed some work to get it going.

Now Ben felt more certain that Boonzie had borrowed the camper. However rough and ready, it would make the perfect mobile base. And now that Ben knew the vehicle's details, he'd already taken an important step towards finding his missing friend.

He lingered a few minutes longer in the house, wondering

why anyone would have wanted to ransack it, and how much of this was related to the mysterious gold coin Mirella had told him about. But he wasn't going to learn anything more by hanging around here. He left the house the same way he'd come in, and walked back around the rear pathway to the street.

The air temperature had dropped half a degree while he was inside Ewan's place, and though it wasn't yet four p.m. the light was already fading fast. Dusk came early around these parts in the wintertime. The darkening sky was choked with clouds and the first wispy flakes of what threatened to become a heavier snowfall were loosely spiralling down. The scent of woodsmoke was in the air as villagers kindled their log-burning stoves in readiness for a cold night. Ben zipped up his jacket, took a black wool beanie hat from one pocket and put it on. In the other pocket was a fresh pack of Gauloises and his Zippo lighter. He drew out a cigarette and lit up as he walked past his parked Mercedes and kept walking through the village.

Smoking helped him think as he explored his unfamiliar new surroundings. His thoughts were not comfortable ones. He shared Mirella's deep concerns about Boonzie's state of health, and wished that his friend had stayed at home to take care of himself. But Ben's worries went deeper. Though Kinlochardaich might appear quiet and peaceful, even quaint and romantic, his innate sixth sense warned him of menace and dark secrets lurking behind the facade, like the watchful eyes of predators hidden in the bushes.

Suspected murder. Vicious beatings. Illegal house entry. The apparent disappearance of a man who'd come to investigate. The list was growing. And now Ben, too, was venturing into the danger zone.

As he strolled along he smiled pleasantly and said good

evening to a couple of villagers he met. Anyone seeing him would think he was just another visitor to the area: maybe a business traveller passing through, or an adventure tourist on a winter camping expedition into the hills. But for Ben, his casual amble through the village felt like a reconnaissance mission no different from a covert military advance force making a pathfinder sortie deep behind enemy lines. Scouting the lie of the land. Gathering intelligence. Estimating enemy strength and location. Identifying any and all potential threats. His senses were fully fired up and not a single detail of his surroundings escaped his notice as he wandered the streets.

This was his ground zero. His war zone. It didn't appear that way, not yet. But if bad men were out there doing bad things, and if those bad men had been foolish enough to bring any harm to Ben's friend, then it was only a question of time before war erupted here. Ben would rip this place apart until he found whoever was responsible. And they would pay for what they'd done.

The snow was beginning to fall thicker and more steadily as he sighted the warm glow emanating from pub windows further down the street. As he got closer he could see the sign above the door that said KINLOCHARDAICH ARMS. The establishment was set back from the road. A few cars were parked outside, their roofs and bonnets dusted powdery white under the amber light of the streetlamps.

In Ben's experience, there was no better place in which to begin a recce operation than the local public house. He looked at his watch. Only four-fifteen, but the falling darkness and plummeting temperature made it feel much later.

Time for a drink.

He pushed through the pub door and walked inside.

Chapter 15

Entering the Kinlochardaich Arms was like taking a step back into the past. Both in absolute terms, since the pub's interior probably hadn't been altered in any significant way since about 1850, apart from the addition of electric lighting and a jukebox, and also for Ben personally, since the interior with its ancient beams and traditional decor took him straight back to the old drinking dens that had been his haunts back in the years he'd lived on the west coast of Ireland.

The decor, though not the ambience. His favourite Irish pubs had been warm and cheery places filled with lively craic, where the conversation and laughter flowed as joyfully as the Guinness and it wasn't unusual for fiddles, mandolins, tin whistles and bodhráns to materialise out of nowhere for an impromptu cèilidh jam session. But as Ben walked in he quickly understood from the dour atmosphere that strangers to Kinlochardaich couldn't expect to be greeted with much in the way of good old Highland hospitality. Even the log fire crackling in the old stone fireplace felt frigid and reserved.

Most of the drinkers in the lounge bar were gathered around a single large round table near the fire. They were a group of men in their thirties to fifties, hunched over pints and talking among themselves in low, mumbly voices as though they were plotting to overthrow the government. An assortment of heavy winter jackets and fleeces were draped messily over the backs of vacant chairs. At the far end of the lounge bar, a woman with long dark hair and a reedy ginger guy were drinking mugs of something hot and steaming at a table for two by the window. The woman had her back to Ben, and the guy was gazing out at the falling snow and saying something Ben couldn't hear.

The only other woman in the place was the young redheaded barmaid sitting behind the beer pumps, uninterestedly reading a magazine and ignoring the wolfish-looking suitor who was leaning on the bar and doing all he could to impress her with his wit. As Ben crossed the floor the barmaid's eyes darted up from the magazine and dwelled on him for a moment, and she flashed a coy smile. No trace of any kind of a smile, though, from the group at the big table. Some of the looks that turned his way were just checking-out-the-stranger glances, others lingered into hard and overtly hostile stares. The talking died away and the place fell silent for several seconds before resuming in the same mumbly tone.

Ben thought he could probably just about manage to cope with the level of friendliness. He wasn't here to make friends. Paying them no notice he walked up to the bar, took off his hat and pulled up one of the plain wooden stools. The barmaid put down her magazine. Up close, she was more a girl than a woman. She was wearing too much makeup, with glitter on her eyelids. With the coy smile still on her lips and her eyes giving him the once-over she sidled across and asked what he'd like.

A no-brainer of a question, since being in Scotland, the sacred homeland of his favourite tipple, it would have been heresy for him to walk in here and order a pint of ale. Ben ran his eye along the row of single malt whiskies behind the bar. It was a decent collection. Some of the names were pretty obscure, though as something of a connoisseur he'd tried them all in his time. In his book there was no such thing as a bad single malt. He made his selection and asked for a double measure. The barmaid served it with another smile. Which the guy who'd been trying to chat her up apparently didn't like very much, giving Ben sullen eyes as Ben thanked her and paid for his drink. Ben ignored him. She did the same, and after a few moments the guy gave up with a disgusted frown and stalked away to sit with his friends.

She rested her elbows on the bar and leaned forward, tacitly inviting Ben to look down her top which, naturally, he was far too restrained and gentlemanly to do. 'You're no from around here,' she said. Such powers of observation. But that was an invitation Ben did rise to, because it gave him the opportunity to mention the purpose of his visit to Kinlochardaich.

'No, I'm just passing through,' he said, and she looked a little disappointed. He added, 'Came to see a friend.'

'Oh, aye? I know everyone in Kinlochardaich.' She winked. 'Lady friend, is it?'

'Nothing that exciting,' he replied.

Just then one of the group from the round table got up and came over to the bar, thumped his empty pint glass down on a beermat and said gruffly, 'Same again, Holly love.' He was a heavyset man of around Ben's age or a couple of years younger, but four inches taller, which put him at about six-three. His hair was black and curly, his nose broken and crooked, and he had the neck and shoulders of a powerlifter. His sleeves were rolled up, showing muscled forearms inked from the wrist to the elbow with flame tattoos. Ben sat and sipped his scotch in silence while Holly refilled the big guy's glass. The man spilled some cash on the counter, gave Ben the briefest glance which Ben noticed but didn't acknowledge, then stumped back to the table with his beer. The pub floorboards creaked under his weight.

The interruption over, Holly returned to her position leaning against the bar and resumed the flirting. 'So where're you from?' she asked, a lot more interested in Ben than in who his friend might be, and making no attempt to hide it. Nineteen or twenty years old, stuck out here in a lonely rural village with obviously not too many strange and interesting new men passing through her life. She was more the kind of age for Jude, Ben thought. His son was between girlfriends at the moment, still living in the States but talking about returning home to the UK. Maybe Ben should send him up north to hook up with Holly here. She'd certainly make a refreshing change from the last one, a social justice warrior and do-gooder political activist called Rae Lee.

'I live abroad,' Ben said.

'Thought you were English.' That didn't seem to put Holly off, though.

He replied, 'Half Irish. But I don't live there, either.'

'How long did you say you were staying?' Getting bolder with the flirting now.

'Only until I find my friend. Which I'm hoping to do soon. Maybe a day or so.'

'Och, that's a shame. Did you say your friend's a local?'

'No, he's just passing through, same as me. His name's Boonzie McCulloch. He's Ewan McCulloch's uncle. Do you know Ewan?'

She nodded. 'Aye, I know Ewan. Heard he was in the hospital, though. Is he okay?'

'Not really. That's why his uncle travelled to the area. I

was hoping to catch up with him here in Kinlochardaich, but no joy. I wondered if maybe he'd been in here for a drink the last couple of days? Older guy. Shorter than me, wiry build. Grey hair, beard. Speaks like he's from Glasgow.'

Holly looked dubious. 'I don't think I've seen him. I mean, we get a lot of older customers who look like that, but you're the first new face who's been in here lately.' She added, 'I should know.'

'All the same, I have a photo of him, if you wouldn't mind taking a look. Might ring a bell.'

She shrugged. 'Sure, but like I say, I'm pretty sure he hasn't come in here.'

It seemed like a long shot, but Ben took out his phone and went to his stored images. The picture of Boonzie was a few years old, taken when Ben had visited him and Mirella at their place in Italy, but he was confident that Holly would recognise him if she'd seen him. There was only one Boonzie McCulloch in the world and he didn't change much. Ben angled the phone so Holly could see. She leaned further forward across the bar, squashing her chest on the counter and tickling his hand with the dangling tips of her hair. The images were stored in date order with the most recent first. He'd have to scroll all the way back to near the beginning to get to the one he wanted to show her.

But Holly stopped him dead when she saw the very first picture, Ben's most recent addition to the file. It was the image of Ewan's gold coin that Mirella had emailed him earlier that afternoon. Holly spotted it and instantly said, 'Hey, that looks familiar. Did you find buried treasure too?'

Ben stared at her. 'What are you talking about?'

'That.' She pointed at the picture with a long, glittery nail. 'It's not every day you see bling like that getting flashed around. Is it real? Looks real. Just like the other.'

'When did you see something like this before?'

She pulled away from the phone, as if she'd seen enough. 'Och, just a few days ago. He was sitting right there, on the same stool you are.'

'Who was sitting here?'

Holly's brow creased into a frown and she hesitated before replying, 'Ross Campbell.'

'Ross Campbell, the fellow who drowned?'

She nodded sadly, still frowning. 'You must have heard about it back home where you come from, aye?' As though accidental drownings in remote parts of Scotland were big news internationally. 'That was awfy. I didn't really know Ross that well, but I was so upset when I heard.' Holly thought about it for a moment, then added in an undertone, 'You know, some folks're calling it suicide. But I don't believe it. When he was in here that night he looked *way* too pleased wi' himself to be the suicidal type.'

'Explain this to me,' Ben said. 'Ross Campbell was in here a few nights ago and had a gold coin with him, just like the one in the photo? Is that what you're saying?'

Holly nodded again. 'Aye, must've been a day or two before . . . before it happened. Maybe even the very day before. I don't remember.'

'And you actually saw the coin?'

'He showed it to me.' There was nothing in her eyes but blank sincerity. She was telling the truth.

'What for?'

'Well, he was a wee bit pissed, to be honest. Kept going on about he'd struck it rich, found the mother lode, all that. Said he was gonnae leave this shithole, go off to a tropical beach and never come back again. Asked me to come wi' him. Me. Can you believe that?' she added with a brief, wistful smile. 'And then he was dead.'

91

'He had just the one coin?'

She shook her head. 'That's all he showed me, but he said he had a whole load more stashed away somewhere. I wiz teasin' him about it, said, "Ross Campbell, where'd you go gettin' yer hands on a big pile o' gold?"'

'And what did he say to that?'

'Wouldnae tell me. Said it was his big secret, and he was the only one who knew about it. I said, "No much of a secret if ye're bletherin' on about it in this bloody place."'

Ben had forgotten all about showing Holly the picture of Boonzie. This was more important. Now the gold trail led back to Ewan McCulloch's dead business partner and the whole mystery had just grown deeper. More significantly, the single coin had turned into a whole stash of them. And if Holly's account was right, it also meant that Ross alone knew the secret of where the gold had come from. Which implied that Ewan had known little or nothing about any of this himself. He might not even have stumbled across the coin until after Ross's death.

Ben was about to ask her more questions, but he never got the chance. Because at that moment he felt a large, heavy presence come up behind him and a loud voice said, 'What's all this fuckin' shite aboot Ross Campbell?'

Ben turned. The guy with the flame tattoos was back, and he didn't look very happy.

Chapter 16

The guy with the flames stalked up to the bar and planted two big brawny fists on the counter. His knuckles were coarse and laced with little white scars, from fights. Losing some, probably, judging by the broken nose, but his confident attitude said he'd won some, as well. He shot a hostile look at Ben, then scowled at Holly. 'Hear me? Nae mair o' that fuckin' shite talk, understand?'

Ben felt like asking the guy what his problem was, and advising him to take a step back and cool it. But he said nothing yet. Holly fired back angrily, 'Watch your fuckin' language, Angus Baird! And I don't remember asking your opinion, so don't you be thinkin' about causin' trouble in here!'

But Angus Baird hadn't finished yet. He pointed a menacing finger at her and said, even more loudly, 'Ross Campbell was a wee fuckin' clawbaw and he fuckin' knew it. That's why he fuckin' topped hisself, an' good riddance tae bad rubbish. And as fer that other boaby, Ewan McCulloch . . .' Baird spat on the floor.

'Think ye're so special, do ye, ye big worthless bampot?' Holly yelled back at him.

Ben had no clear idea what clawbaws, boabies and bampots were. These people had a language all of their own. But he was watching Baird and knowing exactly what was about to happen next. The guy was a rage volcano waiting to erupt.

Baird yelled, 'Watch what you say to me, ye wee bitch!' In the next instant, just like Ben had predicted, the big right arm lashed out to make a swipe at Holly. She dodged out of the way, but even if she hadn't, the blow would never have reached her. Ben snatched Baird's hand out of the air, trapping it by the thumb and using it as leverage to twist his wrist around and back on itself in a painful lock. Baird let out a cry of shock and surprise. He couldn't wrench his thumb free for fear of breaking it. All he could do was try to contort his body to relieve the pain, but Ben only twisted it harder. It was the simplest of moves, almost like a card trick. Hardly any effort required, using just two fingers. It didn't matter how big and strong they were when you sent those kinds of pain signals to their brain.

Assuming they had a brain. In Baird's case, Ben was even a little surprised that the lock worked so well. He said, 'Hitting women is just not a nice thing to do, Angus. Didn't your mother teach you manners?'

Baird went down on his knees on the pub floor with his arm stuck up in the air, now roaring and braying like a bull trapped in the castration pen. Two of his friends from the round table were instantly up on their feet and ready to come to his rescue. Ben had seen that coming, too. One of them snatched up an empty pint glass and broke it over the edge of the table. He pointed the jagged teeth Ben's way and snarled, 'Let him go, ya basturt!'

'Not until he's apologised for his antisocial behaviour and agrees to leave here quietly,' Ben said. 'The lady and I were having a private conversation.'

'Kenny Mitchell, put that glass down!' Holly screamed. The girl had spirit, that was for sure. But neither Kenny

Mitchell nor his buddy who had flown to Baird's aid were inclined to back down. They advanced another few steps towards the bar, ready to rush Ben both at once. The usual routine. Their strategy, crude but theoretically effective, would be to come at him in a pincer movement and overwhelm him with a furious barrage of blows. Once he was on the floor, it would be game over.

That was the idea, at any rate. But what made this situation a little trickier was the broken glass in Kenny Mitchell's hand. He looked fairly serious about using it, and getting glassed on his first day in Scotland wasn't Ben's idea of a fruitful trip. This would have to be dealt with in an appropriate fashion.

He said, 'Sorry about the mess, Holly.'

She looked at him. 'What mess?'

At that moment the pair came charging in. Mitchell on Ben's right, brandishing the glass like a dagger, and his pal on Ben's left, with his fists balled and teeth bared. Ben used the leverage on Baird's arm to force him to his feet and propel all two hundred and fifty pounds of him into the guy on the left. The impact sounded like two rugby players slamming full pelt into one another. Baird was heavier, and the other toppled backwards with the crushing weight sending him sprawling into the round table. The table capsized and glassware and beer flew everywhere. Their friends, who until that moment had remained seated, now all jumped up, but nobody else looked ready to join the fight.

Which left all of Ben's attention focused on the more serious matter of Kenny Mitchell, who was still in mid-charge with the intention of slashing him open with the jagged shards of his pint glass.

Ben had about half a second to consider his tactical options. For him, half a second was like half an hour. He

95

could have made a detailed list of all the ways he could permanently disable this idiot and make him eat the damn glass before Mitchell even knew what was happening. None of which were acceptable options. Ben hadn't come here to make friends, but he hadn't come here to kill anyone either. Not unless he truly had to. And getting arrested for assault wasn't going to serve his cause too well either.

So Ben simply waited until Mitchell was almost on him, then neatly sidestepped out of his way and tripped him up. Mitchell might have fallen on the broken glass, which wouldn't have been healthy for him but would have been entirely his own fault. In the event, the glass flew out of his hand and went skittering off into a corner as he belly-flopped to the floorboards with a crash that brought down a sprinkling of dust from the ceiling beams.

Then it was Angus Baird's turn to re-enter the contest to see who could get most badly damaged. He came at Ben with a demented screech of fury. Normally, in combat against worthy opponents, Ben wouldn't repeat the same trick twice. But these were not worthy opponents, and the same trick worked just fine. Ben had his back to the bar. As Baird rampaged towards him, big knuckly fists ready to pulverise this impertinent stranger who had dared to humiliate him, Ben danced aside, gently grabbed Baird by the collar on his way past, and simply allowed the big man's wild momentum to carry him headlong and face-first into the solid oak counter. Baird's thick skull slammed into the hard wood with a sound like a rifle shot and an impact that made the bottles behind the bar tinkle and rock. He slid to the floor, his body went limp and he lay there very still with his nose smeared sideways across his left cheek like a squished tomato.

'That mess,' Ben said to Holly.

Chapter 17

Holly leaned over the edge of the bar to peer down at the shape on the floor. Baird looked like a beached whale. 'Jesus Christ. Is he dead?'

'No, but I hope there's a pharmacy in the village. He's going to need some headache pills when he wakes up. Not to mention a little reconstructive facial surgery.'

Baird was completely out cold and would be for some time. His friend Kenny Mitchell was dazed and groaning on the floor and the third guy was still buried in the wreckage of the capsized table. Three for three, and Ben hadn't thrown a single punch or kick. Most of their other drinking buddies had now gallantly fled the building rather than stand up for their mates. None of the remaining pub clientele were coming anywhere near Ben or the bodies on the floor.

Except one. It was the woman he'd noticed when he'd come in, sitting by the window at the far end of the room with her back to him. Now she came marching over, clutching a handbag she'd brought from her table. She was maybe about thirty, with tight jeans and dark eyes that matched the colour of her hair. Her gingery man friend stayed in his seat and looked nervous, but she had a purposeful and self-possessed manner that Ben admired even before he knew who she was.

The woman stepped up to Ben and flashed a warrant card from the handbag. 'Police officer. You stay right where you are.'

The name on the card was PC Grace Kirk. Ben replied, 'Afternoon, Constable. I wasn't going anywhere. I haven't finished my drink yet.'

'They started it,' Holly protested, pointing past Ben at the slumped shapes on the floor.

'I saw what happened.' PC Kirk glanced down at the inert body of Angus Baird, then over at the other two.

'They'll be fine,' Ben said. 'Just had a little too much beer and got themselves all worked up over nothing.'

She stared at him. 'Who are you?'

Ben gave his name, slipped his wallet from his jacket and flicked out his driving licence to show her. She took it from him and checked it over, warily comparing his face to his photo and back again. He asked, 'Are you arresting me, officer?'

'I'm thinking about it.'

'For what? I barely laid two fingers on them. Like handling butterflies.'

She thought about it for a few moments longer, then seemed to make a decision and handed him back the licence. 'Fact is, Mr Hope, I wouldn't know what to arrest you for. You were only defending yourself and Holly here. I can't charge you with assault if you used minimal force. And you hardly seemed to do very much at all.'

'I didn't have to,' Ben said. 'They're not really bad boys. They just think they are.'

'Tell that to all the other people they've had a bit more success trying to beat up. Looks like they came unstuck this time. Even three against one, with a broken glass. Hardly a fair fight.'

To have had any chance of a fair fight against Ben, the likes of Angus Baird and his pals would have had to arm themselves with more than a broken glass. Thirty-millimetre cannons might have equalised things a little, as long as they knew how to use them. But Ben kept that opinion to himself. It might not be what PC Grace Kirk needed to hear.

'So, all things considered, no, consider yourself lucky because I'm not arresting you,' she said.

'Thank you, officer.'

'But consider yourself cautioned. No more trouble, okay?'

'Why would I cause trouble? I'm just an ordinary traveller minding his own business.'

Grace Kirk looked at him curiously, as though she'd never encountered anyone quite like him before and wasn't sure how to deal with him. 'Are you sure you're okay? Do you need to sit down? Talk to someone? Shock can affect people in all kinds of ways.'

'Do I look in shock to you?'

'No, in fact I'd say you look incredibly calm and collected, Mr Hope.' She glanced back at the casualties. Kenny Mitchell was beginning to stir and try to pick himself up off the floor. 'Excuse me for a moment while I deal with this gentleman, before he decides to make his exit.'

'You need some help?'

She gestured for him to stay where he was. 'You just sit tight and finish your drink. I'd like to ask you a few more questions afterwards.'

'I told you,' Ben said. 'I'm not going anywhere just yet.'

He sat and watched as Grace Kirk attended to Kenny Mitchell. In all his dealings with law enforcement, one thing he'd always respected was the coolness and bravery of female officers when dealing with large, aggressive men twice their strength. After informing Mitchell that he was under arrest, she calmly and efficiently secured him with a pair of hand-cuffs she was carrying in her handbag. A good cop is never off duty. Ben thought she was probably carrying an extend-able baton and pepper spray in there as well. Next it was the other idiot's turn. Angus Baird was still out for the count. Grace got on her phone and made some calls, speaking too low for Ben to hear, but he guessed she was calling in police backup as well as maybe an ambulance. No telling how long the response time would be, out here in the sticks.

Soon afterwards the pub door opened, and along with a flurry of snow in came a middle-aged couple who turned out to be the owners, horrified and shaking their heads at the state of the place. Grace Kirk explained to them that there had been a brawl, and said they were waiting for her colleagues from Fort William to come and take away the offenders. Ben wasn't mentioned. Meanwhile, Holly was busy cleaning up broken glass and spilled beer from the floor, pausing now and then to smile at him.

The ginger-haired guy who'd been sitting with Grace Kirk at the window table quietly finished up his coffee and then left, waving goodbye to her on his way out. Grace was still talking to the owners when blue lights appeared outside. Moments later three uniformed officers with snow sprinkled like dandruff on their shoulders pushed through the door, followed by a pair of paramedics from the ambulance that had arrived with the police response cars. They hadn't made bad time, Ben thought.

By then, Angus Baird was starting to come round while his two handcuffed friends were fully conscious and loudly protesting their innocence. 'It wiz that basturt there! He fuckin' attacked us!' The medics gave Baird a check-over before he was formally arrested and loaded into the ambu-lance, while the uniformed police led the other two outside and placed each in the back of a separate car. Grace accompanied her colleagues outside. Ben could see her through the window, and watched as she hopped into the front passenger seat of one of the cars. When she got out again a couple of minutes later, he was pretty sure she'd been running a search on his name on the national crime database. She wouldn't have found anything there. The kind of files that existed on him required deeper digging, as well as a high level of official clearance.

Once out of the car, she lingered for a few moments in the snowy street to talk with the uniforms. Then the procession of vehicles set off, lights flashing. Grace came back inside the pub, shook the powdery white flakes from her hair and clothes, then walked over to where he was sitting. The owners had seemed too preoccupied with the damage to have noticed him at all, and had now disappeared through a STAFF ONLY door. Holly had vanished too. It was difficult to tell whether the pub was open or closed at this point. Though with the snow coming down harder than ever outside, it seemed unlikely that any more customers would venture from their homes any time soon.

Grace pulled up a bar stool next to Ben's and sat down with a sigh. 'All done and dusted. The things you have to do when you're off duty.'

'I'd offer you a drink, but there's nobody tending the bar,' he said.

'Thanks for the thought. I don't drink, anyway.'

'You said you wanted to ask me some questions.'

'Just a formality. You're free to go if you want.'

Ben looked out of the window. The snow wasn't showing signs of stopping. 'I'm all yours.'

Chapter 18

The fire was dying. Alone inside the empty pub, they moved over to the fireplace and Ben laid a few sticks of wood from a wicker basket onto the embers, with larger logs on top. Soon the blaze was crackling back into life again. Grace sat close to it and held out her hands to warm them by the heat of the flames. 'We don't get a lot of strangers passing through Kinlochardaich. Especially not ones like you.'

'Is that a question?'

'I'm just curious, that's all.'

'Don't worry, I'm not planning on staying any longer than I have to.'

'May I ask what's the nature of your visit?'

Ben replied, 'Personal.'

'As in, you don't want to say?'

'No, as in I'm a personal friend of the McCulloch family.'

She cocked an eyebrow in surprise. 'You came to see Ewan?'

'Everyone around here seems to know Ewan. Including our friend Angus Baird, who doesn't seem to like him very much.'

She made a casual gesture with one hand. 'It's a small community. We all know each other. Maybe too well, sometimes. People tend to harbour a lot of stuff. Old grudges, bad blood, rivalries that sometimes go back generations. As for Baird, he's just an angry moron who hates everyone. Forget about him.'

Ben was happy to do that. 'How is Ewan? I only just got here and I haven't been to the hospital yet.'

'He's doing about as well as anyone would be doing, after getting half the bones in their body broken and their brains almost beaten out. He still hasn't come around. Maybe he never will.'

'I'm very sorry.'

'Yeah. So am I.' Ben could see the depth of sadness in her expression, and sensed that she wanted to say more. She paused a beat and then added, 'It's been really hard for me, because Ewan and I used to go out. A long, long time ago. How do you know him?'

'I don't. I have to admit, Ewan's not my main reason for being here. His uncle's an old friend of mine. I came to look for him.'

She frowned. 'What do you mean, look for him?'

'I mean, he was here, and now he seems to have vanished.'

Her frown grew deeper. 'You're talking about Boonzie?'

Now it was Ben's turn to be surprised. 'You know Boonzie?'

'Hardly very well, but I liked him. I met him in Fort William, at the hospital. Gave him a lift to the station, and I was there when he talked to DI Macleod and DS Coull. Not a very cordial interview.'

'Boonzie doesn't think much of the police generally. Present company excepted, I'm sure.'

'My superiors weren't too enamoured of him either. Especially when he announced that he was intending to hang around the area and pursue his own private inquiry into what happened to Ewan. I haven't seen him since. I thought he must have just drawn a blank, given up and gone home to . . . Italy, wasn't it?'

'Drawing a blank and giving up isn't Boonzie's way.' Ben paused a moment while he tossed another log on the fire. Thinking about whether he should feed her more of what he knew. His instinct told him no, but despite himself he felt he could trust her. Grace Kirk might just turn out to be a useful contact. Even if she was a cop. He said, 'If he was planning on going home empty-handed so soon, he wouldn't have borrowed his nephew's camper van.'

'He took Ewan's camper?'

Ben nodded. 'I went to the house. There are signs that Boonzie was there before me. And the vehicle is gone. That's good enough for me. I have the registration, if you want it.'

She gave a crooked kind of smile. 'I'm the police, Mr Hope. I think I can get hold of that information. But thank you.'

'You can call me Ben.'

'Okay, Ben. It's too soon to launch a full-on Missing Persons investigation, but we can notify local officers to be on the lookout for the camper. How long do you think he's had it for?'

'Probably since immediately after you met him in Fort William. He'd have returned to Ewan's place to start putting his plans together, and he'd have wanted his own transport.'

She nodded. 'Last I saw him, he was heading back to Kinlochardaich by bus.'

'And as far as I know, nobody's seen or heard from him since,' Ben said. 'Which leaves open certain possibilities.'

'Such as?'

'Well, for one thing, he has a serious heart condition.'

'Shit. I didn't know that. He seemed in great health for a man his age.'

'Nor did I, until yesterday.'

'You think he might have suffered some medical issue?'

'That's one option. The one his wife Mirella is mostly

concerned about. I'm concerned about it too. But I also think he might have got into another sort of trouble. Seems there's a lot of that going on around here. First Ewan McCulloch's business partner, then Ewan himself. Now his uncle.'

Grace looked pensive. She sighed. 'I warned him not to go asking too many questions. I told him I was worried he could get hurt.'

'Why would you tell him that?'

'Because he was convinced that what happened to Ross Campbell and Ewan was connected. And because until we catch the men who attacked Ewan, there are some right nasty bastards out there.'

'Is there a connection?'

She shook her head. 'That's a confidential police matter. I can't discuss it with you.'

'Do the police have any potential leads on Ewan's attackers?'

'Same reply. In any case it's not my investigation. I'm out of that loop.'

'Who's in charge of it?'

'My same two superiors who spoke with Boonzie, Detective Inspector Fergus Macleod and Detective Sergeant Jim Coull.'

'You might be out of the loop, but you still have a personal interest in knowing what happened to him. You must have some idea.'

'As far as I'm aware, no suspects have emerged yet. I'm sticking my neck out telling you even that much. Believe me, I wish I knew more.'

'So do I,' Ben said. 'If only to persuade me I'm wrong. I don't like the way this picture is coming together so far.'

'If you have information to share, I should hear it.'

'Even though you won't divulge any to me?'

'I'm the police. You're a citizen. That's how it works.'

'I'll play your game,' Ben said. 'The first part is just logical deduction. If Boonzie was chasing up leads and getting closer to learning what happened to Ewan, he posed a threat to the bad guys. Then they would have needed to take action before he found out too much.'

'That's obvious enough.'

'The second part is less obvious, unless you know Boonzie McCulloch as well as I do. He isn't someone you can intimidate or scare off. Heart condition or no heart condition, he's tougher than you can imagine.'

'I worked the beat in Glasgow. I'm familiar with what tough means.'

'No,' Ben said. 'You have no idea of what he can handle. For someone to get the better of him, they'd have to be extremely skilled. That's not an idle claim. I know what I'm talking about.'

She narrowed her eyes, thought for a moment, then said, 'Okay, whatever you say. Go on.'

'Therefore, assuming that all of this is connected and that whoever assaulted Ewan is the same person or group of people who would subsequently need Boonzie taken off the table to protect their interests, we're not talking about just your regular provincial crooks. You'd need to be looking at a broader pool of suspects, someone much higher up the food chain. Organised crime gang members, or affiliated to them. Hardcore professionals from the outside.'

'You get all of this from logical deduction?'

'Not all.'

'Seems pretty damned hypothetical to me,' she said. 'To begin with, you've got no motive. No reason to explain why professional criminals from the outside should have any interest whatsoever in what happens in our dull and insignificant wee community of Kinlochardaich. We've nothing to offer them.'

'Actually you do,' Ben said. 'And this part isn't guesswork. I think this is about money.'

Chapter 19

'What money?' she asked.

Ben replied, 'It's not what money. It's what *kind* of money.'

'All right then, what kind of money?'

Ben took out his phone, brought up the image of the gold coin that he'd showed Holly, and held it out for Grace to see. 'The kind that looks like this.'

'You'd better explain.'

Grace listened as Ben told her what he'd learned about Ross Campbell's discovery. 'These coins are hundreds of years old, which I'm guessing makes them worth much more than just their weight in gold. Not just to serious collectors, of which there are probably thousands out there, but also to anyone with the connections to fence stolen antiquities on the black market.'

'Stolen antiquities, is that something you're knowledgeable about?'

'Enough to know that a lot of people in that world will pretty much do anything to make a buck. Including killing off anyone who gets in their way.'

Grace was peering thoughtfully at the picture on Ben's phone. 'There are old stories about hidden treasure in these parts. I never thought there was any truth in it. Where did Ross find them? How many did he have?'

Ben replied, 'Where he found them was his little secret. As to how many, it must have been a few, or else he wouldn't have been going around the village bragging that he was rich enough to leave Kinlochardaich and set himself up on a tropical beach for the rest of his life.'

'You only just got here. How do you know all this?'

Ben didn't want to get Holly mixed up in police business. 'That's classified, officer. I prefer not to reveal my source.'

'Withholding information from the police is an offence.'

'So arrest me.'

She stared at him for a moment, then sighed. 'All right. What else do you know?'

'That Ewan found at least one of the coins that Ross had. It probably happened by chance, because I don't think that Ross intended to let his partner in on the secret, or that he was planning on leaving. But maybe whoever attacked Ewan didn't know that. Maybe they assumed that he was equally involved. Maybe they beat him up to make him reveal where the rest of the gold was. Or maybe it was to force him to cough up the identity of the anonymous witness, this poacher, who claimed to have seen Ross being murdered. Except Ewan had no idea who the poacher was. He needed his uncle's help to find out. That's the reason Boonzie came to Scotland.'

Grace said nothing. Ben could see wheels turning inside her head, but whatever she was thinking she kept to herself.

Ben said, 'The witness is the key that will unlock this thing. If he was telling the truth, then whoever murdered Ross Campbell was after what he'd found, and faked an accidental drowning or possible suicide to cover their tracks.'

Grace remained silent. Still thinking hard.

Ben went on, 'You can be sure that when Boonzie went off in Ewan's camper van, it was to track down the poacher and find out what he knew. That's what I'd do, in his position. It's what the police should be doing, too. Are they?'

Grace shook her head. 'I told you, I can't discuss confidential matters pertaining to an ongoing police investigation.'

'Even if you knew the details, and weren't being left out of the loop by DI Macleod and DS Coull?'

'Correct.'

'Fair enough. Rules are rules. I get that. Did you have any other questions for me?'

'I was curious about what's next for you. Where you plan on going from here.'

'Nowhere. Not until I find Boonzie. Wherever this leads, I'm not ready to leave Kinlochardaich just yet.'

'Do you have a place to stay?'

'I never got around to arranging one,' he said. 'Maybe I'll just buy a tent.'

'In December?'

He might have told her that three months spent living rough in the frozen Hindu Kush of northern Afghanistan while hunting terrorist insurgents had been a far more punishing experience than anything the Scottish Highlands could offer. Winter warfare training above the Arctic Circle in Norway with the Royal Marines' Mountain Leader Training Cadre hadn't been exactly a walk in the park, either. He just said, 'I've had worse.'

'Bad news is there's no camping supplies shop in Kinlochardaich. In fact there's hardly anything much at all in Kinlochardaich. No hotel, not even a guesthouse.'

'Looks like I'll have to kip in the car, then.'

'But I do happen to know that old Mrs Gunn's empty cottage is still up for rent.'

'Mrs Gunn?'

'The village's most senior resident. She seemed ancient

even when I was a kid. Must be a million years old now, but still as sharp as a razor. She'll be happy to let you have it for a few days. You might have to pay her for a week up front, though. She's like that.'

Ben suspected that Grace Kirk was only helping him so that she could keep an eye on him, being the canny police officer she clearly was. But he was happy to play along for now. And sleeping in the car didn't appeal much. Maybe he was getting old and too used to the soft life. Besides which, he could easily give Grace the slip anytime he wanted to. He replied, 'Not a problem. How do I get there?'

'Why don't I drive you over there now and introduce you?'

'My rental car's over at Ewan's place.'

'It's only the other end of the village. You can easily walk back and collect your car afterwards.'

They went outside into the snow and she led him to an old Land Rover that was parked a little way down the street. She noticed him smiling at it. 'What did you expect me to drive, a little pink Fiat with eyelashes on the headlights?'

'I like it.'

'Boonzie liked it, too.'

They clambered inside. The doors slammed with a clang. Grace fired up the engine and lights, and flipped on the wipers to clear the snow from the windscreen. A feeble stream of cold air blew from the heater vents. Grace crunched the stick into gear and pulled out into the empty street.

As they drove through the village Ben asked, 'So do you and your husband live here in Kinlochardaich?'

She looked at him with a blank expression.

Ben said, 'Sorry, I thought . . . maybe I should say "partner", but I hate that word. I saw you sitting together when I came into the pub.'

110

'Lewis?' She laughed. 'Och, no. We're not an item.'

'My mistake.'

'It's okay. I know there's talk about us, but that suits him fine. He likes to keep the fact that he's actually gay from the village gossips. We don't have much of an LGBT community in Kinlochardaich.'

In Ben's world, LGBT was a military acronym for Laser-Guided Bomb Target. But he got the general idea, and nodded sagely as Grace went on: 'You have to work hard to preserve your privacy in this place, you know? They're all watching every move you make from behind their net curtains. As for me, I'm a single girl, if that's what you were trying to find out.'

'I wasn't.'

She smiled. 'Your driving licence says you live in France.' Changing the subject.

'Normandy.'

'What do you do there?'

'I'm in education.'

'Teacher?'

'Of a sort.'

'Before that, were you in the army with Boonzie?'

'He told you he was in the army?' Ben was amazed. Boonzie never talked about his military past.

'And about growing tomatoes in Italy. People tell me things. I don't know why. Just got that kind of face, I suppose.'

'I didn't tell you that about myself.'

'No, but I kind of sussed it out. Not just from the fact that I saw you take down two notorious local hard cases without breaking a sweat or even hitting anyone. It's the way you talk, the way your mind works. You kind of have the look, too, although I imagine your hair would've been a bit shorter back then. How long has it been?'

'My hair?'

She tutted. 'No, silly. How long since you left the army to go and live in France?'

'Your powers of observation do you credit. You should be a detective sergeant, at least.'

'Working on it,' she said. 'So am I right?'

Ben said, 'I've been out for a while.'

'And that's where you met Boonzie, in the army?'

'He'd already been there for ever when I joined. We served together, but only for a short time before he quit. He trained me. Taught me. He was my mentor, and later my friend. He's one of the best people I've ever known.'

'I admire that you came all this way for him. We should all have friends as loyal. Someone who'd drop everything to look out for us, whatever it takes.'

Ben wasn't sure if she was being sincere, or circuitously trying to fish for what his intentions might be. 'I meant what I said about not leaving here until I discover what's happened to him. Nobody's going to stand in the way of that.'

'You sound just like him. Like when he told my superior officers to "stay oot ma road".' She mimicked Boonzie's tone and accent perfectly. 'Frankly, I was a little concerned about him carrying out his own private inquiry. I hope we're not going to have that kind of problem with you. Are we?'

'I didn't come here to cause trouble,' Ben said.

'Or put the local heavies in hospital.'

'That was their choice, not mine. I'm interested in just one thing. The safety and wellbeing of my friend.'

'I'm glad to hear it. I really hope he's okay, too.'

And with that, they had arrived at old Mrs Gunn's place.

Chapter 20

The most senior resident of Kinlochardaich was as wrinkled as a Galapagos tortoise, deafer than a rock, and a nail-hard negotiator with a very definite sense of the worth of her empty cottage next door. The converted mews was attached to the large stone-built house in which Mrs Gunn lived alone on the edge of the village. As a temporary base it suited Ben's needs just fine. The single bedroom was small and basic, the tiny living room had a wood-burner and there was a log pile and a splitting axe in the shed. He always travelled with enough cash to meet unforeseen expenditures, and once the deal had been thrashed out at maximum volume, Ben shelled out a week's rent in advance. Clutching the cash in her bony fist she handed over an iron key the size of a soup spoon, and the cottage was his.

'Welcome to Kinlochardaich,' Grace said when Mrs Gunn had retreated to her house and the two of them were alone. They stepped out into the amber glow of the streetlamp. She asked, 'You want a lift back to your car?'

The snow had stopped and the clouds had cleared to unmask a billion stars twinkling beneath the infinite dome of the inky-black sky. Looking up at the immensity of it made north-western Scotland feel like just another pinprick slowly wheeling around the outer fringes of the Milky Way.

Ben couldn't remember the last time he'd breathed air so pure and invigorating. 'I think I'll walk it, thanks.'

'Well, I guess I'll see you around, Mr Ben Hope. Try not to get into any more trouble, will you?'

'You keep saying that like I'm a disreputable character.'

'No, I'm sure you're really the perfect gentleman. Mr Charm himself.'

He feigned surprise. 'That's what they call me. How did you know?'

'Och, get out of here.'

'I love the way you Scottish ladies say "och".'

She smiled. 'I could still arrest you, you know.'

'It was nice meeting you, Grace.'

'Yeah, right.' Then with a last crooked smile that Ben liked a very great deal, she jumped back into her Land Rover and took off with a puff of smoke and tyres crunching on the snow.

Ben watched her tail-lights disappear up the empty street. Mrs Gunn's curtains were shut, a chink of light peeking through the gap and the blare of the television audible outside. He locked up the cottage, slipped the massive key in his pocket and set off at a slow walk. The temperature had fallen to well below zero and the freezing air was turning the snow on the pavements to a slippery rime of ice. It was only just gone seven in the evening but the village was already settling in for the night, soft lights in the upstairs windows and the smell of woodsmoke on the breeze. He was the only one out walking. He enjoyed the solitude, as he relished the coldness of the night. Taking his time, he passed the old stone church and the graveyard where he supposed Ross Campbell must have been laid to rest not long ago; then a few hundred yards further on, across the street, he saw a pool of yellow light that was the village's only shop, open late.

Ben hadn't eaten since he'd landed in Scotland, and felt suddenly hollow with hunger. He crossed the street and walked into the shop. The sign above the door said KINLOCHARDAICH STORES. An old guy with a bushy white moustache, though probably only about half Mrs Gunn's age, was tending the counter and greeted Ben with a friendly 'Good evening' as he entered.

It was the kind of village general store that sold everything from groceries to hardware and farm supplies. Ben perused the shelves, tossed a few tins of meat stew and a bag of rice into a basket along with a jar of instant coffee, the real thing being too much to hope for. Living in France had given him a taste for red wine, but he was also wary of the plonk on sale in Kinlochardaich Stores. The beer selection was more promising, if a little offbeat. The bottles of local ale were labelled with fetching names like Sheepshagger, Kilt Lifter and Skull Splitter. He took one of each, and a bottle of single malt whisky. Something to keep him warm on the cold nights to come. Hopefully not too many of them.

As he paid for his purchases he took out his phone and pulled up the photo of Boonzie to show the old guy. 'This is a friend of mine. He's visiting the area and might have been in here. Wondered if you'd seen him?'

The old guy gave Ben a curious look, then peered closely at the phone with narrowed eyes. After a long time he slowly nodded and said, 'Aye, I think so. Couple days ago. I remember, 'cuz he wiz drivin' Ewan McCulloch's camper van.'

We all know each other, Grace had said. Ben could see she'd been right about that. 'My friend is Ewan's uncle,' he said to the old guy. 'I'm trying to find him. Did he happen to mention anything about where he was going?'

The old guy shook his head. 'Just bought a load of stuff and left.'

'What kind of stuff?'

The storekeeper scratched his head, trying to remember. 'Let me see, now. Like he wiz goin' on a campin' trip, at this time of year. Tinned provisions, bottled water, coffee. And something else, too.' He pointed a gnarly finger over at the hardware section. 'Must've known the snow wiz comin', 'coz he bought one of them there shovels.'

Ben looked at the shovels and something with thousands of icy-cold little feet crawled down his spine. They were good quality hardware. Sturdy wooden shafts, big square steel blades enamelled in dull black. And he knew that Boonzie hadn't been thinking of digging snow when he'd bought one.

No, Boonzie was thinking that when he caught up with the men who'd put his nephew in a coma, he wasn't just going to punish them. He was going to kill and bury them.

'Thanks for the information,' Ben said to the old guy.

'Ye're welcome. I hope you find your friend.'

'Yeah, so do I.'

Ben left the store with his supplies jinking inside a carrier bag and walked on to where his car was parked. Ewan McCulloch's house was as dark and silent as a grave. Ben drove the Mercedes back through the quiet streets to the Gunn cottage. His landlady was still watching TV. He let himself back inside his new digs, dumped his canvas bag on the floor and carried the groceries into the kitchen. He searched through the cupboards for a couple of saucepans, filled one with water for the rice and emptied a can of stew into the other. Chunky cubes of beef in some kind of sauce that smelled like something Storm would like to eat, but it would do. Like he always said, he'd had worse.

He sat at the blue Formica kitchen table to eat, and washed his meal down with a pint of Kilt Lifter. Then he rinsed out the glass, grabbed the whisky bottle and wandered through into the living room. It was meat-locker chilly in there, so he piled some kindling and small wood from a wicker basket into the wood-burner along with a crumpled ball of newspaper and lit it with his Zippo. The flue was cold and the fire smoked for a few moments, then bright flames danced up and ate the smoke, and soon the cast-iron box of the stove was clicking and ticking as the metal expanded with the heat.

Ben settled into a fireside armchair, cracked open the scotch and poured out a couple of measures, then lit a Gauloise. Mrs Gunn had said nothing about not smoking, and even if she had, Ben figured he was paying for the privilege. Watching the fire grow and feeling the warmth slowly spread through the cottage, he sipped the scotch and watched his cigarette smoke trickle to the ceiling, and thought about how things stood and what he needed to do next.

The fact was that Boonzie could be anywhere, dead or alive. As skilled a finder of missing people as Ben was, not even he stood much chance of locating his friend in a thousand square miles of hills and forest with only a vehicle number plate to go on. But there was a way he could narrow his field of search to a sharp focus and that was to put himself in Boonzie's shoes. Emulate his methodology. Follow in his footsteps. Arrive at the same point on the road.

Find the poacher.

All the arrows were aligned in the same direction. The poacher knew, or claimed to know, who had killed Ross Campbell. By association, assuming he was telling the truth, he probably also knew who put Ewan McCulloch in a coma. And by further association, if something bad had happened to Boonzie then the poacher's information would potentially lead Ben straight to the door of those responsible.

He set down his glass and took out his phone. Kinlochardaich might be lacking a lot of modern commodities but he was getting a strong mobile signal. He pulled up Google, the oracle with the answer to All Things, and tapped in the search keywords SALMON POACHING SCOTLAND.

Illegal freshwater fishing was a subject Ben knew nothing whatsoever about, and as he trawled randomly from one web article to another he was surprised at what big business it was. From what he could glean, the reason why the Fisheries enforcers had such a hard time catching offenders was twofold. To begin with, it was almost impossible to police the waters of Scotland's thousands of lochs and rivers, whose combined area was larger than some seas. Loch Ness alone held more than seven million cubic metres, more than the total volume of water in all the lakes of England and Wales.

The second reason illegal salmon fishing was so hard to stop was that it was so lucrative, because the untraceability of the stolen goods meant that a lot of it ended up on the tables of top restaurants in Edinburgh or London, who were happy to pay cash and ask no questions in return for quality merchandise.

Put those problems together, and it added up to a highly tempting activity. So tempting, that the authorities had even had difficulties preventing their own enforcement personnel from catching fish on the sly. Even more strongly drawn to the freshwater bounty were criminal gangs, whose members had been known to attack or threaten the Fisheries enforcers at knifepoint when caught in the act.

Ben didn't think that the mystery poacher was one of those. More likely, he was just some local guy putting food on the table or perhaps making a few quid on the side. For legitimate anglers the official salmon season had ended in

October and wasn't due to start again until January or February, after the spawning season had replenished the stocks with a teeming new generation of young fish. But a dedicated poacher who didn't feel the need to abide by the rules and was hardy enough to brave the rough conditions could feel free to harvest the lochs and rivers unimpeded all through autumn and winter.

Which meant there was a reasonable chance of finding the guy out there on the loch in December. The problem Ben faced there was the same one the enforcers faced: that of geography. He closed down his search and jumped over to Google Maps, which told him that Loch Ardaich was twelve miles from west to east. That was a lot of water, and an even larger area of shore, for one man to patrol in search of a small, moving target. Ben would have felt inadequately equipped even with a four-man SAS team and air support.

But again, there were ways to even the odds. According to what few obscure news reports Ben could find online, Ross Campbell's body had been found near the eastern end of the loch, not far from the new Highland Manor golf resort development where his surveying duties had taken him that day. And that enabled Ben to drastically reduce the area of loch he'd need to cover. Ben had hunted many men, during his time in the army and since. He was exceptionally good at it, because he had the ability to put himself in his quarry's mindset, think like they thought. So he closed his eyes now, let his mind drift and thought the way the poacher would think.

If what the man claimed was true, then he was scared as hell. He'd witnessed a murder. He was carrying the heavy burden of a dark and dangerous secret. It was possible that he'd stay away from the loch altogether, stay at home peeking through the curtains. Or that he'd find another loch or river, or switch to shooting deer for a while. But if he did choose to keep poaching on Loch Ardaich, he'd stay as far away as possible from the scene of the crime. Therefore, if there was any chance of catching him at his work, it would be at the opposite end of the loch, the western side. And while the facts pointed to the alleged murder having taken place during the daytime, the poacher would now be much more likely to venture out only under cover of darkness. An extremely cautious man. Paranoid, even. Knowing that the Fisheries enforcers were out at night looking for him. Knowing also that certain others would be strongly motivated to wipe out any witness who could incriminate them. He'd be as wary as a wild animal, and like a wild animal he might easily resort to violence to defend himself if cornered.

That didn't concern Ben. He had gone after warier and more dangerous men, and found them, and survived.

The cottage was comfortable and warm, but Ben had no intention of sleeping there that night. As the hour grew later, he made his preparations.

Time to go hunting.

Chapter 21

The far western tip of Loch Ardaich was Ben's target destination that night, but he didn't drive all the way there. He headed east from the village and circled the twelve-mile length of the loch anticlockwise along the lonely winding roads until he was running parallel about half a mile from its northern shore. An hour's trek from the western end he stopped and left the car hidden deep offroad, concealed in the shadow of the pine trees.

He used his phone to mark the GPS coordinates, then set off on foot with his bag over his shoulder and his boots crunching in the hard-frozen snow. The forest hugged close to the west side of the loch, the pines standing thick and straight as spears with their white-capped evergreen canopy drooping low over the ground. An owl hooted from its unseen perch overhead.

By the time he reached the water's edge a mist was rolling in, drifting like battlefield smoke over the surface and blotting out the stars. It was still and peaceful down here, the only sounds the gentle wind rustling the pines and the soft lapping of the water against the shore. Ben stalked eastwards along the south side, just a slow-moving patch of shadow that paused here and there for long moments to drink in the stillness and observe every inch of his surroundings.

When after two miles he'd seen nothing, he backtracked the way he'd come. At its widest point the loch was several hundred yards across, but at its extreme western end the stretch of water narrowed to a taper, little wider than a stream all choked with branches and floating debris. He skirted around and began to make his way up along the north side. The mist was slowly intensifying, the shadows deepening around him until the inky blackness all but swallowed the trees and the water.

Ben had been following the north shore for a half-hour or so when he saw the lights. A pair of bright white torchbeams, forty or fifty yards up ahead, close to the lochside, sweeping left and right like searchlights. He sank into a crouch and watched them. Behind the lights he could make out the dark silhouetted figures of three men, picking their way through the bushes that skirted the shore. They were heading in his direction, but the range of their torches was too short to reach him yet. They could be a gang of poachers, he thought. If they were, his man could be among them – though Ben's mental profile of the guy suggested he wouldn't be. Or they could be Fisheries bailiffs. Or someone else. Ben was interested in finding out who.

He moved towards the lights, keeping his body low to the ground the way he'd long ago been trained to sneak up on the enemy. Getting closer, he could see that the three men weren't carrying fishing gear. That ruled them out as salmon poachers. But they were carrying something. The lights glinted off the twin barrels of a shotgun. That was when he realised he'd stalked a little too close. One of the torchbeams swept over him, hesitated and came back. A white dazzle seared his retinas. He ducked, but too late. There was a hoarse, excited yell of 'Over there! I think I seen him!'

Ben snaked away into the thick bushes. But the strong white

light followed him. A second later the heavy percussive deton-
ation of a shotgun blast split the night and echoed over the
loch. It was followed by another. The first shot went a long
way wide of Ben but the second clipped twigs off the tree
directly above him and showered him with pine needles and
powder snow. If they weren't poachers, they damn well weren't
official bailiffs either. Not unless their department had adopted
a new shoot-to-kill policy without informing anyone.

Ben moved a little further from the shoreline and then
stopped and remained as still as a rock, listening. He heard
voices. Local accents.

'I think I got him.'

'Which way'd he go?'

The three figures were moving faster now, making a lot
of noise as they hunted for him. One of them shouted, 'We
know ye're there, ye fat scar-faced basturt! Come on oot!'

Which was enough to persuade Ben beyond a doubt that
the men had been hunting someone else. Scars he might
have, but none on his face. And nobody could have described
him as fat.

Then another voice said, 'Split up, boys. He cannae be
far away.' With only a pair of torches between them, two
of the men broke off one way and ventured deeper into
the trees, away from Ben, their beam scouring the undergrowth in front of them. The third man kept moving
towards him, snow and twigs crunching under his feet as
he came closer.

The man was just three or four steps away from Ben when
he halted. Ben heard the clunk of the guy's shotgun action
being broken open. The sound of spent cartridge hulls being
ejected and landing softly in the bushes. A pause as he loaded
two fresh shells into his chambers, then snapped the gun
shut. His voice sounded very close by as he repeated, 'I know

ye're there somewhere, ye big eedjit. Show yerself, or I'll start fuckin' blastin'!'

Which Ben preferred not to happen. If this moron started firing blind at the surrounding trees and bushes, he'd have a pretty good chance of shooting Ben by accident.

Silent as a panther, Ben emerged from his hiding place, came up behind the man and took him down with one hand over his mouth, craning back his head, and the other twisting the shotgun out of his grip. The man could put up no resistance nor make a sound as Ben dragged him into the bushes at the foot of a tree and wrapped an arm around his throat, locking him in a chokehold that starved his brain of oxygen and within a few seconds put him to sleep. Ben pinned him down hard and tight until he felt his body go limp.

Unconsciousness would last no longer than a couple of minutes. By then, Ben was hoping that the other two men would have wandered further away, and he'd be able to make this one tell him the name of the man they were looking for, why and for whom.

In the meantime, Ben wanted to have a look at his victim. He picked up the fallen torch and cupped his hand over the lens, so that the light shone dull and red through his fingers. He flashed it on the guy's head and shoulders. He was a fairly large man of about thirty-five, balding, unshaven, acne pits on his cheeks, earring in his left lobe. He wore a camouflage-pattern winter jacket cinched around his thick middle with a shotgun cartridge belt.

Ben recognised him as one of the men from the pub. A pal of Kenny Mitchell and Angus Baird, evidently. Which Ben was suddenly finding very interesting indeed. He unbuckled the shotgun cartridge belt from around the guy's waist and slung it over his shoulder. Then he searched inside the guy's jacket and found a wallet. He was about to open it up to look for ID when something zipped very close by his head and cracked sharply off the tree trunk right beside him. Flying bark splinters stung the side of his face.

Then a fraction of a second later, trailing in the slipstream of the supersonic bullet, came the muted cough of a silenced rifle shot far away.

Ben was already diving into the bushes, grabbing his bag and the unconscious man's shotgun as he went. A second bullet pierced the night and smacked hard into the ground just inches away from him, blowing a crater in the dirt and sending up a spray of grit and snow. Close again. Too close. Ben kept moving, no longer concerned about making his way silently through the undergrowth because he no longer had that luxury. He cut a path between the trees that curved away from the two other searchers, but as the torchlight now swept back around in his direction he knew that they'd picked up the sound of his movement. They were about thirty yards to his right. One guy pointing the torch, the other clutching a shotgun, tracking him through the forest as though he was a running squirrel. Then the shotgun went off with a loud BOOM and buckshot pellets carved a bite out of a pine trunk in Ben's wake.

He didn't shoot back, because he didn't want to slow down or let his muzzle blast give away his position to the hidden rifleman. He sprinted full-pelt through the trees, leaping over exposed roots and fallen trunks, thick brush and brambles ripping at his legs. At any moment he expected the flash of white light and the tumbling sensation as the shooter's third bullet turned out to be the lucky one that cut him down in his tracks.

After thirty sustained seconds of hard running Ben glanced back and saw nothing but darkness behind him, and realised that he'd managed to put enough distance between himself and his pursuers to lose them. The only sounds were the crunch of his footsteps, the rasp of his breath and the patter of frozen rain that had started falling over the forest. He slowed his pace a little, so that he could continue more silently and with less risk of slamming face-first into a tree.

Ben took more than an hour to make his way back to where he'd hidden the car, stopping every few yards to make sure he wasn't being tracked. As he got close to the car he approached very slowly and with extreme caution. Nothing could spook even the most capable soldier more deeply than the blood-chilling knowledge that a sniper might be calmly watching from a concealed position, eye to his scope, finger on trigger, just waiting for you to walk right into the kill zone. Ben wasn't easily rattled, but the last steps to the car were the most painfully drawn-out and tensest few minutes he'd experienced in a very long time.

But he made it to the car without any silent kill shots finding him from the darkness. He blipped the locks and jumped inside and fired up the engine and headlamps, hating the sudden noise and light that were a beacon for his position and wanting to get away as fast as possible. He tore away over the bumpy terrain, reached the road and put his foot down hard. The icy rain was falling harder and making the road slippery. He was glad of the SUV's fancy traction control as he carved through the treacherous bends at high speed. There were no lights in his rear-view mirror. Nobody was following.

Halfway back to Kinlochardaich, Ben pulled off the single-track road into a passing place, stopped the car and leaned back in his seat to light a Gauloise. He murmured, 'Shit.'

It was only then, trying to steady the trembling flame against the tip of the cigarette, that he realised that his hands were shaking.

Chapter 22

It took two cigarettes to settle him down. As he sat and smoked quietly in the darkness of the car, watching the frozen rain slither down his windscreen, he was trying to understand what the hell had just happened back there.

There was little question in his mind that the men had come to the lochside for the same reason as him: to search for the poacher. Ben knew only that he was overweight and had a scar on his face. But the men hunting him clearly knew much more. The killers had somehow discovered the identity of the star witness and were closing in, intent on taking him out of the picture and thereby covering their tracks. Covering also the connection that Ben now understood existed between the killers and the men who'd tried to assault him in the Kinlochardaich Arms.

Ben flashed back to the events of earlier, and remembered how it had been the talk of Ross Campbell that had triggered Angus Baird's aggressive reaction. It had been more than just bad blood and Baird being an angry moron who hated everybody, as Grace had said. It had been the behaviour of guilty men with something to hide. Knowing that, Ben was getting a strong urge to drive straight to the police station in Fort William, find his way inside the cells where Baird and his pal Mitchell were being held, and extract some truth out of them. Jails were generally easier to break into than out of, in Ben's experience. But a little patience could save him the trouble. A simple affray case like this one, they'd probably be released after a couple of days, pending trial. Ben could catch up with them then.

As much as he was itching to talk to Baird and Mitchell, what he really wanted to know was the identity of the hidden sniper. The more he thought about it, the more he became convinced that the man was a world apart from his companions at the lochside. The goons with the torches and shotguns were noisy, clumsy and amateurish. The rifle shooter was anything but. The time interval between the bullet impact and the suppressed report told Ben that the guy had been some distance away, probably hunkered down in a sniper's nest on higher ground with a decent view of the terrain below. Shooting in pitch black conditions meant he was certainly using some kind of infrared night-vision scope, Gen 2+ image intensifier technology or better. Expensive, professional kit. And the fact that he was capable of making accurate shots through thick cover hinted at skill and training that was far beyond that of the stooges he was with.

They might have been working together, but this guy wasn't one of them. Ben was certain of it. Which suggested a hierarchy of command in operation. It was almost as though the sniper was using his lower-rank underlings as beaters to flush out his quarry so that he could execute him from a distance, clean and surgical.

And that fate had very nearly been Ben's when the killers had mistaken him for the poacher. The first bullet had missed his head by maybe an inch and a half. In those conditions, such a near miss was still excellent marksmanship. The bullet's trajectory might have been slightly deflected by a tree branch midway to the target; if it hadn't, it would have struck exactly to point of aim and Ben would not have been sitting here wondering about it. He'd be a semi-headless corpse lying in the woods. And that was an unsettling thought. Sometimes you got a brush with death so up-close and personal that you could smell it. Ben was smelling it now. *Get over it,* he scolded himself.

One thing he couldn't get over was his deepening worry about what might have happened to Boonzie. He remembered his words to Grace earlier: *For someone to get the better of him, they'd have to be extremely skilled.* And that's what the rifleman was, for sure.

Ben vowed that he would find him, too. To get close enough to do that, he was going to have to equip himself appropriately. That would be tomorrow's mission.

It was not yet dawn by the time he got back to his base, tired and aching and demoralised. The icy rain had turned the snow on the pavements rock-hard and slippery smooth. Inside the cottage, the fire had died and the rooms were cold. Ben relit the wood-burner, stripped off his damp clothes and hung them over the back of a chair to dry. He took a shower and changed, then drank a pint of hot black instant coffee and napped for an hour in the armchair by the fire. Feeling a little revitalised when he woke, he dropped to the floor and forced his weary muscles to pump out a hundred press-ups and a series of stretching exercises.

The double-barrelled shotgun he'd taken from his opponent last night was still in the car, tucked out of sight behind the front seats. He went outside with a blanket to roll it up in, then carried it around the side of the cottage to the shed, where he found an old hacksaw with a reasonably sharp blade hanging on a nail above the workbench. He clamped the shotgun in the bench vice and used the saw to chop the barrels off flush with the wooden fore-end, about twelve inches long. Then he did the same at the other end, removing the stock to leave just the pistol grip. He now had a twelve-bore hand cannon that was useless for most normal purposes a shotgun was good for. But if a man wanted a devastating close-range combat blaster that would fit unobtrusively into a bag, he need look no further.

Back in the cottage, Ben swallowed another pint of black coffee while he searched the internet for stores in the area dealing in hunting and outdoors equipment. He found one in Inverness, and the 140-mile round trip duly became his first task for the day.

The shop stood between a newsagent's and a small restaurant on a narrow street opposite the sloping, sculpted rear lawns of Inverness Castle, seat of the city's Sheriff Court. Ben was waiting outside when the owner opened the place up for business. A little bell jingled as he pushed through the door and was hit by the unique smell of outdoor clothing and hunting supplies stores: a scent of burnished leather and slightly musty waxed cotton, blended with the mixed aromas of boot polish and gun oil. The place was an Aladdin's cave stacked from floor to ceiling with shelves and display units, stuffed and mounted deer heads and antlers occupying every area of unused wall space. The proprietor was a flabby middle-aged guy with a threadbare comb-over hairstyle and glasses thicker than pint-glass bottoms that magnified his eyes like a bush baby's. Ben nodded him a polite good morning and set about threading his way through the maze of country wear, fishing tackle, camping equipment, hiking accessories and firearms-related apparel to pick out the items on his list.

Next to a rack of tartan-lined shooting jackets of the sort upper-class ladies and gents might wear to an exclusive pheasant massacre at a Scottish manor estate, Ben found something altogether more utilitarian and suited to his purpose. The two-piece ghillie suit was the kind of outfit used by deer stalkers and woodland hunters as well as military snipers, covering the wearer from head to toe in artificial mossy foliage like something that had just crawled out of a thicket: the best form of camouflage clothing ever devised. Ben pulled it down from its hanger, laid it on the counter and went on shopping.

He paused to gaze at a display rack of scoped hunting rifles, one of which would have nicely complemented the ghillie suit if he'd possessed the necessary UK firearms licensing paperwork. Instead he made do with something much quieter and just as deadly, a Ka-Bar survival knife with a razor-sharp black carbon steel blade. The last item on Ben's list was the most expensive, a pair of infrared night-vision goggles. Several hundred pounds for a piece of kit indistinguishable from what Special Forces had been using fifteen years earlier, now available to the general public. Just the thing for prowlers, voyeurs, perverts and folks who needed to be able to stalk dangerous killers at night in a dark and remote forest.

The shop owner was all smiles as Ben dumped the rest of his purchases on the counter and took out his wallet to pay. 'Don't sell that many of the ghillie suits, even fewer of the night-vision goggles,' he commented happily. 'Then all of a sudden, that's two of each sold in the same week.'

Ben looked at him. The shop owner went on grinning and nodding. 'Aye, sold the last pair to an older gentleman. In fact, strangely enough, he bought the exact same items as you. It's almost uncanny, thinking about it.'

Ben felt something click inside his mind. He took out his phone and brought up the photo of Boonzie to show him, the way he'd done with Holly the barmaid and the old guy in the Kinlochardaich Stores the day before. 'Would this be him?'

The shop owner peered over the rims of his glasses to get a focus on the photo, then looked up again, nodding in recognition. 'That explains it. Friend of yours, then?'

'My dad,' Ben said. 'We were planning on doing a bit of woodland stalking. Then maybe take a trip down to Glen Etive to see if we could bag a red deer.'

Dad. Boonzie would have killed him for this.

'Och, that's nice,' the shop owner said. 'Father and son. Just like the old times. How it ought to be.'

'I thought we were going to get kitted up together, but the crafty old so-and-so's very competitive. Always trying to get the jump on me, like he's got something to prove.' Ben smiled and shrugged. 'Just his way, I suppose.'

'I know what you mean. My father was just the same, God rest his soul.' The bush-baby eyes clouded with tender nostalgia.

'So you say he bought the exact same items?' Ben asked.

'As far as I remember.'

Great minds think alike, as the saying went. But trained minds think even more alike. Boonzie had been following the same trail as Ben, only he was several steps ahead. Ben had to hope he could race fast enough to catch up. He asked, 'When he was in here?'

'Two or three days, I think.'

'Two? Three? Which? I'd be much obliged if you could tell me exactly.'

Maybe if Ben hadn't been forking out several hundred pounds the shop owner might not have been so willing to help, but he reflected for a moment and then said with a smile, 'My memory's not what it used to be. Hold on, I can tell you exactly.' He spent a few seconds tapping and prodding his computerised till with rectangular reflections of the screen showing on his lenses. 'Here it is. It was four days back. I remember now. Your dad was the last customer of the day. He turned up just as I was about to close.'

Ben worked out the timeline. Four days ago meant that Boonzie had visited the shop on his first day in Scotland, just a couple of hours after he'd last spoken to Mirella.

The shop owner said, 'And, my mistake, your dad did make one extra purchase that doesn't appear to have been on your list.'

'What?'

'One of those.' The shop owner waved at a hanging display above the counter. Ben looked up and saw that it contained an assortment of crossbows. Most of them were plasticky and toylike, but a couple of them looked like highly effective weaponry that could drive a razor-tipped bolt through the side of a rhino and penetrate a couple of brick walls on its way out.

Those were the ones the shop owner was squinting at through his glasses as he went on, 'Excalibur, made in Canada. The most powerful of their kind on the market. No licence required. Your dad asked for the screw-on hunting arrow tips. I reminded him that it wasn't legal to hunt live quarry with in the UK, but he bought it anyway. Said that wasn't a problem.'

Ben pointed. 'Could you take one down for me, please?'

The shop owner lit up. 'You want to buy it too?'

'I want to see it first.'

The shop owner took one down and passed it to Ben. You could feel the latent power flowing through the weapon like electric current. It felt light and balanced. Ben put it to his shoulder and trained the onboard telescope sight through the window onto the street. The scope was hi-tech stuff, with an inbuilt laser rangefinder and an electronic red-dot optical reticule that glowed brightly against the target for shooting in low-light conditions. Mil-dot elevation increments to show where to hold the aim for longer ranges, to compensate for the forces of gravity. Once skewered, nothing could survive. The bow was an eminently lethal piece of kit, even more so when placed in the hands of a warrior like Boonzie McCulloch.

Ben could see the methodical steps his friend had taken as he prepared for the task ahead. The camper van. The supplies. Now the ghillie camouflage suit, the combat knife, the NV goggles and the high-powered bow completed the picture. Boonzie wasn't going after red deer. He knew the dangers; he was taking no chances. And since four days ago, he'd been actively in pursuit of his quarry.

But was Boonzie the predator in this hunt, or was he the prey?

Chapter 23

Four days earlier
The day before Boonzie is taken

Boonzie had almost forgotten how much he'd loved this game, once upon a time. The thrill of the hunt took him back decades to his military days, tempered only by the bitter ache in his heart every time he thought about Ewan lying in the hospital and the men who put him there.

On his return from Inverness he'd hidden the camper van deep in the shady heart of the forest near Loch Ardaich, where he'd spent two hours that afternoon diligently cutting pine branches with his new knife and laying them over the vehicle until it was virtually invisible. More work than draping camouflage netting, but far more effective.

He'd spent the rest of his day hunkered inside his concealed command centre, working out his strategy. By a process of logical elimination he'd come to the conclusion that his best chance of finding the poacher was at the end of the loch furthest from where Ross Campbell had been murdered. Unless, that was, the poacher had simply escaped the area after the incident. But Boonzie had to try, because if he failed to find this man he might never discover the truth.

He hadn't spoken to Mirella since leaving Ewan's house earlier that day, but he thought about her frequently and it hurt him to think about her sitting alone and fretting back home. When this was over, he promised himself, he would never leave her alone for another minute of his life.

Boonzie bided his time inside the camper until long after nightfall, consuming a simple meal of beans and coffee and keeping himself warm by the flame of his gas stove. Then, as midnight approached, he took the crossbow out of its bag and loaded six of his hunting bolts, with their shaving-sharp arrowheads fitted, into the weapon's onboard quiver. Boonzie had little reason to think that the poacher would pose any significant threat to him, but under the circumstances he had no intention of going unarmed. Next he put on the ghillie suit, the trousers first and then the top, leaving the headgear until last so that he could wear it over the head harness of the night-vision goggles.

When he was ready, he slipped out of the camper van and began to make his stealthy, silent way through the dark forest towards the north-west shore of the loch. With the goggles over his eyes, his surroundings turned into a shimmery, watery-green world, as though he was walking on the ocean bed. It would have been easy to make too much noise crunching over the frosty ground, but Boonzie moved the way he'd trained men to move, back in the day. The skills he'd taught to his trainees were so deeply ingrained into his mind that the passing of the years had done nothing to dull them.

Quarter of a mile from the edge of Loch Ardaich, the snap of a twig nearby made him freeze, the mossy and leafy contours of the suit allowing him to merge into his environment so that he was just another patch of foliage in the darkness. A moment later the sea-green figure of a deer

136

stepped into his field of vision. She was a young doe, foraging alone among the trees. Her eyes were two shining emeralds as she glanced around her, alert and ready to flee at the first sign of danger but perfectly oblivious of his presence.

Boonzie smiled at the sight of her. He'd hunted and killed many animals for survival during his military past, but the taking of any innocent life sickened him. He wouldn't have dreamed of hurting this beautiful creature. She passed within a few feet of him, then moved on. Boonzie waited until she was gone before he continued on his way, so as not to alarm her with any sudden movements.

Forty more minutes passed before he reached the lochside. Beyond the fringe of the pine forest the waters were still and smooth, shrouded here and there with pockets of eerie drifting mist that the NV image made appear like a toxic fog. Boonzie slipped along the shoreline for half a mile. Then half a mile again. He saw nothing, but kept moving with the indefatigable patience that had served him so well in the SAS.

Then, just as he thought his night hunt would prove fruitless, he spotted the distant green beacon of light dancing on the edge of the water, and gut instinct told him with a glow of satisfaction that he'd found his man.

Boonzie edged closer, silent and unnoticed. If he could sneak up on a wild deer, then no human quarry had a chance of sensing the approach of the camouflaged figure creeping along the grassy shoreline. The poacher was a large and chubby individual, dressed in waders and a long waterproof winter coat. A wool cap covered his head. He appeared to be winding up his night-time fishing session and getting ready to leave. A few minutes later, and Boonzie would have missed him.

Boonzie halted and crouched rock-still in the frosty

bushes, watching as the poacher packed up and tidied away his kit. From the shadows of the trees near the shoreline protruded the rear end of an old Subaru four-wheel-drive that had been backed down a track through the woods. The poacher had opened up the tailgate. Boonzie observed the greenlit figure going back and forth with bits and pieces of equipment to stow in the boot, taking his time, very much at home in his element and quite unaware he was being observed. He struggled up the bank to the 4x4 with a large oblong box that reminded Boonzie of a military ammo crate. Boonzie guessed it contained the poacher's haul of fish. Judging by its weight, it looked like he'd had a successful night.

Soon the poacher would be ready to leave. Then would be the time for Boonzie to make his move.

After four hours of freezing his bollocks off out here, Jamie McGlashan was looking forward to getting back to the bothy, polishing off his quarter bottle of Bell's with two or three slices of rabbit pie and crawling into his sleeping bag with a nice hot water bottle. Tired and cold and wet he might be, but satisfied in the knowledge that his night's catch would put a couple of tasty meals in his belly and bring him in a few quid besides.

It was still a damn sight better than working for a living, that was for sure. Jamie had never had any luck in that department, and had given up on it long ago. He wasn't much of a people person. He loved the solitude and the silence of the remote wild places where he'd spent all of his life. This was where his heart was. Plus, nothing the outside world had to offer could possibly compare with the rush of clandestine excitement when you snagged a big juicy salmon. The thrill of forbidden fruit. Maybe that was why he kept coming back to his favourite loch, where he'd been fishing man and boy. It was kind of an addiction.

Hooked. Jamie had to chuckle at his own joke. As he sat on the edge of the tailgate to yank off his waders, he reflected more seriously that a person would have to be bloody addicted, not to mention a total daftie, to venture anywhere near the spot where, helpless and transfixed with horror, he'd seen a man being murdered. He would never forget Ross Campbell's screams as the killers hurled him into the water. The poor bastard's last moments of panic when they pushed him under the surface. The awful instant when the wild splashing and gurgling finally ended and he bobbed back up to the surface, face down, slimy with weeds and very obviously dead even from where Jamie had been watching it all take place.

But what troubled Jamie even more profoundly than the haunting vision of Ross Campbell's last moments was the knowledge of who the killers were. Two of them, at any rate.

Knowing what he knew, a sensible man would have stayed away from here. Not Jamie McGlashan. Still, he had taken what he considered to be reasonable precautions. Such as giving the murder scene a wide berth by sticking to the far western end of the loch, nearly twelve miles away; and such as not returning to the shithole mobile home that his housing benefit cheques paid for, and instead living rough in the stone bothy where he'd camped with his father as a boy, when the old man had taught him the poacher's craft.

Those were mixed memories for Jamie. His father had been a brutal and volatile tyrant whom he'd loathed as much as he'd loved. Every time he thought about him, Jamie touched his scarred lip and thought about the legacy it had left him with.

The bothy was little more than a ruin now, but he was

content to stay there until all the heat died down and he could be certain that the killers had no interest in him.

He stuffed his waders into the bin bag he kept them in, chucked it into the back of the Subaru and pulled on his boots. Out of habit he took out his phone to check his Facebook page, though he had no real friends and wasn't expecting anything. Reception was crap out here anyway. He replaced the phone in his breast pocket, then stretched and yawned, closed the tailgate lid, dragged his weary feet around to the driver's door and hefted his bulk in behind the wheel. He was getting fatter all the time, not that it worried him that much any more, with nobody around to taunt him about it.

The Subaru's interior light hadn't come on when he opened the door. Which didn't surprise Jamie, because virtually everything else about the old wreck was failing. He reached up and prodded the switch, and the car's interior filled with a dim yellow glow.

And Jamie McGlashan let out a scream as he saw the figure sitting in the passenger seat next to him.

The apparition was more like a creature than a man. It looked like something that had crawled out of a swamp, all covered in leafy foliage and green dangling mossy fronds. For a bowel-loosening moment Jamie thought it was one of the mythical beasts that had filled his grandfather's stories. But mythical beasts didn't wear hi-tech night-vision goggle apparatus and go around with crossbows. This one was cradled in the swamp thing's lap, cocked and loaded and pointing a razor-tipped arrowhead right at Jamie's big round stomach.

Jamie instinctively made a grab for the door handle, wanting to throw himself out and bolt away in terror through the woods. That was when the creature spoke. It said in a strong Glaswegian accent, 'Dinnae even think aboot it, son. Stay right where ye are.'

Someone had injected icy loch water into Jamie's veins where his blood used to be. He could barely breathe, but he managed to blurt out: 'W-who are you?'

The creature replied, 'Never mind who I am. Let's talk aboot who *you* are. What's yer name, son?'

All kinds of terrible thoughts flashed through Jamie's mind. The most frightening of which was that this man had been sent to murder him. His worst nightmare had come true. The killers knew about him! He stared at the crossbow and the thought of being skewered against the inside of the car door made him want to puke with terror. 'J-J-J-Jim,' he stammered. 'Jim S-S-S-Smith.'

The creature said nothing, contemplating him for a moment. Then a mossy hand flashed out as quick as a snake and plucked the mobile phone from Jamie's coat pocket. The crossbow stayed trained on Jamie's vitals as the creature swiped the screen to unlock the phone, and spent a moment glancing through it. Jamie swallowed as he remembered his still-open Facebook page.

The creature had already found it. And seen his real name.

'Lie tae me again, Jamie McGlashan, and ye're a dead man.'

Jamie's heart lit up with hope. Maybe that meant the creature wasn't an assassin sent to murder him, after all. 'A-all right! I'm sorry. I'm Jamie McGlashan.' As a glimmer of courage returned he repeated, 'Who are you?'

The creature reached up and removed its leafy hood, and Jamie could see the face of the man inside the ghillie suit. His features were lined and his hair and beard were white. The stranger's eyes were as cold as Loch Ardaich in January and as inscrutable as a dead salmon's.

'The name's McCulloch. I'm Ewan's uncle.'

Jamie was totally confused. All he could mutter was 'Shite.' An instant later, he knew that his expression had betrayed him.

Ewan McCulloch's uncle said, 'Ye spoke tae my nephew. The night of the murder. Before Ewan was attacked.'

'I—'

'Nae mair bullshit, Jamie. I can see it in yer eyes. It's you. Ye're the one who saw Ross Campbell killed.'

There no longer seemed any point in denying it. And in the strangest way, it felt good to talk about it. 'Yes! I watched the fuckers drown the poor guy. I won't forget it as long as I live.'

'I didnae come here tae hurt ye, Jamie. But hurt ye I will, if I havtae. Ye'll disappear in these woods and no trace o' ye will ever be seen again. If I'm makin' that extra clear, it's because I dinnae want it tae happen.'

Jamie tried to shrink away, but there was nowhere to go. He quavered, 'Then what do you want?'

'Information. Details. Descriptions. Faces. Names. All that ye know. You do that for me, I'll let ye go. Okay?'

'And if I don't?'

The dead fish eyes gave the slightest of twinkles. 'I think you're gonnae talk tae me, son.'

And Ewan's uncle was right. Jamie told him everything.

Jamie McGlashan had an old scar on his upper lip that looked like a twisted worm. It gave him a slight speech impediment. In his lispy voice he described how he had witnessed four men murder Ross Campbell. Boonzie didn't want to know the details of how, only the names of who. Two of the names, he'd never heard before. But McGlashan was keeping the best for last. When he heard the other two

142

names, Boonzie understood why the poacher was so afraid.

Those two names were Detective Inspector Macleod and Detective Sergeant Coull.

Their mention was enough to make Boonzie lose his famous steely composure. 'Ye'd better be tellin' me the truth,' he growled at McGlashan with such ferocity that the poacher turned ghastly pale in the dim light of the car. 'Or I swear tae God, ye'll be sorry. I found ye once. I can find ye again. And next time I'll kill ye.'

'I'm not bullshittin' you! That's who I saw!'

Boonzie eyed him with suspicion. 'How did ye know them?'

'I've been arrested four times for poachin'. I know every pig in the region. Trust me. I'm no gettin' this wrong. It was Coull and Macleod.'

'Swear?'

'On my mother's grave, man!'

Boonzie stared deep into Jamie McGlashan's eyes and believed him. 'All right.' He leaned back into the car seat and fell into a long silence. He had sat face to face with these same bastards and listened to their assurances that they would catch the attackers who'd beaten his nephew almost to death. If McGlashan was right and Coull and Macleod were the very same men who'd helped to murder Ewan's friend, then they were almost certainly deeply involved in what had happened to Ewan himself.

The rage made Boonzie's heart thump dangerously fast and heavily. Even in the subzero temperatures of the winter night he felt as though he was on fire inside. A wave of nausea washed over him. He had the urge to swallow one of his pills, but resisted it.

'What are you goin' to do?' McGlashan asked tentatively.

Boonzie did not hesitate in his reply. 'I'm goantae find

them. Make them confess. Hurt them back for what they've done. And then I'm goantae put them six feet below the groond, where they belong.'

McGlashan swallowed hard and glanced at the crossbow. 'No, I meant, what aboot me?'

Boonzie shook his head. 'I'm not an animal, son. Ye've played fair wi' me an' I willnae hurt ye. Go home.'

The poacher's eyes filled with tears of relief and he looked as though he was about to cry. 'Mr McCulloch?'

'Aye?'

'I'm so sorry aboot what happened to Ewan. I tried to warn him.'

'I ken ye did, son. And I appreciate it.'

'I hope he's goin' to be okay.'

Boonzie nodded gravely. 'Thanks, son. You take care, noo.'

'I will.'

'But if ye want my advice, get as far away frae this place as ye can. All hell's aboot tae break loose.'

And then Boonzie pushed open the car door, stepped out into the night and was gone.

Chapter 24

Just a few hours after Boonzie McCulloch had talked to the poacher, another face-to-face conversation was about to take place.

The man who had been summoned to the big house was called Carl Hacker. He hadn't been given a lot of notice and had been over 5,000 miles away when he'd received his instructions that his employer's personal G5 jet was waiting to fly him back to Scotland immediately. The silver Rolls Royce Cullinan had picked him up from Glasgow International just after dawn and whisked him, smooth and fast, to the magnificent two-thousand-acre property 150 miles north of the city.

The splendid castle was in fact a relatively modern construction, built in mock-eighteenth-century style to the exact specifications of its owner. It stood majestically nestled at the foot of a mountain, with panoramic south-facing views of a country estate that stretched as far as the eye could see. Hacker's employer had various other residences, including a villa in the Bahamas, a luxury apartment in Monte Carlo and a small chateau in Brittany, where he believed his family to have originated; but he considered the castle his home and spent nearly all his time there. It comprised more than enough bedrooms for Hacker to have been allocated his own personal quarters on the first floor, though his international travel commitments gave him little chance to use them.

Hacker made his way through the stately corridors and up a sweeping staircase to the third-floor study. If he was jetlagged from his long journey, he didn't show it. He was a man of great composure, whose face never betrayed what was going on in his mind. Physically he was tall and lean and looked younger than his forty-one years, his buzz-cut brown hair just beginning to silver at the temples. He wore an immaculate dark suit whose cut accentuated his broad shoulders, tapered torso and narrow waist.

Hacker knocked, stepped into the study and quietly closed the double doors behind him. The walls were rich with ornately carved oak panels and the golden early-morning light from the east-facing leaded windows reflected off shiny dark green buttoned leather and the arrays of antique weaponry displayed around the room. A pair of enormous claymore two-handed swords hung crossed against a banner of his employer's family tartan and the clan crest with the motto VIRECIT VULNERE VIRTUS. *Courage grows strong at a wound.* Hacker knew a little about courage, and wounds too.

Outlined against the window was the back of a large leather swivel chair, turned away from the desk to face the view of the estate. Hacker walked up to the desk and stood with his hands clasped behind his back. He said in his calm, soft voice, 'You wanted to see me.'

The chair slowly swivelled back around. Hacker's employer looked tired, with dark circles under his eyes as though he hadn't slept. He didn't thank Hacker for having dropped everything and travelled halfway round the world at such short notice. That wasn't the kind of relationship he had with anyone.

'Yes, Hacker. I called you back from Korea because your skills are needed here in Scotland. There's some urgent business that has to be attended to.'

Hacker replied levelly, 'I thought I was already attending to business. You sent me to Seoul to stop Kang's people taking over our interests there. Which, as your international head of security, I was in the process of dealing with when I received your message.'

'Yes, yes. But never mind Kang for now. I need this poacher person found and dealt with instead. Plus this old fool McCulloch is turning into a real headache, poking his nose in where it's not wanted.'

Hacker was already fully briefed on the events that had been taking place here during his absence. He replied, 'With all due respect, need I remind you that McCulloch and the poacher are scarcely in a position to cut you out of a multi-million-dollar property investment deal? While I can assure you that Kang and his gangsters are busy doing just that, now that my back is turned.'

His employer waved that irritating distraction away, like swatting a fly. 'It's all a matter of priorities, Hacker. My current ones are closer to home.'

'You don't have to worry about the poacher,' Hacker said. 'He'll be found and taken care of, just as you wish. Easy meat.'

'Good. As for Ewan McCulloch's uncle, this "Boonzie" person, I'm concerned that we may have a real problem here. The poacher is just some local idiot who saw too much. But McCulloch is a professional. I never bargained for someone like this getting involved in our affairs.'

'I thought you had local muscle keeping tabs on him,' Hacker replied. 'Baird and his cronies.'

'I pulled Baird off the job. Perhaps a little rashly, I'll

confess. But I didn't trust him. The man's an inbred cretin. And knowing what we now know about McCulloch thanks to our sources in local law enforcement, I was worried that he might spot Baird, catch him and make him talk. That would have been an unmitigated bloody disaster.'

Hacker nodded in agreement. 'If you recall, I did advise you not to hire Baird in the first place. That goes for all these local yokel morons you've picked up. What did you do, put an ad in the paper saying "Henchmen wanted"?'

'All right, all right, I get the point.'

'More than just a moron, Baird's also a coward with a big mouth. You're right – McCulloch would probably have made mincemeat out of him, *if* he'd got too close. But it would still have been worthwhile letting Baird stay on his tail, at a discreet distance. Do we have any idea where McCulloch is now?'

Hacker's employer threw up his hands with a sigh of exasperation. 'None. He's dropped completely off our radar. If he'd given up and gone back home to bloody Italy, we'd have known about it. All we know is that he's driving the nephew's camper van, because Baird saw him leaving the house in it. But there's been no trace of him since. It's as though the wily old bugger has disappeared into thin air.'

'It's not entirely surprising. Men like him are trained to do just that.'

'And men like you. You're one of their kind. You know how they operate, how their minds work.'

Hacker's own past history was known to very few people outside of this room. '*Was* one of their kind,' he corrected his employer. 'Only I was better. Still am.'

'Exactly. Why else would I have brought you all the way back here and risked letting a third-rate bandit like Kang shaft a property deal I spent months setting up? Just tell me you can deal with my problem.'

Hacker considered for a long moment, watching his employer's eyes and seeing that he was serious. Hacker's boss was not the wealthiest business tycoon in the world, but his net worth nonetheless extended comfortably into nine figures and he was the kind of person who would pay whatever it took to get things done. He was also not someone to be trifled with by refusing his wishes. Not even for Hacker, who was more direct with him than any other man in his employ.

Hacker nodded. 'I can deal with it.'

'Excellent.'

'But we have to catch him first. From what you tell me, McCulloch could be anywhere in the western Highlands. We don't have the resources to track a tough target like him over thousands of square miles of wilderness. Unless . . .'

His employer looked at him with penetrating eyes. 'Unless?'

'It all depends on how badly you want to locate this man.'

'I said it was an urgent matter. That's what it is, Hacker. I want him found yesterday.'

'In which case, it's simply a matter of expanding our resources. Money and manpower, plus the usual ancillaries, such as equipment and transportation.'

'Money's not a problem,' Hacker's employer said, with a note of irritation. 'As for the rest, that's your department.'

Hacker nodded. 'I have certain contacts, yes. I can make the necessary calls.'

'How quickly can you get hold of these contacts?'

'I can think of four men based in London who can make themselves available to us at a couple of days' notice.'

'No quicker than that?'

'These are busy people,' Hacker said. 'And they're expensive.'

'Of course. Are these men part of your . . . organisation?'

'It's more of a brotherhood,' Hacker said. 'A fraternity of

men with a shared background and set of values. There's a whole network of us, but the four I have in mind are Bobby Banks, Kev O'Donnell, Liam Carter and Mitch Graham.'

'Call them. I can have the jet pick them up as soon as they're ready to travel.'

'They'll want to know exactly what the job entails. Therefore I need to know what your intentions are. Once we find McCulloch, what then?'

'I would say that's self-evident. He needs to be taken out of the game. And I don't mean paid off to keep his mouth shut. I mean eliminated, properly and permanently, like the other two.'

'But preferably with a little more expertise and neatness,' Hacker said. 'The Campbell business was clumsy, at best. To say nothing of the complete dog's breakfast they made of "eliminating" McCulloch's nephew.'

'I accept that some mistakes have been made,' his employer said, a little stiffly. 'It can't happen again.'

Hacker nodded again. 'And if I'm in charge of this operation now, we do things my way. Agreed?'

They shook hands. Hacker left the room and got straight on the phone to the kinds of people he knew he could trust to come on board.

McCulloch had no idea what he'd got himself into. The fool was already as good as dead.

Chapter 25

The morning after her meeting with Ben Hope, Grace Kirk was at her desk in the police station in Fort William, staring at a pile of administrative work in front of her without really seeing it. She was having trouble devoting her undivided attention to a recent spate of farm machinery thefts in the area, and kept drifting off to think about more pressing matters.

Before her day's shift had begun she'd detoured by the hospital to check on Ewan and been allowed in to see him, just for a few moments, by the careworn Dr Fraser, who was obviously concerned that his coma was persisting without sign of recovery. Grace had sat by Ewan's bedside and clasped his hand while speaking to him softly. 'Ewan, it's me. It's Grace. Won't you please come back to us?' It was so awful to see him lying there, hooked up to machines and covered in tubes and wires. He looked shrivelled and lifeless and it was impossible to know what, if anything, was happening inside his mind. She had left the hospital in tears.

Also distracting her from her work was the memory of her encounter with the intriguing stranger she'd met last night, and the perplexing things he'd told her. She couldn't get them out of her head. She'd lain awake half the night, puzzling.

Nor could she forget the sound of his voice or the intensity of his eyes as he'd talked. It had been as though nothing and nobody else in the world existed at that moment. Just her, him and the crackling fire that flickered in his pupils. There was something about this guy Hope. Maybe he was crazy. Maybe he was something else entirely. She liked him. In fact, if she was honest with herself, maybe she liked him a little too damn much.

When she finally got sick of writing reports about stolen tractor parts, she switched into another part of the police computer system and made a couple of calls to check on what was happening with Angus Baird and his two brawler friends. She was gratified to learn that all three of them were scheduled to appear before the Sheriff Court in three days' time, accused of breaching the peace. Baird was still in hospital with concussion, which came as no surprise to Grace. The other two were being bound over in jail until their court date, because of their previous convictions for violence. Silly bastards.

The office space that Grace shared with her fellow officers was a cramped cubicle that smelled of laundered police uniforms, the aftershave of the mostly male coppers, and the bad coffee from the machine down the hallway. The peculiar brown liquid it dispensed was generally referred to as 'the shits', but they all nevertheless consumed it in endless quantities. She was thinking of going to fetch a cup when one of her colleagues, a somewhat hyperactive young constable called Pete Finnigan, came by with one of the ready smiles he always had for her, and some surprising news.

'Hey, Cap'n.' He thought it was amusing to call her that, because of her surname. Spot the *Star Trek* geek.

Grace wasn't really in the mood for a chat, but she offered back a friendly smile. 'Hi, Pete.'

'Heard the latest? They made an arrest in the McCulloch case.'

Grace's smile dropped and she stared at him. 'Seriously? Who?'

'Watkins.'

'The Greenie?' Grace knew about Geoff Watkins from all the fuss in recent months over the Highland Manor project. He and some of his fellow ecowarriors had set up a tipi camp near the main gates of the development site and resolutely vowed to remain dug in there for as long as it took to force the contractors to pull out once and for all. Watkins had specifically come to the attention of the local police due to the extensive criminal record he'd accrued pursuing his ideological crusade back in his native England, which included everything from scuffles with officers during rowdy climate protests to attempted arson attacks on butcher's shops. It seemed that some people just had nothing better to do. He'd spent a couple of months in jail in 2016, following a particularly nasty hunt saboteur incident in which a horse had been badly injured and its rider nearly killed. Since his arrival on the local scene, Watkins had been suspected of taking part in the vandalism of construction equipment at the Highland Manor site but there'd been insufficient evidence to charge him with criminal damage.

'I shit you not,' Finnigan said with a smirk, pleased by the look of amazement on her face. 'Brought him in early this morning, after our officers hit the camp in a dawn raid led by none other than the heroic DI Macleod himself, with his wee lapdog Coull scurrying at his heels.' Finnigan should have been a small-town reporter instead of a police constable. He glanced around in case any of the office tattle-tales were listening.

Grace said, 'I'd no idea that Watkins was a suspect in the investigation.'

'Kind of a no-brainer, really. It was common knowledge that McCulloch & Campbell were the surveyors for the Highland Manor project. Makes perfect sense for a nutcase like him to target the firm director for intimidation. With his form, you wonder why Macleod and Coull didn't jump on him sooner.'

'Is motive all they've got on him? Is there any direct evidence?'

Finnigan shrugged. 'Just telling you what I know, Cap'n. Not like we shit-kicking bottom feeders in the lower ranks have the inside track on what the brass are up to, is it?'

Grace was frowning. 'What about Ross Campbell?'

'What about him?'

'If the Greenies had motive for assaulting one member of the McCulloch & Campbell firm, then that works for both.'

'Aye, I suppose so, but as far as I know, the thing with Ross Campbell is still down as an accidental drowning.'

'Seems like a bit of a coincidence, don't you think?'

Finnigan shrugged again. 'Hey, shit happens.' Then his smirk grew wider and he lowered his voice. 'But listen. Never mind all that. I've got to tell you what Cammie Linton told me just now. He was on the raid. Made me *so* fuckin' wish I'd been there too, man.'

'Why?'

'Och, you wouldn't believe it. So when the troops landed on the camp, right, there's Watkins and about a dozen of his hippy friends all huddled under blankets around this brazier to stay warm, right? Then Watkins sees the officers running towards him, and he jumps up from under the blanket and he's stark fuckin' bollock naked.'

'Oh, come off it. No way.'

Finnigan's grin was spread so far across his face that it looked as if it was going to split. 'You heard me. It's, like, minus two degrees and this bawheid's in his birthday suit. Maybe they use some kind of wacko Zen meditation to control their body temperature while they're communing with the Being. Anyhow, then Watkins takes off and starts legging it like a bat out of hell through the snow with Coull and six more officers chasing after him. But then it gets even better, because Watkins' hippy friends – they're all totally in the scud too – they start yelling and screaming at the top of their voices and pelting our guys with turds. Fuckin' *turds*, man. Like they were keeping them handy to use as ammunition or something.' He shook his head in wonder. 'You couldn't make this up. Anyhow, they ended up making five more arrests. Grace? You okay?'

Grace's mind had drifted off while he was talking. Naked hippies flinging excrement didn't interest her too much, and in any case PC Cammie Linton was notorious around the station for spinning all manner of weird and wonderful yarns that only a dork like Pete Finnigan would fall for. Instead she was thinking that if Watkins was responsible for the attack on Ewan McCulloch, then whether or not the Campbell drowning was connected it went against everything Ben Hope had told her about the gold coins, and about his fears for what might have happened to his friend Boonzie. If the eco-warrior was indeed the culprit, Hope was on a wild goose chase and the apparent disappearance of Ewan's uncle was still unaccounted for. Unless Ben Hope was getting that all wrong, too.

Then again, Ben Hope didn't strike Grace as a guy who got things all wrong.

Finnigan looked a little peeved that she wasn't cracking up at his account of the dawn raid. 'What's the matter with you? That's the best fuckin' story I've heard in yonks. Almost shat myself laughing when Cammie told me.'

She asked, 'So has he put his hands up to it?'

'Who?'

'Watkins. Has he confessed to the assault?'

'Cammie said that when they took'm away he wiz screamin' that he was innocent, had nothin' to do with it and they got the wrong guy, and that this was a government conspiracy to persecute him for his beliefs. But then they all say that, don't they?'

Which told Grace that Macleod and Coull were probably still down there in the austere, windowless interview room, working on grinding a confession out of Geoffrey Watkins. 'To be continued, I suppose. Thanks for filling me in, Pete. Appreciate it.'

'Hey, no problemo. You want a cup of the shits? I was just on my way.'

'No, I'm good.'

'Whatever you say, Cap'n. Gotta rush. See ya.' Finnigan sauntered off, whistling a cheery tune.

When Finnigan was gone Grace went back to her pile of work, but any faint hope of being able to get any of it done was now dashed. She leaned back from the desk and gazed out of the window at the grey skies over Fort William and the snow-capped hills in the distance and tried to get her thoughts in order.

Whichever way she tried to look at it, the Watkins arrest just didn't make sense to her. The logic worked, as far as it went: Watkins' history of ideologically inspired thuggery loosely explained the motive for the attack, and certainly nobody could say the guy didn't have a violent streak. But the more Grace thought about it, the more she doubted that Macleod and Coull had anything solid to pin on Watkins. There were just too many boxes left unticked to convince her.

Casting her mind back to the meeting between Macleod,

156

Coull and Boonzie McCulloch, she remembered how quick her superior officers had been to dismiss the notion that the assault on Ewan and his business partner's drowning were somehow connected, implying that Ewan's suspicions about Ross's death, and the involvement of the poacher, were no more than a tall tale. As though they were trying to give Boonzie the brush-off by discrediting that whole line of enquiry. Yet just moments later they'd been expressing a particular interest in the gold coins that Ross Campbell had somehow come by, and asking Boonzie what he knew about where Ross might have found them. The mention of the coins had caught Grace's ear at the time, though it hadn't meant anything to her – nor to Boonzie, as she'd later confirmed with him. Macleod and Coull had tried to act all casual, but their questions had been none too subtle and Grace had thought she detected an underlying sense of anxiety in their tone and manner. The real bullshit note had sounded when Boonzie had challenged Macleod and Coull about it, and they'd shut him down by saying the matter was related to a separate investigation.

Really? What investigation? The weirdness of her superiors' line of questioning had struck Grace sharply at the time, and been on her mind ever since. After the things Ben Hope had told her last night, she'd been thinking about it even more. It was as though Macleod and Coull were playing a double game, hiding something while fishing for information and secretly anxious to find out who else might know. Now the Watkins thing had entered the equation, it just didn't fit right and felt a little too convenient for Grace's liking. If Ewan was beaten up because of his involvement in the Highland Manor development, where did that leave Ross's stash of valuable gold coins that Macleod and Coull had been so keen to know more about?

She was at a loss to piece the facts together, but she sensed that something odd was going on. Even if Macleod and Coull succeeded in extracting a confession out of Watkins, she knew she'd never feel comfortable with that outcome. Because this was about Ewan. Though their relationship was far in the past, she still cared about him deeply as a dear friend. Thanks to all this, he was lingering in a coma from which he might never awaken.

She couldn't bear that thought.

She needed to know the truth.

The only problem was how to set about finding out. Even under normal circumstances a lowly PC couldn't go poking her nose into her superior officers' investigation without getting stonewalled, at best, and more likely treated to a severe bollocking. In any case if her hunch was right and Macleod and Coull had some kind of hidden agenda, the last thing she needed was to draw their suspicion on herself.

But then Grace had an idea, and thought that maybe there was something else she could do.

Chapter 26

Three days earlier

Following his encounter with Jamie McGlashan, Boonzie had worked his way back through the woods to where he'd hidden the camper van. He had stripped off the ghillie suit and warmed his chilled body by the flame of his gas stove.

He'd already known then what he had to do next. Nothing else mattered. His mission commitment was unwavering and his plan was sharp and focused in his mind. Yet the white-hot rage he'd felt on hearing the poacher's testimony had not left him. A terrible burning pain had spread through his chest and down his left side, and racked him until he had eventually given up trying to fight it through willpower alone, and swallowed down two of the pills from his bottle. He hated himself for his weakness. When at last the agony had diminished, he had been able to curl up under his blanket and snatch a few hours' sleep.

Long before daybreak the following morning, Boonzie set off for Fort William. For the first few miles a fresh snowfall overnight had all but swallowed the lonely road under a virgin carpet of white and he drove carefully until he reached the A82. The council gritter trucks had been out last night to salt the roads, and the tarmac was a clear, twisty black ribbon cutting through the wintry landscape.

Reaching Fort William just after eight a.m. he passed the hospital where Ewan was, and seriously considered stopping off there to check on him. But he had other matters to attend to first. From the hospital he followed the route by which Grace Kirk had driven him to the police station. It was still dark when he got there, but traffic was already filtering through the building's main gate as the early birds reported for work, and he hoped he wasn't too late.

In a more urban environment Boonzie would have chosen to find a parking position on the street somewhere opposite the building, from which to mount surveillance on his target. The Fort William police headquarters sat alone in the middle of a large area of wasteland, off the town bypass close to a roundabout, and there was nowhere to set up his observation point outside the grounds. Instead he drove straight inside and parked in a side parking area for visitors, within view of the building's entrance.

If anyone came over and asked him what he was doing there, he'd say he'd come to talk to DI Macleod or DS Coull about his nephew's assault. Which was essentially the truth, anyway. Although what Boonzie had in mind went beyond mere talking.

The camper van was a fine surveillance vehicle. It had a side window veiled with a lace curtain, and below it a berth that folded up into a bed-settee when not in use. Boonzie detached the scope from the crossbow and settled on the sofa cushions so that he could watch from behind the lace as staff cars arrived and their occupants entered the building some sixty yards away. With the scope's magnification screwed up to the max, he could easily make out their faces from this distance.

Within a minute of his arrival a silver Ford sedan turned in through the gates and parked in the staff parking area, followed by a small blue Kia. He watched as their drivers, a man in his thirties and a woman with bleached-blond hair respectively, got out and pushed inside the building's front doors with his scope crosshairs centred on their faces. Neither of them was of interest to him. He went on waiting.

Boonzie had Jamie McGlashan's mobile phone in his pocket. He had taken it from the poacher in case it came in handy, preferring the anonymity of using someone else's rather than having to purchase one in his own name. He could feel it there, burning a hole in his side, telling him he should use it to phone home. He took the phone out and gazed at it, torn by indecision. Part of him badly wanted to talk to Mirella, to check on how she was doing and to tell her he was okay. But he knew she'd be very emotional, and feared that the sound of her voice and her tears might break his resolve and make him want to give up his quest and rush back home to be with her again.

Instead he used the phone to look up the number for Belford Hospital online, dialled it and got through to the main reception desk. He identified himself, asked if Dr Fraser was available and was told she'd just come in. While waiting for the doctor to come on the phone, he watched three more cars arrive. A yellow VW, a brown Land Rover Discovery and a purple Suzuki hatchback. Two females, one male, all unfamiliar faces and of no importance to him.

At last, Dr Fraser came on the phone, having only just got into work and already sounding as though she was running in eight directions at once. Boonzie repeated who he was and asked about Ewan. He was ready for the worst, but even so the news that there had been no discernible change in his nephew's condition left him feeling flat and grim. He thanked her for the update anyway, gave her his number and asked if she would call if there were any developments, good or bad. Dr Fraser promised that she would.

Boonzie put the phone away and continued waiting and watching. At 8.47 a.m. the first glint of the sun's disc peeked over the hills in the east. Two and a half minutes later, at precisely ten to nine, a black Jaguar luxury estate veered in sharply through the gates and rolled up in front of the building. The driver's door swung open and Boonzie felt a small, sharp blade of pain and fury stab his heart as his Number One target, Detective Inspector Fergus Macleod, emerged from the car, grabbed a briefcase and raincoat from the back and then marched up to the entrance. Macleod's face was blotchy and red and he walked uncomfortably, as though he'd overstuffed himself with fried eggs and bacon that morning. Boonzie thought briefly about reattaching the scope to the crossbow and pinning him like a butterfly to the doorway before he made it inside, then dismissed the idea as maybe not practical. Macleod disappeared into the building. Boonzie made a note of his car make, model and registration.

He was finishing scribbling down the number when a red Toyota Corolla arrived and parked a few spaces away from the black Jag. Boonzie put the telescope to his eye and saw that it was Jim Coull. He observed his Number Two target enter the building, took a note of the reg number and settled back for the wait.

From nine a.m. onwards the police station gradually came to life. Vehicles came and went from both the staff and visitor car parks. Boonzie brewed up a mug of strong black coffee and kept watching the building in case either of his targets left. Time passed. If anyone had even noticed the camper van sitting in the visitor car park, it seemed nobody was interested enough to come and check it out.

Boonzie didn't care how long he needed to wait. He had food and water, heating and toilet facilities, and could remain there all day if necessary. In the event, he didn't have to bide his time for too long. Three hours after reporting for duty, DI Macleod and DS Coull emerged together from the building. Macleod had on the raincoat and still looked blotchy. They appeared deep in serious conversation as they walked towards the car park. The pair hovered there for half a minute longer, still talking, the winter wind ripping at their hair, then split up and walked to their vehicles. Boonzie wondered where they were going. He moved up the narrow aisle to the driver's seat as the black Jaguar took off, followed by the red Toyota. Boonzie started up the camper van and let it roll gently out of the visitor car park after them, making sure to keep a good distance behind.

As they reached the gates, the Jag turned left towards the bypass roundabout and the Corolla headed in the opposite direction. Now Boonzie was torn as to which one to follow. He opted to go after Macleod in the Jag.

Boonzie hung back and allowed a few other vehicles to slip between himself and the Jag as Macleod led him around the snowy-edged bypass skirting Fort William. A couple of miles later they entered a residential area on the edge of the town, filled with white-roofed modern houses that all looked like clones of one another. By now the vehicles spaced between them had filtered off, and Boonzie had to be careful not to be spotted while at the same time not losing sight of the Jag for too long, in case it disappeared among the Legoland warren of suburban streets. Finally Macleod pulled up in the driveway of a large detached residence with a prim garden and a double garage. Boonzie slotted the camper by the kerb eighty yards back, moved quickly back to the net-curtained side window and grabbed his telescope to watch Macleod climb out of the Jag and walk up to the house.

It looked as though the cop was coming home for lunch, in which case he might be there for a while. Boonzie decided to follow Macleod inside and confront him there. If the man was alone, so much the better. If not, Boonzie would have to deal with it. His plan was to force Macleod to confess everything, then make him call his minion Coull to get him to come over to the house on the pretext of needing to have a secret meeting.

Then Boonzie would decide what to do with the pair of them. His current favoured option was to drive them out into the middle of nowhere and slit their throats before he buried them.

He reattached the scope to the bow, then cocked the weapon and fitted a hunting bolt before applying the safety catch and slipping it into its carry bag. Just as he was about to step out of the camper and start making his way over to the house, he saw Macleod re-emerge from the front door and stride quickly back towards his car, speaking on a phone. He dived behind the Jag's wheel, and moments later the car reversed sharply out of the driveway and sped off. Wherever he was going in such a rush, Boonzie intended to follow.

Macleod's Jaguar led him out of town, and it wasn't long before they were miles out into the snowy countryside. Boonzie was still hanging right back, partly to avoid notice in Macleod's rear-view mirror, but partly also because the wheezy old camper van was hard pressed to keep up with the fast car.

More than eight miles into the middle of nowhere, the Jaguar turned off the road and went bumping and sliding down a twisty track with dilapidated barbed-wire fencing and overgrown gorse bushes and brambles on both sides. Boonzie waited until the car was out of sight, then cautiously followed. He continued along the track for a hundred yards, until he could see the Jag parked another hundred yards ahead at the bottom of a slope, next to a dead tree and the ruins of an old grey-stone chapel.

Boonzie pulled in behind a clump of gorse and got out of the camper with the cocked crossbow in his hands and his sheathed knife and a handful of extra hunting bolts stuck in his belt. The icy wind wrapped itself around him and his breath clouded like smoke. He had no idea what Macleod was doing, but saw his chance to catch the bent cop alone where there would be no witnesses. Eyeing the lie of the land he saw a natural path through the bushes and over a snowy rise from whose top he would be able to work his way around the back of the ruined chapel and approach Macleod by stealth. The ghillie suit would do him no good in this terrain, even if he'd had time to put it on.

Boonzie cleared the barbed-wire fence and scrambled up the slope, gorse overgrowth scratching at his legs and his feet sinking into deep snow. As he made it to the top of the rise he flattened himself low to the ground and crept forward until he could see Macleod's car from a different angle. And something else he hadn't been able to see from the track: another car, parked a few yards away from the Jaguar around the side of the ruined chapel. The second car was a big silver tank of a Rolls Royce. Boonzie realised that Macleod had driven out to this remote spot for a rendezvous with someone he obviously didn't want to meet in public.

This could be interesting.

Boonzie scrambled the rest of the way down the slope and approached the back of the roofless old chapel. He could hear the sound of voices: two men in conversation, though he couldn't make out what they were saying. Peering through a crumbled window he saw Macleod standing below the remains of an archway, talking with another man Boonzie had never seen before. The other man was older and trimmer than Macleod, and much better dressed in a tweedy suit under a long cashmere overcoat. His hair was silver like his Rolls Royce, expensively styled and swept back from his high brow. Boonzie wondered who he was.

Only one way to find out.

He stepped around the corner of the chapel and pointed the crossbow at the two men.

They stopped talking and stared at him. Macleod's florid features went the colour of beetroot and he said loudly, 'What do you think you're doing, McCulloch?' He looked angry, but strangely unsurprised by Boonzie's sudden appearance.

Boonzie kept the bow levelled in their direction. He stepped closer.

'You're making a very big mistake, McCulloch.'

Boonzie took another step and shook his head. 'That would be you,' he replied, 'when you and yer pal Coull killed Ross Campbell an' put my nephew in a coma.'

'You're out of your bloody mind.'

'Shut yer hole,' Boonzie snapped savagely at him. He jerked the bow towards the older man. 'Who're you?'

The older man smiled. 'Come, Mr McCulloch, let's be reasonable about this. Why don't you lower the weapon and we can talk?' His voice was smooth and mellow, the accent perceptibly Scottish but attenuated.

'On yer knees,' Boonzie grated.

But Macleod and the older man didn't move. 'You're going to regret this, you know,' the older man said.

That's when Boonzie saw what at first glance looked like a large red insect hovering in front of his chest. Except it

166

wasn't an insect. It was the bright red dot of a hidden marksman's laser sight drawing a bead on him from a distance.

And at that moment he knew that he had walked into a trap.

'As you can see, you're not really in a position to dictate terms, Mr McCulloch,' the older man said. 'Now, you have three seconds to drop your weapon or my security employee, who currently has a high-powered rifle aimed at your heart, will shoot.'

Boonzie might not have been as fast as he once was, but he was still fast. He made a dive for it. There was an explosion of dirt and snow as the rifle bullet blew a crater in the ground behind where he'd been standing a split-second earlier. Macleod and the older man retreated behind the stone archway. Boonzie's blood was frozen in his veins as he raced towards the cover of the dead tree near the ruins, ducked behind its thick trunk and pressed up tight against it. Glancing past its gnarly edge he saw four more men stepping out of the bushes and striding towards him.

Men with pistols.

Boonzie knew he was cornered, and the sudden realisation started up a heavy thudding in his heart.

The armed men were coming closer. Someone called out, 'Give it up, McCulloch, you're done!'

Boonzie began to sweat. The perspiration sheeted down his face and prickled his eyeballs. The thumping in his chest was so strong it felt as though it would shake his ribs apart. A ripping pain seared his whole left side, from hip to shoulder. He blinked to try to clear his vision, which had suddenly gone blurry. Something was happening to him. Something catastrophically bad that he had no strength to fight back against.

In the next moment, he was staring up at the grey sky.

He realised that he'd fallen over and was sprawled on his back on the hard, cold ground.

In his last moments before he fell into a faint, the men reached him. Through his blurred vision he caught glimpses of their grinning faces. He could hear their laughter. Felt their hands taking away his weapons and searching through his pockets. They found McGlashan's phone and took it.

And Boonzie's final thought before the world went black was that he hadn't called Mirella.

Chapter 27

On his return from Inverness around ten-thirty that morning, Ben stopped off at the Gunn cottage for a bite to eat, to inspect his purchases and phone Boonzie's wife.

Mirella had still heard nothing, and she sounded as if she was falling apart from worry, grief and lack of sleep. She was sobbing bitterly when she picked up the phone, and the tears barely stopped flowing during the three minutes they spoke. From the beginning he sensed from her tone that something had changed. He was right.

'It's not that I don't trust you, Ben. I wouldn't have asked for your help otherwise. But—'

'But?' Ben guessed what was coming next.

'The days are going by. I feel so helpless sitting here waiting for the phone to ring. I can't eat. I'm up all night pacing. How long before we have to admit you can't find him, and we need to involve the police?'

'If I was unable to find him, what do you think the police could do?'

'What about INTERPOL and people like that? They have all kinds of ways to help, don't they? Helicopters and sniffer dogs and things.'

Just what the world needed. Another botched police operation with too many chiefs and not enough Indians, which would send the bad guys running for the hills and virtually guarantee that Boonzie was never found, dead or alive. Assuming that the joint powers of European law enforcement bothered to do anything at all. But Ben couldn't tell her that. 'I'm close, Mirella. So close I'm following right in his foot-steps.'

'I don't know what to do.'

'It's your choice, Mirella. Whatever you decide, I will respect it. But I won't give up.'

'Another day,' she said with a sniff. 'Twenty-four hours. Then I think I'll call them. I'm sorry, Ben. I'm going to go crazy if I don't *do* something.'

'You do what you feel is right,' he said with a sinking heart. 'And call me anytime, day or night. Okay?'

She was still crying when she ended the call. Ben gazed out of the window at the snowflakes spiralling from the grey clouds, and heaved a deep sigh. Twenty-four hours to find Boonzie before his wife pressed the panic button, come what may. Perfect.

There was no time to lose. Ben finished packing his equip-ment, wrapped up his weapons and then went out to the car and sped off along the now-familiar road out of the village leading towards Loch Ardaich. Now that he knew for certain that he was on the right track, he needed to believe that his second attempt to find the poacher would bear fruit. If the bad guys didn't find him first.

Whoever the bad guys were. Ben had no idea. But their involvement in this situation offered him a new lead to follow. Whatever information they already had about the poacher, he could use that knowledge to his own advantage by tracking their movements. He was looking forward to meeting them again, especially the rifleman. And he was sure he would. Their next encounter would be a different game entirely.

Out of caution he left the car hidden in a different spot from last night, nearly half a mile away among the dense pine cover close to the western shore. It was cold out here. Seriously cold. Stepping from the warm Mercedes into the subzero wind chill made the skin on his face feel raw and papery-thin. Snow clumped heavily on the pine branches, dragging them low to the ground. Now and then one would shake itself free of its load and spring up, adding a cascade of powdery snow to the depth that was already on the ground. The going was tough in these conditions. An ordinary person would have left a trail of prints that a blind man could follow. But Ben Hope was no ordinary person. Moving slowly and carefully without leaving a trace of his passing, he spent nearly an hour working his way back to the spot where only luck had spared him from getting shot the night before.

Surveilling the terrain by daylight only confirmed to him what he'd already known. Whoever had been behind the rifle was a hell of a shooter. Probably almost as good as Ben was himself. Only a supremely skilled marksman would have attempted to steer his bullet through dense tree cover, in darkness and fog. There weren't many angles from which he could have done it; and it was by calculating the bullet's likely trajectory over the challenging terrain that Ben was able to work out the possible origin of the shot. His best guess told him that the shooter had been positioned on a tree-lined ridge to the west, about sixty metres above the waterline. Ben used the crossbow's laser rangefinder to confirm the range. Two hundred and eleven yards.

It took another thirty minutes to trek around the shoreline and clamber up the ridge. When he finally got there, Ben soon found that his best guess had scored a bullseye. Fresh snowfall couldn't quite mask the man-sized indentation in the ground where the sniper had lain marking his target. But the real proof was the small hole in the snow a few inches to the right. Ben dug his fingers into the hole and found the ejected shell casing which, hot from the rifle's breech, had melted the hole and buried itself among the grass underneath. The case was shiny and new. The headstamp markings on its base said .308 WINCHESTER. A chambering almost identical to the military 7.62 round used by NATO forces. It could punch through a human target with devastating effect at over a thousand metres.

Ben was feeling luckier than ever.

He dropped the cartridge case back into the snow, then looked around him. The sniper's position was a fine vantage point, with a sweeping view over the loch's western end and the frozen whiteness of its shoreline. Ben couldn't have chosen a better one, and he decided to make use of it for a while. He fully intended to stay out here all day and all night, if that was what it took. With no other leads and the clock in his head ticking away the twenty-four-hour countdown until Mirella involved the authorities in the search, he was feeling the pressure.

Ben unpacked the ghillie suit from his bag and put it on over his clothes. It would help to keep him warm as well as unseen. When he lay down in the snowy undergrowth he looked like just another immobile patch of vegetation, invisible from more than a few steps away. Now it was just a question of waiting and watching. Two things Ben Hope was exceptionally good at. He was good at a lot of things. And like all high-achieving people he was confident in his talents and hard-learned capabilities. When you took the kinds of risks he'd taken in his life, you needed to be. Because if you didn't believe you were up to the challenge, then you were already setting yourself up to fail.

But Ben was still just a man, and in common with all his fellow humans he wasn't immune to self-doubt. There had been times in his life when his belief in his abilities had hit rock bottom, when he'd felt as lost and weak and helpless as a rudderless ship in the teeth of a raging storm. As he lay there now, his body slowly numbing in the cold, watching the empty loch and the icy wilderness that hugged its banks, he could feel those same old haunting doubts and fears closing over him like a curtain of darkness.

What if nobody turned up, neither the mysterious poacher nor the men who were hunting him? What if Ben was just chasing shadows and squandering what little precious time remained to him, while his friend was still out there somewhere, maybe sick, maybe hurt, maybe dead?

What if Mirella was right, and it was time to hand the search over to someone else?

Those were the bleak, crippling thoughts that were swirling uncontrollably inside Ben's head at that moment, threatening to undermine everything he was. But for every ebb of the tide there must be a balancing swell. And so a counter-voice, a very old voice that had been there all his life, now found itself and began to speak, deep within his being. *Because no matter what happens; no matter what shit you have to deal with; no matter what kind of hellfire the sky decides to rain down on you; this is where you are right now, and this is who you decided to be and take upon yourself; and you will damn well lace up your boots and pick up your weapon and put all that shit behind you and stand up and be the man you are.*

No doubts. No second guesses.
Eyes wide open and no fear.
It's who you are, soldier.
So fucking be it.

And then Ben suddenly spotted the distant figure moving along the lochside, and realised that he was no longer alone.

He watched the figure through the crossbow scope and turned the magnification up full to get a closer view. Whoever the person was, they were dressed in a heavy black quilted winter jacket that bulked out the contours of their body, with a hood pulled down low over their face to protect from the biting wind. They had emerged from the trees and were slowly making their way along the shoreline in Ben's direction. Was it the poacher? He wasn't carrying any fishing gear.

As Ben went on watching the figure in black, it seemed to him from the way the person moved, pausing every few steps to look around them, that they were searching for something or someone. But the angle of the hood kept hiding their face. The hopeful notion that it might be Boonzie flashed briefly, though only briefly, through Ben's mind before he dismissed it as wishful thinking.

After a few moments the figure turned and began moving in the opposite direction, away from Ben. He was concerned that they might disappear back among the trees and be lost from view. If he wanted to find out who the person was, he would need to get closer.

He left his sniper's position and zigzagged his way down the slope of the ridge, moving carefully and unobtrusively between rocks and bushes. From this distance, without binoculars or a telescope, it was unlikely the figure in black would spot him. Ben reached the foot of the ridge and stalked along the shoreline like some strange leafy predator, using the cover of the lochside shrubs and trees to hide his approach. The figure in black was moving more slowly and out in the open, making no attempt to conceal themselves as they ambled along the waterside and kept pausing now and then to gaze left and right. What, or who, were they looking for?

Ben was fast catching up. When he was just sixty yards behind, he sank down behind the thick base of a pine trunk and shouldered the crossbow once more to observe the figure through the scope.

Even from the rear, he instantly knew for a fact that the person wasn't the poacher, or Boonzie McCulloch, or any other man. It was a woman. The heavy coat didn't completely obscure the feminine contours of her body.

Then the woman turned to look about her again, and this time Ben was able to get a glimpse of her face.

It was Grace Kirk.

Grace hadn't seen him yet, and he didn't want her to, not looking like a bogeyman from the forest. Still behind the tree, he quickly stripped off the ghillie suit and bundled it away out of sight along with the crossbow. Then he stepped out from behind the tree and broke into a jog to catch up with her, calling her name.

She stopped and turned, pulled back the hood and stood there planted halfway up to her knees in the snow, staring at him as he approached. Her cheeks and nose were flushed red from the cold and her hands were hidden under big woolly mittens. She raised one of them to brush away a lock of black hair that had fallen across her face. Her breath billowed in clouds. Her eyes were shining with excitement and she looked as though she was about to say something, but Ben spoke first.

'What are you doing here?'

If Ben was surprised by her presence here by the loch, her reply was even more unexpected.

'Looking for you,' she said. 'I had a feeling I'd find you here.'

'Why were you looking for me?'

'To tell you that I found the poacher. I know who he is.'

Chapter 28

That moment changed everything. Ben was full of questions, but Grace was so cold that she could hardly speak. The temperature had to be minus six out here. He said, 'Let's get you somewhere warm, and talk there. Where's your car?'

She pointed a mittened hand towards a gap in the trees. Her teeth chattered as she replied, 'There.'

The opening in the trees led to a rough track that sloped upwards from the lochside. Her old Land Rover was parked on the frozen ground a couple of dozen yards away, icicles hanging from its roof guttering and the battered bodywork glittering with frost. It felt like a fridge inside, too. Ben got behind the wheel, found the key in the ignition and started it up. The vehicle's heating system was feeble at best, consisting of two small air vents on the dash and a fan that couldn't have made a candle flicker. It took a while with the engine running before anything resembling warmth began to filter through and thaw Grace sufficiently to tell her story.

Ben listened as she told him about Geoffrey Watkins' arrest for the assault on Ewan McCulloch. 'Last I heard, they were still working on getting him to confess to it. Except I don't think he will, Ben, because I don't buy that he did it. There's more going on, and the Watkins arrest is a blind. You said this was about money. I think you were right.'

'And I thought you couldn't discuss confidential matters pertaining to an ongoing police investigation.'

'Tactical flexibility is the essence of good strategy. I'm prepared to bend the rules a little here and there.'

'No bad thing. But why the sudden change of heart?' he asked.

She pulled off her mittens and held her hands above the heater vents, flexing and unflexing her fingers to get the blood running again. 'Yesterday in the pub,' she said. 'Something you told me stuck in my mind. I kept thinking about it afterwards. It was bugging me all night long.'

'What did I say?'

'You said that Ewan had no idea who the poacher was.'

'That's what Boonzie's wife Mirella told me. Ewan received an anonymous call. The poacher was too scared to give away his identity.'

She nodded. 'But later I remembered that what Boonzie said to me was different. The call was anonymous, yes, but Ewan told Boonzie that he thought he knew the guy. The voice sounded familiar to him, he just couldn't put a face or a name to it.'

Ben frowned. 'Go on.'

'Then there was something else you said last night, that the witness was the key to this whole thing. I wasn't too sure at the time, because I couldn't get my head around the idea that Ross's death was connected to what happened to Ewan. But now the way they're trying to pin the assault charge on Watkins makes me think someone's trying to cover up the truth and pretend like Ross's gold coins never existed. See?'

'Okay.'

She went on, 'So this morning I got thinking about all this, and none of it was making any sense to me, so I went into the arrest records. I feel like shit for not having done it days ago. I could've helped Ewan's uncle. Whatever's happened to him might not have happened.'

'What arrest records?'

'Every now and then the Fisheries enforcers catch someone illegally catching salmon on the lochs. In the olden days they used to just beat the crap out of them. Nowadays they have to report it to the police. Which works out much cosier for the poachers, since they don't get much more than a slap on the wrist. But they still get a criminal record, of course, and it's all on file.'

'That's where you found our poacher?'

'Actually I found a whole bunch of them,' she said. 'Some were repeat offenders, others one time only. I took down the names and ran a check on each one in turn. The first was Hamish Galloway. Arrested seven times for illegal salmon fishing, the last time in March 2014, which was just two months before he died of emphysema. So that's him crossed off the list. Second was a guy called Clark Duff. Again, I ran him through the system. Turns out poaching is the least of his crimes. He's currently halfway through serving a six-month sentence for shoplifting. Strike him off the list, too. And on, and on. Some of them have left the area, some are still around. Dozens of names. But that didn't stop me from nailing our boy.' She grinned. 'Jamie McGlashan. King of the heap, with an undefeated eleven past poaching convictions to his name. Never married, never had a real job. Lives alone and on benefits. He's our guy.'

'How can you be so sure?'

'Because Ewan and I both went to the same school as him. I didn't know him all that well. Nor did Ewan, as I remember, because people tended to keep their distance from Jamie. He was a rough kind of kid, used to get into fights, act moody, and didn't have a lot of friends. We were all vaguely aware of some problems he had at home. The rumour was that his dad used to hit him, but back then dysfunctional family issues weren't openly talked about. One day Jamie came into school with a split lip that was all sewn up and swollen like a rugby ball. After that, he always talked with a bit of a lisp, and it left him with a nasty scar that kids used to make fun of. So, more fights, more trouble, more suspensions. It was sad. He wasn't a happy boy. Then he started developing a weight problem, which made him even unhappier.'

Ben recalled the taunts of the men who'd been out hunting the poacher the night before. *Fat, scar-faced bastard.* It sounded as though Grace had nailed it. 'And you think maybe that's why Ewan recognised his voice on the phone, because of the lisp?'

'The way Jamie talked could have sounded vaguely familiar to him, but still just a half-memory he couldn't pin down. The mind works like that sometimes, doesn't it? Especially when it was so long ago. I mean, we were just eight or nine years old.'

Ben thought about it. The unhappy, overweight, scar-faced kid who went on to become a loner, preferring the solitude of the wild open spaces. Who had felt impelled to come forward and spill what he'd witnessed to an old school acquaintance, maybe out of some kind of nostalgic spirit. Maybe also because of his own history of childhood physical abuse. The psychology fitted plausibly. But the only way to know for sure was to talk to McGlashan in person.

Grace said, 'I cross-checked the police records with the DVLA. He drives a blue Subaru Forester, year 2000 model. Current address is a rented trailer home about half a mile outside Kinlochardaich. I reckon we can find him, easy.' The redness had faded from her cheeks and nose. Her eyes were alive with exhilaration.

'This is good work, Grace. Excellent work.'

She gave him the crooked smile that he liked so much. 'Do I get a gold star, or what?'

'Only if McGlashan does actually turn out to be the right person. Have you told anyone else about this?'

She shook her head. 'Just you. And nobody else would be wise to the school connection between Jamie and Ewan. So I'd reckon it's safe to say we're the only ones who know.'

'Only, I was wondering how this would sit with your superiors, DI Macleod and DS Coull. This is their investigation. As their subordinate, you can be fired for withholding information from them. And I don't suppose they take a favourable view of officers conducting their own private inquiries. Why go out on a limb like this?'

She looked at him, and he could see the hardness in her eyes. 'I love my job. I'm good at it and I don't take the risk of trashing my career lightly. But my instincts are telling me that something about this whole business isn't right. If someone's lying, that's going to piss me off a great deal. For Ewan's sake, and for my own, I want to find out what the hell is happening here.'

'And bring me along for the ride? Why?'

'Because we share a common purpose. Because two heads are better than one, like they say. And because I don't feel safe pursuing this on my own. Whoever's behind all this, they're obviously prepared to get rough. So before I made any moves I wanted to come and find you. I went to Mrs Gunn's cottage, but you weren't there. She told me she'd seen you drive off earlier. From the things you said last night I had a pretty good idea you might be checking out the loch.'

'All twelve miles of it.'

'I know. But I'm a persistent cow when my mind's made up. I drove up and down for an hour before I spotted your car. That told me what end of the loch you were scouting. Which makes sense. The furthest point from where Ross Campbell died. If McGlashan came back here, this would be the spot.'

'Smart thinking, officer.'

'I'm a top cop. Then I went looking for you. Turns out you found me instead, just when I was about to freeze my arse off. So here we are. What do you say?'

'You barely know me. Why would you trust me?'

'I see a guy who knows how to handle himself, with the brains to figure things out and the integrity and courage to do whatever it takes to help a friend in need. I've a good eye for people, Ben. And I don't think you're so bad. You'd make an excellent police officer.'

'Insulting me now?'

'Come on, Ben. I'm serious.'

'So am I, Grace. No offence, but what makes you think I'd want to tag along with you?'

She rolled her eyes. 'Oh, purlease, not the "I work alone" thing. Why shouldn't you want to? Because of what I do for a living? Are you scared of me?'

'No, I'm not scared of you.'

'Maybe you're worried you'll compromise yourself. What are you gonna do, shoot someone?'

He said nothing.

She gave him the smile again. 'Besides, if you don't agree to work along with me on this, I won't tell you Jamie McGlashan's address.'

'A trailer home half a mile from Kinlochardaich. You've already told me enough to find it.'

'Yeah, but what if I was spinning you a load of crap to put you off the mark? Then you wouldn't have a chance in hell.'

He said nothing.

'You know you need me. In fact you can't do without me.'

He was quiet for a few moments longer. Then asked, 'When do you have to go back to work?'

Grace looked at her watch. It was coming on for two p.m. 'In about six hours from now. My turn for the evening shift. Lucky me.'

Ben said, 'Then let's waste no time.'

Chapter 29

Three days earlier
After Boonzie is taken

'Is he dead?'

The group of men by the ruined chapel were looking down at the unconscious body on the ground. Hacker knelt down and took Boonzie McCulloch's pulse, then looked up.

'He's not dead.'

'What's wrong with him? People don't just keel over for no reason.'

Hacker said, 'It's his heart.'

Hacker's employer looked at him. 'You know that, do you? Are you a doctor now?'

Hacker didn't reply, just showed him the pill bottle they'd found in Boonzie's pocket. Hacker's employer glanced at the medicine, then slipped it into the pocket of his cashmere coat. He said, 'What else have you found on him? Show me that phone.'

Hacker passed him the phone they'd taken from McCulloch. His employer examined it. He spent a few moments tapping and swiping at the screen, then frowned and said, 'Well, well.'

Hacker said, 'Well well what?'

'It isn't his. This phone seems to belong to someone called

Jamie McGlashan. Here's his Facebook page.' He tapped and scrolled a bit more, then his eyebrows rose. 'Hmm. Very interesting.' He tossed the phone back to Hacker, who looked at what his boss had found. The screen displayed a selfie image of a fat man he'd never seen before. He was standing by what was obviously a Scottish loch, hills and mountains in the background, clad in waterproofs and wearing a big goofy grin because of what he'd just caught and was proudly holding aloft.

Hacker handed back the phone and said, 'It's a picture of some pork-chop moron with a harelip and a large, dead fish in his hand.'

'Yes, Hacker, that's what it is. But it might also be something more than that.'

Hacker couldn't give a damn. It was too bloody cold to be standing out here debating. He was here to do a job. One that was currently only half done, as far as he was concerned.

'So what now?' asked Bobby Banks, one of the crew who'd arrived from London just hours before. Like Hacker, they were all keen to finish what they'd come here to do, collect their very generous paycheque and be flown home.

'Shoot him,' Hacker said.

'No problem.' Without hesitation, Banks walked over to Boonzie, bent down and pressed a pistol to his head.

DI Fergus Macleod hovered nervously in the background. Even though he'd been personally present at the drowning of Ross Campbell and taken part in the beating of Ewan McCulloch, he still had no stomach for this kind of thing. None of the others paid him any attention and were not remotely concerned that they were in the presence of a senior police officer. Macleod was in far too deep to be any kind of a threat to them.

As Banks was about to pull the trigger, Hacker's employer held up a hand and said sharply, 'No. Wait.'

Banks stopped, lowered the weapon and looked uncertainly at Hacker, who was staring at his boss as though he were an idiot. 'You said you wanted this man eliminated,' Hacker said. 'Properly and permanently.'

His employer shot him back an acid look. 'I don't need to be reminded, Hacker. I know what I said. I'm simply considering the advantages of temporarily delaying his elimination.' He held up the phone, like a lawyer brandishing Exhibit A in the courtroom. 'McCulloch might be old and sick, but he's no fool. He's obviously been on the same trail that we are. Hunting for the poacher, but for the opposite reason. I'm betting that this McGlashan is our star witness. If McCulloch has his phone, it means that he's been in contact with him. Which in turn means he must know more about this whole affair than I'd so far given him credit for. And that being the case, I can't help but speculate what other information McCulloch might be privy to. Things his nephew might easily have told him before he met with his little mishap. Such as the location of the spot where Ross Campbell found my lost property and took it for himself.'

My lost property. Hacker could see no trace of doubt in his employer's eyes. The guy really believed it. His delusion was the driving force behind all that had happened, and Hacker often wondered where it might end. He didn't question the boss's intelligence. He was probably the cleverest and wiliest person Hacker had ever met. But there was no doubt in Hacker's mind that the man was insane.

'Could be a long shot,' Hacker said. 'Hard to say for sure.'

'Only one way to find out, isn't there? And we won't achieve that by killing him.'

Hacker made no reply. The men didn't look pleased. Hacker's employer could see the looks passing between them, and he knew what they were thinking: that a job half done would be a job half paid for.

'Don't worry,' his employer said. 'I still want him dead, and you'll still receive the agreed fee. Plus an additional bonus of five thousand each. *If*,' he added, 'you can find out what he knows, and on condition that it's of value to me. Otherwise, not a penny more.'

Hacker nodded. The rest of the men appeared reassured, with the exception of Macleod, who looked even more nervous now that kidnapping and possible torture were about to be added to the list of crimes to which he was an accomplice.

'And I'm also commissioning you men to carry out another job for me,' Hacker's employer said. 'Now we have reason to believe that this McGlashan is the witness, I want you to find him and get rid of him for me.' He motioned at Macleod, without looking at him. 'I'm sure that Macleod here will be able to supply you with his home address.'

Hacker truly didn't care whether McGlashan was the witness or not. 'You want us to find out what he knows, too?'

'No, just kill him. He's caused us enough trouble already.'

Just then, the unconscious body on the ground stirred and let out a pained groan. Banks said, 'McCulloch's coming round.'

Hacker's employer tossed Banks the bottle of pills. 'Give him a couple of these, if that's what he needs. Then get him loaded into the van and we'll bring him to the estate.'

The snatch had worked perfectly. The one good thing Angus Baird had done was to alert them to be on the lookout for Ewan McCulloch's camper van. Macleod and Coull had spotted it in the police station car park the moment they'd arrived for work that morning, notifying Hacker's employer just moments later. The plan had taken shape quickly and efficiently. Their preparations made, Hacker and the newly arrived crew had sped from the castle to the chosen ambush spot in their unmarked van, following their employer's silver Rolls Royce Cullinan. Now they not only had McCulloch, but the name of the poacher, who would be dealt with soon enough.

First it was McCulloch's turn. By the time he recovered consciousness they were already en route back to base and he awoke to find himself bound and gagged in the back of the van. His captors removed the tape from his mouth long enough to dry-feed him two of his heart pills. Boonzie kicked and struggled as best he could, but he was still weak and soon gave up trying. By the time they arrived at their destination, he was asleep again, his breathing shallow. They bundled him out of the van and carried him to the secure, inescapable place beneath the castle in which they intended to keep him for the rest of his life.

While the crew took care of their task, Hacker's employer climbed the stairs to his study. He closed the door, hung up his coat and loosened his tie, then lit an Arturo Fuente cigar and settled in a plush leather armchair with a satisfied smile on his face. He had a great deal to be satisfied about, and not just because his current plans were moving along so nicely. Whenever he sat here in the luxurious splendour of his private domain overlooking all his stately acres and surrounded by the trappings of wealth, it was impossible not to be reminded of how very far he'd come from his comparatively humble roots.

His name was Charles Stuart, but it hadn't always been. He had been born and raised Peter Charles Johnson and only much later, as an ambitious young man setting out to make his first million, adopted the surname that he believed reflected his true birthright and identity.

The Johnsons hadn't been a poor family, but hardly rolling

in wealth either. Alan Johnson had practised as a gastro-enterologist at Western General Hospital in Edinburgh and his wife Susan had taught history at a local comprehensive school. Susan Johnson had been an excellent teacher and an even better storyteller, and her only child had grown up listening to his mother's spellbinding tales of their country's rich and romantic past, from the coming of the Romans to the reign of Arthur; from Robert Bruce to Mary Queen of Scots; and the Scottish Wars of Independence from the time of the celebrated freedom fighter William Wallace through to the later bloody battles waged by the Scots Jacobites versus the English Redcoats and the adventures of the Young Pretender, Prince Charles Edward Stuart, more popularly known as Bonnie Prince Charlie. The man who'd tried, and failed so gloriously and somehow magnificently, to claim the British throne for a Scottish king to sit on. What a moment that would have been.

Peter had been enthralled by those stories and soon began delving into the history books to learn more for himself. It would set him on a course that would change his life.

Susan Johnson's fascination with history, and especially the turbulent times of eighteenth-century Scotland, went beyond simple academic interest. Her maiden name prior to marrying Peter's father had been Stuart, the French form of the ancient Scottish dynastic surname Stewart. The clan's ancestral origins dated all the way back to a Breton knight who had come to Britain soon after the Norman invasion of 1066 and quickly established an Anglo-Norman noble house. Centuries later, Sir John Stewart of Bonkyll died fighting alongside William Wallace at the Battle of Falkirk in 1298.

In the modern age there were more than seventy thousand people in Britain bearing the name Stuart or Stewart, all of them potentially eligible to claim descent from Scotland's royal dynasty. But Susan Johnson, née Stuart, had been more tenacious than most in tracing back her genealogy through a centuries-long forest of family trees, and convinced herself beyond a shadow of a doubt that she, and hence her son also, belonged to the line of the noble Stuart clan.

The connection, Susan maintained, came down the female line and led back to Charlotte Stuart, whose mother Clementina Walkinshaw had been Charles Edward Stuart's mistress – the pair having first met during the rebellion of 1745 when he was unsuccessfully battling the English to regain the British throne for his father, James Stuart, the 'Old Pretender'. Charlotte had been the only one of the couple's illegitimate children to survive infancy, herself eventually dying young at the age of thirty-six. Her relationship with her biological father had been a difficult one, but the Bonnie Prince eventually legitimised her in 1784 with the title of Duchess of Albany, whereupon she more or less abandoned her own three children and spent most of her remaining years caring for the elderly prince, by now a physically decrepit alcoholic and a far cry from the glamorous image of the heroic, albeit failed, defender of Scottish glory.

Charlotte's children had been raised in anonymity, their identities hidden behind aliases to protect them from scandal. The trail was obscure, but by a convoluted process of deduction Susan Johnson had come to the unwavering conclusion that she was personally descended from Charlotte's elder daughter Marie-Victoire Adelaide, born 1779, who had found herself in Poland following the outbreak of the French Revolution and there married a Polish nobleman by the unwieldy name of Paul Anthony Bertrand de Nikorowicz, with whom she had a son; and on it went.

In short, it was a complicated business. Young Peter hadn't

189

quite been able to keep track of it all, but never doubted his mother's claim. And when a young boy grows up believing that royal blood runs in his veins, it can have a profound effect.

In Peter's case, it had been a mixed one. He'd worked extremely hard academically and, to his parents' joy, at seventeen had gained a place at Cambridge to study economics. But it hadn't been an easy path for him. At university he'd often felt inferior to the wealthier students, suspecting that they resented this comprehensive school kid from Edinburgh and didn't consider him as one of their peer group. By the end of his first year, he'd become hardened to the class division he felt existed between them, and developed an aggressive chip on his shoulder. What had kept him going was the thought of the day when they'd all find out that he, Peter Johnson, was the descendant of a genuine true-blue prince. Let all those toffs eat shit for having snubbed him. One day, he was going to rub their snooty fucking noses in it.

And so that was exactly what he'd done. Fired by a combination of his ancestral pride and his hatred of his peers, one of his first acts after graduating from Cambridge with his first-class degree was to change his name by deed poll from Peter Charles Johnson to Charles Stuart. His second action was to found the stock brokerage company that would, within just a few short years, make him super-wealthy.

The newborn Charles Stuart was relentlessly ambitious and worked eighteen hours a day. He'd made his first million while still in his twenties. By the age of thirty-five he was the owner of one of Scotland's best private art collections. By thirty-eight he'd bought his first aircraft, built a stable full of racehorses, purchased the villa in the Bahamas as a holiday residence and the chateau in Brittany – from where his beloved, now sadly deceased, mother had told him the Stuarts had originated. Then on his fortieth birthday he'd lavished a multi-million-pound fortune on buying the two-thousand-acre estate in Scotland and started building his dream castle.

The castle was Charles Stuart's pride and joy and was still, in many ways, a work in progress. He had designed the place to be as historically authentic as possible, albeit with all the trappings of modernity cleverly concealed behind its thick stone walls. One of his nods to authenticity was the underground chamber he'd had built deep inside his fortress's foundations. He had passed it off to the architects as a wine cellar, but it contained no wine and was in fact a dungeon, modelled on real-life examples from the historic castles of Edinburgh, Loch Leven and, grimmest of them all, the bottle dungeon of St Andrews, a seven-metre-deep hole cut into solid rock and from which there could be no escape.

Stuart had been morbidly fascinated by dungeons ever since reading Walter Scott's *Ivanhoe* as a boy. In fourteenth-century France these dark and dreadful pits of incarceration had been called *oubliettes*: in translation, a place where the hapless prisoner would be left to rot and be forgotten. The delicious sadism of it still sent a shiver down Stuart's back. He'd often fantasised about hurling his enemies into his very own dungeon and throwing away the key.

And so, the dark, dank pit beneath the castle was where Boonzie McCulloch was to remain a prisoner until he told them what he knew, which would also be the day he died.

Then, or so Charles Stuart hoped, he would be on track to reclaim the one thing he so badly wanted and money couldn't buy.

The lost treasure of his ancestor. The remainder of the legendary Jacobite gold that Stuart now knew for certain was buried somewhere beneath the ancient pine forest of Loch Ardaich.

Chapter 30

The primitive stone bothy had played an important role in Jamie McGlashan's life. Once upon a time the remote, weather-battered shelter had served its traditional purpose as a means for roving hunters like Jamie and his father to take refuge from the elements and cook fish and rabbits over an open fire. Years later it had become Jamie's regular hideout when he was on one of his intensive poaching sprees and sometimes wouldn't return to his trailer home for weeks on end. And since Ross Campbell's murder it had provided a very convenient hiding place for an eye-witness too terrified to go home.

It was nearly four days since Jamie's encounter with Ewan McCulloch's uncle, the wild old nutcase who'd appeared out of nowhere dressed like a yeti and threatening him with a crossbow, and to whom Jamie had confessed his secret. Jamie hadn't seen him again, and probably never would. Which pissed him off somewhat, because it meant he'd likely never see his mobile phone again either. But the old guy's haunting final words of advice had kept replaying inside his head ever since.

Get as far away frae this place as ye can. All hell's aboot tae break loose.

With no cash for travelling and nowhere else to run but

the bothy, Jamie had spent these last days keeping his head down in even greater paranoia than before, shivering miserably through the freezing cold nights and dozing for most of the daytime in his sleeping bag, living off his diminishing catch and only sneaking outside to forage for firewood now and then.

As much as part of him enjoyed the total reclusion, he couldn't stop his imagination from running riot. What the hell had the old guy been planning on doing? Jamie lay there for hours visualising scenes of mayhem and bloodshed, Ewan's crazy ninja killer uncle stalking the streets like Rambo hellbent on revenge. The look in his eye had been so terrifyingly sincere that Jamie had no problem believing he would carry out his threat to put his enemies six feet under the ground. For all Jamie knew, the nutter had already wiped out everyone connected with his nephew's beating and had either been shot to death in a massive gun battle with the police or was now locked up in jail. Which, with the bad guys dead, would mean it was now safe for Jamie to leave his hiding place. Not knowing what was happening out there was eating him alive.

So was his worry about another problem. Every two weeks, Jamie was obliged to jump in his Subaru and make the tedious drive to Fort William to sign on for his benefits. Poaching wasn't quite a lucrative enough profession for him to give up his dependency on those Jobseeker's Allowance cheques, not to mention his housing benefit payments. And today was signing day. If he didn't show up at the Job Centre to make his mark and verify that he was actively seeking work, etc., etc., then the Nazis in the dole office would give him grief and threaten to stop his benefits.

As Jamie ruminated over his problem, it suddenly occurred to him that his signing-on book, that all-important document required to demonstrate his feeble and mostly spurious attempts to find work, was sitting on his bedside cabinet in the trailer.

Jamie stamped about the bothy in a rage yelling 'Ahh, fuck! Fuck!' But stamp and yell all he wanted, he knew he had little choice but to venture back home for the first time in days, grab his signing-on book and hustle over to Fort William to keep the Nazis happy and the dole cheques rolling in. His duty done, he could decide afterwards whether or not to return to his hideout.

He packed up his stuff, tossed everything in the back of the Subaru, dusted the snow off the windscreen and managed to get the engine started. With a lot of sliding and skidding around, he negotiated the mile-long track to the main road, and set out towards Kinlochardaich.

He rented the trailer from the farmer who owned the neglected field half a mile from the edge of the village. At some point in the far-distant past the farmer had planned on turning the whole field into a caravan park but run out of interest after the first mobile home was installed, and for the last several years had been content to let Jamie live there as his sole tenant for £30 a week. Home sweet home was a solitary, lichen-streaked 25x10ft prefabricated box with a leaky roof and cracked windows, surrounded by a wasteland of junk and resembling a landfill on the inside.

Jamie ploughed the Subaru across the rutted, frozen field, parked up and tramped through the falling snow and up the slippery metal steps to his front door. He never locked the trailer, since the lock was broken and there was nothing worth stealing in there anyway.

The flimsy door creaked open and Jamie stepped inside without bothering first to kick the snow from his boots. Wasting no time, he headed for the bedroom. The trailer was filled with the familiar old smell of stale cooking oil, unwashed clothes and rising damp. His bed was a mildewed single mattress on the floor and his bedside cabinet was a scabby kitchen unit he'd rescued from a skip. There among the clutter of mouldy mugs and crumpled magazines lay his damn signing-in book, just where he'd remembered it.

'Ya basturt,' he muttered. He looked at his watch. It was nearly two-thirty p.m., giving him plenty of time to get to Fort William. He scooped the book up and thrust it in his pocket and turned towards the door.

And was unable to react, flinch or utter anything but a gasp of horror and surprise as the two figures blocked the doorway and one of them punched a long, slim knife blade deep inside Jamie's stomach.

Jamie staggered back a step, too stunned to compute what was happening to him. As fast as it penetrated his vitals the knife withdrew and then came at him again, stabbing at his chest. This time Jamie instinctively raised a hand to protect himself, and the razor-sharp blade slashed across his palm and severed his little finger. Then the second figure stepped forward, clutching another knife, and Jamie felt an unimaginable shock of agony as the cold steel plunged into the soft flesh of his neck. His mouth opened to scream, but what came out was an unearthly, inhuman shriek, like the sound of an animal being slaughtered.

And it was only then, in a strangely detached moment of comprehension as though he were observing it happening from the outside, that Jamie McGlashan realised that he was being brutally murdered.

Chapter 31

'I just have to ask one thing,' Grace said, shivering. 'Can we go in your car? Because I think I'm about to die of cold pretty soon if I don't get to a proper heater.'

It was a ten-minute drive from where the old Land Rover was parked to where Ben had hidden his Mercedes. He replied, 'Whatever you want', jammed the Landy into gear and got it turned around on the track, then headed up to the winding narrow road that snaked around the perimeter of the loch. The thing was primitive, just a thumper diesel bolted to a chassis, more a tractor than a car. He wondered how generations of SAS soldiers, including himself, had coped with such basic machinery back in the day. That thought took him back to thinking about Boonzie again, and he shut his mind down and resolved not to think so much.

He soon found the spot where he'd left his car. The tyre tracks leading to the hiding place were mostly snowed over, as he'd been betting on for concealment from less benign eyes than Grace's. He parked her Landy next to the Mercedes, and they switched vehicles.

'Life saver,' Grace sighed as they set off towards Kinlochardaich and the blasting heat started to permeate the inside of the Mercedes. She snuggled back into the soft leather seat like a cat draping itself over a warm radiator. 'Nice car. I could get used to such luxuries. Whatever they pay sort-of-teachers in France, it's obviously way more than my meagre police wages.'

'It's not mine,' he said.

She looked at him. 'Please don't tell me you stole it.'

'I nearly had to. The rental companies don't like me too much.'

'Why not?'

'Long story.'

Ben glanced at the dashboard clock. Their diversion to switch vehicles had delayed them a few minutes and it was now 2.23 p.m. He was anxious about the passing of time, fretting over Mirella's deadline for calling in police involvement from her side and hoping he was about to finally meet the man he'd been trying to find for two days now. His one consolation was that, thanks to Grace's digging, they were a step ahead of the others searching for Jamie McGlashan.

Ben was soon to discover he was wrong.

He drove faster, the big car's traction control gadgetry effortlessly tackling the wintry conditions as they sped towards the village. The sky was leaden with cloud and the snow was falling more heavily. He flicked the wipers to full speed to clear the screen.

'Cold winters you get up here,' he said.

She nodded. 'Getting colder year on year, too. Not like you'd think it, from all the climate change crap on the news saying we're all about to roast to death.'

'I have a solar physicist friend who'd tend to agree with you,' Ben said.

Grace raised an eyebrow in surprise. 'Is that what you teach, solar physics?'

Ben had to smile at that. 'Not exactly.'

At 2.26 p.m., as the first village houses were coming into view up ahead, Grace pointed at a minor junction cutting off to the left, the edges of the road hard to distinguish from the verges. 'Turn left here.' Then shortly afterwards, she pointed to the right and said, 'Take that one.' He could see she was directing him around the edge of Kinlochardaich.

Minutes later, as they were heading beyond the village outskirts and the dash clock hit dead on half past the hour, Ben glimpsed the lone, sad trailer sitting in the middle of a snowy field ringed by a barbed-wire fence and an old blue Subaru Forester parked beside it, and knew he was looking at the McGlashan residence.

'So you weren't bullshitting me. He lives just where you said he did.'

'More like a double bluff,' Grace replied, with a smile. 'Threw you right off the track, didn't I?'

'I'd still have found it without you.'

'Yeah, I'll bet you would've.'

The field gate was open. Ben slowed for the entrance and drove on through, following a set of fresh tracks that cut across the open ground towards the trailer. It must have been years since the field was in any way tended. Under the layer of snow and ice the ruts and holes were rock hard, making the Mercedes lurch and bounce. Three sides of the plot were open, the fourth a thick line of trees at its eastern perimeter. There were no other houses or vehicles in sight within the wide expanse of whiteness.

As they drew closer to the trailer home Ben could see the mess of junk lying all around it. The fresh tyre tracks led up to McGlashan's Subaru, which was parked with its front end up close to a stack of old gas bottles and other detritus. The trailer home itself was raised on blocks with a set of rusty metal steps leading up to the door. Its roof was layered with four inches of snow, like everything else around except the car, which was only lightly dusted with fresh flakes. If McGlashan was home, he hadn't been home for more than a few minutes.

Ben pulled up behind the tail of the Subaru, blocking it in lest its owner get any ideas about trying to escape. He was half expecting the poacher to come bursting out at any moment, but there was no movement. He killed the engine, said, 'Right then, let's go and say hello,' and swung open his door.

Ben was stepping out of the car when two things happened.

The first was the terrible, wailing scream that came from inside the trailer. For a split-second Ben froze where he stood and locked eyes with Grace, who was climbing out from her side. She stared back at him, her face tightening into a hard frown. Each of them thinking the same thing. Each recognising a sound that Ben had heard before, and which Grace hadn't, but which the human brain is naturally hard-wired to identify as the cry of a fellow human in extreme, off-the-charts agonising physical distress. The same awful sound that mankind's primitive ancestors learned as their signal to run for their lives when one of their number was suddenly clasped in the jaws of an attacking cave bear or sabre-toothed tiger.

The sound of pressing, ultimate, primal danger.

Then the second thing happened. Which was that the trailer door crashed violently open. But instead of Jamie McGlashan bursting out through it as Ben had been half-expecting moments earlier, what emerged were two large men. Both dressed the same, in black quilted winter jackets and black woollen beanie hats and black leather gloves and black combat trousers tucked into military boots. Neither of them looked remotely like a benefits scrounger and part-time poacher disturbed from his slumber by unexpected visitors. They looked exactly like two men who'd just been interrupted in the act of doing something very nasty and violent to a helpless victim. Their faces, the fronts of their jackets, their hands and forearms were spattered and glistening with blood. So was the long knife that each of them was clutching as they leaped down the steps from the trailer entrance. And Ben had a pretty good idea whose blood it was.

He sized the situation up in a flash. First, the fact that there were no vehicles parked nearby except for McGlashan's blue Subaru and his own. Which meant these two guys had made their way here on foot, although he was betting their car or van wasn't far away behind the trees that backed onto the eastern edge of the field. Then there was the lack of snow on the Subaru's windscreen and the recent tracks on the ground, showing it hadn't been parked there long. If McGlashan was inside the trailer, and if that was his blood, then it meant he'd only just arrived home and these two guys had been here waiting for him, knives ready to move in for a quick, dirty and silent kill.

But knives weren't all that they had brought with them. As the first guy to reach the bottom of the steps took to his heels and ran, the second guy threw down his blade and ripped a large black pistol from his jacket. With an angry snarl on his face he pointed the gun towards Ben and Grace and opened fire, fast and wild.

Grace yelled out in alarm and threw herself on the ground behind the Mercedes as gunfire raked the screen and punched holes in the bodywork. Ben ducked behind the open driver's door. Which wasn't a safe place to be, because anything flimsier than an armoured limousine door skin could offer scant protection from pistol bullets. He managed to thrust an arm between the front seats and grab his bag from the rear before the shooter redirected his aim away from Grace and the driver's window burst apart and a shower of glass fragments rained down over his head and shoulders.

Ben dived to the ground and rolled and scrabbled under the bottom door sill as more bullets smacked and ricocheted and blew up puffs of snow inches away. Still the guy kept firing, BLAM-BLAM-BLAM, filling the air with noise.

The Mercedes sat high off the ground, but the snow was deep. It got into Ben's eyes and nose and mouth and for a few moments he was thrashing blindly to crawl out from under the other side of the car. Knees and elbows, his back raking against the car's underbelly. He rolled out from underneath and dragged his bag with him. Grace was three feet away, cringing under cover. The shooter had paused firing and was moving around the front of the car with the pistol in both hands, hunting for his targets. In about two seconds he was going to have a clear shot at them. Grace first, because she would be the closest. Then Ben.

No way. Not going to happen.

Because now Ben's hand was inside his bag. Fingers closing on the butt of the sawn-off shotgun within. Two twelve-gauge buckshot rounds loaded in the chambers, strikers already cocked and ready. No time to take it out. No time to hesitate. No time to take aim either, but with a sawn-off hand cannon at short range no aim was necessary.

He didn't want to do it. Hated it with all his heart and soul. But the shooter was leaving him no choice. The guy was coming on another step around the front of the car. The gun tightly clasped in his black-gloved hands. His eyes burning with the heat of battle and his cheeks flushed red and steam billowing from his open mouth like dragon's breath. Fresh from the last kill and ready for more. Seeing his targets hunkered down in the snow. Raising his pistol to open fire on them.

Ben's thumb found the safety catch. A simple sliding button on the tang, backward for safe, forward for fire. He felt the click. Forefinger on the trigger, the whole bag raised in the air with the gun still inside it, pointing at the shooter's chest. Then the resistance of the trigger broke and the weapon went off like a grenade and kicked back hard against the palm of Ben's hand as it blasted its devastating payload out of the bottom of the bag.

The heavy thump of the gunshot echoed over the field, far louder than the snappy reports of the pistol. The shooter caught the full blast of the twelve-gauge buckshot round square in the chest and went straight down, arms outflung. He crashed backwards into the snow, and it was over.

Chapter 32

The exchange had lasted less than five seconds. Ben ejected the smoking shell from his weapon. He wouldn't be needing the second one. The guy was lying on his back as limp as a boned duck, the white snow turning pink all around him, eyes staring straight up at the clouds.

Ben strode over to him and took the pistol from his curled, dead fingers. The weapon was a Glock 21, a full-size combat auto in forty-five calibre. Totally illegal to possess as a civilian in the UK. Which in itself said interesting things about the identity of the shooter. The gun's grips were sticky with blood from the guy's gloves, which were smeared and glistening with it. Ben dropped the magazine from the mag well and racked the slide to pop out the remaining cartridge from the chamber. The guy had managed to fire off seven rounds to Ben's one. He still had seven left. A lot of bad things could have happened in those seven rounds.

Once Ben had the dead guy's weapon secure, he went over to Grace. She was slowly picking herself up from the ground, clumps of snow falling from her clothing, and took the helping hand that he offered her. Her fingers felt very cold. Her mouth was hanging open in shocked disbelief and her eyes were darting back and forth between the dead guy and Ben.

'Jesus Christ,' was all she could say. 'Holy shit. What did you just do?'

He said, 'What I teach.'

'Killing people?'

'Saving them.' He checked her briskly over. 'You're not hurt.' Then he glanced over the field and his eyes followed the tracks in the snow left by the escaping attacker, who was now well out of sight. The tracks headed straight for the trees on the eastern edge of the field, where Ben had guessed the men's vehicle was hidden. He was momentarily torn between going after him and going into the trailer. As he was making up his mind, he heard an engine firing up somewhere behind the trees and revving hard away. He thought, *Fuck it*, and let it drop. He hurried over to the trailer. Bounded up the slippery metal steps to the door and pushed inside.

The victim was in a mess. Still alive for the moment, though most of his blood was no longer inside him. His throat had been slashed wide open and more than a dozen deep stab wounds perforated his portly torso. The poor guy had been virtually eviscerated. His eyes were all out of focus and rolling wildly. As Ben crouched over him, the dying man seemed to register the presence of a helper and tried to speak, but all that came out was a wet gurgle and a blood bubble that swelled from his lips and then popped. Then his eyes rolled over white, his last breath rasped from his scarred mouth and his muscles slackened as death settled over him like a blanket.

There was nothing Ben could do here. The victim had done all the talking he was ever going to do.

Should have gone after the bolter, Ben thought. Bad decision.

Sensing Grace's presence behind him, he stood and turned

204

to face her. She looked grim and sickened, but then he figured that a cop who had worked the mean streets of the big city had seen plenty of blood before and wasn't about to start puking or fainting on him.

Ben shook his head. 'He's done.'

'Yeah, I think I can see that.'

'Is it Jamie McGlashan?'

She nodded. 'I haven't seen him in a long time. He's put on a lot of weight. But I recognise that scar on his lip. It's Jamie.'

They left the trailer and descended the steps. Silence had returned. The gentle whistle of the wind blew the falling snow into their eyes and hair. Ben walked over to the body of the first guy, crouched down next to him and started going through pockets. The shotgun blast had torn him wide open and the snow all around him was stained pinkish-red.

Grace stood watching what Ben was doing. She shook her head. 'You know, when I asked if you were planning on shooting anybody, that was kind of meant to be a joke. I didn't realise you actually were.'

He stopped and looked at her. 'You think I planned this?'

'You're carrying a sawn-off shotgun. I don't think you brought it along for crows.'

'Are you going to ask where I got it from, officer?'

'No.'

'Are you going to arrest me for possession of a prohibited firearm?'

'No.'

'Sorry that I shot the bastard?'

She folded her arms, thought for a moment, and then shook her head again. 'I'm not sorry that he's dead and we're not. And I'm still not sorry that I asked you to come here with me. In fact right now I'm feeling pretty damn glad. But

205

before long I'll be thinking about all the stuff I *should* be sorry for. Like holding back information from my superiors. Inviting a civilian to participate in an unauthorised independent inquiry. Colluding in the illegal killing of a suspect.'

'And fleeing the crime scene,' Ben said. 'That is, unless you want to call this in and wait for your colleagues to turn up.'

She gave a dark laugh. 'Whatever. I don't care. I just want to understand what the hell happened here.'

'What happened is that we got here too late. A few minutes sooner, Jamie McGlashan might have had something useful to tell us. But now we'll never get to hear it, because the other people who've been hunting for him got to him first.'

'But this says something,' Grace said, pointing at the blood and the dead guy.

'Damn right it does. It says I'm pushing on with this. What about you?'

'What about me?'

'You don't have to do this, Grace. It's not too late.'

'You mean, not too late to go back to my cosy little world as a provincial backwater copper and forget this shit is happening right under my nose?'

Ben said nothing and set about checking the dead shooter's pockets. They were completely empty, except for a spare loaded magazine for his Glock. There was no wallet, no cards, no cash or change, no keys, no phone, no form of identification whatsoever. It was pretty much what Ben had expected.

As Ben was finishing up, the dead man's head lolled over to the side – and that was when Ben spotted the tattoo inked onto the side of his neck, just visible over his collar. A sinister human skull enmeshed in a Gothic-script capital D that passed through one eye socket and between its grinning jaws.

Two crossed military daggers behind the skull formed an X.

It was a distinctive design. And to Ben, one that held a very particular and interesting significance. He reached down and picked the dead man's floppy right arm out of the snow. Yanked off the blood-spattered glove and rolled the guy's jacket sleeve up to the elbow. Nothing.

Grace looked puzzled. 'What are you doing?'

'Looking for something.' Ben picked up his bag. It was a wreck, with a big ragged hole in the bottom that he'd have to patch up later. From it he took the Ka-Bar survival knife that he'd bought in Inverness. He unsheathed the black blade and used the razor-sharp tip to slash open the dead guy's jacket sleeve all the way to the shoulder. The dead guy was wearing a fleecy cold-weather shirt underneath. Ben slashed that too, exposing the pallid, rapidly cooling flesh of his upper arm. And there was the second tattoo he'd been looking for. Older, less sharp and more faded than the skull on the dead guy's neck.

Ben said, 'Bingo.'

Grace peered. 'So he had tattoos. So what?'

'Not just any tattoos,' Ben said. 'The one on his arm is the regimental wings of the Parachute Regiment. He's ex-military.'

'Maybe. Or maybe the tat's a fake.'

'It could easily be. There's a lot of losers and wannabes running around harbouring infantile warrior fantasies. But the one on his neck suggests that it's real. See?' Ben used the knife to slash the jacket collar so that Grace could get a better look at the skull-and-daggers Gothic D.

'I see it, but I don't get it. D could just be his initial. How do you know his name isn't Dave, or Donald, or Darren?'

'Trust me. Even if it was, this is something else.' He put the knife away, took out his phone and used its camera to snap three images, one of each tattoo and one of the dead guy's face.

She frowned. 'How can you be so sure?'

'Because there aren't too many people in the world wearing this tattoo,' Ben said. 'In fact it's extremely rare, because it takes a unique kind of qualification to even be allowed to wear it. This is the first one I've ever seen in the flesh. I'll explain it to you. But first I think we ought to get out of here.'

Chapter 33

Grace said, 'What about Jamie? We can't just leave him here to rot.'

'I wouldn't worry about that,' Ben replied. 'If nobody else finds them in the next few hours, Jamie and our friend here will ice up like a couple of frozen chickens. They probably won't thaw out until next year.'

'God, this is awful.' She watched as Ben stuck the dead guy's Glock in his belt. 'What, you didn't have enough guns already?'

'Better to have them and not need them than to need them and not have them,' he replied. 'And I think we're going to need them.' He gathered up his bag and jumped in behind the wheel of the Mercedes as Grace piled in the other side. The screen was cracked and there were several bullet holes in the bodywork. He had to hope that the damn thing would still go.

It did. They took off across the field, exited the gate, and Ben skidded out onto the road heading back around the village outskirts.

'Where to now?' Grace asked.

'First I'm taking you back to your car. Your shift starts in a few hours, remember?'

She shook her head vehemently. 'Screw that. I'm calling in sick. You and I are partners in this now.'

'People are getting killed, Grace.'

'So tell me something new. You're not getting rid of me that easily. Either I ride along with you and see this out, or you can consider yourself under arrest.'

'And I thought we had an understanding about that.'

'And I could still change my mind.'

'Arrest me, you'll have a hell of a lot of explaining to do to your superiors. Besides, what if I decide not to come quietly?'

'You want to put that to the test?'

Ben glanced at her. Her eyes were as hard as bullets. He sensed that she wasn't joking. He could easily prevent her from arresting him. But given how determined she was, he'd probably have to kill her in the process. And that wasn't an option for him.

She said, 'So. Partners, or not?'

'Your choice.'

'Yes, it is. And I already made it. Partners?'

He sighed, relenting. 'Fine. Suit yourself. Partners.'

Some of the hardness melted from her expression. 'You can begin our collaboration by telling me what kind of person wears a D tattoo with a skull and crossed daggers.'

Ben threaded the car through the turnings leading them back in the direction of the loch. As they sped along the icy road and the white-capped trees flashed by on either side, he explained, 'The D stands for a small, select group of individuals. Except you might say that "select" is the wrong word. And you'd be right. They call themselves "the Dishonourables". Not everyone in that world even believes that they really exist. They're a legend, almost a myth.'

'But who are they?'

'Ex-military,' Ben said. 'As their name suggests, their careers didn't last long, because they didn't exactly distinguish themselves. Once you get a DD stamp on your record it makes it virtually impossible that you'll ever be readmitted into any branch of HM Armed Forces, for as long as you live.'

'DD,' Grace said. 'As in "dishonourable discharge"?'

Ben nodded. 'The army, navy and air force don't like letting go of people they've invested an awful lot of time and effort into training and equipping. Screw up, and there's no end to the punishments they'll dish out in the hope that you'll straighten yourself out. But for the real rotten eggs, there's no choice but to court-martial them and boot them out as fast and as hard as they can. It's not a decision they take lightly. Getting a DD can ruin your life. It all but destroys your chances of getting decent civilian work in the future. The lucky few might manage to land okay jobs in the personal security industry. A number of them enlist into other militaries, like the Foreign Legion, who aren't too fussy about who they take on. Some might sign up as private military contractors and go off to do the mercenary thing, fighting for cash in dirty little wars and putting down rebel insurrections on behalf of nasty tin-pot regimes in places you've never even heard of. Others just burn out, become junkies or alcoholics and end up killing themselves. But the Dishonourables went a different path, or so the legend goes.'

He eased the pressure on the gas to let the car roll gently over a large patch of ice. A pale mist was descending that made it hard to distinguish the distant hills from the snow-laden sky. Grace said, 'I'm listening.'

Ben continued, 'Nobody knows how they found one another, or who first came up with the idea, or even exactly when it happened. But they discovered a way to turn their badge of disgrace into a mark of virtue, in their way of seeing things, by forming a tightly-knit and loyal band of their own.'

211

'How do you know all this?'

'I was in that world a long time, Grace. You hear things. What I heard was that if the Dishonourables existed at all, they were a mixed bunch from a whole range of different regiments and backgrounds. Some had been drummed out of the forces for selling drugs. Others for using excessive violence and taking part in atrocities against the enemy, or occasionally civilians, in war zones like Afghanistan or Iraq. But what they all had in common was that they were the worst of the worst. Instead of the cream that rises to the top, these guys were the sludge that sinks to the bottom. They were comfortable doing the kind of things that suited them to the line of work the Dishonourables allegedly specialised in.'

'What kind of work was that?'

'Dirty deeds, done dirt cheap. Murder contracts. Intimidation. Extortion. Targeted robberies. Drug smuggling. Human trafficking. You name it. They're said to travel all over the world, taking whatever jobs they can get their hands on, sometimes working together and sometimes alone. No rules, no limits. The story went that to be inducted into the brotherhood, first you had to satisfy the committee that you were the right stuff. Or the wrong stuff, depending on your point of view. Once you'd got through the basic selection process, then came the final test.'

'Tell me about the test.'

'You don't want to hear it, Grace. Seriously.'

'I'm asking.'

'The test was to kill someone. The Dishonourables would single out a victim at random – man, woman, child, didn't matter. The chosen target would be kidnapped and taken to a secret location, like an abandoned building or warehouse, where everyone would gather for the occasion. Then the prospective new recruit would have to murder them in front of the others, in a manner decided on by the group. Gun, knife, hammer, bat, strangulation, dismemberment, flaying, burning alive—'

Grace held up a hand and put the other over her mouth, as though she was going to throw up. 'Stop. Please. I get the picture.'

'I told you you didn't want to hear it,' Ben said. 'The whole show was filmed on a camcorder and multiple copies stored in different safes, their own private collection of snuff movies. That way your fellow Dishonourables would always have a hold over you, in case you ever tried to rat on them. Like the mafia. Once you passed the test and got the ink, you were in for life.'

'I've been a police officer for a long time. But I can still hardly believe things like this actually happen.'

'What, that people could be so evil and warped?' Ben said. 'If you'd seen the things I have, you'd have no problem believing it. But as to whether the Dishonourables really existed or the whole thing was just a wild myth, I didn't have an opinion until today. Now I have to believe it's true.'

'And that guy back there was one of them?'

Ben nodded. 'Looks that way to me. From serving with a top-class regiment like the Paras, to hooking up with the lowest, scummiest bunch of cutthroats money can buy. How and why he managed to fall so far, we'll never know.'

'The one who got away. Do you think he was one of them, too?'

'Makes sense. Same goes for the military-grade sniper who nearly drilled a .308 rifle round into me last night when he mistook me for the poacher, down by the loch. It might have been one of the pair we met today. Or there could be a third player. Or more. There could be a whole gang of Dishonourables out there, working for whoever's behind all this.'

Grace looked at him. 'This is the first I've heard about a sniper shooting at you down by the loch.'

He shrugged. 'I survived. What's behind me isn't important. My concern is what's ahead. And right now the one who got away is heading back to base to report to his employers. He's going to tell them exactly what happened, and describe the man and woman in the black Mercedes who killed his associate. Which means you and I are officially involved in this now. They know we're onto them and they'll be hunting for us, too. Same as they hunted for Jamie McGlashan. Same as I believe they hunted for Boonzie, because he was getting involved and asking questions. They'll go after anyone who stands in their way.'

Grace said in a softer voice, 'You think they got Boonzie, don't you?'

Ben made no reply.

Grace fell into her own silence, deep in thought for a long minute. 'Okay. Let's say you're right about all this. In which case, we've learned something about what's going on here. But we haven't learned anything that can help us. I mean, we have no idea who these people really are, who they could be working for, or anything useful about them. All we know is that whoever hired them is obviously willing to do anything to get what they want. Such as the gold coins that Ross Campbell found, or whatever. But aside from that, we're back at square one, with nothing to go on.'

Ben had already worked through the same thought process ahead of her, and knew what he had to do next.

He said, 'You're right. We don't know much. But there's someone else who might.'

Chapter 34

It had now been three days since Boonzie McCulloch's capture and incarceration inside the dungeon deep beneath Charles Stuart's castle. Three days of total lack of cooperation from the prisoner. Three days of growing frustration for his captors.

Hacker and his men had spent so many hours trying to make the stubborn old bastard talk that at various times he'd had to pull Carter, O'Donnell, Graham and Banks off the job of hunting for the poacher. Which Hacker had deeply resented, because it had meant having to work along with a bunch of Stuart's amateurish local goons. If that situation hadn't been forced on him, the man they'd spotted by the lochside the night before – Hacker had been pretty damn certain it must be Jamie McGlashan, because who else would have been hanging around there in the middle of a freezing cold night? – surely wouldn't have got away.

All to no avail.

Of course, Hacker had known from the start that prising the truth out of Boonzie McCulloch would be problematic. Firstly, they still had no idea whether he actually knew anything of value to them, concerning Ross Campbell's discovery and his nephew's possible involvement in it.

Secondly, it was clear to them that the old guy would

never reveal the location of the gold, not even if he'd been carrying a mental treasure map around with him. This was a man who had been trained not to divulge information to captors, at any cost. Hacker had experienced a taste of that same kind of training in his past, even if the mock interrogations he'd been subjected to were nothing in comparison to the brutality and realism of the capture simulations the SAS had to endure. Hacker understood only too well that they'd have to tear Boonzie McCulloch apart limb from limb before he'd utter a single syllable to them.

And therein lay the problem. Because while Hacker's crew had been champing at the bit to get the cash bonus coming to them if McCulloch talked, Hacker needed to be careful to restrain them from going too far with a prisoner who obviously wasn't a well man. How do you forcefully extract information from a captive you have to pussyfoot around at the same time, in case he ups and dies on you? You can't starve him of food and water, can't overly stress him physically, and certainly can't torture him – an option Hacker knew was uppermost in his men's minds. The Dishonourables were old hands at torture.

Forced to compromise, Hacker had been at pains to ensure that the prisoner's physical needs were met. He'd even been grinding up the pills from McCulloch's medicine bottle and mixing them into his food according to the dosage on the label, which was in Italian and caused him a major headache to translate. Whether or not the diet of pills was preventing the old guy from keeling over again, Hacker couldn't be sure. But nonetheless he worried about what would happen when the bottle ran empty. If the pills were keeping the prisoner alive and he was liable to kick the bucket without them, whatever information he might be withholding would die with him.

Stuart had played this one well, all right, Hacker thought. For all his business genius, he was being a complete fool.

Something more was needed. If physical stress wasn't an option, then perhaps it was time to try a more subtle approach. Hacker had been sitting alone in his private quarters within the castle when the idea had come to him. He'd called his employer on his mobile to run it by him. It had been approved.

And so, a little after two-thirty that afternoon, Hacker went to pay another visit to the prisoner. From deep in the castle's stone passageways he descended the steps to the cellars. There was a whole complex down there, great vaulted storerooms packed with all kinds of junk and antiques. Another flight of steps led down to a dingy sub-basement where Hacker unlocked four heavy padlocks securing a thick steel door that could have contained a bomb blast. He heaved it open and locked it behind him.

From there, using an electric lantern to find his way in the darkness, he descended yet another flight of steps and passed through a steel cage door to an arched stone passageway at whose bottom was the access to the dungeon itself, an iron grid trapdoor held fast by a massive bolt. It was dank and airless down here, making even Hacker feel claustrophobic. The thought of being kept prisoner in such a place was as bone-chilling as the dampness. He slid back the bolt, set down his lantern, raised the trapdoor and lowered the ladder that was the only way in and out of the hole.

Hacker climbed down the ladder and held up his lantern, scanning around him for the prisoner but seeing only shapes and shadows. A steady drip-drip-drip of moisture leaked from the curved stone walls and echoed in the darkness. It was like entering a cave inhabited by a dangerous predator that might suddenly attack out of nowhere. Hacker drew his pistol.

'McCulloch? Are you awake?'

No reply. Hacker took a cautious step deeper into the chamber. He'd seen better conditions than these in the worst Third World prisons, but he felt no compunction for the man locked up inside. He felt only the same tiny tingle of fear that Boonzie McCulloch's unseen presence somehow managed to kindle in him every time he came down here.

'McCulloch?'

Then Hacker saw him. The prisoner was sitting quietly in a corner, back to the wall, totally immobile. Hacker moved closer, holding the lantern and the gun out in front of him, but not too close. Boonzie McCulloch's eyes were shut and he seemed to be barely breathing, sunk into a trancelike state like a Buddhist monk deep in meditation.

Hacker said, 'I know you can hear me, McCulloch.'

No reply. Not a flicker of movement from the prisoner.

'I have to say, you're a disappointment to me,' Hacker told him. 'I'd have expected you to cooperate with us by now. If not for your own sake, then for the sake of people you care about. I mean, that's not just being unreasonable. It's downright selfish.'

No response.

It was time for Hacker to spring the new plan on him.

'Think we don't know everything about you? You'd be wrong. We know where you live in Italy. And we know you have a wife there.'

The inert shape in the corner showed no sign of reaction.

Hacker went on, 'We can get to her, you know. It's just a question of sending a couple of my guys out there to pay her a little visit. And I will, if you carry on refusing to talk. Is that what you want?'

Silence.

'Here's how it will go,' Hacker said. 'First I'll run an extension cable in here and bring down a screen. Like a tablet or a laptop. The biggest one I can find. It'll be hooked up to a live internet feed, so that you can watch the recording of my guys going to work on your dear beloved spouse. They'll take their time. It'll be a long show, and we'll get to savour every moment of it. After they've finished enjoying themselves in every way imaginable, they'll torture her. Believe me, they're experts at it. And then they'll kill her, very very slowly indeed. I'll rig up extra speakers down here so that you can listen to her screams, full volume.'

Still no response from McCulloch. For an unsettling moment, Hacker thought he was dead. But then thought he could hear his breathing, slow and deep. He was awake and conscious, all right. And listening to every word.

'Afterwards you'll be left to rot in here,' Hacker said. 'No more food, no more water, and no more sleep because I'll keep the playback of her screams running day and night. You'll die listening to her pleading for mercy. Knowing that you could have saved her life. Knowing you could have spared her all that terrible suffering, just by telling us what we want to know. Is that what you want?'

Still no response from the prisoner. Only a very long, very still silence.

Hacker was about to say more when Boonzie McCulloch's eyes slowly opened. Just hard little pinpricks in the half-light from the lantern, they fixed him with a look so cold, calm and dispassionate that it sent a frisson of genuine terror right through Hacker.

Hacker had never shrunk from anyone before. He had to use all his willpower not to shrink away now. He swallowed hard.

Boonzie McCulloch said nothing. No words were needed, because there was no promise of hellfire retribution that couldn't have been better expressed by the terrible expression in his eyes.

'You think about what I just told you,' Hacker said, making an effort to keep his voice steady and menacing. Then he backed away towards the ladder and quickly exited the dungeon, leaving the prisoner sitting alone in the pitch darkness.

Chapter 35

Stuart was waiting for him upstairs. Hacker shook his head. 'I told him what we discussed. He still isn't talking.'

'Then it's time to move to the next stage,' Stuart said. 'I want you to go to Italy and take care of this personally. Today. Take Carter with you. He seems like the most reliable.'

'You're sure you want to go to that extreme?' Hacker asked him. 'Bluffing is one thing. Carrying it out, that's a whole other game.'

'I thought you people could handle anything.'

'I'm not doubting whether my associates and I can handle it. I'm questioning whether you want that on your conscience. What we'll do to McCulloch's wife won't be pretty. Plus there'll be no way to make it look like an accident, like with Campbell. The Italian police will be all over it. And by flying me and my guy over there, you're leaving a trail that's connectable directly to you.'

Stuart looked dubious. 'Who would ever make that connection?'

'The chances are slim. But there's still a chance. It's possible that McCulloch's wife has already reported her husband's disappearance to the authorities. If so, specific locations here in Scotland will have been mentioned. Which potentially points at your involvement, if someone flags that a private aircraft just happened to travel from Scotland to Italy and back again, neatly coinciding with her murder. I'm just saying, think about it.'

'Oh, I'm thinking about it, Hacker. I'm thinking you're worried about incriminating yourself.'

Hacker shook his head. 'If heat comes down on me and my people, we can just disappear. That's what we do. What we've always done. But not you. You're a respectable businessman. You'll be fully exposed and on your own.'

'There's no going back now,' Stuart replied hotly. 'I told you I was prepared to do whatever it takes. And so will you be, if you want to go on working for me.'

'Your choice,' Hacker said.

At that moment, Hacker's phone began to vibrate in his pocket. He pulled it out and saw the caller ID. 'It's Banks.'

'I'm assuming this means we're finally rid of our star witness,' Stuart said. 'Some good news at last.'

Hacker's two Dishonourables associates Bobby Banks and Kev O'Donnell had been sent out earlier to finally eliminate the poacher. Their orders had been clear and simple. Kill McGlashan, dispose of the body, destroy the evidence, burn his trailer. As Hacker hit reply, like his boss he was assuming that he was about to be told that the mission was complete and they were returning to base.

But as Banks began to babble in his ear, Hacker realised that something was badly wrong. He gave his employer an anxious look and put the call on speaker so Stuart could listen in. 'Slow down, Banks. Where are you?'

Banks's voice sounded agitated over the phone speaker, and muffled by the noise inside his car as he drove fast. 'On my way back. Alone.'

'Where the hell's O'Donnell?'

'He's dead. I think.'

'You *think*?'

'There was shooting. I looked back and saw Kev go down. If he ain't dead he's in a bad fuckin' way. He was just lying there in the snow, all bloody.'

'Looked back, as in, you were running away when this happened?'

'The job was take out McGlashan,' Banks said. 'Just a poxy fisherman. We didn't know we were going to meet any resistance, did we?'

'I thought you went tooled up.'

'Yeah, but only the one shooter, and Kev had it. What was I supposed to do? The fucker's got a sawn-off.'

'Calm down,' Hacker said sternly. He was getting a headache from trying to figure out what the hell Banks was telling him. 'What fucker's got a sawn-off? McGlashan? Did he shoot Kev?'

'No, not McGlashan. He's fucked, okay? We did the job. I'm talking about the other fucker.'

Hacker's mind flashed back to the man he'd tried to kill the night before, down by the loch. He'd thought he was shooting at the poacher. Maybe he'd been wrong. Maybe a serious new player had arrived on the scene. That might explain how the man had managed to evade him and disappear like a ghost. But who was he?

'This man, what does he look like?'

'Could be late thirties, maybe early forties, but fit. Six foot or a little less. Blond hair, jeans, leather jacket. Turned up in a black Mercedes SUV. There was a woman with him.'

'Did you get the Merc's number?'

Banks wasn't a total idiot. He recited the registration. Hacker made a mental note of it and said, 'Okay, describe the woman to me as well.'

'White, I'd say mid-thirties. Good-looking. Long dark hair.'

'How far out are you?'

'On these roads? Maybe twenty minutes.'

'Copy that. Get here as quick as you can.' Hacker ended the call and heaved a sigh. 'Shit.'

Stuart was glaring at him. 'Well done, Hacker. Top class. All I can say is, your man O'Donnell had bloody well better be dead. If the law get hold of him and he talks—'

'I thought you had the local cops in your pocket.'

'Macleod and Coull are bought and paid for, but it's not as though I control the entire Northern Constabulary. For all I know the whole of Kinlochardaich is swarming with police, as we speak. It's exactly the kind of disaster you assured me wouldn't happen, with your so-called professionals on board.'

'We can fix this,' Hacker said. 'I just need to know who the guy in the black Mercedes SUV is. Once he goes away, the problem goes away.'

Stuart was looking at him in disgust. 'At least I get something for my money.'

'What do you mean?'

'I mean, while you were wasting time with McCulloch earlier, I got a phone call from Fergus Macleod, notifying me of an interesting detail that happened to come to his attention today. It seems that one of his lower-rank officers has been digging around in the database files at police headquarters, looking for convicted poachers in the local area, coming up with the name Jamie McGlashan and crosschecking it with DVLA records to get his current address and vehicle details. Now, apparently, in this wonderful technological new world of ours, officers wishing to access the police computer files need to log in using their own personal access code. Which leaves a record of who's been looking at what.'

'And so?'

'And so I believe I know the identity of the woman who was with the man in the black Mercedes,' Stuart said. 'The officer who was doing all this private sleuthing happens to be one PC Grace Kirk. Who also happens to have been the off-duty constable who arrested Angus Baird and his friends the other night, after a pub brawl which, according to certain eye-witnesses who fled the scene, involved an unnamed stranger from out of town. All that's known about him is that he beat the living daylights out of three large, powerful men without hardly touching them. Does that sound like someone who could potentially get the better of your associate Kev O'Donnell in an armed confrontation?'

Stuart took a phone from his pocket and flashed up a picture. It was an ID photo of a female police officer, taken from some official personnel file. She was in her early thirties. Good-looking. Her hair was dark, tied back but visibly quite long. 'Fits your man's description of the woman at the scene of today's incident, don't you think? All in all, clear enough evidence that PC Grace Kirk is mixed up in this somehow.'

Hacker stared at the photo. The scale of the problem was gradually dawning on him. 'If she's with the police, then who's the guy? He can't be a copper. Coppers don't blow people away with sawn-offs. Not in this country, anyhow.'

Stuart shook his head, putting the phone away. 'Whoever he is, he's just made the mistake of his life, messing with me. Your flight to Italy is now postponed, Hacker. Instead I want you to focus on finding this man before he causes us irreparable damage.'

Hacker asked, 'What do you suppose they know?'

Stuart replied, 'They found McGlashan. They're getting closer. Therefore we have to assume they know everything.'

'If he's not a copper, then what's his motive?' Hacker said, thinking out loud.

'He's obviously after the same thing everyone else is. Money.'

'Or maybe it's something else. Maybe he's a mate of McCulloch's, come looking for him. An army buddy, perhaps.'

Stuart shook his head. 'Too big an age gap, surely.'

'Not if the guy was just starting out on his military career when McCulloch's was coming to an end. They could still have served together, in the same regiment, at the same time.' The more Hacker thought about it, the more the pieces of the puzzle seemed to slot together. The likes of Jamie McGlashan couldn't have got away from him at the loch last night. But an SAS soldier was an entirely different matter. Not to mention the fact that someone of that calibre would be more than a match for a dozen Angus Bairds.

'That's all I needed,' Stuart muttered. 'What the hell do you propose to do about it, Hacker? Hacker?'

Hacker was momentarily elsewhere, staring into space, his head filled with the image of Kev O'Donnell lying there dead in the snow, covered in blood, ripped apart by a shotgun blast. Then Hacker tried to picture the man who had done this.

You kill one of the brotherhood, you face the penalty.

Hacker replied, 'I think you need to call Macleod back right away and feed him the registration number for the black Mercedes. It'll take him exactly two seconds to provide us with its owner's name. Then he can get his brother-in-law, or whoever, to access the guy's military record, like he did McCulloch's. Then we'll see if our theory is right, and we'll know exactly what we're dealing with. Once we know who this bastard is, he'll be much easier to catch.'

'You hope.'

'It's a start,' Hacker said.

'What about Kirk?' Stuart asked him.

'Your bent copper will have her home address, right? So get it. When she gets home from work tonight, we'll be waiting for her.'

Stuart considered the new plan, then took his phone back out and dialled.

'Macleod? It's me again. There are two more things I need you to do for me, so listen carefully.'

Chapter 36

The snowfall was coming back with a vengeance and the early winter dusk was already beginning to descend as the Mercedes reached the lochside track, where Grace's Land Rover was slowly disappearing under a covering of white that filtered through the pine tree canopy like flour through a sieve. As Ben pulled up behind her vehicle, Grace said, 'You still haven't told me who this person is you think can help us.'

Ben replied, 'I don't want to get our hopes up. It could be a dead end. We'll find out soon enough, after I get back to the cottage and make a couple of calls.'

'If you're going back to the cottage, then I'm coming too.'

Ben knew there was no point arguing. She'd only threaten to arrest him again. He opened his door and slid out of the driver's seat, leaving the engine running and the heat blasting. 'You drive. I'll take the Landy and meet you there.'

Grace clambered across the centre console and got behind the wheel. She had to adjust the mirror and rack the seat forward for her shorter legs. Then she shoved the transmission into reverse and backed away down the track. When she was out of sight, Ben ran back to the trees by the lochside where he'd left his things earlier. He carried them back to the Land Rover and tossed them in the back. The ice on the windscreen had solidified into rock-hard rime that he had to scrape away before clambering into the frigid metal box of the cab and firing up the engine. No traction control, no anti-lock brakes, no fancy onboard electronics of any kind. But there was nothing better in the world for driving in deep snow, if you knew how to handle it. He took off and followed Grace's tracks back towards the Gunn cottage.

When he got there, he found the wood-burner already coming to life, the stovetop kettle whistling on the range, and Grace on the phone to the police headquarters, putting on a convincingly croaky and weak voice to spin them a story about having come down with a sudden case of flu. She was a fast worker, that was for sure. Finishing the call she said in her normal voice, 'That'll buy me a couple of days. I'm making a cup of tea. Want some?'

Ben pulled a face at the idea, and went into the kitchen to grab the jar of instant coffee. Two empty mugs stood on the kitchen counter with teabags in them. He fished one of the offensive items out, dumped three heaped spoonfuls of coffee in its place and poured the water in from the kettle. Grace joined him at the counter, and stood next to him to perform the milk-and-sugar ritual. Her shoulder brushed his arm as she stirred her tea with a clinking spoon. Her presence so close by felt comfortable to him. He could smell her perfume and a whiff of some kind of scented soap. He suddenly realised that this little moment was the closest thing to domestic cohabitation with a member of the opposite sex that he'd experienced since splitting up with his fiancée, Brooke, a long time ago. It was a strange feeling.

But the moment was soon over. They carried their drinks back into the cottage's living room and Ben tossed a couple more logs on the wood-burner before taking out his phone. Grace perched on the edge of an armchair, sipping her tea. 'Are you calling the person you reckon can help us?'

229

'No, I'm calling a guy called Chimp Chalmers.'

'Who the hell is Chimp Chalmers? What kind of name is that, anyway?'

'He used to be in British Special Forces. Now he lives in the Czech Republic.'

'Doing what?'

'He sells stuff. Anything from an ex-Soviet tank or attack helicopter to a Scud missile, delivered to the location of your choice, anywhere in the world, for the right fee.'

Grace cocked an eyebrow. 'I see. We're buying a tank now?'

'No, we're asking a favour. Chimp has connections every-where. I'm hoping he can help us.'

Ben dialled the number from memory. After seven rings Chimp's familiar voice came on the line. He was called Chimp because he was built like an ape, long arms, barrel chest, bandy legs and all. He sounded like one, too. The hoarse grunt said, 'Who's this?'

'Hello, Chimp.'

'Well, fuck me if it ain't my old chum Ben Hope. I heard you were six feet under, pushing up daisies.'

'That'll teach you to believe rumours. I need something from you.'

'Music to my ears. Just got in a nice shipment of Israeli surface-to-air missile launchers, brand new in their crates. Do you a good price. Or maybe you're after another aircraft, like last time?'

Ben remembered last time well. On that occasion, when his son Jude had got into trouble off the coast of east Africa, Ben and Jeff Dekker had ended up having to buy a Russian military seaplane to go and rescue him. It had drained most of the cash in the Le Val bank account.

'Nothing like that this time. Just a phone number.'

'You're breaking my heart,' Chimp rasped sourly. 'Whose?'

Ben asked, 'You remember an SRR colonel by the name of Bartholomew Montgomery?' SRR was the Special Reconnaissance Regiment, which had been formed many years earlier to support other UK Special Forces units in counterterrorism. 'He retired a long time ago. Must be well over eighty now. I'm hoping he's still alive.'

'You don't mean Mad Monty, do you?'

'Mad Monty,' Ben repeated. 'The very man.'

'Jesus wept. What the fuck d'you want to talk to that batty old duffer for?'

'Can you get me the number or not?'

'I can talk to a guy who's mates with a guy who knows another guy who might be able to get hold of it. But it's going out of my way, you know?'

'Just get it, Chalmers.' Ben ended the call.

Grace commented, 'That's one way to ask for a favour.'

'He'll call back,' Ben said. 'Because he knows what I'll do to him if he doesn't.'

'You seem to know a lot of very strange folks,' Grace said. 'Do I dare to ask why they call this person Mad Monty?'

'Because he had a habit of believing things that nobody else wanted to believe,' Ben said. 'Maybe because he was way ahead of the curve. Or maybe because he really was crazy.'

Only time would tell. While he was waiting for the call back, Ben unloaded, stripped, cleaned, reassembled the pistol he'd taken from the dead man, then reloaded it and put it in his bag with the shotgun. Next he grabbed the roll of black tape from inside the bag and went out to the car. Grace followed him outside and stood leaning against the open doorway, warming her hands on her mug of tea as she watched him start tearing off two-inch strips of tape and sticking them over the bullet holes in the Mercedes' body-work. Black on black; from a few feet away, if you squinted

231

a little, they weren't too noticeable. There wasn't much he could do about the cracked screen, except hope he didn't get pulled over for it by some overzealous traffic copper.

'I count six holes,' she said.

'Seven,' he replied, pointing out the one she'd missed.

'Hmm. Now I get why the car rental companies don't like you.'

'At least it's still in one piece. That's unusual for me.'

Ben was taping over the seventh hole when his phone went.

Chalmers still wasn't happy to be forced into giving out free information, but he'd moved quickly. The number was a UK landline with a 01298 prefix area code for an area of the East Midlands. Ben went back inside the cottage and dialled it. The voice that replied after just one ring spoke in a very clipped upper-class accent. 'Montgomery.'

Ben knew he was only going to get one shot at this, so he wasted no time in throwing in everything he had, including the most powerful, albeit tenuous, connections he still had in the British Army. He was even prepared to capitalise on his rank title, something he normally avoided at all cost.

'Colonel, we've never met and you don't know me, but my name is Major Benedict Hope, formerly of 22 Special Air Service. I can send you a link to my business website to verify who I am. Lieutenant-General Cedric Grumman, formerly of the Irish Guards, and Brigadier Jacko Jennings of the King's Royal Hussars, will also vouch for me.' Both men, now retired and in their seventies, had served at different times as Director of Special Forces, commanders-in-chief of SAS.

Ben was aware of Grace staring at him in open-mouthed astonishment, but he ignored her as he pressed on: 'I apologise for this unorthodox method of approach, Colonel, but I'm dealing with a specific problem and I believe you're the only person who can help me. It concerns an organisation of former servicemen who go by the name "the Dishonourables".'

There was a drawn-out pause on the other end of the line while Montgomery evaluated whether or not to trust this stranger calling out of the blue. Finally he said, in the same plummy tones, 'It's certainly a pleasure to speak to you, Major. How may I be of assistance?'

At the same moment Ben was talking on the phone to Mad Colonel Monty, Charles Stuart was receiving another phone call from his payrolled underling, Fergus Macleod. The detective inspector was calling from work and speaking so low he was almost whispering, as though frightened that others might be listening at his office door.

'You wanted Grace Kirk's home address. She lives in Kinlochardaich.'

'Give it to me.' Stuart listened, and copied it down as Macleod read it from the personnel file. Stuart said, 'I want to know everything about this bitch. What kind of car does she drive? Is there a husband or boyfriend?'

'She drives a wreck of a '98 Land Rover Defender,' Macleod answered in the same furtive near-whisper. He read off the registration number. 'As far as I know, she's single and lives alone.'

Stuart noted down the reg, too. 'When does she next get off work?'

'She was scheduled for an evening shift tonight, but I'm told she called in a few minutes ago to cry off. She's come down with the flu.'

'And I'm a monkey's uncle.'

'What are you going to do?'

'What do you think I'm going to do?'

Macleod sounded nervous. 'There's something else. I traced the car reg you gave me earlier. It belongs to a black 2018 Mercedes GLS sports utility vehicle that was rented just days ago from a car hire outlet at Inverness airport. The customer's name is Hope, Ben Hope. Lives in France, runs some kind of training centre.'

Stuart smiled to himself. This was excellent news. He noted down the name. 'Are you sure this is the man we're looking for?'

'Aye, perfectly sure. To be certain I ran a check on him through the police computer. No criminal record. But to say there's a bit of a military record would be an understatement. I got my brother-in-law to look into it, like you asked. By the way, he wants to know if there's any money in this for him.'

'You can pay him out of your share. Just tell me what you found.'

'Well,' Macleod said nervously, 'it wasn't easy. Hope's file is so cloaked in Ministry of Defence red tape, I don't think even the bloody Prime Minister would have the security clearance to see all of it.'

'Stop blethering and cut to the chase,' Stuart said urgently.

Macleod replied, 'All right, but you're not going to like it.'

Chapter 37

Colonel Monty was a proud Englishman, patriot and royalist who, ashamed and appalled by the slur on Her Majesty's forces that was the ex-military mafia calling themselves 'the Dishonourables', had devoted the entire two decades of his retirement to tracking them down and bringing them to justice. Or so the story went. The colonel had been widely derided for his obsession with a subject that many within the armed forces believed was pure hokum.

That was how Ben had first come to hear the mess-room chatter about Bartholomew Montgomery, years earlier when he'd still been with the regiment. Like everyone else he'd heard the rumours about the old fruitcake tilting at windmills like a modern-day Don Quixote; and like everyone else, he'd had no reason to take any of it seriously. The nickname 'Mad Monty' had stuck.

But now it looked as if the colonel might have been right on the money, the whole time.

Speaking to him, nothing about the elderly officer's manner suggested to Ben that he was anything less than one hundred per cent mentally sharp and lucid. Ben laid out the facts for him, though he was careful not to say too much over the phone about his encounter that afternoon. It didn't matter. Monty was perfectly astute enough to read between the lines.

It didn't take long for Ben to pique the colonel's interest, since a real-life encounter with members of the Dishonourables brotherhood was a rare and important event. Once Ben had him hooked and wanting to know more, he got down to business. 'In my current situation it's critically important for me to identify the individual in question. I need to know if that's an option.'

'As you know, I've spent many years collating information on the brotherhood,' Monty replied. 'I have dossiers on a number of men whom I suspect to have been inducted into its membership, past and present.'

'And it's possible that this person could be one of them?' Ben said.

'Certainly possible, though by no means guaranteed. I'd have to have a little more to go on. I take it that you have photographic evidence concerning this individual?'

'Taken earlier today, immediately following the incident,' Ben said. Which was enough to convey a clear picture for Monty to visualise: one very dead corpse, still fresh, all ripped and bloody after suffering an extremely violent demise and by no means a pretty sight. Ben added, 'It goes without saying that this is strictly eyes-only material.'

'Of course. I fully understand that, due to the, ah, *sensitive* nature of such evidence, you're far too cautious a man to share it across digital media.'

'Correct. Or else I'd have been happy to email it to you.'

The colonel replied, 'Likewise, in the event that I was willing and able to provide you with information in return – again, far from guaranteed – it's not something I'm prepared to do over the phone. Nothing is secure nowadays.'

'For that reason, I'm hoping you'll consent to a face-to-face meeting. Subject to your verification that I'm who I say

I am. But time is an issue here, Colonel. The sooner we meet, the better.'

'I appreciate the urgency of your situation. But I'm sure you must also understand my trepidation. This is a highly dangerous and sinister group of criminals, who may have become aware of my investigation into their activities, and I'm not in the habit of exposing myself to risk. As genuine as you sound, you could be one of them. And I'm not as capable of defending myself from attack as I was ten years ago.'

'I understand perfectly.'

The colonel thought for a moment, then said, 'Write down this email address, Major. Send me your credentials. I'll speak with Lieutenant-General Grumman and Brigadier Jennings and get back to you within the hour.'

'Whatever you decide, sir, it's been a pleasure talking to you.'

But before he hung up, the canny old fox had a request. 'Tell me one thing, Major. Something nobody else could possibly know.'

If Monty was going to use it to check with two former SAS directors to establish Ben's veracity, then it had to be secret information to which only the inner circle of British Special Forces would be privy.

Ben said, 'September twentieth, 2003. A combined UKSF and Delta Force unit with the codename Task Force Red deployed twenty miles west of Tikrit as part of Operation Citation, under my command. SAS suffered one KIA that day, a thirty-year-old trooper called Jon Taylor who caught an RPG round in a surprise attack by Islamic insurgents. Taylor was from Wakefield. He played the saxophone. His wife's name was Sally and they had a little girl called Charlotte, who'd be twenty-one now, and a Yorkshire terrier called Duke who lost a leg in a road accident when he was a puppy. Jon was upset about it at the time.'

Something nobody else could possibly know. It was Ben's best shot.

'You think he'll ring back?' Grace said when the call was over.

'Only time will tell.'

But time wasn't something Ben had in spades, and every minute spent waiting was painful to him. He stood watching the darkness fall outside the cottage window and chain-smoking Gauloises, unable to silence the clock that was ticking loudly in his head. He was betting the farm on Mad Monty. If this went nowhere, he had no other leads to follow.

'Isn't there some other way?' Grace asked.

'Unless I break into jail and kidnap Angus Baird and his cronies on the off-chance that one of them might be able to tell us something useful,' Ben replied, 'then yes, right now, this is the only way.'

Grace had nothing better to offer. She fell back into her own brooding silence, twiddling her thumbs by the fire. When she spoke again, one hour and five minutes had passed since the end of Ben's conversation with Mad Monty. 'He's not calling back, is he?' she said glumly.

Ben said nothing. One hour and ten minutes. One hour and fifteen.

Grace said, 'He's definitely not calling back.'

Ben still said nothing.

'I can't believe I'm running around with an SAS major.'

'Retired.'

One hour and twenty-one minutes after the call had ended, the phone rang and Ben snatched it up.

Mad Monty said, 'Make your way towards Buxton, Derbyshire. Call me when you get within ten miles and I'll supply you with further instructions.'

'This is much appreciated, Colonel.'

'I look forward to making your acquaintance, Major Hope.'

Operation Citation and Duke, the three-legged pup, seemed to have done the trick. Monty hung up the phone.

'How far away is Buxton?' Grace asked, echoing Ben's own thoughts. So late in the afternoon, there was little chance of grabbing a last-minute flight from Inverness to Manchester. The only alternative was a long drive south.

'Over six hours by car,' he replied. 'I'll go on my own.'

She jutted out her chin in defiance. 'Not on your life, pal.'

'Fine. Do you want to swing by your place and pick up a change of clothes or whatever else you need? We'll be away all night long.'

Grace shook her head. 'Nope. I'm good.'

'Then let's get moving.'

It was 4.52 in the afternoon.

Chapter 38

At 4.55, Carl Hacker was returning upstairs from checking on the prisoner when his phone burred and he saw the call was from his guy Mitch Graham. Over an hour had passed since Graham and Carter had been despatched back to Kinlochardaich in the same fast 4x4 their associates had used earlier in the day, to perform a couple of important tasks. The first of which was to revisit Jamie McGlashan's trailer site, check whether the place was crawling with police, and if not, then to remove O'Donnell's body from the scene.

Once that was taken care of, their second task was to pay an unannounced home visit to the Kirk woman. Their orders were different from those issued to O'Donnell and Banks earlier that day. Rather than be simply slaughtered and left where they found her, Kirk was to be taken alive and brought to the castle for interrogation.

'Well?' Hacker asked. 'How'd it go?'

'We took care of Kev. Cops were nowhere near the place.'

'Good. Where is he now?'

'Boot of the car. Or what's left of him. He was so frozen solid we had to break the poor sod into pieces to get him inside a bin liner. If he starts to thaw, it's gonna make a hell of a stink.'

'What about the woman?'

'No sign,' Graham said. 'Place is empty. Lights are off, no sign of life. Her car's not there either. And it ain't been there any time recently, either. There'd be tyre tracks.'

'You definitely got the right address?'

'Come on, mate. We ain't the local spastics who work for Stuart.'

'All right, all right.'

'Good news is, we found the Land Rover parked outside a cottage at the other end of the village. It's a one-horse town. Didn't take long to scope the place out.'

'Are you at the cottage now?' Hacker asked hopefully.

'Yeah, but don't get your knickers in a twist. Whoever was here, looks like we just missed them. Two sets of fresh footprints in the snow, from the front door to where a car was parked. One set of prints is bigger, tread looks like your typical sort of combat boot. The other smaller, could be a woman's. Tyre tracks are wide apart and have a pretty fat tread. Looking at a big car.'

'Like a Mercedes GLS?'

'Or something like that. It's snowing like a bugger here and the tracks ain't got more than a sprinkling on them. I'd say they were made less than twenty minutes before we showed up.'

'Can you follow them?'

'No point,' Graham said. 'Easy enough to see which way they headed out of the village. But by the time you get onto the main road you ain't gonna see shit.'

The picture was clear to Hacker. The cottage must be Hope's local base, most likely rented like the Mercedes he was driving. Kirk was with him, and the two of them were obviously up to something. More bad news for the boss, on top of what Macleod had revealed about Hope's military background.

'What do we do now?' Graham asked.

'Get inside the cottage. If there's anything more you can find out, call me. Then I need you to stay there until he comes back.'

'And when he does?'

'The boss wants him alive.'

'Not going to be easy.'

'Are you scared of one guy on his own?'

'One SAS guy.'

Hacker snorted. 'Fuck the SAS. The Pathfinders could eat them for breakfast.'

'Then maybe you ought to be here, instead of us mere fucking rear-echelon mortals,' Graham said.

'Get in the damn house and call me back if you find anything.'

Hacker got off the phone and steeled himself for the prospect of breaking the latest news to the boss. Stuart had stormed off in a rage after Macleod's call earlier on, and Hacker hadn't seen him since, presuming he was somewhere within the castle.

Hacker dialled the mobile number, but there was no answer. He wondered where the boss might have gone off to.

Right at that moment, the boss was speeding towards Fort William. The roads were terrible, but the Rolls Royce Cullinan with its four-wheel-drive transmission could munch up the most difficult conditions with ridiculous ease, its engine as smooth and quiet as an electric turbine.

He'd just had to turn off his phone and get out of the house before the frustration drove him insane. Nothing seemed to be going his way. The prisoner still wasn't talking. The sizeable investment he'd made into hiring Hacker's associates wasn't producing the returns he'd hoped for. And now he'd had the aggravating confirmation that this maniac Ben Hope was not only a former military comrade of Boonzie McCulloch's but some kind of super-soldier with a war record apparently so extensive and classified that even regular Ministry officials could only view a fraction of it. How much more bad luck could a man bear?

Worst of all, he, Charles Stuart, was not the tiniest step closer to recovering his natural inheritance. His birthright. His family treasure. All he'd managed to obtain until now were the measly couple of coins that Ross Campbell had been carrying the day of his death, plus the one that Macleod had taken from Ewan McCulloch. The location of all the rest was still a mystery.

Hardly a minute went by that he didn't want to gnash his teeth in fury at what was being withheld from him. He could hardly sleep at night any longer, because every time he closed his eyes he could *see* the masses of his ancestor's buried treasure lurking beneath the dirt and leaves of the ancient forest. In his fevered dreams he found himself wandering lost among an endless wilderness of mossy pine trees, repeatedly falling to his knees and digging like a wild man, only to find nothing but fistfuls of filth and rot.

He knew he was slowly going crazy. And crazy men sometimes did crazy things. On the Rolls Royce's passenger seat was a briefcase containing the largest knife Stuart had been able to find in the castle's kitchen. He was prepared to use it.

His destination that evening was the Belford Hospital. On arrival he marched up to the main desk clutching his briefcase and told the receptionist that he was here to visit the patient Ewan McCulloch.

'I'm sorry, sir,' the receptionist politely replied, 'but visiting times are by arrangement only. I'd have to check with Dr Fraser first.'

Stuart muttered a reply and slipped away from the desk. When the receptionist turned her back to answer a ringing phone, he darted through a doorway and headed down a long, brightly lit corridor. He wandered about the hospital, peering through doorways and following signs. The Belford wasn't very big, and so it didn't take him long to find the room he was looking for. Through a window he could see the inert form of Ewan McCulloch in his bed, all wires and tubes hooking him up to bleeping machines. Stuart lingered outside the door. Nurses and orderlies crisscrossed past him in the corridor, all too preoccupied to pay him any notice. The instant the coast was clear, Stuart slipped inside the room and softly closed the door behind him. He turned off the light so that he couldn't be seen through the window.

Stuart approached the bed and studied the patient in the dim glow of the blinking machines. Ewan McCulloch was very still and appeared almost dead. A monitor bleeped to the slow, steady rhythm of his heartbeat.

Stuart unlatched his briefcase. Slipped a hand inside and took out the carving knife. Leaning over the bed he lowered his face close to the patient's ear and murmured, 'I know you can hear me, you little shit.'

Whether Ewan could hear or not, he made no reply or movement.

'That's not all I know,' Stuart hissed. 'Ross Campbell told you where he found the coins, didn't he? Tell me where they are. Tell me!'

No response. The patient seemed to be a billion light years away, floating in another galaxy.

Stuart said, 'If you won't tell me, then by God I'll make damn well sure you never wake up and steal it for yourself.'

He raised the carving knife. Pressed its sharp carbon steel tip against the soft flesh of Ewan's neck.

Ewan didn't move or make a sound. Stuart's fingers clenched the knife handle tightly. His mouth felt dry. All he had to do was push the blade in. He wondered how it would feel to kill. Would the blood spurt all over him, or would it just gush out like water from a hose? How long would McCulloch take to die?

Do it!

Then the room door suddenly opened, and the light came on.

Stuart whirled around, whipping the knife out of sight behind his back. His eyes widened in shock and alarm at the sight of a female doctor standing in the doorway, who appeared just as startled to see him standing by the patient's bedside. The name on her tag was Dr Fraser. She said, frowning, 'You're not supposed to be in here. Why did you turn the light off? Who are you?'

For an insane moment, Stuart contemplated attacking her and stabbing her to death. 'Sorry, wrong room.' He stumbled towards the doorway and pushed past her and back out into the corridor, keeping the knife hidden. He broke into a run as the doctor came after him, yelling, 'Hey, stop! Hold it right there!'

Stuart kept running. He saw a door on his left and batted through it. Dashed along another corridor and down a flight of steps, nearly knocking over a young guy in an orderly's uniform who was coming up the other way. Stuart reached another door at the bottom of the steps and pushed through that one too, and turned right and ran. Three doorways later, he'd somehow managed to give his pursuer the slip. By pure luck he found a fire exit. The cold night air chilled the sweat on his brow as he hurried around the side of the building towards his parked car. His heart was pounding hard and his breath billowed like a steam locomotive.

Before he got into the car he turned and shook his fist at the hospital, and screamed, 'I'll be back for you too, you bitch!' Then he dived in behind the wheel of the Rolls, cranked the engine and squealed out of the hospital car park and away into the night. Two miles outside of Fort William, he stopped in a layby to get his breath back. Turning on his phone, he saw he had three missed calls from Carl Hacker.

Stuart called him back.

'Where've you been?'

'Watch how you speak to me, Hacker. I've been attending to some important business. What do you want?'

Hacker relayed to his boss the report from Graham and Carter. 'So now we know where Hope lives. When he comes back, he's ours.'

'It's obvious that Hope and Kirk are up to something,' Stuart said. 'We need to act fast before this situation gets any worse.'

'What do you sugg—?' Hacker began, but Stuart cut him off and instantly began dialling Macleod's number.

'I'm at home now,' Macleod complained when he picked up. 'In the middle of my tea.'

'I don't give a tuppenny fuck where you are. I need you to have Ben Hope arrested immediately.'

Macleod spluttered as though he was choking on his pie and chips. 'On what charges? I can't have someone arrested just like that, for no good reason.'

'Try murder,' Stuart said. 'Hope is the prime suspect in the brutal killing of a local citizen called Jamie McGlashan. A name I'm sure you'll recognise. The same man we've spent the last several days trying to identify. And the same individual in whose police files your officer Kirk was showing an unhealthy interest earlier today. Which suggests to me that she may be acting as an accomplice. I've reason to believe that the two of them are together as we speak, and there's no telling what they're up to.'

'How—?'

'Shut up and listen. If you send your officers out to the scene, you'll find McGlashan's corpse inside his trailer. In the meantime, you need to put out a BOLO alert, or an all-points bulletin, or whatever the hell you people call it, on Hope's car. I want him pulled off the streets, and Kirk too. Then I want them both brought to me. Understood?'

'That's insane,' Macleod protested. 'The system doesn't work that way.'

'Then improvise,' Stuart said. 'Make it happen by whatever means possible. Unless you want to find yourself implicated in the murder of Ross Campbell and the assault on Ewan McCulloch. That wouldn't be too beneficial for your career, now would it?'

'You tell on me, I'll tell on you.'

'I'd like to see you try,' Stuart said.

Chapter 39

While the enemy were making their plans, Ben and Grace were speeding southwards through the night. The Mercedes' powerful headlamps probed into the darkness and the wipers were working full pelt to swipe away the driving snowflakes. Once they had left behind the treacherous rural byways their route was all A-roads, where they joined the thickening stream of traffic trickling its way towards Glasgow and the Borders. The wintry weather lashing southern Scotland showed no sign of letting up but the gritter trucks had done their work and the roads were clear, with dirty brown snow and slush piled up all along the verges. On the approach to the city Ben joined the motorway network and let the car settle into a cruising speed of 85, just fast enough to munch the miles without too much risk of the bullet-holed car getting pulled over by the law. At the Scottish border the M74 became the major artery of the M6 that would take them all the way south through northern England to Manchester.

Conversation was sporadic between them, and Grace eventually fell asleep. Ben rolled his window down a crack and smoked, alone with his thoughts and the metronomic swish of the wipers. He had no idea what awaited them at their destination. All he could do was keep ploughing ahead, and let the dice roll.

Time inched by. Ben was tired, and could have done with someone to talk to. But he didn't want to disturb Grace, who was still fast asleep in the big, enveloping armchair of the passenger seat with her head resting on her shoulder, her face partially covered by her long black hair. Now and then he glanced at her and thought how peaceful she looked, and how comfortable he felt in her presence. That strange feeling of cosy domesticity came over him again. But then he thought about the predicament the two of them were in, and the certain dangers that lay ahead. And he wished that she hadn't become mixed up with him in this. If he could find a way to sideline her safely out of it and finish the job alone, he would.

On and on. Lockerbie, Carlisle, Penrith; skirting the edges of the Lake District and passing into the rugged wilds of the Yorkshire Dales. They'd been driving for over four hours when Grace woke up and announced that she was hungry. Soon afterwards a sign for motorway services flashed past, and Ben pulled in. Stretching their muscles they stepped out of the warm car into the cold evening wind that blew off the tall hills and tasted of more snow to come. They wandered from the parking area and saw more signs for Road Chef, McDonald's and Costa Coffee. Anything would have sounded good at that moment. Ben was pretty damn hungry too. Five minutes later, they were seated in a booth for two near a window with their meals on trays. A cheeseburger, fries and a tall paper cup of black coffee for him; some kind of soya-based fake meat concoction stuffed into a sesame roll with bits of salad and a diet soda for her.

'I didn't know you were a vegetarian,' Ben said, eyeing her choice of food.

She shrugged and took a bite. 'I'm not. I'm just careful what I take into my body.'

'What you take into your body.'

She nodded. 'I mean, have you any idea of the crap that's in that thing you're eating? Let me guess. You're going to tell me you've had worse, like the army made you eat fried worms or some such.'

'No, but I ate part of a goat's heart once, in the mountains of Afghanistan.'

Grace wrinkled her nose. 'Yuk. How did you cook it?'

'When your camp's surrounded on all sides by units of enemy fighters who'd be only too happy to chop your head off if they found you, you don't give away your position by lighting fires. So it wasn't cooked.'

'That's so gross. I don't know how people can stand that kind of life.'

He shrugged. 'It was my life.'

'You must have had other things in your life though. Like a wife, girlfriend, someone special, waiting for you at home, praying you'd come back in one piece. No?'

'Not then,' he said. 'Too much complication.'

'What about now?'

'Not now either.'

'Too much complication?'

'Just how it is,' he said.

'What, are you a monk or something?'

'Let's just say I'm between romantic entanglements at the moment.'

Grace took another bite of the concoction and chewed reflexively. 'You don't like talking about yourself, do you? I suppose it goes with the territory.'

Ben knew she was right about that. Maybe he needed to open up a little more. 'I was married once, to someone called Leigh. Engaged another time, to someone called Brooke.'

'Didn't work out?'

'Leigh died.'

'Shit. Sorry I asked.'

'It was a long time ago, but I still think about her very often. Brooke and me, that was years later. Anyhow, she left me because I walked out on her, the day before the wedding.'

Grace shook her head. 'Why did you walk out?'

'Because a friend needed my help,' he said. 'Maybe it was stupid of me. But I couldn't say no. I had to go.'

'Like you did for Boonzie,' she said. 'Taking risks and making sacrifices for friends in need is obviously a strong character trait of yours.'

'You're making me sound like a good person.'

'Aren't you?'

'I'm the wrong guy to answer that question.'

She touched his hand, just briefly, and flashed him a smile. 'Then let me answer it for you. I don't think you're too bad a person.'

'When this is over, you might see me differently. More people are going to get hurt, Grace. I am going to take an active part in that. I don't like it much, but it's going to happen. No way to change it. What we were involved in today, that was just the beginning. And we can't underestimate our enemy's intention to hurt us, too. They're going to fight back with everything they've got, and they're not soft people. One way or another, things are set to get ugly.'

Grace's smile dropped away and she looked at him seriously. 'I thought we'd been through this. Are you trying to tell me I shouldn't be with you?'

'I'm asking you not to make me responsible.'

'For me?'

'For what could happen.'

'I can look after myself,' she said.

When they'd finished eating they walked back to the car

in silence, fuelled up and then resumed their long journey into the night. Sometime after nine p.m., as the motorway cut between the city of Lancaster to the west and the barren moorlands of the Forest of Bowland to the east, the snow dissipated and turned to icy rain. Beyond Preston they switched motorways onto the M61 and their route curved eastwards towards Manchester. As ten p.m. came and went, with less than an hour to go before they hit the Peak District and the old spa town of Buxton, Ben decided it was time to alert Mad Monty to their imminent arrival.

'You don't waste time, Major.'

'I have none to waste. ETA should be around eleven tonight. What's your address?'

Montgomery gave him a sat nav coordinate for a location close to a village called Harpur Hill, on the edge of Buxton. 'There's a disused, flooded quarry known locally as the Blue Lagoon. I'll be waiting for you. If you get there first, don't get too close to the water. It's blue because of caustic chemicals leaching out of the limestone, and as toxic as bleach.'

Following Monty's coordinates, they reached the Harpur Hill quarry shortly after eleven o'clock. A rocky track led them close to the huge square-cut pit, whose edges plunged steeply down towards the water that looked inky black in the darkness. Ben and Grace stepped out of the car and looked around them. The quarry appeared deserted, no vehicle lights or any sign of life to be seen. The driving icy rain was turning into sleet. Grace shivered and wrapped her coat around herself. 'Is it just me, or is this kind of a weird place for a meeting?'

Ben was about to reply when he sensed something wasn't right. 'Shush.'

'What?'

He moved back towards the car and reached for his bag.

But before he could get to the shotgun inside it, a tall, thin shadow detached itself from the darkness and a figure stepped towards them.

Chapter 40

The figure said, 'There'll be no need for that, Major. Move away from the vehicle, please, keeping your hands where I can see them. Your lady friend, too.'

Ben and Grace stepped away from the car. The figure came closer. Tall, bony and stooped, wearing a long dark coat and a broad-brimmed hat that dripped with rain. And clutching an old service automatic that he had pointed at the two of them.

Ben didn't like being sneaked up on, and if he hadn't been tired and bleary-eyed from the long drive, the colonel would never have got the edge over him. Mistakes like that could cost you your life.

'I apologise if I appear somewhat overcautious,' Monty said. 'But one can never be too careful, under the circumstances. I hope you won't mind if I frisk you for concealed weapons?'

'Be my guest, but you won't find any,' Ben said.

Monty was quick and efficient, and as discreet as possible when it came to searching a lady. Her hair was wet from the sleety rain and her eyes flashed a look of fear at Ben. He replied with a smile that said, 'It's okay.'

There were four moments during the search when Ben could have taken the pistol from him and turned the tables, but he held back. Once the colonel was confident that neither of them was armed, he waved the pistol towards the darkness. 'My vehicle is parked over there. After you, if you please. But first, you'll oblige me by giving me your car keys. You can have them back later.'

Ben locked the Mercedes and tossed Monty the keys. Then they turned and started walking in the direction Monty had pointed. He walked five paces behind, still holding the pistol and shining a small torch whose beam showed the way. They headed down a crumbly stone path that wound to the quarry's edge, where a plain Ford panel van was hidden behind a stack of huge limestone boulders. Monty blipped the locks and said, 'Now, if you'd be so good as to get in the back, we can be on our way.'

The van's twin rear doors were plain metal with no windows. Ben yanked on the handle and opened up the back. A dim light came on inside, showing the thick plywood sheets attached to the interior.

Grace looked at Ben and shook her head. 'You've got to be shitting me.'

'Come on,' Ben said softly. He helped her into the van, then climbed in after her. The only seating in the rear cargo area was the hard metal humps of the wheel arches, one on each side. Monty closed the door and locked it. They heard his footsteps crunching on the rocky path, then the sound of the driver's door opening. As the engine rasped into life, the interior light went out and they were in pitch blackness.

'What is this?' Grace hissed. 'Are we being kidnapped?'

'No, it's just the cost of doing business,' Ben replied. 'If we want what he has to offer, it's got to be on his terms. Quid pro quo.'

'With a gun pointed at us.'

'I don't blame him for being careful. I'd have done it just the same way, in his position.'

The van bumped and rocked and creaked as it made its way back along the rough track from the quarry. There was little for the rear passengers to hang onto to prevent themselves from getting tossed around, but it wasn't long before the van reached the road and the ride smoothed out.

The drive lasted just fifteen minutes. After a series of twists and turns the van lurched up an incline that felt like a driveway. The engine sound became echoey as they entered an enclosed building, like a garage, then died. Ben heard the whirr and scrape of the electric garage door closing behind them. Their host climbed out from behind the wheel. Footsteps walked up the side of the van.

Ben said, 'Try to be nice, okay? Stay focused on our purpose for being here.'

'As long as he doesn't point that gun at us again. I could have him banged up just for owning it.'

Then the back doors opened, and the plywood interior filled with light.

As Ben had guessed, the van was parked in one bay of a domestic block-built double garage, the other half filled with garden tools and shelving units and all the utilitarian clutter of the typical middle-class suburban home. Colonel Monty's pistol was no longer in evidence, and his manner was courteous and apologetic. 'I do hope you can forgive me for all these precautionary measures. Your telephone call did leave me in something of a quandary. No hard feelings?'

Ben replied, 'None at all, Colonel.' Grace said nothing, obviously not quite yet ready to forgive him.

'Your car keys,' Monty said, returning the Mercedes fob to Ben. He hung his coat on a peg and removed the broad-brimmed hat, revealing a wispy comb-over of white hair. Then he ushered them through the garage to an interior door that led inside his home. The house was large and tastefully furnished, if a little on the formal side, as suited a retired military officer of Monty's generation. One wall proudly displayed a whole montage of framed photographs, the older ones in black and white, dating back through the colonel's career to his early days at Sandhurst. The stooped, crooked Monty of today was a far cry from the dashing, ramrod-straight figure of a man he'd been in his glory years.

'Please, make yourselves comfortable,' the colonel said, showing them through to a sizeable conservatory filled with chintzy woven rattan armchairs and sofas. Icy rain pattered on the windows and glass ceiling, but the room was warm and inviting. As they entered, a corpulent grey-haired woman whom Ben presumed to be Mrs Montgomery appeared in the doorway. She was dressed as though getting ready for bed, in dressing gown and fluffy slippers.

'This is my wife, Eunice,' Monty said. Ben introduced himself and Grace. Eunice was all smiles, as though greeting old friends. 'Grace, that's such a lovely name. You must be hungry after your long journey, dear. Would you like a piece of apple tart?'

'That's very kind of you, perhaps just a small slice,' Grace said, making an effort to be polite.

Eunice beamed with joy. 'That's wonderful. I'll just go and bake one.' She hurried off towards the kitchen, dressing gown swishing around her.

And folks said Monty was mad.

'Will you take a drink?' the colonel asked, opening a cabinet that housed a row of bottles and glasses. Ben asked for scotch, neat. Grace declined. Monty took out a pair of crystal tumblers and a bottle of good single malt, set them down on a glass-topped table and poured out two enormous measures that would have befitted a hard-drinking officers' mess of old. The colonel settled on a rattan armchair. Ben took a seat on one of the matching sofas, and Grace sat next to him.

'I'm sure you're anxious to get down to business,' the colonel said. 'Now that we're free to talk openly, perhaps you'd like to start by describing in more detail your recent encounter? I'm a little foggy on how you became involved in this whole situation.'

'I don't have time to go into it all, colonel,' Ben said. 'Let's just say, as I told you on the phone, that circumstances have led us into conflict with some unpleasant people, who have some even worse people working for them.' He reiterated the story, exactly as events had unfolded from the moment he and Grace had arrived at Jamie McGlashan's trailer.

If Colonel Montgomery was mildly disappointed that one of the two killers had managed to escape, his pleasure at hearing of the other's fate more than made up for it. 'You mentioned you had photographic evidence to show me?'

Ben took out his phone and scrolled up the three images of the dead man for Monty to see. The colonel examined the close-ups of the tattoos first, the regimental ink on the corpse's upper arm and the Gothic D, skull and daggers adorning his neck. 'You're quite correct, Major, this is indeed the insignia of that disgraceful organised crime gang, the Dishonourables. And the older tattoo indicates that this piece of scum previously had the undeserved privilege of serving with the Parachute Regiment.'

'The third image shows his face,' Ben said.

Monty brought the picture up and feasted his eyes for a moment on the sight of the bloody corpse in the snow. 'You seem to have made a thorough job of it, Major. I commend you. In fifteen years of chasing these filthy scumbags I'm yet to have had the satisfaction of personally seeing one sent to hell where he belongs. You've no idea how happy this makes me.'

Monty *really* didn't like the Dishonourables.

'But is there a chance we might be able to identify him?' Ben asked.

'You could have gone the route of accessing the military records of all servicemen dishonourably discharged from his regiment over, say, the last twenty-odd years and working through them until a match was found,' Monty said. 'A long and arduous task. However, the good news is that the legwork has already been done, thanks to my own humble efforts. I have the names and pictures of every single man DD'd from the British armed forces, going back decades. And I'm also pleased to inform you that this particular scumbag's face looks vaguely familiar to me.'

'His name?' Ben asked.

Monty shook his head. 'You'll have to excuse an old man's memory for being a tad less sharp than it once was. So if you'll follow me, let's go and consult my records, shall we?'

Chapter 41

They left the conservatory and the colonel led them through the house and upstairs, past more collections of family photos on the walls showing grinning, gap-toothed kids and grandkids. Passing an open bedroom door, Monty stopped at the end of a passage and produced a ring of keys with which he proceeded to unlock another door. He flipped on a light switch and led them inside. At one time, the room had been a little girl's bedroom and still had faded pink wallpaper with small teddy bear motifs. But the Montgomerys' daughter had long since grown up, and now the room served as the colonel's study. Two tall filing cabinets stood beside a desk piled high with folders and papers.

'You're looking at twenty years of work,' the colonel said as he pulled open a filing cabinet drawer and began sifting through cardboard suspension files. 'I've called in more favours than I care to mention, spent fortunes on private investigators, surveillance and bribes to informants or for obtaining illegal copies of police reports, staked my entire reputation and at times risked alienating my own family. An obsession, I'll admit, but in my opinion a worthy one. The sooner the Dishonourables are rounded up and jailed, or preferably strung up, the better. Now let's see if we can't find your man somewhere among this lot.'

The files were arranged by regiment and subdivided into squadron and unit, according to where each subject had been in his military career when it had all come to a crashing end. Monty had hundreds of individual dossiers on dishonourably discharged former soldiers covering a period of many years, and the job of sifting through them all would have taken hours if the dead guy's regimental tattoo hadn't narrowed things down for them. Monty lifted out the file for the Parachute Regiment and carried it over to the cluttered desk.

Ben had known a lot of Paras in his time, and admired them enormously. He was happy to see that relatively few men from that elite airborne infantry unit had ever fallen so low as to receive a DD. Of those twenty-nine whose dubious activities over the years had caused them to be included in Monty's records, some of the dossiers were thicker and some scantier depending on how thoroughly he'd been able to research the man's background. Eight of the older files were stamped DECEASED. Monty explained how, where his investigations had led him to suspect involvement in the Dishonourables' organisation, he'd marked the file with a big red capital letter S. Others were labelled with a black capital C for 'confirmed'. Whatever its status, each dossier bore the individual's service number and, more importantly for Ben's purposes, a photocopy or scan printout of their official military ID photo.

It didn't take very long to match one of the ID photos to Ben's phone image of the dead man in the snow. It was Grace who found it, inside one of the active dossiers marked C. 'Got him,' she said instantly.

Ben looked. The soldier's name was Kevin O'Donnell. His military photo showed a much slimmer and smoother-featured young soldier, but there was no doubting that it was the same guy. O'Donnell was forty-three years old. He'd been just seventeen when he'd first signed up as an army recruit, twenty-four when he'd enlisted with the Paras, and thirty-two when he'd tested positive in a random drugs test at Colchester Garrison and duly been booted out of the regiment.

As Monty recounted, for the next six years after his discharge O'Donnell had drifted aimlessly from one thing to another, before getting his first conviction for aggravated assault. Four years later, during which time he'd been in and out of prison for increasingly serious crime and somehow hooked up with the Dishonourables, he and a fellow ex-soldier had been pulled in as suspects in the particularly violent London gangland assassination of a known police informer, one Lyle Cunningham. Both had been questioned by CID detectives, but then released due to insufficient evidence. 'It's all in here,' Monty said, tapping the photo-copied police report. 'Since then the two have been occasional associates, involved in a variety of dirty dealings for which, sadly, they've been too clever to get caught. But I happen to know plenty about their activities.'

Monty flipped through the file and pulled out a set of grainy photos that looked as if they'd been covertly shot from the back of a surveillance van. They showed O'Donnell walking down a city street in conversation with another man, taller, slimmer, meaner-looking and maybe a year or two younger. The pictures had been taken in summer. O'Donnell was wearing a T-shirt with a palm tree on it, and his friend was clad in a sleeveless hoodie that showed off his toned arms. And the unmistakeable Dishonourables tattoo on his right deltoid.

'What's the second guy's name?' Ben asked.

'Oh, you can read all about him, too,' Monty replied. He

returned to the filing cabinet, rooted around for a moment, and came back to the desk with another file that was thicker than O'Donnell's. As Ben began to leaf through it, Monty said, 'A real beauty, this one. His name is Carl Hacker. Born in London, joined the army at eighteen. Promising start, showed great ability, and he quickly worked his way up to join the Pathfinders, where he was promoted to staff sergeant.'

Ben was surprised, because he knew all about the Pathfinder Platoon. Primarily a recon unit, they often worked in an Advance Force operations role as support to SAS. Their troopers were some of the toughest and most disciplined in the business, who received a level of training second only to the most elite regiments of the joint Special Forces family.

'Of all of them, you would say that Hacker was the biggest waste of a good soldier,' Monty said. 'By all accounts he was a master with a rifle, too. Won first-place medal in the AOSC long-range sniper event, two years in a row.'

AOSC stood for Army Operational Shooting Competition, the British Forces' premier marksmanship tournament, held annually at Bisley in Surrey. To even qualify, you had to be excellent. To come away a winner was a superlative achievement. Ben had only won it once.

'And then it all went badly awry,' Monty went on, shaking his head. 'As you'll see from his file, Hacker earned his DD eight years ago following his alleged involvement in a gun-running racket supplying weapons, ammunition and explosives that had been magicked out of British military arsenals to members of organised crime gangs in the UK, Sweden and Germany.'

'Tell me more about him,' Ben said.

Monty replied, 'Turn to the last page of his dossier and you'll see that he's now employed as international head of security for an independent investments company called

Stuart Corporate Enterprises Ltd, based in Scotland but with offices worldwide. I did some digging into the firm in case it was some kind of front for illicit activities. You never know. But it all seems perfectly above board, and quite a large-scale set-up. Which makes Hacker one of the fortunate few with his background who still somehow manage to land cushy legitimate jobs despite their dubious past history. But then, he was always one of the clever ones.'

Ben and Grace exchanged glances. Ben asked Monty, 'Based where in Scotland?'

The question caught the colonel off-balance. He puzzled for a moment, scratching his head. 'Lord, I forget exactly. I'd have to check. As I recall, it was somewhere in the Highlands. An unlikely location, I remember thinking at the time. Fort something. The company owner is some multi-millionaire or other who owns a castle up there. It's coming back to me now. Charles Stuart, that was his name. Like Bonnie Prince Charlie, the Young Pretender.'

'There are three Highland forts,' Grace said. 'Spaced out in a diagonal line spanning northern Scotland from the Firth of Lorne to the Moray Firth. Fort George in the east, Fort Augustus in the middle and Fort William in the west. So which is it?'

'Fort William,' Monty remembered suddenly. 'I'm sure it was that one. Yes, yes, of course. That's where the Commando monument is, at Spean Bridge. Where Churchill sent our boys to train with the American Army Rangers during the war.'

Ben was already delving into his phone to search online for Stuart Corporate Investments Ltd. He quickly found the company website, which was just as impressive as Monty had described. The site proudly vaunted its international footprint but capitalised most of all on its Scottish roots, getting maximum wow-factor value from the multiple panoramic shots of the magnificent estate and spectacularly grand Highland castle that served as its corporate headquarters.

But it was its location that mainly interested Ben at this moment. The damn place was just a few miles north of Fort William. Which also placed it just a few miles south of Kinlochardaich. Almost exactly equidistant. Slap bang right in the middle of all the action that Ben and Grace had just left behind. And to which they'd soon be returning.

Ben had been around long enough, and seen enough weird and crazy things, to know that coincidences did happen. But this connection was hard to dismiss so easily.

He said, 'Grace, I think you and I need to head back north and go and say hello to this Mr Stuart.'

Chapter 42

At the same moment Hacker was getting on the phone to Graham, who was still hiding at Hope's cottage with Carter.

Hacker asked, 'Well? Have they come back yet?'

Graham replied impatiently, 'If they'd have come back yet, don't you think I would've called you? How much longer do we have to sit here freezing our bollocks off?'

'Quit whinging. You're getting well paid for it. Call me the moment anything happens.' Hacker ended the call and turned to Stuart, who was pacing the floor in agitation with his hands clasped behind his back. They and Banks were in the industrial-scale kitchen in the bowels of the castle. The room was filled with the rich aroma of Italian dark roast coffee filtering through a percolator on a range the size of a locomotive. Banks was sitting hunched over the enormous table with a steaming mug and the dismantled pieces of a pistol in front of him, which he was assiduously cleaning with a copper wire brush and a rag.

Hacker said, 'Hope and the woman are still out there somewhere.'

'I know they're still out there somewhere,' Stuart snapped back at him, still pacing. 'I'm not deaf. Or stupid. Which is why Macleod and Coull have been instructed to keep an eye on every inch of road for a fifty-mile radius in case they show up.'

'On their own?'

Stuart gave a derisive snort. 'The payroll doesn't stop with Macleod and Coull, you idiot. I have my hierarchy of minions, they have theirs. That's what makes this operation so damned expensive. Every local Keystone Cop with a second mortgage, a nasty gambling habit or a sprog studying for some worthless university degree wants to get his fingers in the money pot. And meantime I still don't have any better idea of what's going on than I did hours ago. Where's Hope? Where's Kirk? What are they up to? I can't stand not knowing. *You* said you were going to deal with this situation.'

Hacker glanced at Banks, not liking being reprimanded in front of a fellow Dishonourable. Banks went on cleaning the gun components and didn't look up, as though oblivious of the conversation.

Hacker replied, 'I'm doing the best I can. But with one guy down, two staked out in Kinlochardaich and two needed to take care of things here at base, our manpower resources are stretched thin. When you first involved me in this matter, we were going after an old man with a weak heart. That was before this Ben Hope came into the picture. He changes everything. If and when we do catch up with him, or your Keystone Cops somehow manage to deliver him to us, either way we're going to have our hands full.'

Stuart stopped pacing and looked at him. 'I thought you said the Pathfinders could eat him for breakfast.'

'We could. But there's only one of me here.'

'So you're saying you need additional manpower. Fine. Bring them on. How many more can you get hold of at short notice?'

Hacker glanced at Banks again, and this time Banks looked up. 'Mikey Creece is looking for work,' Banks said. 'So's Phil Buckett. Ran into them in a pub in King's Cross the other week.'

Creece was an old crony of Hacker's from back in the day. The two of them had been mixed up together in the lucrative gun-running scam that had ultimately ended Hacker's military career. Creece had since gone on to better things. Hacker said, 'I thought Mikey and Phil were in Ukraine, shooting rebels for the Russians.'

'They were, but you can't trust fuckin' foreigners to keep a proper war going these days. Every time there's a fuckin' ceasefire it's down tools and you don't get paid for sitting around on your arse. They got pissed off and came home. Reckon they'd be up for it. And they'd probably be able to round up a few more of the boys, too.'

Hacker nodded. 'Especially if it means taking out some SAS piece of shit who killed one of us.'

'Call them now,' Stuart said. 'Get five, ten, twenty, whatever it takes. I want a regiment here, with all the weapons and ammunition you can scrape together out of the pits of the criminal underworld. I've had enough of this Hope meddling in my affairs. I don't want him dead. I want him obliterated, vaporised and erased from the face of the earth as if he'd never existed. And then I want what's rightfully mine. DO YOU HEAR ME?'

Meanwhile, deep below them, Boonzie McCulloch was sitting very still but wide awake, resting with his back to the cold, dank dungeon wall. After days of confinement his vision had adjusted to the near-total darkness of his surroundings, to the point where he imagined he could make out a single photon of light. In his experience you could get used to just about anything. But the stone floor that was all he had to sleep on wasn't getting any softer, and the damp felt as though it was creeping a little more into his bones with every passing hour. He was raw with fear and anger, and hunger pangs gnawed fiercely at his belly. The food dish his captors had brought him earlier was empty. Cold rice and beans, and a plastic teaspoon to eat them with in the darkness. The bitter aftertaste of the ground-up heart pill they'd mixed up into his food was still on his lips.

Boonzie understood why these men were keeping him alive. What they wanted from him was the same thing they'd thought Ewan had. Something that Boonzie simply couldn't give them, even if he'd wanted to. And that wasn't good.

Boonzie also understood that things weren't going well for his enemies. Day on day, he could sense the change in their manner. They were beginning to panic. Their plans were falling apart. Something new was happening that they weren't telling him about, but it was frightening them. Boonzie knew the smell of fear and he could smell it on these men. Which intrigued him, but also worried him deeply, because it meant that the danger to Mirella was no idle threat.

Something had to be done.

And Boonzie was working on it.

He'd been working on it for the last three days, ever since he'd thought he could hear the sound of water gushing somewhere behind the wall of his prison and had figured out where it was coming from. His fingertips were ragged and bleeding from his efforts, but the soreness in his hands mattered no more to him than the jolts of pain that now and then shot through his chest as he worked. He'd rest a while, then keep at it until the aching tiredness washed over him, then rest again. All around the clock. Day and night were the same down here.

Now Boonzie decided that he had rested long enough. He rocked his body forwards onto his knees and crawled silently across the dungeon floor so that he could go back to work on the loose stone block in the wall.

Chapter 43

On the drive back northwards, Ben plugged his phone into the Mercedes' hands-free system and called Mirella. The landline call rang a few times before it was redirected to a mobile. A moment later, a confused-sounding Mirella picked up. It was only then that he realised how late it was; even later in Italy.

'I'm sorry I woke you.'

'I wasn't asleep. It's impossible for me to close my eyes.' Mirella tearfully explained that she'd gone to stay with her brother's family in Rome, unable to stand being alone any longer. She was going out of her mind and, to Ben's relief, was still procrastinating over whether or not to call in the authorities.

'Hold on just a little longer, Mirella. I might have found out something important.'

'*You found him?*' It was agonising to hear the rawness of emotion in her voice.

'I didn't say that, Mirella. I'll call you back when I know more. Sit tight and take care.'

'You look exhausted,' Grace said, looking at him with concern when the tough call was over. 'When's the last time you got any shuteye? You ought to be resting.'

She was right, of course. Mad Monty had offered them

the use of two spare bedrooms for the night, but Ben had declined the invitation and decided to press on. At two a.m., three hours after meeting their host at the Blue Lagoon quarry, they were hitting the road again. Ben couldn't deny that he was badly in need of sleep, but he felt fired up by a renewed sense of purpose. Mad Monty had come through for them in fine style; the coming day would tell whether the things Ben had learned had set him on the right track.

'When this is over, I'll rest,' he replied.

'You want me to drive? It's a hell of a long way back to Kinlochardaich.'

'I'm fine,' he said. 'Just keep talking to me.'

'What do you want me to talk about?'

'Anything. I don't care. So long as I can hear your voice.'

Grace smiled. 'That's sweet.' She thought for a moment about what to say. 'I'd never been to Buxton before. Had you?'

'Can't say that I had.'

'It's a very historic place. Did you know that Mary Queen of Scots spent a lot of time there?'

Ben dimly recalled having read something once. 'I think she spent time everywhere, locked up in one castle or another while she was Queen Elizabeth's prisoner.'

'That's true. But Elizabeth let her visit Buxton often to take the waters there, on account of her bad health. She wasn't a well person. And the spa waters were supposed to have amazing healing powers.'

'Did it work?' Ben asked.

'I don't think it did a lot for her. Then Elizabeth stopped her going anyway, because she was nervous about Mary getting involved in plots against her if she was given too much freedom.'

'And then she chopped her head off.'

'Not for a few years afterwards. That was one execution warrant Elizabeth really didn't want to sign. She delayed it for a long time. But as she saw it, politically she had no other choice.'

'I never knew all that,' Ben said. 'How come you're so clued up?'

'Someone had to pay attention during history class at school. I actually liked learning about Scotland's past. All the famous figures from our history. William Wallace, Robert the Bruce, Rob Roy, Bonnie Prince Charlie, Flora MacDonald—'

'Who was she?'

'A real Scottish heroine, who helped Prince Charlie escape after the English hammered his army at the Battle of Culloden in 1746. She managed to smuggle him to the Isle of Skye on a boat, disguised as a woman. You know the Skye Boat Song? I mean, who doesn't? Anyway, that's where it came from.'

Ben looked at her. 'Bonnie Prince Charlie, the great Scottish hero, dressed up as a woman to get away from the English?'

She nodded. 'Yup. Petticoat, stockings, garters, and all. Posing as an Irish maid called Betty Burke. Actually, the pattern of material his dress was made of became all the rage for fashionable Jacobite ladies in the late 1740s.'

'Kind of gives a new meaning to the term "Young Pretender",' Ben said.

'Shocked?'

'Not really,' he replied. 'An SAS squad once dressed up as Muslim women, the full head-to-toe garb, so they could infiltrate an ISIS terrorist cell in Raqqa.'

'Bet that gave them a surprise.'

'Especially when the troopers pulled submachine guns out from under their burqas and blasted them,' Ben said.

'But they were attacking, not running away. The SAS don't do running away. And I'd like to see anyone try getting any of the guys I knew into stockings and garters.'

'Oh, and Prince Charlie wasn't really Scottish either,' Grace said.

'He wasn't?'

'His father James II was half French and born in London, and his mother was from Silesia, now Poland. He was born and raised in Italy, spent less than fourteen months of his entire life in this country, and if he spoke English at all it was with a foreign accent. I mean, European royal families were always a mixed bag, inbreeding all over the place. But if Prince Charlie could claim he was Scottish, then with a name like Kirk that goes back to seventh-century Norway, I'm definitely a Viking.'

The journey continued. Ben kept Grace talking, to help him stay awake through the long hours. It wasn't just the sound of her voice he liked. It was her warmth, her wit, and her company generally. He was starting to like her. Maybe too damn much.

They stopped at the same services they'd used on the way down, and ate pretty much the same meal as before. Then, just as they'd done the previous evening, they returned to the car and kept moving. Hours later they left the motorway north of Glasgow and the night-time traffic, already thin at that hour, dwindled away until the Mercedes became just a solitary bubble of light speeding through the empty darkness. Grace kept offering to take over at the wheel until she dozed off herself, leaving Ben alone again with his troubled thoughts and the endless road snaking hypnotically towards him out of the night. The further north they travelled, the lower the outside temperature reading on the dash dropped. Frozen rain mixed with hail and sleet needled the windscreen and formed a glacial slick over the roads and snowy verges, forcing Ben to relax his pace for fear of hitting a patch of black ice.

Nothing happened for a long while.

And then, on the lonely road pushing into the Highlands, something did happen.

Chapter 44

Just past six in the morning, carving through the frigid black heart of the wilderness somewhere between Crianlarich and Glen Orchy, the monotony of their journey came to a sudden halt with the screech of a police siren behind them and flashing blue lights filling the rear-view mirror. Grace had still been half-dozing in the warm comfort of her seat, and woke up with a start. 'Shit! What's happening?'

'Looks like we might have company,' Ben said. He'd been watching the solitary headlights creeping up on their tail for the last few minutes, and wondering about them. He slackened his pressure on the gas a little but kept moving, in case the patrol car was about to push past them and speed onwards in pursuit of dangerous criminals elsewhere.

Some chance. The patrol vehicle stayed right where it was, blues and twos going full blast. Ben thought *fuck it*, flicked his indicator like a good citizen and gently pulled in towards the snowy verge. The cops pulled in behind.

Grace said, 'What's this about? Were you speeding?'

'On these icy roads? The sixty limit's faster than even I'd want to go.'

'Then what do you think they want?'

'I reckon we're about to find out.' Ben stepped out of the Mercedes into the night-time chill. The patrol car was a

Mitsubishi 4x4 with POLICE and the Gaelic POILEAS emblazoned across its bonnet. Both doors swung open and both cops climbed out. Two men, thirties, bulky with black winter coats over their uniforms, batons and cuff holders and Taser holsters dangling from their thick middles, cap peaks pulled down low. Ben supposed that was to make them look mean. It didn't. They just looked tired and sour, as if they'd been driving around half the night. Ben could empathise with that, though he might have been able to empathise more if he hadn't just been pulled over in a bullet-holed car containing a bag of illicit guns and ammunition.

The cops walked around the front of their vehicle and came striding over, lit from the rear by their own headlamps and from the front by the red glow of the Mercedes' tail-lights. Puffing billows of steam on their breath, like bulls. Radios crackling and fizzing. Long metal torches in their gloved hands. Definitely trying to look as intimidating as they could.

Ben closed the driver's door. He stepped around the rear of his car to see if maybe something wasn't working properly back there. Tail-lights: check. Number plate light: check. Indicator: ditto. The taped-over bullet holes weren't visible from the rear, either. And he'd been going steady at about 1 mph below the limit. No obvious reason why he should have been stopped.

He greeted the approaching cops with a pleasant 'Anything in particular I can help you with, officers?' He got no answer, only a couple of ugly stares in return. One of the cops was wearing the hint of a smirk on his face. The other one just looked surly.

Ben said, 'Maybe you're lost and you need some directions. Bad luck, I'm not from around these parts.'

Still no reply. The smirking one stood a few feet away and

aimed his torch in Ben's face. The surly one stepped around the passenger side of the Mercedes and shone his beam through the window. He glared for a moment at Grace inside the car, then turned and gave his colleague a confirmatory kind of nod. His colleague nodded back, still wearing the smirk. Maybe he had Bell's palsy or something. Not taking his eyes off Ben he pulled out a phone, jabbed keys to make a call, and a moment later muttered in a low voice, 'It's me. We found them. Uh-huh. Copy that, it's Hope and Kirk, all right.'

Which Ben thought was a little strange. Because in all the countries of the world where he'd ever been pulled over by the cops, he'd never met one yet who used a phone instead of his radio. Nor had Ben ever encountered a police officer with the gift of prophecy. But this guy seemed to know the names of both occupants of the Mercedes, before he'd even asked them a single question.

At that moment Grace pushed open her passenger door and got out of the car. The surly cop moved back a few steps, but kept his torch shining on her. The cold wind streamed her hair across her face. She brushed it away, flashed her police warrant card at the two cops and said breezily, 'PC Kirk, based in Fort William. How are we doing this morning, gents?'

No replies, no smiles of greeting to a fellow officer. Ben looked at Grace and saw the slight bemusement in her eyes that these two weren't acting quite normal. Then he looked back at the surly cop who was standing a few steps away from her. The cop was holding his torch in his left hand. Ben saw his right hand slip inside his police overcoat and come out with something he definitely shouldn't have had in there. It was a high-voltage cattle prod.

At the same moment, the smirking cop suddenly came

towards Ben with an identical device clenched in his hand. A nasty glint of something in his eyes reflected in the red glow of the Mercedes' tail-lights.

Ben had no idea what was going on. But he knew what was about to happen in the next instant, unless he took the appropriate action, and fast. He jumped back along the driver's side of the car until he was level with the windscreen. Planted the flat of his hand on the cold metal of the wing and in an explosive burst of energy vaulted feet-first across the Mercedes' wide bonnet. Sliding across it at a sharp angle. Crunching down into the snow and ice of the verge on the opposite side, shoving Grace bodily out of the way and throwing his weight hard against the open passenger door as the surly cop came at her with the shock prod in his hand. The edge of the door slammed into the cop's chest and side and the violent impact knocked him off balance. He staggered backwards with a grunt of pain and fell heavily into the snow.

Then Ben was all over him, trampling him hard and brutally so that he had no chance of getting up, and ripping the shock prod from his hand. The cop tried to flail at Ben with the torch in his other hand, but Ben blocked the blow with his foot and kicked the torch away. Then he drove his knees downwards into the cop's chest, punching all the air out of his lungs, and jammed the high-voltage device against the guy's throat.

No hesitation, no mercy. This bastard didn't get a second chance. A harsh electrical crackle and a high-pitched choking scream of pain filled the air, together with Grace's confused yell of 'Ben! No!'

Ben ignored her and held the powerful voltage against the cop's throat for just an instant longer, until he was confident that the guy was well out of the fight before he ever got into it. Then Ben looked up and saw the second cop backing away, his smirk replaced with a look of startled fear. Turning. Feet slipping and sliding on the compacted roadside snow. Tripping over himself in his jittery haste to sprint back to the relative safety of the patrol vehicle.

Not moving anything like quickly enough.

Ben launched into the chase and caught up with the fleeing cop like a lean, hungry panther running down a fat, lumbering wild hog. The guy let out a gasp of shock and fright as he was slammed to the ground and his face crunched into the snow. His torch went tumbling out of his hand and clattered onto the road. He tried to twist and roll onto his back, lashing out in self-defence with the identical shock prod he'd produced moments earlier. His weapon of attack was now his only chance of protecting himself against his would-be victim who'd so suddenly and violently turned the tables against him.

But that chance was short-lived and futile. The sole of Ben's left boot came stamping down hard and pinned the cop's wrist to the icy road. Then Ben dropped his right knee to pin the cop's other arm. He saw the terror flash in the guy's eyes. Then came the fizz, crackle and scream as the metal contacts of the shock prod pressed into the soft flesh under the cop's chin and let loose with several thousand volts of electricity. A small taste of his own medicine before Ben decided to be merciful and knocked him senseless with a hard crack to the side of the face.

Grace was standing on the verge, staring at Ben as though he'd lost his mind. She yelled again, more loudly, 'Ben! What the fuck?'

Ben ignored her a second time, though he knew he'd have to explain things to her before long. He quickly rifled through the cop's coat pockets and found his police ID in its leather holder and a thick wallet. When he opened up the wallet he wasn't surprised by its contents. He gave them a sniff, then checked the ID. The cop's name was PC Murray Brown.

'Nice meeting you, Murray.' Ben stood up, stepped away from the unconscious heap in the snow, and turned to look at Grace. Explanation time. Her hair was all awry in the cold wind and the look of wide-eyed bewilderment on her face was lit blue and red by the patrol car's swirling roof light.

Ben pointed at the two inert shapes on the ground and said, 'I thought you people were trained in unarmed combat. These two could barely wrestle their way out of bed in the morning.'

Grace could hardly speak. Her mouth opened and closed twice before she managed to say, 'Ben, what the hell are you thinking? Those are *police officers* you just assaulted!'

Ben shook his head and replied, 'No, they're not.'

Chapter 45

Ben said to Grace, 'They're not police officers. They're *bent* police officers. That's a whole other matter. When they chose not to play by the rules, they gave away all privileges of their office and opened themselves up to the consequences.'

Grace just shook her head in bemusement. Ben opened up PC Brown's wallet to show her what was inside. 'How many cops you know are running around with two months' salary in crisp new fifty-pound notes stuffed in their pockets?'

'What are you talking about?'

Backlit by the patrol car lights, Ben walked over to the first cop and knelt beside him. The guy stirred and groaned, showing signs of wanting to wake up. So Ben tapped him on the skull and put him to sleep again, then went through his coat pockets. Same result. Another bulging wallet containing a thick wad of cash. He sniffed that one, too. The name on the police ID was PC Douglas Rennie.

Ben tossed the wallet to Grace, and she caught it one-handed. He said, 'This payoff happened so recently, the notes smell like they just came out of the machine. And whoever gave these jokers all this cash also gave them these little toys to play with.'

He tossed her the shock prod, which Grace deftly caught with her other hand. He said, 'Four thousand volts gives

282

quite a jolt, as you saw. People use them on pigs and cattle. Those things have skin like leather. We don't. It hurts like hell, but that didn't stop your colleague PC Rennie from wanting to use his on you. Correct me if I'm wrong, but I don't think they're part of official police kit.'

Grace stared at the banknotes she was clutching in one hand, then at the shock prod in the other, then down at Rennie, then up at Ben. 'I don't—'

He said, 'I do. Because if you're an officer playing by the rules, you've got to account to your superiors for every time you use your Taser. These two were working off the books. Hence the need to keep it under the table and improvise a little. Hence also the other item of kit they're not using tonight.' He pointed. 'Look at their uniforms. No body cams. Most forces are issued them now, including yours. But this was one "arrest" they didn't want anyone to see.'

He left her struggling with her inevitable conclusions and went back over to the slumped heap that was PC Murray Brown. The phone that the cop had used to make his call moments earlier was still in his coat pocket. Ben fished it out. 'Just like he was using this to tell his bosses that he'd found us, instead of calling it in by radio. One look at our faces, they knew it was us, because they'd been tipped off in advance. It's a no-brainer, Grace. No other way to see it. Now do you understand?'

Ben checked the phone and saw that Brown's call had been to another mobile. He would have bet all the cops' payoff money that the number belonged to a disposable pay-as-you-go job, bought for cash, no names, no questions. The call record showed that several more calls had been made that day, to and from the same number. Nothing before then.

Grace said, 'Yeah, I think I do understand. So what the hell are we going to do now?'

283

'Much as I'd love to make a citizens' arrest and watch these chumps getting dragged off to jail, we have no way of knowing who else in the local force has been bought off. So I vote we get out of here. But first I want to make sure our friends Murray and Dougie can't follow us, when they wake up.'

Ben walked over to the police car, stepping over the unresponsive PC Brown. He opened up the driver's side and groped about under the steering wheel until he found the bonnet release latch, tugged it and heard the pop of the lid. Then he walked over to the edge of the road, where Brown's torch lay. He picked it up. A solid fistful of black metal tube, about a foot and a half long. Just the job, for what he had in mind. He carried the torch over to the car and tucked it between his knees while he lifted the bonnet lid the rest of the way up and held it in place with its support strut. Once that was done he snatched the torch back out from between his knees, turned it on and shone the strong beam around the engine compartment in search of the battery.

Ben was no kind of an expert car mechanic, and had pretty much forgotten everything of the army courses he'd been made to take back in the day, the aim of which was to teach Special Forces operatives how to reactivate derelict old motors they might need for transport deep behind enemy lines, when things got rough. Or how to sabotage working vehicles in order to compromise enemy movements, which was more to the point in this instance. But even a non-mechanic like him knew what a battery looked like. A square plastic box with two metal terminals about twelve inches apart, positive and negative. Brimming with volatile chemicals and large amounts of latent electrical energy that could all too easily be abused, for destructive purposes. That was one army course Ben remembered well.

He yanked the red and black plastic covers off the battery

terminals. Laid the metal torch sideways across the battery so that it was touching both contacts, shorting out the battery. Sparks fizzed, and kept fizzing. The current flowing across the shorted terminals would generate a lot of heat very quickly. Ben closed the bonnet lid, jamming the torch in place. As he turned and started walking back towards Grace and the Mercedes, thick acrid smoke was already billowing out from under the bonnet, followed seconds later by the first flash of flame. It wouldn't be long before the patrol car caught fire. He grabbed PC Brown by the ankles and dragged him a few feet further from the vehicle, so he wouldn't burn to death. Sometimes you needed to show consideration for your enemies.

Grace watched the flames pouring and curling out from under the patrol car's bonnet with her hands on her hips and a raised eyebrow. 'Couldn't you just have slashed the tyres or something?'

'It's a chilly night,' Ben said. 'We wouldn't want your police colleagues to get hypothermia.'

'Not to mention that you have a flair for the dramatic. Admit it.'

'Something tells me things are going to get more dramatic from here,' he said.

Chapter 46

They got back in the Mercedes and took off, leaving the burning police car and the two unconscious cops by the roadside. Grace sat in silence, frowning deeply. Ben lit a Gauloise. It was still two hours before daybreak. The snow had died away and the clouds had rolled aside to uncover an inky sky studded with bright stars. He turned off the road two miles later at the first exit, and followed a maze of narrowing lanes for several more miles until their route took them close by the edge of a still, milkily starlit body of water with looming black hills in the background.

The sat nav showed that they were close by the shores of Loch Bà. The place was as desolate and empty as any wilderness Ben had travelled in. He turned off the road and bumped over rocks to pull up on the slope of the shore, the car's nose pointing down at the glistening water.

'This is a good spot,' he told Grace.

'For what, sightseeing?'

'We need to dump this car,' Ben replied. 'It's got a big red flag on it. And I couldn't have returned it to the rental company anyway.'

'You could have said you were shot at by bandits.'

'That probably happens all the time around here, doesn't it?'

She sighed. 'Damn it, I was getting to like this car. And we're miles from anywhere.'

'We shouldn't have too far to walk to find alternative transport,' Ben said.

'You're not going to find a bus out here at this hour, or any other.'

'A bus wasn't what I had in mind.'

'Not too many car rental outlets either. For what good it would do you.'

'Don't rub it in,' Ben said.

Ben got out of the Mercedes and Grace reluctantly followed. The stars cast their light over the dappled waters of Loch Bà. They gathered their things from the back of the car. Ben made the choice to leave the crossbow, the ghillie suit and the unused night-vision goggles behind. He regretted ditching them, but he needed to travel light. Then he put the transmission in neutral, let off the handbrake, and they stood back and watched as the Mercedes rolled down the slope. Slowly at first, then gathering speed, bumping over the rocks and snow, until it splashed nose-first into the loch. Ben had chosen the spot well. In moments the deep black waters closed over the bonnet, then the roof; and then it was gone.

He sensed Grace's tension and put his arm around her shoulders to give her a reassuring squeeze. Said softly, 'It's going to be okay. Trust me.'

Grace was shaking her head. 'It's not, though, is it? I can't believe what's happening. It's like I'm having a weird dream that I can't wake up from.'

'Then let's prove that we're not dreaming,' he said. 'We can do that with one call.'

'To who?'

'I don't know yet. But I can guess.' Ben took out the phone

he'd captured from Murray Brown. Slid his thumb over the screen to unlock it, and saw that there was just one bar of reception out here in the wilderness. One was enough. He redialled the number Brown had called earlier. It rang several times, then just as Ben was expecting the call to go to voicemail a gruff voice, irritable with lack of sleep, grumbled 'Macleod. So what's happening, Murray? Do you have them or what?'

Ben's guess had been dead right. He smiled and said, 'Detective Inspector Fergus Macleod?' As he said the name, he glanced at Grace and saw her flinch as though she'd been slapped.

Grace wasn't the only surprised one. There was a stunned silence on the other end. A smart guy would have ended the call right away. Except it was already too late, even for that.

'Murray can't come to the phone right now,' Ben said. 'He's too busy having a party with all that money you gave him. I presume it wasn't your own money. You were just passing it down the line, weren't you?'

'H-Hope?' Macleod stammered.

'Give your boss a message from me,' Ben said. 'Tell him that I have something he wants. Tell him that if he's interested, he can phone this number and we'll talk business.' He ended the call.

Grace's expression was as tight as violin strings, her mouth a thin clamped line. Ben said, 'So there it is. Sorry, Grace, but your bosses Macleod and Coull are in on this whole thing. Supplementing their police pay by moonlighting for the main man.'

Grace said tersely, 'Charles Stuart.'

Ben nodded. 'Ninety-nine per cent for sure. First we find out that a member of the Dishonourables, the gang that killed Jamie McGlashan and tried to kill us, is working for

288

Stuart. Now this. Doesn't take a fortune to persuade the likes of Macleod and Coull to switch sides. Especially if they're also mixed up in murder, attempted murder, and maybe kidnapping too. And Stuart has a lot of money. The kind that buys a great deal of influence and protection. With enough resources on tap, you can even own the local law.'

'We're living in modern-day Scotland. It's not the Wild West.'

'Times change,' Ben said. 'But people don't. Power and money hold as much sway over men's minds as they did all through history. That's not my opinion. That's a fact.'

'But what did you mean, "Tell your boss we have something he wants"? We don't, do we?'

'No, but we can trick him into thinking we do, and we can use that to draw him out. Macleod will already have told him by now, and he'll be going crazy wondering what we're offering him. When he gets in touch, then we'll be able to eliminate that one per cent of doubt that Stuart is the person behind all this.'

'I can't wait,' she said sourly.

'You won't have to. I don't think he'll hang around too long to call. In the meantime, let's get moving. We've a lot of ground to cover.'

All that was left of the sunken Mercedes was a few bubbles and spreading ripples on the starlit surface of the loch. Ben shouldered his bag. They turned away from the shore and started walking over the rough ground back towards the road. Grace asked, 'Which way?'

'Left,' he said, pointing.

'Any particular reason?'

'If in doubt, I always turn left. Doesn't really matter which way we go. We're bound to find something sooner or later.'

'Fine, then left it is.'

They headed up the road, keeping to the apex where the snow was thinnest. Hitching a ride to the nearest town or village was an option that floated in Ben's mind. Out here you would hear a car or truck coming from a mile away, but the only sound was the soft moan of the wind and the crunch of frozen snow under their feet. Ben had Brown's phone in his hand and kept waiting for it to ring.

Nobody called. Ben and Grace kept walking, speaking very little, both of them focused on keeping moving and staying warm. They walked a mile of the lonely, dark, winding road without seeing the slightest sign of human habitation. Then another. After a long silence she asked, 'Do you think Boonzie's still alive?'

'I have to,' he replied.

'And that Stuart's got him?'

'That's what I believe.'

'If they thought he knew where the gold was . . .' Her voice trailed off.

'They'd torture him,' Ben said. 'For days on end. Until he talked.'

'Who are these people, who would do such things?'

'Dead men walking,' Ben said. 'That's who they are.'

On they walked. Then, at exactly eight a.m., with the dawn still some forty-five minutes away, Brown's phone began to buzz in Ben's hand.

Chapter 47

It was a man's voice on the phone, deep and resonant, not old, but not young, with an accent whose audible Scottish-born origins had been smoothed around the edges by decades of international business travel. He sounded outwardly calm and cool, but Ben sensed an undertone of agitation, like ocean currents swirling beneath Arctic sheet ice. The voice said, 'Am I to presume that I'm speaking with Mr Ben Hope? Or perhaps I should address you as Major?'

Ben replied, 'And am I to presume that I'm talking to Mr Charles Stuart?'

'We meet at last. I wish I could say it was a pleasure.'

'That's the nice thing about business negotiations,' Ben said. 'You don't have to like the people you're dealing with.'

'I take it, then, that I'm correctly informed and you wish to do business with me?'

'When one person is in possession of something that the other would do anything to obtain, a sober commercial transaction is the more mature way to resolve things for everyone's benefit. As opposed to, say, going to war. I don't think that either of us wants to do this the hard way.'

'As I think you know, I'm fully prepared for that option.'

'Nobody's ever fully prepared for a war,' Ben said. 'I'm

offering you a far preferable alternative. One that you get to walk away from unhurt.'

'Then you do have something that I want?' Stuart was doing his best to sound composed, but as they circled the main issue it was becoming harder for him to contain his anticipation.

'I'd say you want it more than anything else in the world,' Ben said. 'Considering the risks you're obviously prepared to take to get hold of it.'

'You have my attention. So what exactly are you putting on the table here?'

'Rather than take my word for it,' Ben said, 'why don't you let me show you? Give me an email address and you can see for yourself, right now.'

Stuart reeled off the address. Ben took out his own phone and sent him the image of the gold coin that Mirella had forwarded to him three days ago. Ben waited for the email to land. When it did, he could almost palpably sense Stuart getting all pepped up and jumpy on the end of the line. Ben said, 'If that looks like something you might be interested in, then I can tell you it's only a tiny sample of what I've got. There are thousands more.'

Now Stuart was fairly hopping. 'How many thousands?'

'As part of our negotiation process, you'll be allowed to view the merchandise in person, and count and recount them to your heart's content,' Ben told him. 'For the purposes of this discussion, suffice to say that there are enough of the damn things to fill two medium-size vans. Except if you did, the weight would bust the suspension. It took us weeks to dig it all up. Took even longer to count it all, once we'd smuggled it away and stashed it safely where nobody could find it.'

'Where did you find it?'

'Right from under your nose, Stuart. It's been sitting buried in the middle of the Loch Ardaich pine forest all these years. Personally, I have no interest in where it originally came from or who put it there. If it was up to me, I'd melt the whole bloody lot of it down into bars.'

'If you did that, it would instantly be worth half as much. This is about historical value, not just gold.'

'Yeah, well, history isn't my thing, Stuart. And a pile of obsolete currency isn't much use to me. But of all the people in the world who'd love to get their hands on them, something tells me you're first in line. Are you ready to make me an offer I can't refuse?'

Stuart warned, 'You'd better not be leading me on, Hope.'

'I always deliver on my promises,' Ben replied. 'Trust me when I say that you'll get what's coming to you.'

'Then let's get this started. How do you wish to proceed?'

'Are you at home right now?'

'I have several homes,' Stuart said ostentatiously. 'I'm presently staying here at my Scottish residence, if that's what you mean.'

'Then here's what you're going to do,' Ben told him. 'If you can bear to come down off your high perch and mix with us poor common folks for a couple of hours. You're going to take a drive out to Kinlochardaich. I presume you know where that is.'

'Is that your current location?'

'My current location is of no concern to you,' Ben said. 'But I'll be at the village pub at one o'clock this afternoon. Not because I'm interested in socialising with a scumbag like yourself, but because it's a public place where I can be reasonably assured that you can't bring your henchmen to cause trouble for me.'

Stuart chuckled. 'You're a very careful man, aren't you?'

'Which is why, if I catch even the tiniest whiff of a trick or a trap, this deal is instantly void and you can forget about ever seeing a single one of these coins. I'll simply go to another buyer. I have several more interested parties already lined up.'

'Really? Who? I know most of the collectors.'

'Again, not your concern. Don't waste my time. Will you meet me, or are we done here?'

'Very well. I'll agree to your request. Keep talking.'

'Needless to say, you come alone. You won't see me when you get to the meeting place, but you can be sure I'll be watching every move you make. Park your car out front where I can see that nobody else is inside it. Then walk inside, go to the bar and order a pint.'

'I don't drink beer.'

'Then order a glass of wine.'

'The wine there is paint-stripper.'

'You don't have to drink it,' Ben said. 'Because you won't be staying in the pub long. Once I'm satisfied that you haven't brought along any of your little friends to intrude on our private conversation, I'll make myself known to you and we'll go for a spin together in your car.'

'How nice. Where will we be going?'

'To the actual meeting place,' Ben said. 'We'll be joined there by my associate.'

'That would be Miss Kirk.'

'I'm not the only one who's been doing his homework,' Ben said.

'And then what?'

'And then we can get down to brass tacks. Or, in this instance, gold ones.'

'Why should I believe any of what you're telling me?'

'You don't have to. You'll see for yourself soon enough.'

'Only your involvement in this matter seems, well, a little perplexing to me. I can't quite work it out.'

Ben paused a beat. He was venturing even deeper into the realms of fiction here, and couldn't afford for Stuart to sense the deception. 'It's not rocket science, Stuart. Ross Campbell was the one who made the discovery, and told his business partner Ewan McCulloch. Then Ewan's uncle and I got involved, because of our expertise. Ewan and Ross were a little concerned about security. They had this crazy, weird idea that someone might try to hurt them and snatch the gold for themselves. Imagine that.'

Stuart said nothing, waiting for more.

'But Ross didn't trust the McCullochs,' Ben went on. 'He thought Ewan was planning on running out on him. So he never told him exactly where the loot was hidden.'

Grace had been listening intently, gleaning as much as she could of the conversation from Ben's end. Now she frowned, not understanding why he'd said that.

'Are you saying that you and Ross Campbell dug it up together?' Stuart asked. 'Because my sources happen to have informed me that you left your home in France for Inverness just days ago, after Campbell was already dead. Which would then point to a lie. And I don't truck with liars.' Charles Stuart, paragon of moral virtue.

'Your bought police stooges are only half right. They can't know that I was in London on other business the week before Ross Campbell drowned, and drove up.' The bluff sounded pretty wild to Ben, but Stuart couldn't disprove it, and Ben was counting on him being too fixated on the gold to pick apart the logic. 'He took me to the forest and showed me where he'd found the first coins. We soon found the rest, and we stashed it somewhere safe before I had to return to France for a few days. Now that Ross is dead, I'm the only one who has any idea where it is.'

Stuart mulled over Ben's story for a few moments, and

seemed to accept it as truth. 'Then it appears I'm speaking with the right person. So let me get this straight. I view the merchandise, we agree on a cash settlement, you get your money and I don't hear from you again?'

'The money's all I give a damn about,' Ben said. 'What else could possibly matter?'

'I thought perhaps you might be somewhat concerned about your friend. McCulloch the elder.'

Ben had to use all his willpower to keep his tone unemotional. 'I told you, Ross didn't trust the McCullochs, either Ewan or his uncle. They were too greedy for their own good. So whatever happened there, happened. No use crying over spilt milk. I don't have a problem with it. If I choose to be unbothered, ethically or legally, then, I suppose, so do you.'

Now Grace was staring at Ben as though he'd lost his mind. She held her arms out with her fingers splayed wide and mouthed, 'WHAT?'

'As you say, spilt milk,' Stuart replied casually. 'But what you tell me is interesting. It explains why the old man didn't appear to know anything about all this, even after we pressured him a little. I have to say, I was rather disappointed by his apparent recalcitrance, at the time. Now I understand.'

A chill went through Ben's whole body. He had the phone so tightly clamped to his ear that it hurt. He was trying very hard not to picture the kinds of things men like this would have done to make Boonzie talk. 'I wouldn't waste my time putting any more pressure on him, if I were you.'

'I'd already come to that conclusion myself.'

Ben closed his eyes, dreading what might be coming next. 'So what'd you do, get rid of him?'

'Oh, no, he's still enjoying our warm hospitality here. Though after this conversation, that situation may come to a swift end. What do you think?'

'Do what you like with the old git,' Ben said nonchalantly. Inside, he was screaming. 'Makes no difference to me. Just make sure you turn up to our meeting' – glancing at his watch – 'just under five hours from now. Remember, Stuart, this is strictly a one-time offer. Don't screw it up.'

'I'll be there.'

'I know you will,' Ben replied, and hung up the call.

'Oh my God, Ben,' Grace said. Still staring at him in blank incomprehension.

Ben reeled. He doubled over, breathing hard and as badly winded as if a heavyweight boxing champion had landed the hardest knockout blow of their career to his solar plexus. Because Ben had just taken the biggest gamble he'd ever taken in his life, and put that of his friend in the balance.

Grace said, 'I'm seriously at a loss as to why you would play it that way.'

Ben took a few deep breaths to clear his head. He looked at her, saw the pain and confusion in her eyes. It took him an effort to speak. 'Because I needed to make this as easy and straightforward as possible for Stuart, if there was any chance of luring him in. He has to believe that all I care about is the money. We get him on his own, he's ours.'

'I get that part. It's the not giving a shit about your friend that I'm not understanding. Just when you found out that Boonzie's still alive after all, you gave Stuart the green light to kill him. What the hell were you thinking?'

Ben said, 'I was thinking two things. First, if I'm the only one who knows where the gold is, it takes away their incentive to torture the truth out of him. If he's still alive after all this time, it's because they couldn't really be sure what he knew or not. They've been hedging their bets. Second, I was thinking that a man like Stuart would never trust a living soul. He's always going to give himself a back way out.'

'So?'

'So he won't kill Boonzie. Not if he's serious about meeting us alone. Because there's no way he would just believe what I said, and he needs some leverage against me if things go bad. I try to double-cross him or back out of the deal, he has Boonzie as a bargaining chip.'

'So when we meet with Stuart tonight, the plan is to grab him, right? But how does that work, if his men still have Boonzie hostage?'

'I just have to trust that our hostage is worth more to them than theirs is. Stuart's the one paying their wages.'

'So they have to release Boonzie if they want their boss back. Which they're not going to get.'

'Correct.'

'And then we've still got the Dishonourables to deal with.'

He shook his head. 'No, *I* still have the Dishonourables to deal with. That part, I'll handle alone.'

'It's messy as hell,' Grace said.

'Those are the cards we've been dealt. It's the only way to play them.'

'And dangerous.'

Ben nodded. 'Yes. It is. For everyone. But especially for them.'

Grace sighed. 'So what now?'

'Now we have until one o'clock to get to Kinlochardaich and put this in motion.'

Chapter 48

As the dawn eventually began to break, the reds and golds and purples of the rising sun appeared like a distant firestorm over the hills. Another mile; then another. No houses, no cottages, no farms. Ben began to wonder if he should have turned right after dumping the car. Grace was saying nothing, strolling quietly beside him with cheeks as red as apples from the cold – but he sensed she was thinking the same thing.

They kept walking. Still nothing. The morning was crisp and beautiful. The kind of morning that should fill a person's heart with joy and make them feel that all was well with the world. If only it had been. Time was slipping by too quickly. They now had just three hours before Ben's rendezvous with Stuart.

Then, just as it seemed the empty wilderness would go on for ever, they came across the farm at the bottom of its own long dirt track.

More correctly, it was a rural property that had once been a farm, back in the days before it had become a semi-ruin. The house's stone walls were mossy and many of the panes in its rotted window frames were broken. It stood in a cracked concrete yard surrounded by outbuildings in an even more neglected state. The place appeared as if it had been uninhabited for the last thirty years, except for the two cars parked out front: one a rough old Mazda estate, the other a VW with one headlight missing and rust holes big enough to stick your fist through.

'You think anyone's at home?' Grace said.

'Let's find out.'

Ben was carrying enough cash to buy both bangers. But he needed only one, and had already set his sights on the Mazda as he went to knock on the farmhouse door. Not everyone was happy to sell a car to a total stranger, but it was amazing what a smiling face and a fat handful of crisp banknotes could do.

Nobody answered the door, so Ben pounded harder. After about a dozen hard thumps he heard footsteps and someone yelling, 'All right, I'm comin', I'm comin'!' The lock rattled and the door creaked open a few inches, and the gaunt face of a skinny middle-aged guy with a shaven head peered through the gap. He said in a slurry voice, 'Aye? Jonesy, is that you?'

One look at him was enough to tell Ben that the guy was blasted out of his skull on some kind of illicit substance, whose scent wafting from the open doorway only served to confirm that impression. His bleary eyes took a few instants to focus on the two unexpected visitors on the doorstep and realise that neither of them was Jonesy, before they suddenly widened in alarm and he came to life and shot panic-stricken back into the house, shouting 'Fuck! Fuck! It's the polis!'

Ben called after him, 'Hey, it's okay. We're not the police.' Technically speaking, only half true. But either way, the house's occupants weren't interested in hanging around to find out. Several more voices were raised in panic from inside. A woman let out a raucous shriek and someone else started screaming, 'Why the fuck d'ye open the door?' To which the slurred voice of the shaven-headed guy yelled back, 'I thought it wiz fuckin' Jonesy, didna?'

'Looks like we interrupted something,' Grace said drily. A second later, they heard a back door crash open and the sound of multiple running footsteps escaping from the rear of the house.

Ben stepped into the front hall. Dustballs the size of dead rats covered the floor and the walls were streaked with mildew. Three nails had been hammered into the plaster near the doorway, with car keys dangling from them. He selected the one with the mouldy leather Mazda fob, and plucked it from its hook.

'That was easy,' he said. 'If the thing starts, we're out of here without further ado.'

'Thought you were going to buy it,' Grace said.

'I don't get the impression the residents of this hippy commune, drug den, cannabis social club, or whatever it is, would spend the money wisely or responsibly,' he replied.

'Probably right about that.'

'I wouldn't feel comfortable about supporting their unhealthy lifestyle.'

'It's the moral choice,' she agreed.

'So we'll just nick their car.'

'Gets my vote.'

They walked back outside. Four men and a woman were hurriedly scrambling away across the half-frozen slushy field adjoining the house. Staggering, in the case of two of them. Ben shook his head and tried the Mazda's door. It wasn't locked. He tossed his bag in the back, got behind the wheel, stuck the key in the ignition, said a quick and silent prayer, and gave it a twist. To his relief and actual surprise, the engine coughed into life instantly.

Grace said, 'Oh-oh. Maybe this won't be so easy after all.'

Ben looked where she was pointing. Two of the fleeing druggies had turned back, having apparently realised that they weren't about to get arrested after all, and that the unexpected visitors were in the act of stealing one of their vehicles. One was the shaven-headed skinny guy. The other was larger, and angrier-looking. As they ran back towards the yard they disappeared inside a lean-to toolshed and came back out a moment later brandishing a shovel and an iron bar.

'They can't do us any harm,' Ben said.

'Maybe not, but they can get in that crappy old VW and come after us.'

'If it goes.'

'We cops are drawn to a good car chase like midges to a lightbulb. You want to attract more unwanted attention?'

Ben sighed. 'Christ. The things you have to do.'

'Don't pout. This was all your idea.'

The shaven-headed skinny guy and his angry pal were still about thirty yards away and closing fast when Ben stepped out of the Mazda with the sawn-off shotgun in one hand and two spare shells in the other. The two druggies skidded to a halt at the sight of the weapon. Ben kept his finger deliberately off the trigger as he pointed it their way, purely for effect. Then he swung it in a big dramatic arc to aim at the old Volkswagen. With a noise like a thunderclap that echoed around the farmyard he discharged one barrel into the old car's bonnet lid. The heavy buckshot round perforated the rusty metal and turned it into a colander. Then he lowered his aim a few inches and squeezed off the other barrel.

BOOM. The car's front grille dematerialised and bits of twisted plastic flew in all directions. Fluid gushed from a ragged hole in the radiator.

Ben broke open the shotgun and the smoking cartridges ejected. He loaded the two fresh rounds into the chambers and snapped the gun shut. By now, the two druggies had dropped their improvised weapons and were stumbling off as fast as they could in the opposite direction. Just to reinforce the point Ben blasted one front wheel of the VW, then the rear. The car sank lopsidedly down on its shredded tyres. A shattered wheel trim rolled away across the yard. The echo of the gunshots drifted away in the cold morning air, and would sound like crow bangers to a distant ear. Just another day in the countryside.

He got back in the car and stuck the gun under the driver's seat. 'Happy now?'

'Whatever gets the job done,' she said.

'What kind of police officer are you, anyway?'

'Hanging out with a guy like you changes a girl.'

Chapter 49

Ben drove fast away from the farm, and within minutes they were twisting through the maze of country lanes as they worked out the rest of the route northwards. By Ben's reckoning Kinlochardaich was still at least fifty miles away, which meant they had little time to waste.

Their stolen car was functional enough, but handled evilly after the modern sophistication of the Mercedes, its worn tyres pattering and slithering on the bad roads and the tired suspension creaking and groaning as he ploughed ahead with his foot hard on the gas. With the fuel gauge deep down in the red they had to stop for petrol before hitting the A82 highway, the main route from the south, near a place called Black Mount. An hour later they were racing through the spectacular scenery of Glencoe, climbing to over a thousand feet over the great wilderness of Rannoch Moor before slowly descending through the glen itself.

'To live in such a beautiful country,' Grace murmured, more to herself than to Ben, 'where so many terrible and ugly things happen.' Snapping out of her reflective moment she turned to him and said, 'There's one thing we haven't talked about. We need to think of an alternative meeting place to bring Stuart to. Assuming we even get to that stage.'

'It has to be somewhere out of the way,' Ben said. 'Very private, and not too far to drive to. Any ideas?'

'I was thinking, there's an abandoned sanatorium about six miles north of the village. At the turn of the last century they treated tuberculosis patients there. Then it was used as a billet for troops in World War Two, and that was the last time it was ever used for anything. Supposed to be haunted, according to some. If you believe in all that ghostly crap.'

Ben nodded. 'That could work.'

'So let's say Stuart goes along, and you get him out there. How do we deal with it?'

'We lead him to the secret room where we tell him we stashed all the gold,' Ben said. 'We throw open the door. He's distracted for a second, seeing nothing but an empty space, and before he knows what's happening he's waking up strapped in a chair, gagged and bound with a hell of a headache, where none of his men could ever find him.'

'Okay. And what then?'

'Still working on that one,' he replied. 'I'm kind of making this up as I go along. But I'll think of something.'

'I wish I had your confidence.'

At that moment, Ben could have used some of that himself. But he didn't admit it to Grace.

Soon after, the iron Ballachulish Bridge carried them across the narrows of Loch Leven. From there, the gently undulating highway hugged the shores of Loch Linnhe, miles of white-capped forest on one side of the road and the slate-grey waters on the other, all the way north to Fort William. The winter traffic was ponderous but steady. Ben had been closely watching the clock throughout the journey, and to his relief they were still an hour ahead of schedule as they approached Kinlochardaich.

Grace asked, 'Okay, so what's the plan?'

'Show me the way to the sanatorium. I'll drop you off there, then come back to the village. All being well, next time I see you I'll have Stuart with me.'

'You must be nuts if you think I'm hanging around in a spooky old building by myself for over an hour.'

'I thought you didn't believe in all that ghostly crap.'

'And I'm totally famished. Couldn't we grab a bite of breakfast first?'

'Hell of a late breakfast,' Ben said.

'Call it an early lunch, then.'

'There isn't time.'

'Come on. Twenty minutes, tops. We can afford it. After all that hiking in the freezing cold this morning, what I wouldn't do for something warm and filling.'

'More soya meat-surrogate with yesterday's limp salad?'

'I was actually thinking of whizzing us up a plate of bacon, eggs and beans. You look like you could do with it yourself.'

Ben had to admit it sounded good. 'I think we can make time for that.'

'My place, then. I've got all the necessaries in my wee kitchen.'

He shook his head. 'No chance. After what happened last night, it's a bad idea for either of us to go back there in case they've got more people waiting for us. Whereas nobody knows about the Gunn cottage.'

'Your place, then. Except that it'll be like an icebox in there. You drop me off, and I'll get the fire lit and everything ready in two shakes of a lamb's tail while you swing by the village store and pick up the food. Okay?'

The joys of domestic living. Too tired to argue with her, Ben shrugged again and said, 'Whatever. Fine by me.'

And so it was decided. Ben pulled up outside the cottage long enough for Grace to hop out and catch the key that he tossed her. She gave him the crooked smile and said, 'See you in a minute, babes. Don't forget the cooking oil.'

He drove off still seeing that damned smile in his mind's eye and wondering whether he'd ever been called 'babes' before. Not that he could recall. But then, he'd never started really getting to like a quirky, dark-haired Scottish police-woman before, either. And a voice in his head had to remind him that, in the midst of all that was happening, this was neither the time nor the place to start liking someone.

Confusing. Ben lit a Gauloise as he drove over to the village stores. The midday sky had choked up with white clouds and it was beginning to snow again. He parked the Mazda outside the shop and went inside. The same old guy with the bushy white moustache was tending the counter. They exchanged a nod and Ben set about culling the items he needed from the shelves. A pack of streaky bacon rashers, a box of farm-fresh eggs, a large tin of baked beans and the bottle of vegetable oil he'd been specifically ordered not to forget. He shelled out a twenty from the bent cops' payoff cash, waited for his change, bagged up his stuff, thanked the old guy and walked back outside into the falling snow.

That was when PC Brown's phone rang a second time.

Ben halted in the middle of the pavement. Large fluffy snowflakes settled on his hair and shoulders. A cold trickle went down the back of his neck. He didn't move for a second. Brown's phone kept ringing. Ben was wondering who was calling. He had a bad feeling about it.

Slowly, he reached into the pocket where the phone was and took it out. Hit reply and held it to his ear.

And then the worst happened.

Stuart's familiar voice said, 'Change of plan, Mr Hope.'

Whatever this was about, Ben didn't like it. 'So you've decided you don't want what I have to offer?'

307

'Not at all. I just decided to change the terms of our arrangement.'

'Then there is no arrangement,' Ben said.

Stuart gave a laugh. He sounded confident and in control. Almost happy. Ben didn't like that either.

'I think you'll come around to seeing it differently,' Stuart said. 'Considering that now I have something else of yours that I'm sure you'd like to have back in relatively undamaged condition. All the time you and little Miss Kirk have been spending together lately, it seems you've grown quite fond. Call it a trade. You give me the gold. And you get to see her again, alive and intact. As opposed to diced up into small pieces.'

Ben said nothing. He felt suddenly very cold, as though his blood had frozen to a standstill. The world seemed to have tilted sideways. His feet felt cemented to the pavement.

Stuart chuckled again. 'Hello? Are you there?'

Ben took a long, slow breath. The ice water in his veins began to grow hot as volcanic lava. 'Where is she?'

Stuart said, 'At this moment she's on her way to my home, in the capable hands of two of my employees whom I had stationed at your cottage in your absence, awaiting your return from wherever it is you've been gallivanting off to. I understand she's a little bruised, having put up quite a spirited fight. But otherwise unharmed. For the moment.'

'If you hurt her, this will go badly for you.'

'As if it wasn't going to already, had I gone along with your plan? You must think I'm an idiot, if you expected me to believe I'd walk away unscathed from our so-called business meeting. So here are the new deal terms. If you prefer not to see Miss Kirk hacked up into dog meat, I suggest you get yourself over here as fast as you can.'

'I know where to find you.'

'Good. I don't think I need to specify that you come alone, because now you really *are* alone. Then you can deliver me the merchandise. Whereupon you get your lady friend back, and we shake hands like gentlemen and carry on our separate ways. Agreed?'

'Doesn't sound as though I have much of a choice.'

'None whatsoever, Mr Hope. Now I really think you ought to get on your way. I'm not the most patient man, and I've already waited far too long to get what's mine.'

Chapter 50

As a child, Ben had been haunted by a nightmare that visited him often, always the same. In the dream he found himself trapped in an empty house, whose dark and menacing corridors he wandered alone, lost and frightened. The house had many doors, but every time he came to a door in the hope that behind it was a way out of his prison, he was too afraid to open it in case of some unimaginable terror lurking there. One by one, bit by bit, every possible escape route was closed off to him, until none remained and he knew that he was doomed to remain locked in there for ever with the monsters from the encroaching darkness. But dreams being dreams, just as all seemed lost Ben had always woken up and found himself mercifully transported back to the sanctuary of his bedroom, shaken but safe.

Now the nightmare was for real. He was trapped with no way out, no chance of waking up. Just the knowledge that only pain and death lay behind every door in front of him. He couldn't afford trying to recruit outside help from the stalwart comrades he knew would rally to his side, because the sand would too quickly run out of the hourglass before he could make that happen. Couldn't break the rule of a lifetime and run to the police, because there was no way to tell which of them he could trust and which were corrupt. Couldn't leave

Grace in the hands of Stuart and the Dishonourables. Couldn't turn away from Boonzie, now that he knew for sure that his friend was alive and a prisoner.

Only one path remained open. Ben just had to accept that Stuart had him by both balls. And that his sole option was to face the man and do whatever he needed to do to make things all right. Or to die knowing that at least his friends hadn't suffered alone.

If need be, Ben was good with that option.

There was a litter bin outside the village shop. He dumped the bag of groceries into it. Wouldn't be needing them. Then snapped Brown's phone in half and dropped the pieces in there, too. Would no longer be needing that, either. He felt suddenly clear-minded and focused as he walked to the Mazda, got behind the wheel and restarted the engine.

Here we go, then.

The map in his mind told him how to get to Charles Stuart's castle, just a few miles south of Kinlochardaich. He sped out of the village, wipers slapping away the beating snow, the tyres battling for grip on the icy road, and a deathly stillness in his heart.

Ben knew he was getting close to his destination when he reached the bottom of a long, wooded road and saw the estate gates in front of him. The spiked wrought-iron railings stood twenty feet high. A pair of stone lions, not much less than lifesize, eyed him from atop the tall gateposts. He pulled up and waited as two men emerged from a gatehouse. Neither of them looked like the kind of individual who might join up with the Dishonourables. Permanent security staff, Ben guessed. One of them stepped through an inset gate and approached the driver's side of the Mazda, giving it the eye. Most visitors to the estate probably didn't show up in twenty-year-old rust buckets stolen from dopeheads. Ben gave his name. The security guy signalled to his colleague and they opened up the main gates and waved him through.

The private road continued through the estate, ascending towards the foot of a tall mountain whose wintry slopes loomed above the trees, its peak wreathed in mist. Ben passed a keeper's cottage and a field where Highland cattle foraged for grass among the snow. Finally, the tree-lined avenue turned a bend and Ben caught sight of Charles Stuart's Scottish residence in all its grandeur before him.

The spectacular images on the company website hadn't quite managed to convey the scale of the place. Nor its contrived artificiality. Carved into the foot of the snowy mountain, Stuart's castle with its ivied turrets and towers and battlements was like some Hollywood set designer's overblown fantasy made real, a wildly romanticised vision of a historical era that only really existed in movies where kilted heroes gallantly ran around rescuing beautiful ladies with long tresses, galloping white stallions through the heather-filled glens and battling their enemies on mountaintops with rapiers and claymores while delivering their stirring lines in a voice-coached twang that was more California than Caledonia.

Except that what was happening here inside these castle walls was very genuine. Nobody was acting. And any blood spilled would be real.

Ben passed between tall gates set into a perimeter wall and entered a courtyard. He pulled up at the foot of a broad sweep of stone steps, stepped out of the Mazda and was met there by three more men with grim faces and hard eyes. The man on the left, Ben had never seen before, but he had the look about him that the security guards on the gate hadn't. The man on the right was the killer who had fled from the scene of Jamie McGlashan's murder.

The one in the middle was Carl Hacker. He looked a little older and a little leaner than he had in Mad Monty's file photographs. He was wearing a suit and tie that made him look like a corporate bodyguard or a secret service agent. Ben could see the lump of the concealed pistol under the tailored line of his suit. The other two were wearing bulkier jackets that made it harder to spot the hidden weapons underneath, but they were there. Ben could almost smell them. Like he could smell their nervousness at meeting him face to face.

'Arms out to your sides,' Hacker said. 'Feet apart.'

Ben allowed himself to be frisked, which Hacker did very expertly and thoroughly while his two men searched the car and examined the contents of his bag. Ben had stopped off by the shores of Loch Ardaich en route to the castle, to dismantle his weapons and fling their components and ammunition into the deep, dark water.

Hacker took Ben's wallet and phone. Said, 'He's clean.'

'Nothing here either,' Jamie McGlashan's murderer called from the car. Hacker nodded. He took a step away from Ben and looked him hard in the eye. 'So you're the SAS high-roller we've all been dying to meet.'

'And you're the Pathfinder who lost his way.'

Hacker flushed an ugly colour. 'Let's go. He's waiting for you.'

They escorted Ben up the steps to a tall carved-oak double doorway and inside a grand hall with a flagstone floor and mounted suits of armour clutching a pike and a halberd guarding the entrance. He momentarily wondered how easy it would be to snatch one of the polearms from its knight's gauntlets and use it to disembowel all three of his escorts right there in the hallway. Probably not too hard, but he dismissed the idea.

'This way,' Hacker said. They led him from the hall down a wide corridor whose walls bristled with stuffed deer heads, with spiky antlers and staring glass eyes that seemed to watch you as you went by. Gleaming oak doors stood to the left and right. Like the ones in Ben's nightmare, they might offer an escape from his predicament or they might lead to a painful death for him and his friends. He calmed the butter-flies that were fluttering in his stomach, and walked on. At the bottom of the corridor was another tall double doorway. McGlashan's killer and his associate stood closely at Ben's sides as Hacker stepped to the door, knocked and pulled it open. Turning to Ben, he jerked his head and said, 'In there.'

They ushered Ben through the doorway without touching him. Wise move, because one shove and someone would have earned themselves a snapped finger. He stepped into a palatially sized room with dark carved-wood panelling and rich fleur-de-lys drapes. The parquet flooring was like a mirror, the centre of its expanse covered with a lush hand-woven carpet of Celtic knot design. More gleaming suits of armour stood around the walls clutching two-handed broad-swords. A rack held a decorative display of old flintlock muskets and Scottish daggers. At one end of the room was a vast sculpted stone fireplace in which a pile of logs was blazing fiercely. Above the mantelpiece hung an enormous gilt-framed oil painting of a historical figure.

At the other end of the room, standing gazing out of a ceiling-height leaded window overlooking the snowy castle grounds, was Charles Stuart.

Chapter 51

The great man slowly turned around as Ben stepped into the room. He was wearing a handsome tweed suit with an open-necked silk shirt and loafers. His silvery hair was slicked back and caught the light from the window. He was smiling the kind of self-congratulatory smile that he probably wore when he'd just come away triumphant from a boardroom battle or trampled one of his corporate rivals in a bidding war.

'Ben Hope. Welcome to my humble abode. So glad you could make it.'

Hacker and Jamie McGlashan's killer stepped into the room after Ben, the third guy remaining outside in the corridor. Hacker closed the door. He and his associate each stood to one side of the doorway, pistols now drawn and eyeing Ben warily, as though they expected him to try to tear their employer apart with his bare hands. That wasn't actually too far away from Ben's own thoughts, at that moment.

Ben repeated the question he'd asked earlier. 'Where is she?'

Stuart made an airy gesture. 'Somewhere nearby, where you'd never find her even if you could try. Hacker's man Graham is looking after her, equipped with an extremely sharp knife that he'd just love to get stuck in with. But don't worry, she's in good health. Whether she remains so is dependent on the degree to which you're prepared to cooperate.'

'It would be in your best interests that she does,' Ben said. 'Because if anything happens to her, you and I are going to have a serious problem.'

'I'd say you're the one with the problem, to put it mildly.'

'The worst that can happen to me is that I die trying. Nobody will ever be able to say I lived an unfulfilled life. Whereas you'd die knowing that you never even came close to getting the thing you most wanted.'

'I'm a businessman,' Stuart replied. 'I understand all about leveraging a deal. Though I wouldn't get too cocky if I were you. You're not in a strong position here, to say the least.'

'Boonzie McCulloch,' Ben said.

'What about him? Are you suddenly concerned about his welfare now?' Stuart gave that triumphant smile again, even more widely. 'Come, come. Surely you didn't think you had me convinced earlier, when you so artfully pretended not to be? Nice try, but I know every trick in the book. I practically wrote the damn thing myself.'

'Then he's alive.'

'Oh, very much so, in no small part thanks to our efforts in keeping him that way. But only two kinds of people exist in my world, Mr Hope. The ones who can be of use to me, and the ones who can't. Now that I have you exactly where I want you, I'm no longer feeling quite so motivated to play nursemaid to some sick old codger. Your friend just became surplus to requirements. Bad luck for him.'

'Same terms apply,' Ben said. 'Boonzie gets hurt, you can say bye-bye to your precious loot.'

'I really don't give a damn if he lives or dies. I'm interested in one thing only. Getting what's mine.'

Mine. Stuart's eyes flashed with a sort of manic glee when he said the word. There was something wrong inside his head. Something deeper and more dysfunctional than just obsessive greed or cold-blooded acquisitiveness. Ben could see it stamped all over his face.

'I don't get it, Stuart. You've got everything in the world, and yet you'd risk it all for a bunch of shiny coins.'

Stuart chuckled. 'Well, now, the word "bunch" would be something of an understatement, as you and I are both very well aware. To my certain knowledge, until your associate Ross Campbell got very lucky indeed, no more than a single bag of French Louis d'or had ever been recovered out of the one million, two hundred thousand livres of foreign aid that were secretly shipped to Scotland in September 1746 by French warships carrying munitions and funds to support the Jacobite uprising against the British crown.'

'So you're a historian now,' Ben said.

'Oh, I'm a little more than that. The man who led that uprising was my direct ancestor. That makes it highly personal to me.'

'Bonnie Prince Charlie.'

'None other. The seven large caskets containing the payroll for his rebel army were moved some twenty miles inland and buried in the ancient pine forest somewhere near the loch. Which means that the vast bulk of the gold has remained hidden there ever since, until now. In modern currency, something in the region of ten million pounds' worth. But of course, I needn't tell you that, since it seems you already have it in your possession.'

Ben said nothing. He was acutely aware that his subterfuge was running out of road here. All he could do was keep the lie going for as long as he could ride it, and hope that either he found a new way to use it, or something better came to him – fast.

Stuart was all lit up, possessed with a kind of electric frenzy that made him pace the floor in agitation as the words tumbled out of him. 'It's unbelievable. I've had experts hunting for it for years. We scoured every likely location for miles around. Spent months on end searching for Cluny's cave, where the Prince is said to have hidden from the English after his defeat at Culloden. I thought he might have stashed the treasure there, but we never found any such cave. I wasn't about to let that defeat me, however. Next I had historians analyse the letter that was found in a secondhand shop in Winchester in 2003, purporting to detail the deathbed confession of Neill Iain Ruari, who claimed to have witnessed the Jacobite clansmen burying the gold. Nothing came of that either. So I dug into the Clan Cameron archives, which tell of the efforts of one of the Prince's loyal followers on a covert mission to Scotland in 1753 to recover the lost treasure and plot the assassination of George II and the royal family. Zilch. Every historical text has been thoroughly examined. No stone left unturned. And yet this numbskull Ross Campbell, some local pipsqueak surveyor, somehow manages to stumble across what people have been dedicated to finding for centuries.'

'Just pure chance,' Ben said. 'The find of a lifetime. Not that he lived very long to enjoy it.'

'That's right, he didn't. You know how the saying goes, Mr Hope. To the victor belong the spoils. That would be me. And here's the part I like the most. I have no intention of paying for it. Nada. Not one penny. Am I clear? There will be no cash settlement involved in this trade.'

'I'd have thought a few million was peanuts to a man of your wealth.'

'And you'd be right,' Stuart said. 'But you won't be getting any of it. How's that make you feel? Knowing that you're the loser, and I'm the winner? My kind will always be. Genetics. Try not to feel too bad about it.'

The guy was so conceited that Ben almost wanted to tell him that there was no gold, just to see the expression on his face.

'Your illustrious ancestor,' Ben said, jerking his thumb back at the painting over the fireplace. 'I suppose that'd be him up there, would it?'

He hadn't given the painting any real notice before, but now he turned to give it a better look. He was no art connoisseur but it seemed to him the typical eighteenth-century portrait, a highly posed hero shot of a nobleman wearing one of the powdered wigs that had been all the rage back then, and shiny body armour draped across one shoulder with a splendid red cape. The intended effect had no doubt been to depict the subject as gallant and virile, a righteous and chivalrous warrior, but to Ben's eye it came across as somewhat camp and affected.

But there was something else about the picture that made Ben look twice. As he studied the face of the man in the portrait he realised that, although a good few years younger, it was the face of the real-life Charles Stuart standing with him in the room. This maniac had had an artist knock up a reproduction of an old painting in his own likeness.

Stuart gazed at the portrait with the look of a man who had seen God. He slowly nodded. 'Indeed, it's my honour to belong to his royal bloodline.'

'That's quite an impressive pedigree, isn't it?' Ben said. 'To be able to trace your heritage straight back to a real Scottish hero.'

Stuart gave a haughty smirk and was about to reply when Ben went on, 'A real Scottish hero who in fact was an Italian coward, who dressed up as a woman to escape the enemy while his loyal followers who stood their ground on the battlefield were slaughtered and persecuted. So much for genetic superiority. I wouldn't be too proud to belong to that line.'

Stuart's smirk died away and became a hard glare.

'Still, with all that gold up for grabs,' Ben said, 'I'd have been surprised if other real Scottish patriots like yourself didn't try to stake their ancestral claim. I hope you've got ironclad proof of yours.'

'Don't you worry about what I can prove or not. The gold's mine, and I'll have it.'

'Only on my terms,' Ben said. 'You'll get it once I get what you have to trade me in return.'

'I have a reputation as something of a tough deal-maker,' Stuart said, getting angry now. 'Don't push your luck, because I don't tolerate it when people try to stand in my way.'

'Looks to me like I'm in your way,' Ben replied. 'Whether you tolerate it or not.'

Stuart stabbed a furious finger at Ben. 'Here's how it's going to be. I don't do deals with people like you, so stick your terms up your arse. But make no mistake, you *will* talk to me.'

'You'd have to say "Please",' Ben said. 'Or try very hard to make me.'

'Let's see about that.' Stuart snapped his fingers. Hacker and his associate stepped forward from their places either side of the doorway, ready for action.

'Bring Miss Kirk in here,' Stuart ordered them. 'Let's see how cocky he is while he's forced to watch his girlfriend having her throat slit open.'

'It's a nice rug, boss,' Hacker said, pointing. 'You sure you want it all bloodied up?'

'Then you can put her eyes out with a hot poker,' Stuart said, motioning towards the fireplace. 'Then strangle the bitch right there on the hearth.'

Ben shook his head. 'No. You're not going to do that.'

Chapter 52

In reply to their stunned silence Ben said, 'I'll tell you why. Because Grace Kirk knows everything I know. That makes her your best insurance policy, if I decide not to talk. And cutting out your insurance policy isn't a smart play. That's why you smart guys aren't going to hurt a hair on her head.'

Hacker and his crony exchanged glances. Stuart's eyes stayed on Ben, narrowing to slits. 'Bullshit. Another lie. You told me you were the only other person apart from Ross Campbell who knew everything.'

'That's what I told you this morning. And it was true then. But this morning was hours ago. I had plenty of time to fill her in on all the details while we were on our way back here.'

'So where the fuck exactly were you?' Hacker asked.

'I was on a fact-finding mission. Learning about a gang of degenerate dirtbags called the Dishonourables. In case you were wondering, I'm not the only one who knows all about you. So do the authorities. The walls are closing in, boys. Not just on you, but your new employer, too.'

Ben knew that the mention of the authorities wouldn't scare men like Hacker and his friend. But Stuart was made of softer material. His cheeks flushed and he chewed his lip and Ben could tell he was succeeding in getting the man flustered. Flustered wasn't the same thing as hopelessly defeated and begging for mercy, but it was a start.

Stuart hesitated a moment longer and then snapped, 'All right, then. So what? You don't think I can make her talk?'

Ben said, 'Doesn't always work that way with torture. Sometimes they just go into shock and close down on you. Other times, they'll tell you all kinds of nonsense, just to make it stop. It's not exactly a fine art, never was.'

Stuart sneered, 'You'd know all about torture, would you?'

'We were taught how, in the SAS. When it comes to hurting people, I'm a master. As you'll find out the hard way, Stuart. It's just a question of time as to how, and when.' The first part was a lie. The second was not.

'Oh, I will, will I?' Stuart was breathing hard with anger but a deepening shadow of doubt had crept into his eyes. 'Fine. Let's play it your way for now. In the meantime, let's try something else. Hacker, go and fetch that old fart McCulloch from the dungeon. Seeing as the stupid bugger apparently doesn't know anything after all, that makes him expendable.'

Hacker smiled. 'Now you're talking. That'll be my pleasure.' He said to his crony, 'Banks, you stay here and make sure the major doesn't do anything stupid. We wouldn't want to have to educate him in the art of fucking people up.'

The one called Banks looked happy to oblige. Ben stared at him and said, 'Banks is pretty good at that, all right. Especially when he's sent to butcher some poor unarmed victim on their own and he can run away afterwards. Maybe he could have dressed as a woman, too.'

Banks didn't look so happy now. Hacker turned towards the doorway and was halfway there when Stuart seemed to remember his expensive hand-woven Celtic carpet and said, 'Wait. No. On second thoughts, take Hope down with you to the dungeon. That way you can bloody the place up as much as you like. Let's see if it doesn't loosen Mr Hope's tongue to see his old comrade getting sliced like a kebab.'

'Works for me,' Hacker said. 'You coming, too, boss?'

Stuart peeled back the sleeve of his tweed suit jacket to consult the gold ingot on his wrist. 'I think not. It's time for my lunch.'

'Enjoy it, boss. What's on the menu?'

'Poached salmon,' Stuart replied, and they laughed.

Hacker pointed his pistol at Ben. Not getting too close, not making the fatal error of allowing his weapon to get within intercept distance of the enemy, lest it suddenly be snatched from his hands and turned on him with savage efficiency by someone who'd been expertly trained for the job. The Pathfinders weren't the SAS, but near enough for Hacker to know the ropes. He said, 'C'mon, fucker, let's get moving.'

'I'll see you later, Stuart,' Ben said.

Hacker and Banks escorted him out of the room. The third Dishonourable was still waiting outside the door. Hacker said, 'Come with us, Carter.'

'Where're we going?'

'Downstairs. To have some fun.'

The art of marching a dangerous prisoner any distance was a tricky business fraught with potential pitfalls, even for trained men. The gang grouped around Ben as cautiously as game wardens relocating a captured tiger. Each man perfectly aware of how fast things could go south for them, if he let his guard down for an instant. Banks and Carter were focused so hard they were sweating. Only Hacker was able to maintain his cool, at least outwardly. Ben could have played it awkward by refusing to move and there wouldn't have been much they could have done to force him. But he was as deeply anxious to see Boonzie again as he was worried about Grace. He let himself be walked through the castle's winding corridors and hallways, thinking and waiting and watching.

Hacker said, 'You know something, Hope? I'm as excited as a kid on Christmas morning. Because I can't wait for you to be dead. And I won't have to wait too long to watch it happen. With any luck, the boss will let me do it myself.'

'You're being a bit over-optimistic. There are only four of you.'

'Four plus the others who're on their way here as we speak,' Hacker said with a grin. 'Oh, yeah. That's right. I got the call this morning from my old mate Mikey Creece. He and nine more guys flew up from London an hour ago. Should be arriving any moment now. They're looking forward to meeting you, Major.'

Ben looked at Hacker and wondered whether he was telling the truth or not. He could see no lie in the man's eyes.

'Two things we hate,' Hacker said. 'One is stuck-up SAS scum like you. Think you're so high and mighty and better than everyone else. But what we hate even worse is anyone who hurts one of our gang.'

'Then you're going to hate me a lot more pretty soon,' Ben said. 'Because splatting a piece of shit like your friend Kev O'Donnell made me feel so warm and fuzzy inside, it gave me an appetite for more. Now I'm wondering if fourteen dead Dishonourables is going to be enough to satisfy me.'

Hacker shook his head. 'Unbelievable. Will you listen to this guy?'

'I'm wondering how it is that you came to fall this low,' Ben said. 'From Pathfinder staff sergeant and twice winner of the AOSC, to joining these vermin and ending up as some gun for hire working for a lunatic. How did that happen? Was it just bad luck, or do you have a few loose screws of your own?'

'I should have shot you while I had the chance,' Hacker said. 'Down by the loch.'

'Except you didn't,' Ben said. 'Because you missed. Just like your whole life is one big miss. How does it feel to know that?'

Hacker replied, 'The more you talk, Hope, the more fun this is going to be.'

They marched Ben deep into the castle's maze of stone passageways to a studded oak door, from where a flight of steps led down to a basement floor with numerous other doors running off it. From there, a narrower and dingier stairway led further downwards into growing darkness and an intensifying smell of damp. A pair of electric lanterns hung from a recharging station on the sub-basement wall. Hacker and Banks grabbed one each, turned them on and the shadows were chased away by strong bright light. Ben saw a steel door ahead, thick and heavy like something that would protect a bank vault. Carter and Banks backed him against the wall with their fingers on their triggers while Hacker produced a key and used it to open four large, sturdy padlocks holding the door. Stuart wasn't leaving much to chance, when it came to prisoner security.

Hacker heaved the vault door open, then signalled to Banks and Carter to move Ben along. Hacker went through the door first, backwards with his gun trained on Ben's chest. Carter and Banks brought up the rear, pointing their weapons at Ben's back. 'Nearly there,' Hacker chuckled to Ben. 'Bet you must be so happy to see your old mate again.'

They moved on through a stone-block tunnel whose craggy walls were streaked with mould and mildew. A few dozen metres further, a third flight of steps took them still deeper below the castle. Ben guessed they must be right down in the foundations by now.

The Dishonourables were still being extremely careful not to get too close to Ben. He could sense their growing anxiety. They kept moving. Next they reached a steel cage door held fast with more padlocks, which opened into an arched stone tunnel more cramped than the one before it. The swaying lanterns made eerie shadows on the walls. The dank airlessness down here was oppressive. It was like walking back into the darkest, ugliest parts of history. Nothing else about Stuart's castle felt authentic, but this did. It was easy to imagine the horrors experienced by prisoners of bygone centuries, left to rot and starve in black holes where rats scuttled and feasted on the remains of the dead. Ben thought of Boonzie McCulloch being kept in such a place. The anger only made his resolve stronger.

Then Hacker said, 'Here we are, boys. End of the line.'

The tunnel was blocked off ahead. Ben had expected something like a barred prison door inset into the end wall, but saw nothing until he looked down at Hacker's feet and realised that the entrance to the dungeon was an iron grid trapdoor with massive hinges cemented into the floor, and secured by a long bolt. A collapsible aluminium ladder lay beside the opening.

Hacker slid back the bolt with his foot. Then he had to set down his lantern in order to use both hands to heave up the heavy trapdoor. Ben tried to peer in through the hole, but saw nothing but blackness. It was impossible to tell how deep it went down. The smell of human confinement wafted upwards. Inside the hole, it must be unbearable.

'Jesus, what a stinker,' Carter muttered. 'The old ratbag must've just pinched one off.'

With the lid raised, Hacker grabbed the ladder and lowered it into the hole, releasing the catches to allow it to extend full-length. Its aluminium feet hit the bottom with an echoey clang. Hacker yelled, 'Hey, McCulloch, wakey wakey! You've got company.'

Chapter 53

Stuart's dungeon was literally a hole in the ground, a bottle-shaped chamber whose design would have made it impossible for anyone trapped inside to get out. Ben had seen some fairly inescapable prisons in his life. Sometimes from the outside, and occasionally from the inside, though he'd never met one that could hold him long. This was the worst.

Hacker yelled again, 'Hear me, McCulloch? Get ready, 'cause it's party time!'

There was no reply from the darkness. Banks said, 'Maybe the old fucker's finally snuffed it. That'll be a shame.'

Hacker shook his head. 'Nah, he's always quiet. Likes us to think he's sleeping, but he watches everything without saying a word. That'll soon change when we get to work, though. Hope your knives are nice and sharp, boys.'

'Too fuckin' right,' Carter replied with a leer.

As he said it, Carter allowed his guard to drop for just a moment and Ben saw a window of chance flash open. He took a half step closer to Carter. His muscles tensed like springs, and in his mind he was already launching into the attack that would leave the man disarmed and permanently crippled. But Hacker saw his intention and snapped the pistol towards Ben's face. 'Uh-uh. Not so fast, my son. Any tricks, I've got seventeen Hydra-Shok hollowpoints in here with your name on them.'

'Shooting me won't go down well with your boss,' Ben said. 'He wants his gold, remember.'

'Gold,' Hacker spat. 'That prick might be too blind to see it, but I'm not an idiot. You're just telling him what he wants to hear. You don't have any more gold than I have.'

'And yet you'd gladly torture a man to death, just to make me tell where it is.'

'No, I'd do it just for kicks. And to give you a taste of what's in store for you.' Hacker cocked his head towards his men. 'Watch this bastard, boys, he's awful tricky. Banks, you're first in the hole. Move it.'

Banks reluctantly stepped to the edge of the hole and started clambering down the ladder, his footsteps resonating inside the hollow chamber. His lantern light darted around as he descended, and Ben was able to catch sight of parts of the curved inner walls, the stone blockwork wet and glistening with damp and condensation. Then Banks reached the bottom and shone his lantern upwards.

Hacker said to Ben, 'You next.' He stepped away to keep his safe margin of space as Ben approached the edge of the hole. Ben climbed down the ladder with two pistols pointing at him from above and a third from below. He was keeping his breathing slow and deep and steady, calming himself for whatever was about to happen next. Which could be a lot of things. Some of them bad, some of them worse.

Step by step, he descended into the pit of hell where his old friend had spent the last several days incarcerated in deplorable conditions, sick and maybe injured, and now set to die a horrible death if the Dishonourables had their way. The stench in the hole grew more choking with every downward rung of the ladder. Banks was standing at its foot looking up, his face contorted in disgust at the smell.

Ben stepped down one more rung and felt the solid floor underfoot. Banks backed away, keeping the pistol pointed at him and the light aimed in his face. 'Move a muscle, twitch a finger and I'll blow your fuckin' brains out, get it?'

Boonzie still hadn't made a sound. Ben tried to peer past the dazzling light shining in his face so he could search for his friend, but could make out only shadow and darkness. Above him, Hacker's footsteps were ringing on the ladder rungs, quickly followed by Carter's; and seconds later all four of them were standing inside the pit of the dungeon. Hacker shone his lantern around the chamber. 'McCulloch?'

Ben stood very still with two guns pointed at his head. As he watched the sweep of Hacker's lantern around the dungeon walls, he was steeling himself for the sight of his friend in God knew what kind of state.

But then two things happened that Ben couldn't have foreseen.

The first was that Hacker's lantern light completed its 360-degree sweep of the chamber without revealing anything but bare stone blockwork. Then it suddenly jerked to a halt and remained fixed and trembling on one spot. Not on the huddled and abject figure of a sick or dying prisoner – but on a neat rectangular hole in the wall where a stone block had been removed.

Ben's heart jolted as if defibrillator pads had been pressed to his chest. The dungeon was empty. Boonzie was gone. Stuart's plan had just become half-unravelled.

Hacker yelled out, 'He's not fucking here!'

Ben suddenly wanted to burst out laughing. *Go, Boonzie.* Looked like there was life in the old dog yet.

Carter and Banks still had their guns pointed right at Ben, but the muzzles were wavering with uncertainty. And that was when the second thing happened. Which was that Hacker's phone rang. He thrust his pistol in his belt, ripped the phone from his pocket, slammed it to his ear and almost screamed, 'WHAT?' In the next instant his anger turned to alarm. 'Graham? What happened?'

Ben could hear the caller's distressed voice on the line, hoarse and high-pitched. He couldn't make out the words. But Hacker heard them up close and clear. His eyes popped wide and his jaw sagged. He gasped, 'She *what*? What the fuck do you mean, *she stabbed you*?'

In that moment, Stuart's plan had suddenly unravelled all the rest of the way. Because somewhere up there inside the castle, Grace Kirk had just managed to turn the tables on her guard.

And that was a game-changer, not just for her but for Ben as well.

Hacker and his associates were stunned by the news. Only for an instant, but an instant was long enough for Ben to see his second and last window of chance open up in front of him.

Banks and Carter were standing roughly three feet apart and five feet away from Ben, Banks to the left and Carter to the right, marking two points of an isosceles triangle with Hacker as its third point in the middle a few steps beyond. This time it was Banks who was closer to Ben.

And so Banks was the target Ben chose now. In one lunge he slammed into him, twisted the gun out of his hand, felt the pencil-snap of finger bones as the weapon ripped free, turned it around and shot him square in the middle of the face.

One down.

Even as the 9mm bullet was still in the air and the spent case was spinning from the cycling breech, the muzzle of the gun was swivelling the three feet to the right to engage Ben's second target. By the time it was pointing at the astonished Carter a tiny fraction of a second later, the next round was chambered and the trigger was reset, and before Carter could even flinch or crap his pants Ben double-tapped him, centre of the chest. Two down. Carter and Banks were always the weakest links. They'd never really had a chance, once the right moment came. And it had come.

But Carl Hacker wasn't going to be so quick and easy to take out.

Chapter 54

Hacker dropped his phone and clawed out his pistol, twisting and dropping into a combat posture with such violence that he let his lantern fall and it went out. He punched his gun out in a two-handed grip and let off a wild string of shots. Seventeen rounds in his magazine, all with Ben's name on them.

But Ben wasn't about to let any of them find him. He dived to the hard stone floor and came lunging up in a fast, explosive forward roll to catch Carter's corpse even as it was still collapsing. He clasped the dead man's body against his own as a shield and felt the thudding impacts of the bullets slamming into Carter's back. Ben had been willing to gamble that Hacker's 9mm hollowpoints would mushroom to a halt inside the body and not penetrate all the way through. It was a hell of a way to put a theory to the test. He fired back over Carter's shoulder, two rapid snapping rounds, but Hacker was already dancing away into the dark recesses of the dungeon, a flitting patch of darkness in the shadows that was hard to pinpoint in Ben's gunsights. The shots ricocheted off bare stone and hummed all around the chamber like angry bees. Firing blind in this place was a recipe for getting hit with your own bullet.

Now Ben had a problem, because he couldn't see Hacker,

332

but Hacker could see him by the light of Banks's fallen lantern. Ben quickly crunched it with the heel of his boot; and now the whole chamber was plunged into blackness. He darted away from where the light source had been, merging into the shadows like Hacker.

This was the moment Ben most wished he still had those damn night-vision goggles. There was dead silence in the chamber, apart from the ringing in his ears. He could sense Hacker slowly circling, watching, peeling the layers of darkness apart with his eyes to discern where his enemy was. A second later there was another deafening gunshot and a white spurt of muzzle flash from the other side of the chamber as Hacker let off another round at the spot where he thought Ben was lurking. He was six feet off target. The bullet struck sparks off the wall and carved its deadly ricochet trajectory all over the place, coming closer to hitting Ben than the original shot.

Now Ben knew where he was, and fired back. But Hacker was fast, too, and in the instant it took for Ben to register the location of the flash and set his sights on it, Hacker had already skipped away and was lost in the darkness.

Silence again. Both men waiting, watching, listening, each afraid to betray his position to the other. They could just keep playing this cat-and-mouse game until someone got hit, either by design or by chance, with their opponent's bullet or their own. Ben didn't like the odds much.

Neither did his opponent. There was a sudden rush of footsteps and a furious metallic clatter as Hacker raced to find the ladder and started wildly clambering up it. Ben fired at the sound and his blind shot howled off an aluminium rung. He fired again. But Hacker was leaping up the ladder like a scalded wildcat and he made it to the top before Ben could get a fix on him. In two bounds Ben was at the foot of the ladder and ready to storm up after him, but a hail of gunfire blasted down all over the inside of the chamber, bullets bouncing everywhere and forcing Ben to dive away from the ladder, roll and take cover.

In the next instant he heard the scrape of the ladder being withdrawn, and then the echoing clang of the iron trapdoor being slammed back down and the bolt being kicked home. More muzzle flashes lit up the mouth of the chamber as Hacker jammed his pistol muzzle through the iron grid and loosed off another five rounds. Ben came back at him with two, three, four return shots, aiming behind the flashes. Hacker's gunfire ceased. Ben heard running steps escaping.

Then nothing. He was alone again down here in the subterranean blackness, with the sudden silence and the sweetish tang of burnt powder mingling with the stench of the dungeon. He patted himself all over for injuries. In the heat of combat you could take a hit without even realising it. He was unhurt. Ben allowed himself a grim momentary pleasure at the rising enemy casualty toll. The score stood at three dead Dishonourables, plus a fourth incapacitated with a knife wound. The colonel would be happy. He'd be even happier by the time this was over.

But it was a long way from over. Ben was still at a serious tactical disadvantage because now Hacker was heading back up there to go after Grace, and Ben was trapped down here with two corpses and unable to do a damn thing to help her. Not good.

He took out his Zippo lighter and thumbed the flint, and the orange flame cast its halo glow through the darkness. Worried that it was low on fuel and would soon gutter out, he searched around for Hacker's fallen lantern and found it, hoping that it wasn't irreparably damaged. To his relief, after a few shakes and knocks it started working again. He put away the warm lighter and set the lantern down on the floor next to him as he took the pistol from Carter's body and stuck both weapons in his belt. Carter and Banks each had a spare magazine in their pocket. Thirty-four more rounds of the same hollowpoints Hacker was using. Not sufficient ammo to start a war with, but plenty enough to put an end to Stuart's operation. The dead men had phones, too, which Ben lifted as well. Next, picking the lantern up again, he made his way over to the mysterious hole in the wall that was all that remained of Boonzie's presence in the dungeon.

How Boonzie had managed to work the stone block loose, Ben couldn't begin to imagine. With no tools to work with, it must have taken him dozens of hours and left his fingers raw. There were dried bloodstains on the block, which stood up on end near the hole with a jagged chunk broken off one corner.

The bad smell was noticeably stronger over by the hole; Ben didn't realise why at first, until he leaned in and examined it more closely by the lantern-light, and understood. Boonzie's escape route was, literally, a tunnel: a large-diameter sewer pipe running through the castle foundations past the curve of the dungeon wall.

Ben shook his head in amazement at his friend's resilience. Boonzie must have been drawn to the spot by the sound of water gushing through the pipe. Maybe the mortar holding in the block had become weakened by moisture leaking from some small crack over time. A few well-aimed kicks might have been enough to start the process of loosening it, before the endless labour of doggedly working it back and forth and inching it from its space. After he'd finally managed to work the block all the way loose he'd smashed it down on the dungeon floor to break off the smaller chunk, which he must have then used to bludgeon a hole in the pipe big enough to crawl into. It had been a desperate gamble taken by a desperate man. His escape through the sewer pipe must have been indescribable.

And now Ben was about to find out for himself. Because there was no way out of here except to follow in his friend's footsteps. If it was good enough for Boonzie McCulloch, then it was good enough for him.

Ben got down on his knees, took a deep breath and then poked his head into the shattered pipe. The smell of effluent made his eyes burn. His one consolation was that the castle would have its own private sewerage, so it was only the shit of its owner, henchmen and various staff that he would now have to go crawling through for an unknown distance. He pushed one arm into the pipe. His outstretched hand sank into the three inches of foul-smelling, icy-cold water running along its curved bottom. Then his torso, one leg, then the other, and he was in. Boonzie was a smaller man and would have fitted just a little more comfortably inside the pipe, if comfort was the word. But Ben could make it.

He started to crawl, pushing the lantern along in front of him as he went. The light illuminated the rounded walls of the pipe for a few feet ahead, dissolving into a circle of darkness beyond. A terrible claustrophobia gripped him as he left the hole behind with nowhere to go but forwards. Where he was going, he had no idea. But anywhere was better than here.

And so on he went. Hands and knees, head down, sloshing through the filthy water and the sediment of foulness that was accumulated in the bottom of the pipe, breathing through his mouth to minimise the stench that made him want to puke, trying not to think about Hacker hunting for Grace up there in the castle and what he'd do if he found her.

336

Ben kept pushing forwards. Twice he found himself verging close to panic, becoming utterly convinced that there was no way out of here, and having to pause while he closed his eyes and steadied his breathing and thought of sunny green hills and wildflower meadows. *Get a grip*. Boonzie had made it out, and so would he.

Soon afterwards, Ben realised that he could see a faint glimmer of daylight in the circular mouth of the tunnel ahead. Galvanised by the sight, he crawled faster towards it and the daylight grew brighter. It was shining down from a round aperture where the horizontal pipe was jointed at a right angle to a vertical outlet. Step irons were inset into the brickwork and led up to a manhole cover several metres above. Someone had left the iron manhole cover open. There was wonderfully fresh, cold air blowing down it, bringing little snatches of snowflakes that spiralled down and pattered on his face as he raised himself onto his knees and craned his neck upwards to fill his lungs. What must it have felt like for Boonzie, getting his first taste of fresh, beautiful air for the first time in days?

Ben left the lantern behind and scrambled up the step irons. Pushing his head and shoulders out through the open manhole he looked around him to get his bearings. Wherever he was now, it was some considerable distance from the castle. He couldn't see it at all, because during his time underground the snow had started again and was now blowing up into a blizzard.

Ben clambered out of the hole and scooped up handfuls of powdery snow to wipe the filth from his clothes and hands. The strong wind tore at him and snowflakes whipped into his eyes and nose. He began to shiver violently and knew he had to find shelter and warmth before he froze to death out here. The afternoon was already fading fast into

337

twilight and the temperature would soon start to drop like a stone.

He staggered through the snow, sinking in up to his knees in drifts that piled up on the uneven ground. The whirling blizzard seemed to be gathering strength with every passing moment, becoming a near-total whiteout. Visibility was no more than a few metres ahead and his sense of direction was almost non-existent. But then, half-blinded by the force of the driving snowflakes filling his eyes, he saw the dark shape of a long, low building ahead and began to make his way towards it.

At first he thought the building was a stable block or an animal shelter, but as he stumbled closer to it he realised it was some kind of groundskeeper's hut or storage shed. The wind was drifting the snow high against its slatted wooden sides. He reached an end wall and worked along its length until he came to a flimsy wooden door, warped and weathered. He pushed through the doorway.

It was semi-dark inside the hut, with only two small windows, both rimed with snow. The ambient temperature was noticeably higher than outside. There was a smell in the air as though someone had been using a propane stove or heater in here not too long ago.

In the murky half-light Ben could make out piles of agricultural equipment, building materials and tall shelving units covered with paint cans, tools and assorted boxes. A large object stood draped with a tarpaulin in the middle of the hut. He tugged at the tarp and saw that underneath was a rugged Polaris all-terrain, two-seater utility vehicle. A cross between a golf cart and a military assault buggy, the kind of thing that estate keepers would use to patrol the grounds and lug trailers of logs and fertiliser around.

So much for that. Ben let the tarp flop back down, and

turned away. He was shivering so hard that his teeth were chattering, and his mind was suddenly on relighting that propane heater, wherever it was. He needed to find warmth and get the circulation going in his numb fingers and toes. He started exploring the rest of the hut. The light was fading quickly as the blizzard outside intensified even more. Up on one of the shelving units was another rechargeable lantern. He reached out to grab it.

And that was when a figure rushed up from behind and attacked him.

Chapter 55

Ben's attacker wasn't a big or heavy man, but he was hard and wiry. He launched into Ben with ferocious violence, knocking him off balance. In the next instant an arm wrapped itself like a steel band around Ben's throat, threatening to crush the air out of him. Ben tried to wrench free of the stranglehold and throw the man off him, but he was clinging on tighter than a mongoose with a death grip on a cobra. Ben was fighting to breathe, and losing fast. In seconds he'd start to black out.

He wheeled around and backed up hard into one of the metal shelving units, bringing down an avalanche of hardware and tool equipment. The impact drew a grunt of pain from Ben's attacker and loosened his hold around Ben's throat just enough for Ben to be able to get his fingers around the strangling arm and relieve the pressure so that he could snatch a gasp of air.

The guy was unbelievably strong and tenacious. But now Ben had a solid purchase on his arm, and used it to throw his attacker over his shoulder and send him slamming to the floor. The man hit the boards with a crash that shook the hut and would have knocked most opponents half unconscious, but he was instantly starting to writhe back upright as Ben stormed in to launch a stamping kick to the guy's face.

If the kick had landed, it would have smashed his jawbone,

rammed his teeth down his throat and been a definitive, spectacular fight-finisher. But just as Ben was gathering his strength and momentum for the killer blow, he hesitated. Stopped. Froze.

The hard, wiry figure of the attacker clambered quickly to his feet. The *very familiar* hard, wiry figure, whose silhouette was dimly backlit against the hut's snowy windowpane. Ben stared at him. The figure stood still and stared back. Neither spoke. The only sound was the moan of the wind outside and the patter of snow against the hut roof.

Ben broke the silence. Said, '*Boonzie?*'

And the man who just a moment earlier had been viciously trying to kill him replied, '*Ben?* Holy shite. Is that you?'

A thousand emotions rushed together in Ben's heart and he embraced his dear old friend so tightly that he realised he was crushing him. Boonzie might have still been as strong as an ox and dangerous as a leopard, but he felt thin and frail after his confinement.

'It's good to see you, Boonzie. You had me a little worried.'

'Damn guid thing I recognised ye when I did, laddie,' Boonzie rasped. 'I might've kilt ye, thinkin' ye wiz one o' them murderin' basturts.'

'You'll be pleased to hear there's a few less of them now.' Ben stepped over to the shelving unit and took down the lantern he'd been about to grab when Boonzie had surprised him. He turned it on but kept it angled away from the window in case anyone saw the light.

Boonzie did appear leaner, and older, than when Ben had last seen him. His cheeks were hollow and more deeply etched with lines, and his hair was whiter and thinner. His clothes were torn and soiled from the dungeon and the crawl through the pipe. He looked like he'd been through hell. But he was the same old Boonzie, as tough and sour and mean

341

and indefatigable as ever, with a twinkle in his eye that no force on earth could quite extinguish.

'What in the name o' jumpin' Jesus are ye doin' here, Ben?'

'Mirella sent me to find you. She was getting a little concerned, too.'

Boonzie's expression crumpled into a look of agonised emotion at the mention of her name. Maybe some forces on earth could extinguish the twinkle after all. 'Is she okay? When did ye last speak tae her? That piece o' shite Hacker said he wiz gonnae hurt her. If anythin' happened tae that woman—'

Ben shook his head and assured him, 'Not going to happen. She went to stay with her brother in Rome. She's safe. Out of her mind with worry, but safe.' Remembering that he had Carter's and Banks's phones in his pocket, he fished one out and offered it to Boonzie. 'You should let her know you're okay.'

Boonzie's shoulders sagged with relief. He gazed at the phone and seemed about to take it, then hesitated and shook his head. 'Aye, I should. But somethin' tells me we're no oot o' the woods yet, laddie. Mebbe that's one conversation that can wait.'

They sat on the floor of the hut with the lantern light between them, and Ben quickly filled Boonzie in on the events of the last few days. Mirella's call; his encounters with Stuart's local heavies and Hacker's associates; the fate of Jamie McGlashan; Grace Kirk's involvement; and the historic cache of gold coins whose accidental discovery had sparked this whole affair. Boonzie listened intently with a face of granite, then asked, 'Have ye seen Ewan? How is he?'

'Still the same, last I heard. I'm so sorry.'

'Fuckers. They're gonnae pay for what they've done. Stuart, his cop pals, the lot o' them.'

'You've done enough, Boonzie. Let me take it from here.'

'Oh, aye? And tell me why would I dae that?'

Ben sensed the warning in his friend's voice, but he pressed on anyway. 'Because Mirella told me you were sick. At times during these last two days I was pretty sure I was looking for a dead man. Now you're alive, I need you to stay that way. For her, and for me. Okay?'

Boonzie glowered at Ben. The twinkle in his eye had chilled to the dangerous glow that had cowed many a bigger, brawnier SAS soldier in its day. 'Haud yer wheesht. Sick, my arse. Takes more'n a wee bit of a dodgy ticker tae bring doon auld Boonzie McCulloch. Them fuckers have it comin' and I mean tae be there when it happens.' He raised a finger and pointed it at Ben like a gun. 'An' dinnae even think o' tryin' tae stop me, laddie. Or—'

'That's what I thought you'd say.' Ben took one of the captured pistols from his belt and held it out it to him. Boonzie eagerly grabbed it, handling the weapon as though he'd been born with it in his hand. Ben had sometimes wondered if that might be the case. He said, 'Remember how to use one of these things?'

'Aye, an' I can still show you a thing or two.'

'Then we need to get moving,' Ben told him. 'Because Grace is running scared somewhere inside that castle with Stuart and Hacker. Ten more of their people could be arriving any time. I've got to go and find her before they do, or they're going to kill her.'

'So what's yer plan, laddie?'

'Just like always,' Ben said. 'We go in, shoot the bad guys, get out and go home.'

'Aye, not a bad idea. But I've got a better one. I wiz workin' on it when you turned up.'

'What?'

Boonzie gave a sly chuckle. He picked up the lantern, stood and beckoned for Ben to follow him. 'Come an' see what I found, laddie. I think ye'll find it interesting.'

Chapter 56

Carl Hacker swore as he made his way from the basement floors of the castle, not just because everything was coming apart at the seams. Ben Hope's last shot had punched a 9mm hollowpoint deep into the meat of his left shoulder and done massive damage in there. Bones were shattered and nerves were shredded. His arm dangled limp and unresponsive. His whole left side was still numb, though when the pain kicked in it would be murderous. His shirt and jacket were soaked with blood and he was leaving a thick trail of red splashes behind him. Sweat poured from his brow into his eyes.

As he struggled up the flights of steps to the ground floor he used his good hand to call Stuart on his phone and tell him the bad news. Stuart had only just finished his lunch, and sounded as though he'd washed down the poached salmon with a quart of fine wine. His eruptive reaction to the news was pretty much what Hacker had expected.

Hacker got off the phone as quickly as he could and hurried the rest of the way to the buttery room where the castle's large supplies of booze were stored under lock and key. It was also the room in which Mitch Graham had been charged with guarding their new prisoner, Grace Kirk. When Hacker had left his guy in there with her, the door had been securely bolted from the inside. Now it was hanging half

344

open. A trail of red footprints led out of the door and up the passage.

Hacker burst inside the buttery room and saw Graham sprawled out with his arms and legs akimbo, still clutching his phone. He wasn't moving. The woman had gone. Broken glass littered the floor. It looked as though dozens of bottles of Charles Stuart's best-quality claret had been emptied around Graham's slumped body. Except the glistening red pool wasn't all wine, because there was a large amount of blood still pumping from the wound in his right thigh. Graham's own very large and very sharp bowie knife was protruding from his leg six inches above the knee.

Hacker staggered over to him and almost slipped and fell in the slick of wine and blood. Kneeling beside his stricken associate, he clasped the hilt of the knife with his one usable hand and tried to yank it out, but the broad blade was so tightly clamped by Graham's perforated quadriceps that he couldn't shift it.

'Graham! Mitch! Talk to me!'

No response. Graham was deeply unconscious from shock and blood loss. Hacker couldn't move him. He was still trying to figure out what to do when, a moment later, Stuart came crashing through the buttery room door. His lunchtime tipple hadn't just affected his voice. He stumbled to a halt on the edge of the red pool, swaying slightly on his feet as he surveyed the scene. 'What the hell's happening?' he demanded. 'Where's the bitch gone?'

'Obviously somewhere she doesn't want to be found,' Hacker snapped back at him, wishing he'd just piss off.

'Go and find her. Now!'

'You've got much bigger problems than just the Kirk woman. McCulloch's escaped, and right now I can't say exactly where Hope is either. I locked him in the dungeon but it would seem it's not as secure as you thought it was. He's probably loose by now.'

'What the hell are you talking about?' Stuart raged at him. 'Are you telling me that you ran away from your post and left him down there unattended?'

Hacker blinked sweat from his eyes. 'For God's sake, man, look at me. I'm wounded. I'm not able to deal with him on my own, okay? Not until Mikey Creece and the others get here. That's not what I get paid for.'

'I'll be the judge of what you get paid for,' Stuart yelled. 'I told you to go and find that fucking woman, for a start. Then you're going to put right the rest of what you screwed up!'

'Are you blind? I've a man down here. He matters more to me than your bullshit about a load of gold that probably doesn't even exist.'

'Is that a fact?' Stuart reached inside his tweed suit jacket and came out with a small, shiny automatic pistol that Hacker had never seen before. Before Hacker could react, Stuart pointed the gun at the unconscious Graham and squeezed the trigger. The ear-splitting crack of the shot made him flinch, but at short range his aim was good enough. A pink mist sprayed from the side of Graham's head. He twitched once and flopped back down into his blood pool.

Stuart said, 'There. Now he doesn't matter any more, does he? So go and do what I tell you. Find the woman. Find Hope. Do your blasted job.'

Hacker stared down at his dead crony. Stared up at his employer. In that moment he forgot all about his own injury and the useless arm that might never function properly again. A surge of rage filled him with renewed strength and he grasped the hilt of the bloody knife, ripped it clean out of Graham's leg and reared up towards Stuart, wanting to slice his guts open.

Stuart's face blanched and he stumbled back towards the doorway, raising the gun again. 'One million pounds, Hacker. Cash.'

Hacker stopped. Still clutching the knife. 'One million?'

'One and a half. Two. I really don't care, all right? Just do it.'

Hacker stood there glowering at him, hating this cowardly little bastard who thought being rich was his magic ticket out of trouble, no matter what. What most pissed Hacker off about that was that it was usually true.

Hacker said, 'Lose the gun. I don't trust you.'

'I've nothing to gain by shooting you, Hacker. Listen to reason. We can still work together.'

'Lose the gun,' Hacker repeated.

'Only if you drop the knife.'

Hacker paused a beat. He let the knife slip from his hand and splash into the blood pool at his feet. Stuart put the gun away. Hacker said, 'All right. Two million, cash. For that you get whatever you want. Except one thing. When this is over, Hope is mine, and mine alone. You started this whole mess, but I'm going to finish it. After that, I don't work for you any more. Because I quit. Understand?'

That was when Hacker's phone rang. He didn't take his eyes off Stuart as he answered it.

The call was from Mikey Creece. Telling him that he, Phil Buckett and the other eight Dishonourables who'd flown up from London with them were en route and just thirty minutes out.

347

Chapter 57

In retrospect, Grace knew that her escape had been down to pure luck. Luck that they'd allocated only one man to guard her. Luck that they'd stuffed her in a faraway corner of the castle, where nobody else could hear the commotion. And luck that the idiot they'd put in charge of looking after her was a filthy would-be rapist with neither brains nor self-control.

Right from the moment they'd overpowered her in Ben's cottage and dragged her out to the car, she'd been aware of the way he was looking at her. She'd known that, sooner or later, he was going to make a move. They'd been closeted alone in the room together for less than an hour when he'd done exactly that.

The room was where the castle's owner kept enough booze to cater for a hundred lavish banquets. Sitting quietly on an ale cask next to a tower of wine boxes, her hands tied behind her back with a plastic cable tie, Grace could feel her captor's eyes on her. He was leaning casually against the opposite wall, smoking a cigarette and thinking thoughts that left a dreamy kind of half-smile on his face. The knife he held loosely in his hand was bigger than a meat cleaver, shiny and curved. After a while he said, 'You know what's going to happen to you, don't you, darling? You're not getting out of here.'

'I'm not your darling.'

He shrugged. 'I hate to think what they're going to do. I could help you.'

She said nothing. Refusing to play his game.

'But if I was to help you,' he added, 'then you'd have to give me something in return.'

In your dreams, she thought. She kept silent, but her heart stepped up a beat and she tried not to let him see her swallow.

'Maybe you ought to let me try out the goods first,' he said. 'You know, get a taste. Like a sampler. To help me decide if I want to help you or not. I mean, it's a risk for me. I've got to think it's worthwhile, know what I mean?'

That was the moment when she knew it was going to be more than just talk. He crushed out his cigarette and flicked away the stub. Pushed away from the wall and took a couple of steps towards her. Studying her intently. Virtually licking his lips. He pointed the knife casually at her chest and said, 'Got a shirtful there, aintcha, darling? You could start by letting me take a peek at those. How about you take your top off for your uncle Mitch?'

She gave him a flat look and said, 'My hands are tied, moron.'

He grinned and replied, 'So what you're saying is, if your hands weren't tied you'd show me what you've got? Yeah?'

'Hey, you never know your luck.'

'That's just for starters. You don't buy the car till you've had a test drive, right? So I still need to see the rest of the goods. Right?'

'Suit yourself,' she said. 'But my hands aren't going to untie themselves, are they?'

He came forward two more steps, close enough that she could smell his bad breath. 'Stand up then, darling. Let me cut you free. Then we can have a bit of fun, you and me. Well, me more than you. But that's how it goes.'

She stood. Her heart was running so fast there were virtually no gaps between the beats. He came behind her, chuckled and said, 'Careful now. Wouldn't want you to get cut.' Then she felt the cold steel flat of the knife blade touch her wrist. She could barely breathe. The blade was so sharp that the plastic cable tie holding her hands parted in seconds.

Her arms dropped to her sides. Her wrists ached from the bite of the plastic. She slowly turned to face him. Up close, he had a complexion like corned beef. His face was livid and his eyes were bulging. A bead of sweat rolled down his temple.

'Now,' he said. 'Get your kit off. Nice and slow.'

Grace crossed her hands in front of her as though she was about to reach for the hem of her jumper and peel it off. Then, so fast that her movement was a blur, she made a fork of the index and middle fingers of her right hand and jabbed it as viciously as she could into his eyes.

He let out a scream. 'Arrgh! You fucking *bitch*!' Half blinded and streaming tears he tried to lunge at her with the knife, but she easily ducked out of the arc of the blade and then launched a savage kick that caught him squarely and solidly in the testicles. He screamed again. But now his blood was up and he was raging like a wounded bear. The knife whooshed at Grace again, and this time she almost didn't manage to get out of its way before it slashed her to the bone. Grace staggered back, tripped over the ale cask and fell.

'I'll cut your fucking liver out!' He towered over her. The knife started coming down. Trying to wriggle away but knowing she'd never make it in time, she lashed out another kick and struck him in the knee, knocking him off balance. He wobbled for an instant and then crashed headlong into a stack of wine crates, which toppled over and sent loose bottles cascading all over the floor. Glass smashed and red claret splashed everywhere as he floundered about trying to regain his balance. But his foot connected with a rolling bottle and he went down again, losing his grip on the knife. Grace snatched it up as it clattered to the floor. He was already struggling to his feet, grabbing the broken neck of a wine bottle.

Grace had followed all the police self-defence courses. She could take down a violent offender in one stroke of an extendable baton. Pin a strong man to the floor with an arm lock and cuff him before he knew what was happening. But in no way was she capable of surviving a knife fight against a large, murderous, military-trained killer who at this moment wanted nothing more than to slash her head off with a broken bottle.

And so she stabbed him, hard and fast, before he could do the same to her. The razor-edged blade sank deep into his thigh. Blood spurted in her face. He let out an animal howl like nothing she'd ever heard before, and fell back clutching his leg.

Grace was already racing for the door, petrified to open it in case more men were in the passageway outside, running to their crony's aid. But the coast was clear. She sprinted away from the open doorway. A corner. Some steps. Another passage. This was the service section of the castle, where the walls were plainly whitewashed and the floors bare stone, and everything looked the same.

The men would soon be hunting for her all over. Maybe they already were. Grace had no idea how many more of them Stuart might have working for him. There could be half a dozen. There could be ten. But the castle must have a hundred rooms and a thousand nooks and crannies in which she could hide, so that she could gather her wits and figure out what the hell to do next.

She passed under a stone arch and found herself coming into the residential part of the rambling castle, where the walls were covered with rich tapestries and paintings and the floors were polished marble. She spotted an open door, peeked through to check the room behind it was empty, then darted inside and closed the door behind her.

She was inside the biggest dining room she'd ever seen. Her reflection in the vast gilt-framed mirror on the wall looked tiny and horribly vulnerable. One cheek was smeared with blood. She could still taste it on her lips. She spat and wiped her face, and looked around her. The room had a long, wide dining table set for sixteen and draped with an embroidered satin cloth that hung nearly to the floor. At one end stood a marble fireplace almost half as tall again as she was; at the other, sumptuous floor-length curtains framed a bow window overlooking the grounds. Outside in the dimming afternoon light the snow was plummeting down like crazy, erasing from her mind any thought of fleeing the castle. She wouldn't survive long out there in that blizzard.

She dropped to her knees and crawled under the dining table, blinking in panic, breathing hard, and tried to focus her scattered wits.

Now what?

Chapter 58

Hacker was in a bad state. On his way upstairs to his quarters he passed out twice and thought he wasn't going to make it. But in the course of his career he'd been shot, stabbed and burned enough times to know from personal experience that it could have been worse. It was a peripheral injury, he told himself. No way was he going to let a poxy little 9mm bullet wound take him out.

His reason for dragging himself up here was the kit bag he kept in his room. Inside was a little box of tricks that came in useful at times like these. After he'd dosed himself with two syrettes of morphine and snorted a couple of hits of crystal methamphetamine, he reached for a syringe device that was designed to inject small, expandable cellulose sponges into a gunshot wound, soaking up blood flow and plugging the hole like a flat tyre. It was only meant as a temporary battlefield measure. His left arm still wouldn't work. But with two million pounds coming he was willing to get the job done first and worry about it later.

By the time he'd finished patching himself up as best he could, he still had a few minutes left to find the Kirk woman before his reinforcements arrived to join him in the task of cornering Ben Hope. Now the meth and the morphine were kicking in nicely and he felt a ferocious buzz of energy course through his veins as he hurried back downstairs from his quarters to the buttery room. Stuart had vanished; Hacker didn't give a damn where to. Graham's body would have to be cleared up, but that could wait too.

Hacker tracked the trail of footprints from the buttery doorway. Half an hour had now passed since Graham had alerted them to the woman's escape, and the bloodstains on the ground were already drying russety-brown. They led up the passage and around a corner. After a few dozen yards the trail was beginning to fade out; but then he spotted a partial print on one of the steps leading towards the stone arch and the residential part of the castle's ground floor. Hacker knew there would be more blood tracks to follow. After escaping the slaughterhouse mess of the buttery room, she wouldn't just be trailing it on her shoes. It would be spattered on her clothes, her hands, her hair, her face. Sure enough, a few yards on he came across a sticky red palm print on the wall where she'd gone racing around a corner.

Okay, bitch, he thought to himself with a grim smile. The effects of the meth and morphine were spiking inside his brain. He was burning with elation and as micro-focused as a fighter pilot. He drew his pistol, clutching it in his one hand and ready to spray lead at anything that moved. She had to be somewhere in the castle, searching for a place to hide rather than take her chances out there in the cold. He walked slowly further up the passage, his footsteps clicking on the marble floor.

That was when he spied the red smear of blood on the brass handle of a door up ahead. It was a room Hacker had entered only once before, Stuart's formal dining room where he liked to treat his dickhead corporate pals to orgies of food and champagne.

Hacker's grim smile spread into a crocodile grin. He pressed an ear to the dining room door, listening for sounds of movement inside. Then pushed the door open and quickly stepped inside the room. In a taunting, singsong voice he said, 'Come out, come out, wherever you are!'

Hacker gazed at the table. The satin cloth hung down almost to the floor, like a tent under there. He moved quickly over to it and lifted up a corner of the cloth, bending down to peer underneath with the gun pointed.

She wasn't there. He let the cloth drop. Looked over at the window, and the heavy floor-length curtains either side. *Of course.* He walked over to the right-hand curtain and jerked it abruptly aside. Nothing behind it but sumptuous wood panelling. Then he tried the other. Same result.

Fuck this rotten bitch. She had to be in here somewhere.

—And she was.

Grace had heard the approaching footsteps on the marble floor just in time to scrabble out from under the dining table and scurry desperately across the room to the only other place she could think of to hide. The huge marble fireplace stood over eight feet tall with a polished, ornate bronze chimney hood the size of a steam-train cow-catcher. The grate was stacked up with a mountain of logs and kindling ready to light. Grace clambered up on top of the woodpile, ducked her head and shoulders up inside the hood, stretched both arms above her and found a brick ledge to get a purchase on. At the same instant that she managed to hoist herself up inside the chimney breast and tuck her legs out of sight, she heard the dining room door swing open.

'Come out, come out, wherever you are!' said the sneering, mocking voice from inside the room. Grace had encountered a lot of meth and crack addicts when she'd worked the beat in the big city. This guy sounded off his face on the hard stuff, and that only frightened her more. She held her breath and clung on tight. Hanging there precariously in that dark, dirty, carbon-stinking space, terrified that the slightest movement would dislodge a cascade of soot that would alert him to her presence – or worse, that she'd lose her grip and come tumbling down out of the fireplace right at his feet. She could hear him moving around the room, searching here and there.

After a few moments that seemed like for ever he snarled, 'All right, bitch. But I'm going to find you. And when I do, I'm going to slice your fucking face off and have my guys wear it like a fucking mask while they're taking turns banging you to death.'

Then Grace heard the door open and close, and the sound of his footsteps disappearing up the passage. She waited another thirty seconds. When she was as certain as she could be that he was gone, she let out the biggest sigh of her life and lowered herself out of the chimney. Again, she caught a glimpse of herself in the huge gilt-framed mirror. Small, vulnerable, and a mess of black filth. But alive. She dusted the worst of it off her clothes and kicked away her shoes, scared of leaving a sooty trail out of here. She darted over to the doorway, peered cautiously out of the gap and saw that the coast was clear.

So Grace swallowed a giant breath and ran for it. Not knowing where she was going. Losing herself in the maze of the rambling castle.

A pair of armoured knights on plinths stood flanking a broad staircase that led up to the next floor, each clasping a long sword in its gleaming gauntlets. Grace clambered up onto the nearest plinth and yanked the weapon from its occupant's clutches. The sword was nearly as tall as she was, heavy and unwieldy, but the first man who tried to slice her face off would get to watch his own guts spilling on the floor before he came within a yard of her. Grasping its hilt with both hands she ran up the stairs to a galleried landing. Left or right?

If in doubt, always turn left, Ben had said. She took his advice. The landing narrowed to a corridor with magnificent burnished oak doors on both sides, any of which could burst open at any moment. With her heart in her mouth she scurried past two, three, four of them; and then saw a fifth that was open a crack.

She paused and peered through the door into a luxurious empty bedroom. A large key protruded from the inside of the door lock. She slipped inside the room, closed the door and locked herself in. Feeling only slightly more secure, she looked around her for another hiding place. There was an antique wardrobe big enough for five people to huddle inside. A huge four-poster bed she could crawl beneath.

Then Grace noticed the dainty little bedside table next to the four-poster. And what was on it. The phone was a clunky, obsolete type of thing with a dial and a receiver connected by a cloth cord. Ancient technology. She hadn't used one like it since childhood. She laid the sword across the bed, hesitated for a moment and then picked up the phone. Pressed the heavy receiver to her ear, inserted a blackened fingertip into the dial and forced herself to remember a direct number for the Divisional Headquarters of the Highlands and Islands police.

When the voice came on the line she said urgently, 'This is PC Grace Kirk from Fort William. I want to speak to Detective Chief Superintendent Allison.'

'I'm afraid DCS Allison is in a meeting.'

Grace chewed her lip. 'Then let me talk to his deputy.'

'I'm sorry, what did you say it was concerning?'

'Just do it, will you?'

'Hold the line, please.'

Grace waited. And waited. Tension locking her muscles as hard as wood. Staring at the locked door. Expecting the pounding and the rattling to begin at any instant. But then the waiting was over, and she was put through to someone who was neither the DCS nor his deputy, but an officer from Inverness CID who was still way up the chain of command from Grace herself.

As calmly and quickly as she could, she told the senior officer what was happening. Her current predicament and location. The murders and the kidnappings. The payoffs to Macleod and Coull and an unknown number of their subordinates. The voice on the line sounded sceptical at first, but the more Grace told him the more concerned he became. 'This is not a prank call,' she assured him more than once. 'I swear to you. This is real and I need urgent assistance.'

Then the call was over. She'd done all she could and now she just had to hope something would happen. She replaced the receiver on its cradle and crept to the door, pressed her ear to it and listened. She could hear nothing outside, so she went over to the window. On a clear day she would have had a sweeping view of the hills and mountains in the distance. Nearly forty minutes had now passed since her escape from her would-be rapist, and the afternoon was fading fast into twilight. She could see snow coming down hard in swirls and flurries over the castle grounds, settling thick and deep everywhere.

And she could see the headlights of three black 4x4s burning through the murk as they passed single-file into the courtyard and pulled up below.

It wasn't the police.

Chapter 59

Hacker was still ripping his way furiously from room to room through the castle when his phone rang again.

'Oy, mate, where is everyone?' rumbled the deep voice of Mikey Creece. 'Some bleedin' welcome committee this is. No way to greet an old pal.'

'Where are you?'

'Right outside the front fuckin' door. Someone gonna let us in, or what? It's taters out here and we're freezin' our bloody nads off.'

Hacker paused for another snort of crystal as he hurried across to meet them in the castle's great entrance lobby. Stuart was nowhere to be seen. Mikey Creece and the other nine members of his crew were all clad in heavy winter coats and boots. Five of them were carrying bulging black military holdalls whose contents Hacker didn't need to guess at.

Creece was a large, bulky man with the physique and flattened features of a backstreet prize fighter. His crony Phil Buckett was his physical opposite, scrawny and short and nervy with darting eyes. The others were a motley bunch of Devil's rejects named Fish, Meeks, Colvin, Hardstaff, Biggs, Walker, Khan and Davies. If Creece was a big guy, then Fish was a monster, six-eight and made of solid muscle with a neck thicker than his head. Chaz Colvin had only one ear, and 'Socket' Meeks wore a patch over his left eye.

Creece ran a hand over his scalp to wipe away the snow-flakes melting into the stubble of his hair, and eyeballed the state of his old Dishonourable buddy. 'Jesus H. Christ, pal. What the fuck happened to you? You're all fuckin' shot to bits.'

'Me? Never better,' Hacker replied. Kaleidoscopes of brilliant white light were spangling and blossoming inside his brain. He felt exhilarated and hyper-alert, and his useless arm seemed to belong to someone else. Who needed doctors and hospitals? 'It's good to see you, Mikey.'

'Lucky we got here at all,' Creece said. 'Fuckin' pilot was gettin' jumpy about landing in this shit weather. Airfield was like an ice rink and these roads ain't much better. But never mind us. Looks like you're the one having the problems. Where's Banks, Carter and Graham?'

'They're dead.'

Creece was a calm and ruthless stone killer, and he accepted the news without a flicker of emotion. 'Plus Kev O'Donnell. You saying one man did for four of our lads?'

The drugs might be having weird effects on Hacker's brain, but they hadn't scrambled his logical capacity. To tell Creece that Stuart had murdered one of their brotherhood would amount to a death warrant for his boss. Not that Hacker cared, but he wanted his money first. He wasn't prepared to tarnish Mitch Graham's posthumous reputation in his comrades' eyes by admitting that he'd been bested by a woman, either. He nodded. 'Yup. Hope took out the lot of them.'

'If you tell me this bastard ain't here any more, then we're gonna be mightily disappointed.'

'He's still here. And now that you are, we can nail the fucker.'

'Then it looks like we came to the right party,' Creece said. He nodded to his men holding the bags. 'Open them up, boys. Show him what we brought to play with.'

Aside from mercenary work and related odd jobs, one of Creece's more lucrative business enterprises was supplying smuggled Romanian full-automatic AK-74 battle rifles to organised crime gangs in London and Manchester. The unzipped holdalls contained ten of them, fitted with folding stocks and tactical lights and lasers, along with spare magazines amounting to over a thousand rounds of ammunition.

'That ought to do it,' Hacker said. 'Okay, fellas. We've got work to do. Hope's somewhere down below. Or was, until everything went tits up. My guess is that he's loose in the grounds.'

'If he's loose in the grounds, then what's stopping him from legging it the fuck out of here?' Buckett asked.

'Because of the woman,' Hacker replied. 'You can bet your arse that he'll come back to find her.'

Creece frowned. 'What woman?'

'She's a cop,' Hacker said. 'Got herself mixed up with Hope, and now she's somewhere in the castle. We've got to find her, too.'

Which was all the information Creece and his men needed to know. As a rule, the Dishonourables had very scant regard for the police, and even less so for female ones. 'She's toast,' Creece said.

Hacker nodded. 'And then some. But the boss wants Hope to be taken alive. That's going to be the hard part.'

'Why alive?'

'Because the boss reckons he knows where there's a ton of gold bullion hidden.'

'Is that a fact?' Creece said with great interest. And from the sparkle in his eye, Hacker immediately knew that Creece

361

was seeing an angle here. If Hacker had believed in the gold, he'd have been quick to see it too. Get Hope, grab the loot, and then maximise profits by cutting all ties – including Stuart.

'One more thing,' Hacker said. 'Just a detail. But there's a second guy involved. A burned-out old fart, used to be SAS too, about a billion years ago. If he's still breathing, he's either dug in somewhere or he and Hope have hooked up together.'

'Doesn't sound like a problem. The boss want him alive too?'

Hacker shook his head. 'He's target practice.'

'Works for me,' Creece said. 'Okay, boys, time to go hunting. But first, time for a nice warm cuppa.'

For a second, Hacker thought he was having an auditory hallucination from the meth. 'We're on the clock here, Mikey.'

But Creece was adamant. 'Sorry, pal. Nothing gets done without we have a cuppa. We're cold and we ain't had a bite to eat since this morning. Right, boys?'

'Right,' came the murmur of agreement from Phil Buckett and the others.

'Whatever,' Hacker said resignedly. 'Follow me.'

He led them down to the castle kitchen, where the kettle was soon on the boil and ten mugs and enough biscuits to fatten the British Army were laid out on the steel worktop. 'Nice gaff your boss's got here,' Creece commented. 'Suit me down to the ground, this would.'

'He's rich.'

'Lucky for some, eh?' Creece slurped down his tea with gusto, smacked his lips and said, 'Ahh. That hit the fuckin' spot. Right, lads. *Now* let's get to fuckin' work.'

The AKs were quickly unpacked from the bags and distributed among the crew. The kitchen resonated with the clacking of metal on metal as, brisk and businesslike, they slapped in loaded magazines and cocked their weapons ready for action. With only one arm, Hacker couldn't handle a rifle and would have to make do with his pistol.

Phil Buckett brandished his weapon with a psychotic grin plastered across his face. 'Ready to rock'n'roll. This Hope prick might've got lucky so far but he ain't got a chance against ten of—'

But Buckett's last word was drowned out by the sudden massive explosion that rocked the building.

'What the—?'

No sooner had the explosion stunned them all, but the ground under their feet seemed to shake as though from some powerful underground tremor. The surreal thought flashed through Hacker's mind: *earthquake*. But it wasn't. Instants later they felt and heard the crashing impacts of an aerial bombardment slamming into the castle. Plaster dust showered from the ceiling and they all ducked their heads in fear that it was about to cave in on top of them.

'We're under attack!' yelled Meeks, his one eye opening wide.

Everyone stared in horror at Hacker.

Hacker had no idea what was happening, but of one thing he was certain. 'It's him. It's Hope.'

Chapter 60

'Come an' see what I found, laddie,' Boonzie had said, beck-oning. 'I think ye'll find it interesting.'

And he hadn't been wrong.

Ben followed, mystified, as Boonzie led him over to the far end of the hut, cupping a hand over the lantern to shade its light away from the windows. In the hours since his escape from the dungeon Boonzie had made himself a little work-space back here, and he'd spent his time productively. The propane heater whose fumes Ben had been able to smell sat beside a rudimentary bench table with an upturned packing case for a chair. On the bench lay two large cardboard boxes and some odds and ends Boonzie had salvaged from the stores inside the hut: an assortment of tools and bits of wiring and tape, a small yellow spray-paint can.

Boonzie picked something off his work surface and pressed it into Ben's hand. It was a half-pound lump of what looked like pale white clay, the size of a small potato, cold and clammy to the touch. But Ben knew it wasn't clay, because he'd seen something very much like it before, on quite a few occasions.

'Is this what I think it is?'

Boonzie nodded with a wicked smile that made his teeth gleam in the semi-darkness. 'Aye, it certainly is.'

Ben stared at his old friend and asked, 'Perhaps you'd like to explain to me where you found half a pound of RDX high explosive?'

'Same place as I found the other thirty-nine an' a half pounds,' Boonzie said, pointing at a larger box on a shelving unit. 'In that other box over there, twenty-one detonators. An' that's not all.'

Ben could hardly believe his ears. But then he thought about the stores of building materials inside the hut, and realised. Stuart's castle was just a rich man's folly that hadn't been constructed all that many years ago. The way it nestled into the slope of the mountainside suggested that thousands of tons of solid rock and stone must have needed to be blasted away to level the ground beneath its foundations. Such a major civil engineering project required the unleashing of immense destructive energy.

RDX fitted that bill perfectly. Its proper chemical name was cyclotrimethylene trinitramine but Britain's Royal Arsenal, who had first developed the formula during World War II, had called it 'Research Department Explosive' and the acronym RDX had stuck. It had been used in the Dam Busters raid against Nazi Germany in 1943. In modern times it was still favoured as a component of military bombs, and also terrorist ones, due to its stability, plasticity and extreme potency, which was significantly greater than that of alternatives like TNT or dynamite. And it was safe. You could whack it all day long with a lump hammer, shoot holes in it or set it on fire. Nothing except a detonator or blasting cap could make it go bang. Civilian operators liked it for the same reason; hence, RDX was a primary ingredient of Semtex, used in commercial demolition and quarrying.

'They must have used a truckload of the stuff when they built this place,' Ben mused.

'Wi' just a wee bit left over after the job wiz done,' Boonzie replied. 'Should've been disposed of or kept under lock an' key. Naughty, naughty. An' now it's gonnae bite them on the bum. Look.'

He motioned for Ben to peer inside the larger of the two cardboard boxes on the workbench. Ben looked, and knew what he was seeing. Boonzie had used half of the RDX and all but one of the detonators to rig up an arsenal of twenty small but powerful one-pound bombs. Each device had a yellow number spray-painted onto it.

'Check this oot.' Boonzie showed Ben something that looked like a walkie-talkie. It was a radio remote detonator trigger device with multiple channels allowing one bomb at a time to be exploded at the touch of a button, or all at once.

'Handy toy,' Ben said.

'Aye, an' that's not all the stupid buggers left lyin' aroond for the wrong folks tae find.' Boonzie reached under the bench and pulled out a cable reel wrapped around with what looked like bright blue nylon rope.

'Detonating cord,' Ben said.

'A hundred metres o' the stuff.' Then Boonzie told him how he'd planned on using it, along with the remaining twenty pounds of RDX. 'What dae ye think?'

'I think you're the kind of evil genius that gives evil geniuses a bad name.'

Boonzie flashed a roguish smile. 'Then let's get this show on the road, laddie.'

Which they set about doing as fast as they could, keeping warm by the sputtering flame of the propane heater. Their first job was the one that Boonzie had been about to take care of when Ben had unexpectedly turned up. That was to divide the remaining twenty pounds of RDX into twenty equal lumps, then unravel the hundred metres of detonating cord and attach the lumps all along its length at five-metre intervals, binding them securely in place with tape before fixing the last of the blasting caps to the end of the cord. As Boonzie rewound the cable reel, Ben set about transferring the twenty individual bombs from their box into an old fertiliser sack.

Once that was done, they turned their attention to transportation. They had no intention of trekking into battle on foot through the blizzard that was still raging outside. Ben wasn't surprised to discover that Boonzie had already test-started the Polaris utility vehicle, checked that it had fuel and made sure the tyres were pumped. They whipped off the tarp and loaded the sack of home-made RDX bombs aboard with the cable reel. Ben had the radio remote in his pocket, along with Carter's phone. Banks's phone was now Boonzie's, the pair set up to speed-dial one another in case they got separated.

Then, with no time to waste, they finalised their strategic plan of attack and clambered aboard the Polaris, Ben at the wheel and Boonzie at his side. The 600cc single-cylinder engine thumped into life. The headlights blazed against the doorway of the hut. They buckled up their seatbelts. He turned to Boonzie. 'Ready?'

'As I'll ever be.'

'Then hold onto your hat.'

Ben slammed the auto transmission into drive and stamped his foot on the gas, and the buggy leapt forwards like a spurred horse. The front crash bar burst through the flimsy door and they came storming out into the blizzard. The icy blast enveloped them like a white blanket.

Ben kept his foot to the floor as they set off wildly bouncing over the rough ground, their knobbly tyres and torquey four-wheel transmission making light work of the deep snow. The buggy's powerful headlamp beams cut like lasers through the swirling flakes. The snowclouds had completely blotted out what little was left of the daylight and visibility ahead was poor verging on nonexistent, though Ben was glad of that. It made it less likely that anyone inside the castle would see them do what they were about to do.

But they'd find out soon enough.

Chapter 61

Ben steered across the grounds in the direction of the castle, relying on his natural homing instinct in the low-visibility conditions. All he and Boonzie could do was cling on tight as the Polaris bucked and lurched wildly over the snow. Already his hands and face were getting numb from the icy blast of the wind.

As they approached the castle, Ben was suddenly able to make out the faint glow of its lights through the swirling whiteness. But as the walls drew closer, instead of heading straight towards them he veered off to the right and began cutting a wide circle around. Towers and ramparts loomed above them in the murk. Ben pressed on harder, steering parallel with the east wall and heading straight towards the mountainside that rose up behind it to the north. He could only hope that the howling wind would make the roar of the Polaris's engine inaudible from within the castle buildings.

Now the buggy was reaching the steep terrain of the mountainside, tyres biting and slithering over rocks and ruts. Ben and Boonzie were pressed back into their seats by the sharp upwards angle of their ascent. He kept his foot down on the gas and fought to keep the leaping, bucking vehicle's nose pointing straight ahead as they climbed up and up. It was a long way to the bottom, if he lost momentum or allowed the vehicle to tip over. He gritted his teeth and kept on going. Soon the castle seemed to shrink below them, dwarfed by the vastness of the mountain. Ben could see the lights of its windows and the outline of the main courtyard from above.

Which meant that they had climbed far enough. The next phase of the plan was the most risky. At Boonzie's signal, Ben brought the buggy around in a curve so that they were pointing parallel with the rearward-facing north wall of the castle. The angle of the slope was hair-raising. One more degree of sideways cant, and the buggy would have tipped over and not stopped rolling until it pulverised itself and both men inside it on the rocks below. Another signal from Boonzie, and Ben rolled to a halt. Neither man spoke, or needed to. Boonzie jumped out, grabbed the cable reel from the back of the buggy and rolled out a few feet of detonator cord. Working fast, he wedged the loose end of the cord under a heavy boulder so that it was pinned in place. Then he jumped back aboard the buggy clutching the cable reel, letting it unravel as Ben continued on their precarious path. As intensely cold as it was, they were both sweating. But the buggy clung like a spider to the rock face, and after a hundred anxious metres all of the cord had been used up.

Boonzie pinned that end under a second boulder. With the detonator cord stretched sideways across the sloping face of the mountainside above the gables and towers of Stuart's castle, it was time to begin the next phase of the plan.

The descent was just as dangerous as the climb, as the front tyres pattered and skipped over loose rocks and boulders and the whole vehicle threatened to tip over forwards. Now the looming castle walls were to their left. Ben killed the lights and shifted the box into neutral so he could cut the engine and coast silently back down to level ground. No movement from the castle. The snow kept drifting down over its roofs and courtyard. The place could have been deserted. But in just moments from now, things were set to liven up considerably.

Ben let the buggy roll to a halt thirty metres from the gates, hidden in the lee of the wall. With that, the Polaris had done its work. They disembarked. Ben took the fertiliser sack full of bombs from the load bay. He had the radio remote detonator trigger in his pocket. Glancing at Boonzie he could see a thrill in his friend's face that he hadn't seen since the last time they'd gone into combat together. Wordlessly, noise-lessly, they made their way through the deep snow gathered at the foot of the wall and sheltered just by the gates, hidden from view of the castle windows. Ben peered inside the court-yard and could see the three identical boxy black Audi four-wheel-drives parked in a row out front, snow layered thickly over their roofs and bonnets. The druggies' Mazda was still where he'd left it earlier. The Audis hadn't been there then. Which meant that Hacker's reinforcements had turned up in the meantime. All ten of them, right on cue.

'Cold night,' Boonzie muttered.

Ben took the remote from his pocket. 'What do you say we warm things up a little?'

'Thought ye'd never ask.'

Twenty-one detonator caps, twenty-one channels. Ben dialled up Channel One, said a silent prayer that it would work, and hit the SEND button.

It worked.

Faster than Ben's prayer could have reached the ears of whoever might be listening up there, the radio signal from the remote activated the blasting cap wired to one end of the detonator cord. The cord itself was just a fuse, a hollow tube filled with volatile powdered explosive. But it was a very, very quick fuse. At the press of the button all hundred metres of line went up so simultaneously from end to end that from below it appeared as a single linear explosion, touching off the twenty packages of RDX in a spectacular leaping curtain of flame that lit up the night and seemed to shake the ground.

Ben had seen some impressive pyrotechnics, back in the day. Some of those had involved several tons, not just a few pounds, of high explosive. By contrast their home-made device was a pretty modest affair. But for Ben and Boonzie's purposes that night, it was plenty good enough. Good enough to dislodge a hundred-metre section of loose rock and boulders that erupted from the mountainside in a broad avalanche and came tumbling and spinning and hurtling downwards, gathering speed and momentum as it came. For a breathless moment it seemed to hang in the air.

Then it hit. Rocks the size of small cars smashing into roofs and gables and towers like a missile bombardment from a thousand siege engines of old. Many an ancient castle had been reduced to rubble by the primitive ballistic technology of rock and stone. With Grace still trapped somewhere inside the building, Ben had no intention of wreaking that much devastation. Not yet. He was just getting started.

'The basturts'll ken we're comin' noo,' Boonzie said.

Ben nodded. 'And we're not going to disappoint them. Let's get this done.'

Chapter 62

The assault on Stuart's fortress stronghold had begun. Ben and Boonzie crept inside the gates and crossed the snowy courtyard, keeping to the shadows. Ben had the sack of bombs over his left shoulder. Boonzie was right there behind him as they stalked fast and quietly through the darkness. If Ben had been worried about Boonzie's heart condition, so far it seemed as though his concerns were unfounded.

There was still no visible movement from inside the castle, but Ben could guess at the kind of chaos that his explosive surprise must have triggered among the enemy. Things were about to get worse for them in there. Approaching the row of parked Audis, he reached inside the sack and pulled out a pair of bombs, numbered 2 and 3 in bright yellow. He rolled them under the parked Audis. Two pounds of RDX was easily enough to rip all three vehicles to pieces and give the enemy something more to think about. Ben hurried a safe distance away from the cars and thought about detonating the charges, then decided it could wait.

They were deep in enemy territory now. No telling when the resistance might kick off. Keeping in the shadows of the walls, Ben and Boonzie skirted around the side of the castle and flanked the inside of the west wall towards the rear. As they rounded the north-west corner of the castle Ben could see a dark rubble field of rocks and boulders strewn all over the snowy ground. A portion of the north wall had collapsed under the force of the landslide. A panel van that was obviously some kind of service vehicle for the estate had taken a direct hit from a large boulder and was almost entirely crushed. There were various garage blocks and admin units out back, some of which had suffered damage as well. Among them stood a steel building with louvred doors and high-voltage warning signs, about the size of two large shipping containers standing a couple of feet off the ground on concrete risers. Ben guessed this must be the electrical room that supplied all the mains power to Stuart's residence, filled with essential equipment like voltage regulators and transformers and backup generators. Thick cables snaked from the side of the building and into an underground conduit feeding power to the castle. Ben stepped closer to the electrical room and could hear a droning hum coming from it. Landslide debris lay all around, but the main power source for Stuart's home had been lucky enough to escape damage.

Time to remedy that. Ben took bomb number four from the sack, dropped it on the ground and kicked it under the raised floor of the electrical room. He signalled to Boonzie and they hurried away to take cover behind one of the garages. Ben dialled up channel 4 on the radio remote and hit SEND.

The blast ripped the silence of the night, much louder up close than the explosion on the mountainside had seemed from far away. A percussive shockwave haloed out from the electrical room as it erupted in a fireball and was torn loose from its concrete risers. The mushroom of flame rolled up out of the smoke. Shrapnel and wreckage cannoned off the buildings. The castle windows all went simultaneously dark. Boonzie flashed Ben a grin and made a thumbs-up.

Moving quickly on, they found a rear service entrance to the main building and filtered inside, pistols ready. Ben had been hoping for two effects of his surprise diversion attack. Firstly, that it would disorientate and unnerve the enemy and scatter them through the castle as they responded to go hunting for their attackers. By Ben's reckoning he could expect to encounter eleven armed men in all, including Hacker. His second expectation was that their military training would have impelled them to split up into two- or three-man teams. From the enemy's point of view, the tactic gave them a better chance of flushing out the intruders they would by now expect to be invading their fortress. From Ben's, it also made it easier for him and Boonzie to deal with them, one team at a time.

It wasn't long before Ben's plan turned out to have been right. As he and Boonzie pressed into the pitch blackness of the castle's interior they soon encountered the first attempt at resistance. It came in the form of a pair of bobbing tactical weapon lights that suddenly became visible at the head of a long, broad corridor and came slowly their way, sweeping left and right as the two men holding the weapons to which they were attached searched for living targets in the darkness. Ben had expected Hacker's Dishonourable reinforcements to come heavily tooled up, and this was no surprise to him.

Instead, the surprise was all theirs. Because while weapon-mounted lights offered the user a fine advantage in night-time combat, they also presented the major disadvantage of giving your opponent something to aim at in the dark. And for the SAS, the dark was their element of choice.

The four pistol shots ripped out of the shadows like a single staccato burst from a submachine gun. The two lights faltered and the murky figures behind them crumpled and thumped to the floor. Ben and Boonzie closed swiftly in.

One of the fallen men jerked and struggled on the floor, not yet dead. Ben shot him in the head and he went limp. No time for mercy.

Neither of the corpses was Hacker. One had a missing ear, the other a patch over his left eye. A pretty twosome, bringing Ben's mental tally of enemy casualties to a total of six so far, with nine more to go.

'Just like auld times, eh?' Boonzie chuckled softly at Ben's shoulder. He seemed to be enjoying himself. Ben was about to reply when the one-eyed dead man's phone suddenly started to vibrate in his pocket. Ben hesitated, then crouched down to pick it up and answer the call. He stayed silent as a deep, rumbling voice that wasn't Hacker's said, 'Socket? We heard gunfire. What's happening? You find him yet?'

Ben answered, 'No, I found Socket. Now I'm coming for the rest of you.'

He ended the call before the voice could reply. Pocketed the phone and stuck his pistol in his belt. He and Boonzie took up the dead men's weapons. Romanian military AK-74s, with all the tactical bells and whistles. Loaded with thirty rounds apiece and set to fully-automatic fire. Not the kinds of items readily found in the rural Scottish Highlands.

'Someone wiz expectin' trouble,' Boonzie muttered.

'And they got it,' Ben said.

They turned off the weapon lights and moved on. Like a silent, invisible wave sweeping through the castle. The enemy was not as silent. Ben and Boonzie were drawn to the sound of voices and slamming doors. They stalked around a corner and through an archway to spy a second two-man team busily hunting from room to room and making a lot of noise doing it. Whatever their military background had been, it wasn't top-drawer. Ben and Boonzie got within a dozen metres before they activated their weapon lights and caught the enemy by surprise in a sudden dazzling blaze that paralysed them like a pair of lamped rabbits.

One of them was a scrawny little guy with nervous eyes. The other was a huge musclebound beast who looked like he gobbled steroids for breakfast. Boonzie delivered a burst into the scrawny guy's chest and mowed him down with authoritative force. Ben's triple-stitch of bullets caught the monster at the top of his nose and punched a vertical line of holes up to the crown of his shaven head. He dropped his weapon, staggered and then crashed over backwards like a felled redwood tree.

Body count: eight, with seven to go.

Chapter 63

Ben took the one-eyed dead man's phone from his pocket and called back his associate with the rumbling voice. The guy answered the call without a word. Ben said, 'This is a time-limited offer. Last chance to cut and run, friend. Otherwise we're going to kill you all.'

'Fuck you,' said the deep voice.

So much for trying to be nice. Ben replied, 'Then I withdraw my offer.'

He was thinking of Grace as he and Boonzie moved on. If she was hiding somewhere inside the castle she must be able to hear the gunfire and know that he'd come back for her. Or maybe his assumption was wrong, and she'd managed to escape.

Or not. Maybe they'd got her.

Ben had to put those thoughts out of his mind. If he didn't, he wouldn't be able to function.

The castle was like a labyrinth, with passages and corridors and doors and archways everywhere. They came to a wide, curving flight of stairs, dimly lit from a window on the galleried landing above it. Ben nodded towards the stairs and led the way up to the first-floor landing. The window overlooked the courtyard. All was still except for the steady, unremitting slant-wards fall of the snow. But as Ben was just about to pass by the window, a movement out there caught his eye. Five figures, silhouetted against the white courtyard, were racing from the castle entrance. They might have been ordinary staff employees making their panicked escape, except for the fact that they were all carrying automatic rifles. It looked as though some of the remaining enemy force must have decided to take his offer after all. He watched as they all clambered into the middle of the three parked Audis. By the glow of the inside light as the doors opened, he could see through the car's side windows that none of the five was Hacker.

Like shooting trout in a barrel. Ben reached for his remote. His fingers hovered over the buttons. *Wait for it.*

The last door slammed. The Dishonourable behind the wheel fired up the engine and the SUV's headlights sliced their bluish-tinged xenon beams across the courtyard. The wipers began to slew away the cake of snow piled over its windscreen. Clouds of exhaust billowed in the freezing air.

Now. Just as the car was about to take off, Ben stood back from the window and hit the second and third channels on the remote in quick succession. The pair of RDX bombs lying beneath the Audis went off a second apart. But the destructive power of one alone would have been enough. The middle car and the two either side of it were blown into the air like toys and the violent blast lit up the courtyard like daylight, engulfing and incinerating the five escaping Dishonourables before they even understood what was happening to them. Which was probably more of a humane end than they deserved, but you couldn't have everything.

By Ben's count the overall toll now stood at thirteen, with just two remaining plus Stuart. But among those three was the most dangerous of the whole bunch, Carl Hacker.

He turned away from the burning wrecks of the Audis to look at Boonzie, to say 'Let's go.' But the words never came out, because his blood froze at the sight of his friend, in the light from the window, bent over double and clutching at his chest. This was what Ben had feared might happen. All this excitement and exertion had finally proved too much.

Ben let his rifle drop to the floor and he raced over to grasp Boonzie by the shoulders. 'Boonzie. Boonzie. Talk to me. Are you all right? *Boonzie!*'

Boonzie's weapon dropped from his hand and he slid down the wall to the floor. His teeth were clenched and his eyes were screwed shut in pain. He suddenly looked twenty years older, and terribly fragile. In that moment, Ben truly thought he was about to lose him. When Boonzie was able to speak, after several seconds, it seemed to take a super-human effort to get the words out. 'I'm—I'm fine,' he gasped breathlessly. 'Be okay. Just . . . a wee bit tired. Need tae rest a while. You go on.'

Ben shook his head. 'No way. Forget it. I'm staying right here with you.'

Boonzie spent a few more moments fighting to gather himself. He swallowed gulps of air. Finally he managed to focus his eyes on Ben, and gave him a look so intense that Ben almost backed away. 'I said *go on*, laddie! Move it or I'll shoot ye myself!'

Ben hovered, indecisive, until he realised that the decision had already been made for him.

He left the sack of bombs with his friend and pressed on alone.

The double and triple doses of morphine and crystal meth were wearing off fast, and now the agony of Carl Hacker's shattered shoulder was beating through him like tribal drums as he made his way, groping and stumbling, through the darkness of the castle.

Everything had started going to shit in the aftermath of the first explosion. Then just as he'd been getting his men organised into search teams while he went off looking for his boss, the bloody lights had gone off. Now he was alone, and the sporadic gunfire rattling within the castle walls that he feared was the sound of his gang getting systematically wiped out only made him feel more isolated with every passing moment. He'd tried calling Stuart's mobile, but was getting no reply. Where the hell was the bastard?

Hacker tucked his pistol inside his bloody trouser waistband and was about to try again when his phone rang in his hand. It wasn't Stuart, but Biggs, sounding panic-stricken. 'Sod this, mate, we're getting out! Khan, Hardstaff, Walker, Davies and me. You should come with us.'

'It's only one man,' Hacker muttered through his pain. 'You're not going to run from just one man.'

'Bollocks to that,' Biggs said. 'There's got to be a whole sodding SAS unit going through the place. They're mowing us down like sodding grass!'

'Where's Creece? He with you?'

'No idea, pal. Far away from here, if he's got any sense. So are you coming with us, or what?'

'No,' Hacker replied grimly. 'I'm staying. I need to find the boss.'

'Then good bloody luck, mate. We're off.'

Hacker tried Stuart's phone one more time, but there was still no reply. Hacker could see his promised two million disappearing down the toilet. If necessary, he'd hold Stuart at gunpoint and make him fork out as much cash as he had stashed away within the castle. But he had to find him first, and pray Hope didn't beat him to it.

It was more than just the prospect of the money that was slipping away. The sponge plug in Hacker's shoulder was so saturated with blood that it was no longer able to stem the flow. He could feel it leaking out of him, warm and wet, and with every drop his life energy was fading a little more. He spurred himself on, and staggered up the stairs to Stuart's study.

No Stuart. As Hacker lingered in the room he glanced out of the window and caught sight of the running shapes of Biggs and the other cowards making a break for the cars. Now he really was on his own. *Fine*, he thought. *Fuck them all.*

Hacker was turning away from the window when a thunderclap explosion ripped through the cars and blew all three of them into the air in a flaming tumble of wreckage, the five men caught right in the middle. Hacker gaped at the scene of destruction and bolted from the study. Half-blind with pain, he staggered down the stairs.

Then Hacker found himself suddenly enveloped in a pool of dazzling white light and heard someone say his name, and he stopped dead in his tracks and whirled around.

Chapter 64

The footsteps thudding down the staircase were lopsided and uneven. Just by their sound, Ben could tell that the man was badly injured. He moved closer to the foot of the stairs until he was just a few metres away. The man reached the bottom and was about to pass right by him, his breathing laboured, when Ben activated the weapon light.

In its bright white glare he instantly recognised the man. And at the same time, didn't. Because Carl Hacker looked like a different person from before. His face was drawn and his body bent in pain and defeat. His clothes were black with blood and the arm not clutching his pistol was dangling limp. Maybe he hadn't got away unscathed from the gunfight in the dungeon, after all.

Ben said, 'Hacker. Stop.'

Hacker stopped. Turned, blinking at the light in his eyes. He weakly half-raised the pistol in his one usable hand.

'Don't even think about it,' Ben said. 'You'll be dead before you squeeze the trigger.'

'You want to shoot me, go ahead,' came Hacker's reply. His voice sounded hollow, spent. 'I'm already fucked.'

Ben said, 'Where is she?'

Hacker managed a thin smile. 'Love to know that, wouldn't you?'

'Take me to her, and I'll let you walk out of here. You can survive this.'

'So you're the one making the deals now.'

'First you drop the pistol, Hacker. Let it go.'

Then another voice from the darkness, deep and gruff, said, 'No, mate. You hang onto that. You might need it in a minute.'

In the peripheral glow of the weapon light Ben saw the large figure of a man step from the shadows. Then the man's own light was shining in Ben's face, making him blink. The deep voice rumbled, 'Well, Major. Looks like we gotcha in a clinch now, ain't we?' To Hacker he said, 'Didn't think I was gonna leave you all alone in the shit, did you, mate?'

Ben knew he could get one, but he couldn't get them both. 'Shoot me, he dies.'

The deep voice laughed. 'By the look of the poor sod, you'd be doing him a favour. He's fucked anyway, just like he said. And so are you, pal. Now why don't you drop the shooter, and let's talk.'

Ben didn't move. He kept his gun on Hacker. Blood was dripping from Hacker's side and he was swaying on his feet. Ben said, 'Talk about what?'

'Talk about how your uncle Mikey's gonna get his hands on that nice big pile of gold I heard someone mention earlier. Why else would I really want to hang around in this bloody mess?'

Uncle Mikey. This would be Creece, Ben thought. He said, 'You want the gold, you're going to have to get yourself a shovel and dig for it.'

'Cut the crap. I know you know. And now it's mine. So let's deal. You give me the gold, you go free. How's that for a bargain?'

'Shoot him,' Hacker croaked.

The big guy chuckled. 'What, and let him kill me old pal?'

'He's not that fast,' Hacker mumbled.

'Nobody wants to die here,' Creece said. 'And nobody has to.'

Then a fourth voice said, 'Wrong.'

And Creece let out a sharp wail. His weapon light wobbled and fell. As though in slow motion, Ben simultaneously saw Hacker's pistol begin to move. The finger on the trigger. The sights lining up in his direction. Ben fired. Hacker's head snapped back as the high-velocity rifle bullet hit him square in the middle of the forehead. He collapsed in a dead heap.

Ben whirled around to shine his beam at Creece. Creece was on his knees, his mouth wide open in a red scream. Both hands clawing at something shiny and silvery that weirdly protruded from his stomach and glittered in the light. Ben blinked, realising in that surreal instant what he was seeing. It was the tip and first six inches of a broadsword blade that had penetrated Creece's body back to front. Ben raised the light and saw a familiar figure standing there behind Creece, still clutching the sword's hilt with both hands.

'*Grace?*'

She replied something Ben couldn't understand. Creece was shrieking in a high-pitched yowl three octaves above his speaking voice. Blood gushed from his stomach. Grace yanked and twisted at the sword, but she couldn't get it out.

Ben said, 'Step aside, will you? Fingers in your ears.'

He had to feel sorry for the guy. Or almost. As Grace dropped the sword and did what he asked, he put Creece out of his misery with a bullet to the brain. Creece's yowling instantly stopped and he rolled over flat to the floor with the sword still embedded through his midsection.

'Better,' Ben said. 'I couldn't catch a word you were saying.'

'I said, Hi. Long time no see.'

'Hi yourself. Been looking for you.'

'You found me.'

'Or you found me.'

She shrugged. 'I was hiding back there. Heard the voices. Thought you could use some help.'

'I had it all pretty well under control, but thanks anyway.'

'Bastard. So are you going to give me a hug, or what?'

'Yes, I am,' Ben said. And he couldn't remember the last time he'd meant anything more seriously. He dropped his rifle and stepped towards her, over Creece's body. Grace opened her arms and the two of them embraced in the darkness.

'Are they all—?' she asked.

'To the last man.'

'What about Stuart?'

'No sign.'

'And . . . Boonzie?' She said it tentatively, hardly daring to ask.

'I found him. He's back there. He's going to be okay.'

'Thank God,' she sighed.

Ben had something else to thank God for, too. He clasped her for the longest time, as tightly as he'd ever held anyone before, and he felt the tension oozing out of him like a poison being sucked from his veins. Grace's cheek was wet against his. 'I was so scared I'd never see you again,' she whispered.

'I'm here,' he said over and over. 'I'm here.'

Chapter 65

Boonzie was where Ben had left him, but by now the ailing patient was up on his feet and trying to act as though nothing had happened. Grace flew at him and squeezed him so hard that Ben thought she was going to crush the life out of the poor guy.

'Bless ye, lassie. It's guid tae see ye again.'

Ben said, 'Time to start thinking about making that call to Mirella, Boonzie. She needs to hear from you.'

'Aye, but let's finish this job first.'

'Whatever you say. You okay to walk, old man, or shall I give you a piggy-back?'

'Say that tae me again an' it'll be yer final words, ye bawheid.'

Grace said, 'Whatever's in that bag, I'm guessing it isn't fertiliser.'

Boonzie winked slyly. 'Ye'll see.'

'Well, whatever it is you have in mind, do it fast because we're going to have company. I made a phone call.'

Ben looked at her. 'The police?'

'I am one of them, in case you forgot.'

'Then you'd best turn a blind eye to the next part. We're not done yet.'

'Oh, I'm getting used to turning a blind eye, Ben Hope. Ever since you came along.'

They left their weapons behind and worked their way back through the castle, scattering bombs as they went until the bag was empty. There was still no sign of Stuart.

Outside, the blizzard had finally died down and only a smattering of flakes was spiralling from the evening sky. Grace stared at the still burning wreckage of the cars. The bodies of the five dead Dishonourables were slowly barbecuing inside, blackened and curled, peeling and hairless. She cupped a hand over her mouth and quickly looked away. 'Jesus Christ.'

The druggies' Mazda had been undamaged by the blast and was almost completely covered with a blanket of white. Ben brushed the snow from the windscreen and driver's window, peered inside and by the flickering light of the fires saw that the key was still in the ignition.

Then he took out the remote detonator trigger.

Boonzie said, 'Go for it, laddie.'

Ben scrolled through the individual channel selection menu until he came to the one that said SEND ALL. One touch of the button would set off the remaining eighteen RDX charges. The grand finale.

Ben pressed it.

If Charles Stuart was hiding up there somewhere in one of his ivory towers, then too bad for him. Ben, Boonzie and Grace watched as the percussive explosions tore through the castle, shattering a hundred windows with their fiery breath. They watched as the inferno quickly gained a hold of the entire building from one end to the other, and the roof timbers began to collapse inwards, and the fires reached high into the night, and embers fell like glowing snow from the sky. By morning, all that would remain of Stuart's pride and joy would be a smouldering ruin.

'That's that, then,' Ben said.

'Time to hit the road,' Grace reminded him.

'Yeah, I think you're right.'

'My place?'

'Sounds good.'

The three of them climbed into the Mazda. Ben fired up the engine and lights, got the wipers and heater going, crunched the old car into gear and U-turned around in a snowy courtyard illuminated yellow and orange by the blaze of the castle. He drove out of the gates and they set off.

The goons at the gatehouse were long gone, and the main entrance to the estate had been left hanging wide open as if someone had departed in a hurry. Three sets of tyre tracks were imprinted into the snow, one fresher than the others. Two heading west, the more recent one heading east.

'You think it's Stuart?' Grace asked, frowning.

'He willnae get far,' Boonzie said.

It wasn't until they'd left the estate behind them and were back on the open road in the direction of Kinlochardaich that they heard the chorus of sirens and saw the flashing lights of dozens of police and emergency vehicles filling the horizon. Moments later, the speeding procession screamed past in the opposite direction. It looked like half the Scottish police fleet had rolled out in response to Grace's call.

'Only took them ninety minutes to get their arse in gear,' she remarked acidly.

'Now's your chance to stop and talk to them,' Ben said. 'They're going to have a lot of questions.'

Grace shook her head and smiled. 'Some other time. I'm off duty right now.'

Epilogue

The police did have a lot of questions. An awful lot. But curiously, even after Grace made her formal statement to her colleagues in Fort William, they didn't show any interest in speaking to Ben. It was almost as though he'd never been involved in any of it.

Boonzie voluntarily checked into Belford Hospital the morning after the incident. The same afternoon, Mirella landed on the place like a hurricane, and Ben was there for the tearful reunion. He was also a witness to Boonzie's solemn promise to his wife that his days of danger and excitement were officially over. If Mirella didn't hold him to it, Ben damn well would.

It was while the reluctant retiree was still being fussed over in the hospital that Dr Fraser, the head surgeon, came to deliver the news that Ewan had awoken from his coma and was talking. Even though he could remember little of what had happened to him, his cognitive functions seemed otherwise unimpaired and the doctors expected him to make a full recovery.

The following day, after spending hours with his nephew, Boonzie went home to Italy a happy man. But his parting words to Ben were disturbingly ambiguous, as Boonzie clasped his hand, gave him one of those sly winks and said,

'All's well that ends well, laddie. We must dae it again some-time.'

Ben remained in Kinlochardaich for several more days afterwards, and spent most of that time with Grace. There were moments when he thought he'd just stay there for ever.

Meanwhile, a number of other events began to unfold. The eco-activist Geoffrey Watkins was released from jail with all charges dropped, while Angus Baird and his cronies were heading in the opposite direction. Shortly after Grace submitted her evidence to the police top brass from Inverness, Detective Inspector Fergus Macleod and Detective Sergeant Jim Coull were placed under arrest for their part in the murder of Ross Campbell and the attempted murder of his business partner, along with multiple corruption charges, and more. A growing list of other names quickly became implicated in the affair, including those of constables Murray Brown and Douglas Rennie, who soon broke down under questioning and confessed to their sins. Oddly, the exact details of how Brown and Rennie's patrol car had come to be set alight on the road between Crianlarich and Glen Orchy remained something of a mystery.

The greatest mystery of all, namely the question of what the hell exactly had happened at Charles Stuart's estate that night, continued to baffle the authorities. Grace's story was that she had managed to escape her captors shortly after making her call to the police, and knew nothing of the causes of the fire that had gutted the castle and left dead bodies everywhere. Her superiors might have privately suspected she was hiding something, but had no evidence to prove it.

While all this was going on, more and more criminal charges quickly piled up against the missing millionaire. CCTV footage taken at the Belford confirmed that the man found suspiciously loitering inside Ewan McCulloch's hospital room by the head surgeon, Dr Fraser, was indeed Charles Stuart. More footage showed the suspect fleeing from the scene, clutching a knife. But it was the devastating confessions of Fergus Macleod and Jim Coull that delivered the greatest damage.

Pending a full forensic inquiry, Stuart was initially thought to have perished in the bizarre incident that destroyed his home – but that theory was dropped when, just hours later, his Rolls Royce was snapped by a speed camera doing ninety on the A830 near Arisaig. Soon afterwards, a major manhunt was launched nationwide. By then, the authorities had learned enough to put Stuart away for the rest of his life.

Eight days had gone by when Ben finally had to tear himself away from Grace and return to Le Val. The parting was difficult.

'Let's be honest,' he told her. 'What's the future for a guy like me and a smart lady cop from the Highlands?'

'We could have had fun finding out,' she said.

Ben had been home less than a week and getting back into the rhythm of daily life, often thinking about her, when he received an unexpected phone call. Grace had some news: Charles Stuart had been apprehended by a police patrol vessel while trying to escape across the sea to Ireland. According to the arresting officers' report, in an attempt to evade capture the fleeing suspect had disguised himself by wearing a long blond wig and women's clothing.

Read on for a sneak preview of the
next Ben Hope thriller

The Demon Club

Coming November 2020
Available to pre-order now

PROLOGUE

The pursuit had led northwards from the English south coast into the heart of the Surrey countryside, deep among thick broadleaf woods under a full moon. It was late March, the spring equinox, and the night was mild and balmy and filled with the sweetly pungent scent of the flowering bluebells that carpeted the woodland floor.

The man called Wolf had stalked his target for hours and for the moment he could go no further, waiting and hoping for the opportunity to finish the job he'd started. A job he did not particularly relish and wouldn't have been doing unless he was getting well paid for it. A job he must nonetheless complete, lest he disappoint the ruthless men who employed him.

So far, the assignment felt like it was jinxed. It wasn't Wolf's fault. He'd followed the plan exactly until things had started going wrong. Which had happened very quickly, earlier that evening.

The hit was scheduled for 7.30 p.m. at the target's home outside the pretty West Sussex village of Pyecombe, a few miles from Brighton. Abbott was expected to have been alone, but when Wolf had arrived at the nineteenth-century parsonage at the appointed hour and was concealed in the large garden preparing to make his move, he'd been inter-rupted by the sudden and unanticipated appearance of a gold Range Rover that pulled in through the front gates, rolled up towards the house and crunched to a halt on the gravel driveway next to Abbott's Lexus.

Wolf had watched from his hiding place as the Rover's doors opened and out spilled the target's ex-wife in a red dress, their two young children and a twenty-something brunette that he assumed was the kids' nanny. Wolf's mission file contained details on the former Mrs Abbott (number three, the trophy, the most painful marital misstep of the fifty-eight-year-old politician's career) and the two kids: little Emily, four, and her brother Paul, seven. Since the acrimonious split they now lived twenty miles the other side of Brighton, in a large house provided by the generous divorce settlement and alimony payments that Debbie enjoyed spending on expensive trips abroad. Her lifestyle habits, such as the recent fling with the ski instructor in Zermatt, were well known to Wolf's employers; but none of the clever-dick analysts who provided the background intel had managed to foresee that she'd show up here today to mess up their plans. Typical.

Anthony Abbott emerged from his front door to meet his visitors, his silvery hair uncombed, casually attired in beige slacks and a cricket jumper. To shrill cries of 'Daddy! Daddy!' the kids rushed up and hugged their father. Wolf had a zoom telephoto lens attached to his phone, through which he could see that Abbott was as nonplussed as he was by old Debbie turning up like this. Judging by their facial expressions and stiff body language, relations between the couple were still frosty. Abbott appeared impatient for her to leave and kept glancing at his watch, as though he'd been disturbed in the middle of something important he was anxious to return to. If only he knew, Wolf thought, what her unexpected arrival had saved him from. Even if it was just a temporary stay of execution.

She didn't hang around for long. Eleven minutes later, the Range Rover departed and Wolf watched it disappear up the quiet country lane. He was pleased to see her go, but now he had another problem: it appeared that the purpose of her visit was to dump the kids and nanny on her ex. Wolf wondered whether her intention was to liberate herself for another romantic trip to Zermatt or elsewhere, or whether she wanted to have the house to herself for a tryst at home with another of her numerous beaux. Whatever the case, the unexpected turn of events screwed things up for him. His mission remit was to make this look like a burglary gone bad, taking advantage of the fact that Abbott's financial fortunes had downturned to the extent that he could no longer afford the private protection team that a man of his importance should ideally have had watching over him. Nicely convenient. Wolf was a skilled assassin who had no problem with carrying out a quick, clean murder dressed up as an amateur job.

But he did have a problem, and a big one, with killing kids. Which he'd have little choice but to do if he pressed ahead now, to avoid leaving witnesses. The nanny, too. Messy. Very messy. While others in his profession might not have such scruples, Wolf just wasn't enough of a bastard for that. And so, Wolf decided to hold back and wait. Improvisation wasn't a problem for a man of his training and experience. He settled back and kept watching the house.

At 9.33 p.m., the hit now more than two hours overdue, Abbott re-emerged from his front door and started walking briskly towards his car. He'd changed his casual attire for a suit and tie and was carrying a leather overnight bag. It seemed like he was going somewhere, leaving the nanny alone to take care of Emily and Paul. Wolf had been told nothing of any planned excursions – then again, if not for

397

Debbie's interference, the mission would have been over and he'd have been long gone by now.

Wolf watched as Abbott climbed into his Lexus and set off up the driveway. By the time the car had reached the road, Wolf had already slipped away and hurried back to the Audi saloon he'd hidden around the corner. Like all the vehicles he drove in the course of his work, it had untraceable number plates and officially did not exist. He quickly caught up with the Lexus and followed at a discreet distance as Abbott hustled off down the country lane. Wherever he was going, the man seemed to be in a hurry to get there.

This new twist offered Wolf a fresh opportunity to finish the job, if he could track his target to a more suitable location. Having laid eyes on Abbott's kids he felt a very slight pang that, thanks to him, they would never see daddy again. But that was the nature of Wolf's profession. Life could be a bitch sometimes. He stayed on the Lexus, never letting it out of his sight but with always at least one vehicle between it and his Audi. Politicians, as a rule, weren't very highly trained in recognising when they were being tailed, but you couldn't be too careful.

The Lexus led northwards for fifty miles, taking the A23 and the M25 into Surrey. He seemed to be heading for Guildford, but then turned off the main road and headed into deep countryside. Wolf hung right back and kept following. Then, at three minutes to eleven, Abbott turned into the gates of a manor estate surrounded by woodland. Wolf drove on past the entrance, slowing down just enough to see the Lexus's taillights disappearing down the oak-lined private road and the plaque on the stone gatepost that said KARSWELL HALL. The stately home itself was out of sight of the quiet country road.

Quarter of a mile further along, Wolf found a spot to

hide the car and cut back on foot through the darkness, taking with him the things he needed. Karswell Hall was encircled by a high stone wall that he scaled with ease, and he dropped down inside the wooded grounds and made his cautious way towards the house. From a vantage point among the trees he was able to observe as more cars arrived, one every couple of minutes, and paused at a checkpoint on the private road where security guards checked papers before waving the visitors on through towards the stately home. It looked like some kind of late-evening event or gathering was underway.

It was 11.22 p.m. and he should have reported to base hours ago. Wolf was all too aware that his employers back in London would be wondering what the hell was happening. He faced the choice of whether to abort his mission and admit failure, or stay on his target until a suitable opportunity arose to eliminate him and make it look like an accident.

Wolf had never admitted failure in his life. He was still figuring out his best move when a black Mercedes limousine purred up to the checkpoint and was halted by the security men. The chauffeur rolled down his window and showed them an admission pass. While they examined it, the driver stepped out of the car for a moment to check a front tyre, and the cabin of the limo was momentarily illuminated by the interior light.

That was when Wolf realised, with a shock, that he knew both of the backseat passengers.

Wolf had personally met very, very few members of the secretive agency he worked for. But he instantly recognised these two men as his superiors. One was a much older man, easily eighty-five, wizened and gaunt, wearing a black suit and sitting in the back of the car clutching a cane between his knees. A very distinctive cane, topped with a silver bird's head with a long beak and ruby eyes. Wolf remembered it, though he'd only seen the old man once before. The other backseat occupant, twenty years younger than his travelling companion, was someone Wolf had had occasional contact with over the years.

The car moved on through the checkpoint, but the image of the two men remained burned on Wolf's retinas. What was going on here? Why were his agency chiefs apparently attending the same mysterious gathering as the very target they had directed him to eliminate earlier that day? Wolf generally never questioned the reasoning behind his directives, but this was weird. It seemed to suggest that they were all somehow involved together – though in what, Wolf had no idea. And if that was right, then it meant that Wolf had unwittingly become involved in some kind of plot to eliminate one of their own. But one of their own what?

Wolf drew away from the checkpoint. He kept well out of sight as he worked his way around the side of the big house, threading through the trees. Karswell Hall was a hell of a grand old country pile, a real billionaire pad, its scores of windows lit up like a starship with exterior floodlamps casting a glow over the immaculate lawn that sloped down from the rear towards a gleaming dark lake at whose centre was a small wooded island, all wreathed in shadow. The gathered guests, maybe fifty or sixty of them, were visible through the windows of the manor, standing in groups, talking, sipping drinks. The men-only gathering was obviously a formal event, judging by the sombre suits and ties of everyone present. Wolf noticed that there was not a single woman among them.

Crouched down low and invisible among the trees, Wolf used his compact but powerful telephoto lens to search for Abbott among the guests, but couldn't make him out in the crowd. Maybe he'd get a shot at his target that night, or maybe not. He kept waiting, and watching.

He had no idea what he was soon to witness.

At the stroke of midnight, the ceremony began.

It was like watching a surreal dream unfold. First the lights went out and Karswell Hall fell into darkness, illuminated only by the pale glow of the full moon that hung over the lake. Minutes later, a procession of figures slowly began to emerge from the rear of the house and wind its way down the lawn towards the water's edge. But, as Wolf realised, there was something bizarrely changed about the figures. All fifty or sixty guests were now wearing strange robes, long, dark, and hooded. Their faces were obscured by black masks. Wolf felt a tingle of apprehension as he saw they were animal masks – no, *bird* masks, with curved, sharp beaks that reminded him of the head of the old man's cane.

The procession assembled at the lakeside. They stood shoulder to shoulder with their backs to the trees where Wolf was hiding, all looking out across the water towards the dark, wooded island at its centre as if full of anticipation for something about to happen there. He scanned the crowd, still searching for Abbott, but it was impossible to tell whether he was among them or not. The hooded men were unrecognisable, all except for the thin, stooped figure that walked with a noticeable limp and leaned heavily on a cane.

Wolf breathed, '*What the f*—??' He knew that he had to capture this on video. If he didn't film what was happening he'd have a hard time convincing himself afterwards that he hadn't been dreaming. He quickly set the phone camera and hit the record button.

Now a low chanting broke out from the crowd. Soft at first, building into a crescendo whose weird sound sent a chill down Wolf's neck. It wasn't English. It wasn't any language he had ever heard before. Then, as the chanting reached its peak, a pyrotechnic burst of flames erupted into life on the island and lit up the trees – and now Wolf swallowed hard and blinked in disbelief as he saw the giant effigy that until now had been hidden in shadow. Twenty feet tall, carved out of stone, a quasi-human figure with the body of a man and the head of a bird, long-beaked like a heron or an ibis. The monstrosity appeared possessed with a life of its own as the flames made the shadows dance and cast their flickering reflection across the water.

The chanting of the crowd went on rising in pitch and intensity, the same incomprehensible phrases being repeated over and over like some hypnotic religious catechism that had taken hold of their minds. The chants were joined now by the harsh, rasping blare of musical instruments, like hunting horns, that sounded from the island and echoed over the lake. More flames illuminated the billows of smoke rising above the treetops.

That was when Wolf should have left. Should have just turned and run, got the hell out of there and just kept running and not looked back. But he didn't. He couldn't. Transfixed by the spectacle, almost willing to believe he was being gripped by some nightmarish hallucination, he couldn't help but keep watching.

Then it got worse. And it became too late for Wolf to turn away.

There were people on the island. Still filming the scene with the zoom of his phone lens wound up to maximum magnification, he saw four robed and hooded musicians – if the dissonant blaring from their horns could be described as music – appear as if out of nowhere through the smoke and assemble at the foot of the statue, two on each side. Moments later they were joined by three more figures that likewise appeared to have materialised by magic. Two of them wore the same robes and masks as the chanting crowd watching from across the lake, and carried flaming torches. But the third was something entirely different. It was a female figure, a blonde, clad in a plain white smock dress. From this distance and in the smoke and flicker of the flames Wolf couldn't make out her features clearly, but enough to tell that she was young, perhaps still in her teens, more a girl than a woman.

But what was instantly obvious to Wolf was that she wasn't there by choice. The two hooded, bird-headed men who accompanied her were clutching her by the arms and drawing her towards the base of the statue. She was struggling, but weakly, and her head lolled limply from side to side as though she was inebriated – or drugged. The hooded men thrust her against the base of the statue, pulled her arms out wide and tethered her wrists to what Wolf supposed, though he couldn't be sure, must be iron rings set into the stone. She hung against the foot of the giant bird-headed effigy as though crucified, her long blond hair obscuring her face. As the hooded men who'd tethered her stepped away, another appeared from the smoke.

He was robed in crimson red with some kind of gold hieroglyph symbol emblazoned on his chest. His mask was more elaborate than the others', like a ceremonial headdress or a bishop's mitre. Except that a bishop's mitre didn't have horns. They were curly like those of a ram, rising into points that gleamed in the firelight. In his left hand he held a staff or sceptre. The right hand clutched a long, glittering dagger.

The masked crowd at the lakeside were going wild, baying and howling like a pack of bloodhounds. The horned figure in the red robe stepped dramatically in front of the tethered captive, raised his hands above his head and addressed the assembly from across the water, speaking words that Wolf couldn't understand. His head was spinning and he felt sick as he began to understand what he was witnessing, and what was about to happen. The figure in red was the High Priest. The master of the twisted ceremony unfolding in front of his eyes. And the crowd of lunatics who'd gathered here tonight on this spring equinox were his worshippers.

Wolf had seen many terrible things in his life. Some of them, he'd caused to happen personally. He thought he'd seen everything. Thought that he was too hardened and jaded for anything to get to him any longer. But the scene he was witnessing now made his mouth go dry and his hands shake. He steadied his grip on the phone camera and kept watching and filming, despite himself.

Solemnly, gravely, the High Priest handed his staff to one of the other men. Then he turned to face the girl, reached out to her and ripped away the white smock with a single violent jerk. The crowd screamed. She was naked underneath. The incomprehensible chanting of the crowd became even wilder.

Now the High Priest stepped closer. He raised the dagger to show the crowd, its long, curved blade glittering in the firelight; then in a fast left-to-right movement that made Wolf flinch, he nicked the girl's neck with the edge of the blade. The blood trickled down her throat and chest. The High Priest bent in front of her, and for a few moments Wolf couldn't tell what he was doing. Then he stepped aside, and Wolf saw the five-pointed Pentacle drawn in blood on the girl's stomach.

This was no theatre show. This was real.

Wolf had witnessed enough. He finally averted his eyes and turned away. But he didn't turn away fast enough to avoid seeing the final stroke of the High Priest's dagger that sliced deep into the sacrificial victim's throat and ended her life. Fire and explosions lit up the whole lake island as the chanting of the crowd reached its climax and became a roar of delight and satisfaction.

Wolf staggered to his feet and stumbled away through the trees, twigs whipping at his face as he beat his retreat. To hell with the job. To hell with the agency, the money, the whole damn thing. He didn't care any more. He was out of here. Done with all of it, forever. He already knew where he would run to: a special place in which nobody would ever find him.

Too late, Wolf spotted the gleam of something smooth and glassy, small and round, pointing down at him from the ivied trunk of a tree.

It was a camera. And he'd been caught right on it.

TERROR HAS A NAME.

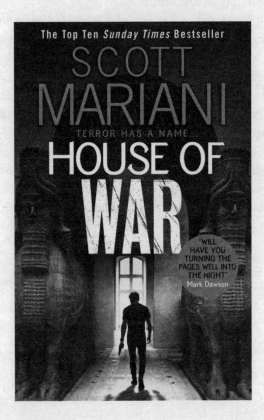

A deadly terror plot. A face from the past.
And a race against the clock for Ben Hope
to prevent the unthinkable.